D0822285

Dear Reader,

The editors at Harlequin and Silhouette are thrilled to be able to bring you a brand-new featured author program for 2005! Signature Select aims to single out outstanding stories, contemporary themes and oft-requested classics by some of your favorite series authors and present them to you in a variety of formats bound by truly striking covers.

We want to provide several different types of reading experiences in the new Signature Select program. The Spotlight books offer a single "big read" by a talented series author, the Collections present three novellas on a selected theme in one volume, the Sagas contain sprawling, sometimes multi-generational family tales (often related to a favorite family first introduced in series) and the Miniseries feature requested previously published books, with two or, occasionally, three complete stories in one volume. The Signature Select program offers one book in each of these categories per month, and fans of limited continuity series will also find these continuing stories under the Signature Select umbrella.

In addition, these volumes bring you bonus features...different in every single book! You may learn more about the author in an extended interview, more about the setting or inspiration for the book, more about subjects related to the theme and, often, a bonus short read will be included. Authors and editors have been outdoing themselves in originating creative material for our bonus features—we're sure you'll be surprised and pleased with the results!

The Signature Select program strives to bring you a variety of reading experiences by authors you've come to love, as well as by rising stars you'll be glad you've discovered. Watch for new stories from Janelle Denison, Donna Kauffman, Leslie Kelly, Marie Ferrarella, Suzanne Forster, Stephanie Bond, Christine Rimmer and scores more of the brightest talents in romance fiction!

The excitement continues!

Warm wishes for happy reading,

*Marsha Zinberg*

Marsha Zinberg
Executive Editor
The Signature Select Program

## MINISERIES

# CHRISTINE RIMMER

# BRAVO BRIDES

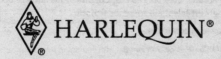

## HARLEQUIN®

TORONTO • NEW YORK • LONDON
AMSTERDAM • PARIS • SYDNEY • HAMBURG
STOCKHOLM • ATHENS • TOKYO • MILAN • MADRID
PRAGUE • WARSAW • BUDAPEST • AUCKLAND

ISBN 0-373-21766-8

BRAVO BRIDES

Copyright © 2005 by Harlequin Books S.A.

The publisher acknowledges the copyright holder of the individual works as follows:

THE MILLIONAIRE SHE MARRIED
Copyright © 2000 by Christine Rimmer.

THE M.D. SHE HAD TO MARRY
Copyright © 2000 by Christine Rimmer.

www.eHarlequin.com

Printed in U.S.A.

# CONTENTS

Dear Reader,

Sometimes my stories have their roots in a character, an intriguing imaginary person who creeps into my writer's mind and won't go away until I tell her—or his—story. And yes, I do spend my days with my imaginary friends. Since I'm an author, this is considered perfectly normal. For anyone else, not so much. <g>

Other times, my stories start out with the great "what if?" Such was the case with *The Millionaire She Married*, the first of the two books in this volume. I had a friend who wanted to remarry—and then she discovered her ex had never filed their divorce papers. They were still man and wife after believing themselves divorced for seven years.

In my friend's case, all was resolved reasonably and simply. Her ex-husband gave her the papers; she filed them. But I found myself wondering...

*What if* her ex had wanted to try again? How could he use the fact that the papers never got filed to create another chance with the woman he'd never stopped loving?

That "what if" became *The Millionaire She Married*. And as I created that story, I became intrigued with the "other" man, Logan Severance, the man the heroine had planned to marry until her ex came back in the picture. Logan was one of those persistent characters who wouldn't go away until he got his own story...and *that's* how *The M.D. She* Had *To Marry* began to take form.

I'm thrilled to see both of these stories on the stands again in Signature Select Miniseries.

Happy reading,

*Christine Rimmer*

# THE MILLIONAIRE
# SHE MARRIED

For my dear friend Georgia Bockoven.
Thank you for the times you listened,
the useful advice and the beautiful books you write.

# Chapter One

The shop, like the steep, rather narrow street it stood on, had a feel of times past about it. The oyster-white sign over the door read Linen and Lace in flowing script. Vines and morning glories twined and trailed in and out of the lettering.

Mack McGarrity stood beneath a striped awning, his hands fisted in his pockets, staring in the window to the left of the shop's entrance. Beyond the glass was a brass canopy bed. The bed was draped with lacy white curtains, covered in filmy white linens and piled with embroidered white pillows.

Next to the bed, on the left, stood a white dresser bearing a white pitcher and bowl. On the right, a white nightstand, with a vase of white roses and a white-shaded lamp. White lacy nightgowns, each one a little different from the next, had been tossed in an artful tangle across the pillows and the filmy bedcovers, as if the lady who owned them all couldn't make up her mind which to wear.

Mack smiled to himself. The fists stuck in his pockets relaxed a little.

On their wedding night Jenna had worn a nightgown like one of those thrown across that white bed—an almost transparent gown, with lace at the collar and down the front. And roses, little pink ones, embroidered around the tiny pearly buttons.

Those buttons had given him trouble. They were so damn small. And he *had* been nervous, though he'd tried not to show it.

But Jenna had known.

And she'd laughed, that soft, teasing laugh of hers. "It's not as if it's our first time," she'd whispered.

"It *is* the first time. *My* first time…with my wife." His voice had been gruff, he remembered, gruff with emotions he'd never allowed anyone but Jenna to see….

Mack turned from the window. He stared across the street, at a store that sold hand-painted furniture. A man and a woman stood at the display window there, admiring a tall bureau decorated with a woodland scene. Mack watched them, not really seeing them, until they disappeared inside.

Then, rather abruptly, he turned back to the shop called Linen and Lace. Two determined steps later, he reached the glass-fronted door. He took the handle and pulled it open.

The scent of the place hit him first—floral, sweet but not too sweet. An undertone of tartness. And something spicy, too. Like cinnamon. It didn't smell like Jenna, exactly. But it reminded him of her. Sweet and just a little spicy.

He'd barely started to smile at the thought when he realized he'd tripped the buzzer that would warn her she had another customer. She turned and saw him just as he spotted her.

When the buzzer rang, Jenna glanced toward the door out of habit, ready to send her new customer a swift, be-right-with-you smile.

The smile died unborn on her lips.

It was Mack.

Mack.

Her ex-husband. Here. In her shop.

After all these years.

It couldn't be.

But it was. Definitely.

Mack.

Her throat closed up on itself. She gulped to keep from gasping.

He looked…terrific. Older, yes. And somehow more relaxed. But in a deep and fundamental way, the same.

He was staring straight at her through those eyes she remembered much too well. Not quite blue and not quite gray, like a sky caught between sunshine and cloudiness.

He smiled at her—that beautiful, half ironic, half shy smile, the one that had dropped her in her tracks nine years before.

He'd lived in an apartment down the hall from her. And she had knocked on his door to tell him that she knew very well he'd been feeding her cat.

When he answered, he actually held Byron in his

arms. That sleek midnight-black traitor had the nerve to purr as if he belonged there.

"I'll have you know, that's my cat," she'd informed him, doing her best to sound bold.

He had smiled, just the way he was smiling at her now—like the sun coming out on a gray, chilly day. She'd felt the warmth, a warmth that reached down inside her and then started to spread.

"Come on in," he had suggested as he stroked her cat. "We'll talk about it."

It had never even occurred to her to say no.

And now, all these years later, just the sight of him made her feel as if something inside her was melting. Her knees wanted to wobble; her pulse knocked in her ears.

Along with the weakness, the unconscion able excitement, she also knew dread.

Why had he come here?

When she had called him three days before, she'd asked one thing of him—made one simple, very clear request. He had said that he would take care of it.

Did his sudden appearance in her shop mean that he had changed his mind?

"Er…miss? Are you all right?"

Jenna snapped her head around and forced a brilliant smile for her customer. "I am fine. Where were we?" She glanced down at the stack of brightly colored linens she clutched in her arms. "Ah, of course. I remember. And I do understand. Not everyone loves white. That's why I wanted you to see these. They're by an English designer I especially like. Summer Garden is the name of this pattern. Beautiful, isn't it? The colors are so vivid, different intensities of green and blue, with the flowers like splashes of pink and yellow and red." She held out the neatly folded pile of sheets. "Feel."

Her customer ran a hand over the fabric. "Soft."

"And durable, too. Three hundred thread count. The finest quality combed cotton, cool in summer, cozy in winter." Jenna slid a glance at Mack. He was watching her. Waiting.

And he'll just have to wait a little longer, she thought. "Come this way." She indicated a display near the far wall. "I have more from this designer. Tell me what you think…."

A few minutes later, Jenna closed a sale of sheets, pillowcases, shams and a comforter. As soon as she rang that one up, there was someone new to wait on. And someone else after that. Since one of her clerks had the day off and the other had taken a two-hour lunch in order to handle a few personal errands, all the customers were Jenna's. And Jenna never liked to make a customer wait.

Still, she could have stolen a moment for the civilities, a moment for hello-how-are-you. An opportunity to find out why Mack had come. She didn't do that. Because she was stalling, foolishly hoping he might just give up and leave.

But no. He wandered the room, examining her merchandise as if he actually intended to buy something. He seemed…very patient, quite willing to wait until she had time to deal with him.

His patience bothered her almost as much as his sudden appearance in her shop. The Mack she had known had been far from a patient man.

But things *had* changed since then. Back then, Mack McGarrity had been a man on a mission. He'd been determined to carve out his niche in the world and he'd driven himself relentlessly toward that goal. Now he had millions.

Maybe having lots of money meant you could afford even more than a mansion in the Florida Keys and a forty-six-foot fishing boat. Maybe having lots of money meant you could afford to wait.

Or at least, maybe it had done that for Mack McGarrity.

The thought probably should have pleased her. For a man like Mack to learn patience—that was a good thing.

But it didn't please her. It made her nervous. Mack had always been relentless. To think that he might now be patient as well could cause her considerable difficulty if, for some reason, he decided to use those characteristics against her.

But why would he do that?

She didn't want to know—which was why she kept stalling, kept letting him wait.

Nearly an hour after Mack entered the shop, Jenna found herself alone with him—save for an elderly woman who came in often to browse. The nice old lady took her time, as usual. Finally she settled on a three-piece set of needlepoint antimacassars. Jenna rang up the sale and counted out change.

"Thank you so much. Come back again," Jenna said as she walked her customer to the door.

"Oh, you know I will, dear. I love your little shop." A cagey grin appeared on the woman's puckered rosebud of a mouth. "And you always do pay such lovely attention to me when I visit."

Jenna pulled open the door. To the accompaniment of the shop's buzzer, her customer toddled outside, turn-

ing to wave as she made her way up the street. Jenna
stepped onto the sidewalk to wave back. Stalling.

And then the time had come. Jenna went inside again
and shut the door.

Mack had moved into the central aisle, only a few
feet away from her. She felt cornered, so near the door
that she kept triggering the buzzer, but distressingly reluctant to move closer to him.

He had the courtesy to back up a few paces. She
moved warily toward him and the buzzing ceased.

There was silence.

She had to force herself to say his name. "Hello, Mack."

"Hello, Jenna."

She stared into his face, a tanned face now, with the
creases around the eyes a little deeper than before. His
light brown hair was still cut no-nonsense short, but
more time in the sun had given it gold highlights. His
eyebrows, too, had gone gold at the tips.

He looked good. He really did.

And she had been staring too long. She cut her eyes
away, not sure what to say next.

She wanted to demand, What are you doing here? To
order, Go away, and don't come back. To insist, I have
my own life now. I *run* my own life. It's a good life, and
it doesn't include you.

But she knew that if she said those things, she would
only sound defensive, would only put herself at a dis-
advantage right from the start. So the uncomfortable silence continued for several more agonizing seconds.

At last he spoke. "Struck speechless at the sight of
me, huh?"

She met his eyes directly, sucked in a breath and
forced out a brisk reply. "Well, I have to admit, I don't

understand why you're here. Key West is a long way from Meadow Valley, California."

Key West. She never would have believed it. Mack, the ultimate workaholic lawyer, living in the tropics, drifting around the Gulf of Mexico in that boat of his. The idea of her driven, success-obsessed husband—correction, *ex*-husband—drifting *anywhere* seemed a complete contradiction in terms.

And she wished he'd quit looking at her with that amused and embarrassingly knowing expression, quit making her feel so…young and awkward. As if she were twenty-one again, a lonely college girl far from home, instead of the mature, settled, self-possessed thirty she was now.

What was it about him? How did he do it? It had been seven years since she'd seen him face-to-face, and five since their divorce should have been final. Still, right now, staring at him, with him staring back at her, she felt exposed. Raw. As if the mere sight of him had ripped open old and still-festering wounds—wounds she'd been certain had healed long ago.

It had been hard enough to pick up the phone and call him, after tracking him down through one of his colleagues at his old law firm. Hard enough to talk to him again, to hear his voice, to ask him to send her the papers she needed.

When she'd hung up, she'd told herself, Well, at least *that's* done.

But now here she was. Face-to-face with him, feeling raw and wounded. Breathless and confused.

It shouldn't be like this, and she knew it. All the hurt and recriminations were long past, not to mention the yearning, the tenderness, the *love*.

By now she should be able to smile at him, to feel reasonably at ease, to ask calmly if he'd brought her the papers.

The papers. Yes. That was the question.

She cleared her throat. "Did you…decide to bring the papers in person, is that it? It really wasn't necessary, Mack. Not necessary at all."

He didn't reply immediately, only kept looking at her. Looking at her so intently, causing that weakness in her knees and a certain disturbing fluttering in her solar plexus.

Now she wanted to shout at him, Answer me! Where are those papers?

But then the buzzer sounded again. Jenna glanced over her shoulder, pasted on a smile. "I'll be right with you."

"No hurry." The new customer, a well-dressed, fortyish woman, detoured toward a display of afghans and furniture scarves hung from quilt stands along the side wall.

Jenna looked back at Mack. He glanced toward the woman over by the afghans, then spoke in a low voice. "I want to talk to you. Alone."

"No!" The word came out all wrong. It sounded frantic and desperate.

"Yes." Lower still and very soft. Gentle. Yet utterly unyielding.

"Miss?" The customer was fingering the fringe of a piano shawl. "There's no price tag on this one."

Jenna realized she was scowling. As she glanced toward her customer, she rearranged her face into a bright smile. "I'll be right there. Just one moment." She turned to Mack again, the cheerful smile mutating instantly back to a scowl. "We have nothing to say to each other."

"I think we do."

"You can't just—" Her voice had risen. She cut herself off, got herself back under control, then went on in an intense whisper. "You can't just wander in here after all·these years and expect me to—"

"Jenna." He reached out and snared her right hand.

Before she could think to jerk away, he tugged her behind a wrought-iron shelving unit stacked with Egyptian-cotton towels and accessories for the bath. Vaguely stunned that he had actually touched her, she looked down at their joined hands.

"Let go," she instructed in a furious whisper.

He did, which stunned her all over again, somehow. One moment his big warm hand surrounded hers—and the next, it was gone.

He said, "I'm not expecting anything. I only want to talk to you. In private."

She could·see it in his eyes, in the set of his jaw. He was not going to just go away. She would have to deal with him, to listen to whatever he'd decided he had to say to her.

Right then, guiltily, she thought of Logan, her high school sweetheart, her dear friend—and now, her fiancé. Logan had waited a long time to make her his bride. And when this little problem with her divorce from Mack had cropped up, Logan, as usual, had been the soul of understanding. He hadn't reproached her, hadn't asked her how she'd managed, over five whole years, to let it slip her mind that she'd never received her copy of the final divorce decree.

He'd just gently suggested that she get the situation cleared up.

So she'd called Mack.

And Mack had said that he did have the papers and

he would sign them, have them notarized and send them to her right away. So she'd reported to Logan that everything had been worked out. When the papers came, in the next few days, she would file them. Within six months she and Logan would be free to marry.

Logan hadn't been thrilled about the waiting period required by California law. But he had accepted it gracefully.

She wasn't so certain how he'd accept the news that Mack had appeared in person and demanded to speak with her *in private.*

But then again, maybe he wouldn't even have to know about this little problem until after it had been resolved.

Logan, who was an M.D. in family practice, had left two days ago for a medical convention in Seattle. He wouldn't return until Sunday night—two more days from now.

By then, Jenna told herself, she'd have everything under control. By then, she would have listened to whatever Mack had to say, taken the papers from him and sent him on his way. The whole situation would be much easier to explain to her fiancé once she had the papers in her hands.

"Miss?" It was the woman over by the afghans, beginning to sound a bit put out.

"Go ahead," Mack said. "Take care of her."

The woman bought the piano scarf. Mack waited, standing a little to the side of the register counter, as Jenna rang up the sale.

Once her customer had left, Jenna sighed and conceded, "All right. I close up at seven. After that, we can talk."

"Good," Mack said. "There are a couple of promising-looking restaurants down the street. I'll drop back by when you close and we'll get something to eat."

Not on your life, she thought. She would not spend the evening sitting across a table from him, fighting the feeling that they were out on a date.

"No," she said. "Come to the house at seven-thirty. We can talk there. Lacey's visiting for a while, but she won't bother us."

"Lacey." He said her younger sister's name with more interest than he'd ever shown in the past. "Visiting? From where?"

"She lives in Los Angeles now."

"What does she do there, rob banks?"

Jenna gave him a too-sweet smile. "She's an artist. And a very talented one, too."

"Still the rebel, you mean."

"Lacey makes her own rules."

"I believe it—and how's your mom?"

Jenna didn't answer immediately. Sometimes she still found it hard to believe that Margaret Bravo was gone. "She died two years ago."

He looked at her for a long moment before muttering, "I'm sorry, Jenna."

He'd hardly given a thought to Jenna's mother while she was alive. Mack McGarrity didn't put much store in family ties. But right now he did sound sincere. Jenna murmured a reluctant "Thank you," then spoke more briskly. "Seven-thirty, then. My house."

"I'll be there."

"Bring the divorce papers. You *do* have those papers?"

"I've got them."

He had the papers. Relief washed through her. Maybe this wouldn't be as bad as she'd feared.

# Chapter Two

Jenna walked home from the shop. It was only three blocks to the big Queen Anne Victorian at the top of West Broad Street where she'd grown up. She enjoyed the walk. She waved to her neighbors and breathed the faint scent of pine in the air and thought about how much she loved her hometown. Tucked into a pocket of the Sierra foothills, Meadow Valley was a charming place of steep, tree-lined streets and tidy old wood frame houses.

At home, Jenna found the note Lacey had left on the refrigerator.

"Last-minute hot date. Don't wait up."

Jenna grinned to herself at the words scrawled in her sister's bold hand. When Lacey said, "Don't wait up," she meant it. Since about the age of eleven, Jenna's "baby" sister had never willingly gone to bed before 2:00 a.m. Lacey loved staying up so late that she could watch the sun rise before calling it a night.

Jenna's grin became a frown.

Without Lacey, she and Mack would be alone in the house.

She crumpled the note and turned for the trash bin beneath the sink. She saw Byron then. He was sitting on the floor to the right of the sink cabinet door, his long, black tail wrapped neatly around his front paws.

"I don't want to be alone with him," Jenna said to the cat. "And do not ask me why."

The cat didn't, only regarded her through those wise yellow-green eyes of his. "Don't look at me like that," she scolded as she tossed the note into the trash bin and shoved the cabinet door shut.

The cat went on looking, beginning to purr now, the sound quite loud in the quiet kitchen. Byron never had talked much. But he could purr with the best of them.

Jenna scooped him up and put him on her shoulder. "If you fall all over yourself rubbing on him, I'll never forgive you." She stroked the sleek raven fur and the cat purred all the louder. "I mean it," she grumbled, but the cat remained unconcerned.

"All right, all right. Dinner for you." She scooped food into his bowl, then left him to his meal.

In the downstairs master bedroom she changed from her linen jacket and bias-cut rayon skirt into Dockers and a camp shirt. She purposely did not freshen up her makeup one bit or even run a comb through her straight, shoulder-length blond hair.

And when she returned to the kitchen for a tall glass of iced tea, she pointedly did not rush around whipping up a little something to tempt a man's palate. She was not dressing up for Mack and he was getting no dinner. She had one order of business to transact with him. She wanted the final divorce papers he was supposed to have signed five and a half years ago. And then she wanted him back in Florida where he belonged.

Ten minutes later she answered the doorbell. It was Mack, grinning that knee-weakening grin of his. A pair of waiters stood behind him.

She blinked. *Waiters?* Yes. Definitely. Waiters. In crisp white shirts, black slacks and neat black bow ties. One carried a round table with a pedestal base, the other had a chair under each arm.

"What in the—?"

"You didn't cook, did you? Well, if you did, save it. I've brought dinner with me."

"But I—you—I don't—"

"You're stammering," he said with nerve-flaying fondness. Then he gestured at the waiters. "This way— Jenna, sweetheart, you'll have to move aside."

"I am not your—"

"Sorry. Old habits. Now, get out of the way."

He stepped forward, took her by the shoulders and guided her back from the door. Then he gestured at the waiters again. They followed him into the front parlor, where they proceeded to set up the table on her mother's hand-hooked Roosevelt Star rug.

In the ensuing seven or eight minutes, Jenna tried to tell Mack a number of times that she wasn't having dinner with him. He pretended not to hear her as the waiters trekked back and forth from a van out in the front, bringing linens and dishes and flatware and a centerpiece of flower-shaped candles floating in a cut-crystal bowl. They also brought in a side table and set it up under the front window. They put the food there. It looked and smelled sinfully delicious.

When all was in readiness, one waiter lighted the candles as the other pulled out Jenna's chair for her.

Jenna sent a glare at Mack. "I don't like this."

He put on an innocent expression, which she did not buy for a nanosecond. "Come on, Jenna. It's only dinner."

The waiter waited, holding the chair.

Jenna gave in and sat down, thinking that Mack McGarrity might have managed to develop a little patience, he even might have learned how to relax. But in this, he hadn't changed at all. He still insisted on doing things one hundred percent his way.

Mack slid into the chair opposite her. He gestured to the waiters and one of them set a bread basket on the table, along with two plates of tempting appetizers: stuffed miniature Portobello mushrooms and oysters on the half shell, nestled in chipped ice. The other waiter busied himself opening a bottle of Pinot Grigio, which Mack sampled, approved and then poured for Jenna and for himself.

That done, Mack signed the check.

The moment the front door closed behind the waiters, Jenna placed one mushroom and one oyster on her plate. She also buttered a warm slice of sourdough bread. Then she rose from her chair. She dished up more food from the offerings on the side table—a good-sized helping of *salade niçoise* and a modest serving of sautéed veal scallops with marsala sauce.

She sat down and ate. The appetizers were as good as they looked, as were the salad and the veal. She did not touch her wine.

As she methodically chewed and swallowed, Mack kept trying to get her talking. He asked about her shop and complimented her on the changes she'd made in the decor of her mother's front parlor. He wondered aloud where Lacey was and tried to get her to tell him more about her sister's life as a struggling artist in Southern California.

Jenna answered in single syllables whenever possible. When the question absolutely required a longer answer, she gave him a whole sentence—and then went back to her meal.

She was finished ten minutes after she'd started. She pushed her plate away. "Thank you, Mack. That was excellent."

"I'm so glad you enjoyed it," he muttered, finishing off his glass of wine and reaching for the bottle again.

She granted him a sour smile. "You've hardly eaten." He'd taken one mushroom and a single breadstick.

"For some reason, I feel rushed. It's ruined my appetite." He poured more wine, set the bottle down.

Jenna smoothed her napkin in at the side of her plate. "Well, then. If you don't feel like eating, then maybe we can proceed to the main order of business here."

He was staring at her engagement diamond. "Nice ring," he muttered.

"Thank you. I like it, too—and can we talk about what you supposedly came here to talk about?"

He gestured with his wineglass. "By all means."

She straightened her shoulders and inched her chin up a notch. "As I told you on the phone, I want to get married again."

"Congratulations." Mack took a minute to sip from his glass. Then he lowered the glass and looked at her straight on. "But don't you think you ought to get rid of your first husband before you start talking about taking on another one?"

"I *am* rid of my first husband," she replied in a carefully controlled tone. "Or I was supposed to be. Everything was settled."

"For you, maybe."

She glared at him. "It *was* settled, Mack."

He grunted. "Whatever you say."

"Well, all right. I *say* that everything was over—except that, for some reason, you never got around to signing the papers that my lawyer sent your lawyer."

Mack studied the depths of his wineglass for a moment, then looked at her once more. "It was a busy time for me. I had a lot on my mind."

She decided to let his lame excuses pass. "The point is, it's over, Mack. Long over. And you know it. I don't know why you're here, after all these years. I don't *care* why you're here."

He sat up a little straighter. "I don't believe that."

"Believe what you want. Just—" *Give me those papers and get out of my life!* she wanted to shout. But she didn't. She paused. She gathered her composure, then asked quite civilly, "Do you have the papers?"

He brought his wineglass to his lips again and regarded her broodingly over the rim. "Not with me."

Jenna could quite easily have picked up the crystal bowl of floating candles from the center of the table and heaved it at his head. To keep herself from doing that, she folded her hands in her lap and spoke with measured care. "You said you had the papers."

"And I do. I just didn't bring them with me tonight."

"You lied."

"I didn't lie. *You* heard what you wanted to hear."

Another lie, she thought, but held her tongue this time. She'd lived with Mack McGarrity long enough to recognize a verbal trap when he laid one. If she kept insisting that he'd lied, they'd only end up going around and around, her accusing and him denying, getting nowhere.

Let it go, she thought. Move on. She said, "You told me you wanted to talk to me. In private. Well, here we are. Just the way you wanted it. You'd better start talking, Mack. You'd better tell me what is going on."

He set his glass on the table. "Jenna, I—" He cut himself off. Something across the room had caught his eye. She followed his glance to the black cat peeking around the edge of the arch that led to the formal dining room. "My God. Is that…?"

"Byron," she provided reluctantly, at the same time as he whispered, "Bub?"

The cat's lean body slid around the arch. Then, his long tail high, Byron strutted over, jumped lightly onto Mack's lap, lay down and began to purr in obvious contentment. Mack petted the black fur in long, slow strokes. Jenna looked away, furious with him for this game he was playing—and moved in spite of her fury at the sight of him with Byron again after all these years.

She stared out the front window at the Boston fern hanging from the eaves of the porch as the sound of Byron's happy purring rumbled in her ears. When she looked back, Mack was watching her. His eyes were soft now, full of memories, of dangerous tenderness. "He has some gray, around his neck."

Jenna's throat felt uncomfortably tight. "He's not a young cat. He was full-grown when we found him."

She thought of their first meeting again, though she shouldn't have allowed herself such a foolish indulgence.

Nine years ago. It seemed like forever.

And also, like yesterday…

She'd been in her junior year, majoring in business administration at UCLA. And he'd been twenty-five, just finishing law school.

Once he'd led her into his apartment, he'd informed her that the cat had adopted him.

"No," she had argued, "That cat adopted *me,* the first day I moved in, three weeks ago."

They were in his living room, which had a shortage of furniture and an excess of books—they were everywhere, overflowing the board-and-block bookcases, in piles on the floor. He petted Byron and he looked at her, a look that made her feel warm and weak and absolutely wonderful. He introduced himself. And he said that he'd named the cat Bub.

She had demanded, "You named my cat Bub?"

"It's *my* cat."

"No, he's mine. And Bub. What kind of a name is that?"

"A better name than Byron—which is just the kind of name a woman would give a black cat."

"Byron fits my cat perfectly."

"No. This cat is no Byron. This cat is a Bub."

"No, his name is Byron. And he's mine."

"No, he's mine."

"I beg your pardon. He is mine."

And about then, Mack suggested, "We could share…." He said the words quietly, looking deep in her eyes, stroking Byron's silky fur and smiling a smile that made her want to find something sturdy to lean against.

"Share…?"

He nodded.

Further discussion had followed. She could no longer remember all that had been said. The words hadn't really mattered anyway. There was his voice asking and her voice answering, his eyes looking into hers, the feeling that she'd knocked on a door—his door—and found a different world waiting beyond the threshold. A magical, shimmering, golden world. A world with Mack McGarrity in it.

In the end, it was agreed. They would share Byron—Bub, as Mack called him. Mack suggested they have dinner together to celebrate. It sounded like a lovely idea to Jenna.

They ate at an inexpensive Italian restaurant not far from their apartment building. And when they returned to his place, he'd asked her in for a last cup of coffee.

She'd stayed, after the coffee. She'd spent the night in his bed—well, actually, on his mattress on the floor. At that time, Mack McGarrity couldn't afford things like beds.

It had been her first time. And it had been beautiful. And after that night, she had moved in with him. Two months later, on November 10, they were married. Jenna had thought herself the luckiest, happiest woman on earth….

"Jenna." Mack was looking at her now, over the shimmering flames of those candles afloat in that cut-crystal bowl. The cat went on purring, and the past seemed a living thing, as real as the cat and the glowing candle flames, a presence in her mother's front parlor with them.

He said, "Since you called, I've been thinking…."

No, she thought. Don't say it. Please don't.

But he did. "You can't marry the med student, Jenna. Not yet."

The med student.

Logan.

Oh, God. What was the matter with her? Taking this dangerous little mental detour down memory lane? Letting herself forget Logan, who loved her and treated her with respect and understanding. Who wanted exactly the same things that she wanted: a partner for life, an *equal* partner. And a big family. Lots of children. Three or four at the very least.

"Logan is not a med student anymore," she informed the infuriating man across the table from her. "Years have passed, Mack, just in case you didn't notice."

He had stopped petting Byron. Those blue-gray eyes bored into hers. "I have noticed, as a matter of fact."

"Logan's finished med school." Her throat felt so tight, it hurt. She swallowed, made herself go on. "He's…done his internship and his residency. He's a full-fledged M.D. in family practice right here in Meadow Valley."

"I don't care if he's Jonas Salk. You can't marry him right now."

She couldn't sit still for that. And she didn't. She shot to her feet. "This is just like you," she accused through clenched teeth. "You appear out of nowhere after all these years and you immediately start telling me how I'm going to run my life. Well, I'm not going to do what you tell me to do anymore. I want those papers you promised you'd sign, Mack. And I want them now."

"I didn't promise."

"That is a lie. You told me on the phone that you would—"

"I know what I said."

"Good. Because what you said was that you'd sign the papers and send them right to me."

"You caught me off guard."

"It doesn't matter how I caught you. You said—"

He waved a hand, then used it to resume stroking her cat. "You'll get what you want. But not right this minute."

I will not start yelling, she silently vowed. No matter how tempting the prospect may be, I will not begin screaming at him.

She asked, "What does that mean—not right this minute?"

"It means I want a little time with you first."

"Time?" It came out as a croak.

"Yes. Time."

Oh, sweet Lord, she did not like the sound of this. She did not like it in the least. She strove mightily for calm—and did somehow manage to keep her voice even. "Time for what?"

Byron chose that moment to leave Mack's lap. The tag on his collar jingled as he jumped to the floor. Landing neatly on the balls of his dainty feet, he strutted across the room, then sat down beneath a marble-topped mahogany side table, where he began bathing himself. Mack watched him.

"Mack," Jenna demanded, to get his attention. He looked at her again. She repeated, "Time for what?"

He studied her before he spoke, his expression arranged into what she always used to think of as his lawyer's face. Composed. Aloof. All-knowing. His eyes looked out from beneath the golden shelf of his brow, seeing everything, revealing nothing.

He said, "We had something good once. And I admit it was mostly my fault that we lost it. I want some time to try to understand what went wrong."

Conflicting emotions swirled inside her. Confusion. Rage. A strange and rather frightening giddiness.

She longed to sit down again, to let her knees crumple and drop to her chair. But she remained upright. "Mack. I just want the signed papers. Please."

And he just sat there, looking out at her through those totally unrevealing lawyer's eyes. "As I said, you'll have them. After you spend two weeks with me."

She gulped. *"Two weeks?"*

"That's right. Two weeks. Alone with me."

She did sit down then. And once seated, she closed her eyes and raked her hair back from her face. "Mack. You cannot do this. I'll…divorce you all over again."

His lips curved, just slightly, as if he found that remark amusing, but only vaguely so. "You're not serious."

She forced total conviction into her reply. "I certainly am."

He reached out and picked up his wineglass again. "Divorcing me all over again will take time." He sipped, settling back in his chair. "It took over a year before, from the date that your lawyer first contacted mine until we reached a settlement. And then we were only fighting over Bub."

Ridiculous, she thought, remembering. Ridiculous and petty. She'd been back home in Meadow Valley when she'd filed, and he was still in New York with that high-powered law firm. He'd hired one of the lawyers from his own firm and instructed him to demand "custody" of Byron. For months, his lawyer and hers had corresponded. And then, out of nowhere, Mack had decided to be reasonable. He'd let her have Byron. Everything had been settled.

All he'd had to do was sign the blasted papers, and everything would have been fine.

He sipped some more. "This time I could fix it so it takes forever. I hope the good doctor will wait for you. But then, I suppose he will. I remember him, how he hung around that one Christmas we spent here. He was waiting for you even way back then—when there was no doubt at all you were another man's wife."

Desperate, Jenna tried another threat—anything, she thought, to make him back down. "I'll get a big chunk of your money if I divorce you now."

He grunted in disbelief and sipped more wine. "Oh, come on. I know you, Jenna. Except for Bub, you wouldn't take anything six years ago. And you won't take anything now."

She gave him her best level-eyed stare. "Don't bet on it. I'm a lot meaner than I used to be. And besides, you weren't a multimillionaire when I divorced you. You were just a lawyer in a big firm, killing yourself and ignoring your wife, spending every waking minute clawing your way to the top. Now you're so rich, I might not be able to resist making a bid for half of all you've got."

"So." He was smiling again. "You know how much money I've got."

The truth was, she *had* followed the stories about him. "I have a pretty good idea."

"From whom?"

She shrugged. "I read the newspapers."

Six years ago, Mack had taken on a class-action suit against a major automobile manufacturer, a suit no one else in his firm had been willing to touch. He'd ended up going out on his own to handle it. And his share of the final settlement had come to ten million dollars.

He advised with some irony, "If you're after my money, you'll be happy to hear that I've at least doubled the ten million I started out with."

"I'm sure you're a very wise investor."

"No, I take big chances. And they pay off."

"Well. Good." She stabbed the air with her index finger. "That means more for me when I take you to the cleaners—which I will, Mack. I swear I will."

He regarded her for an endless count of five. She glared right back at him, thinking how easy it would be to pick up her dinner knife and hurl it at his heart.

At last he said in a musing tone, "You've developed a temper. I don't remember you having a temper before. You were sweet and shy. And you cried instead of getting mad."

She pushed back her chair again and stood. It felt a lot better, looking down on him. "Right. I used to be a wimp. But now I'm all grown up. I make my own decisions. And I have a life. Do you understand that? There is a man I want to marry and a business I need to run. I can't leave my store for two weeks. And I certainly can't leave my fiancé to run off with another man."

"Not just any other man, Jenna. Your husband."

"You are not my husband, not in any but a purely technical sense."

He lifted a brow at her, insolently, as if her assertion didn't even deserve comment. "I'm sure you can find someone to look after your store."

"I am not going to find anyone, because I'm not going anywhere."

He set his half-finished glass of wine on the table and

rose slowly to his feet. "Just leave all this right where
it is. The restaurant will send someone over tomorrow
morning to deal with it." He pulled a business card from
his back pocket and set it on the table. "Call this number. Tell them what time you want them to show up."

She didn't even glance at that card. She looked right
at the maddening man standing across the table from
her. "I am not—repeat, *not*—spending two weeks with
you, Mack."

The look he gave her then was almost tender. "Think
about it, Jenna. Two weeks isn't that long. We'll go to
my place in Key West. I think you'll like it there. The
house is old, like this one. It needs...a woman's touch."

"Hire a decorator."

He didn't reply to that, only looked at her indul-
gently before adding, "Once the two weeks are over,
you'll be rid of me for good—unless we both decide we
shouldn't be divorced after all."

She couldn't hold back one sharp, disdainful cry. "I
don't need two weeks to decide that. I decided that a
long time ago."

He actually had the gall to pretend to be wounded.
"You're really hurting my feelings here."

She gaped at him, wondering how he could joke
about this. It was not funny. Not funny in the least.
"This is...blackmail. It's...it's kidnapping. It has to be
illegal."

He shook his head. "It's not. Trust me. I know. I'm
a lawyer."

"Mack. Please." She pulled out all the stops and
stooped to pleading. "*Please.* There is no point in this.
Don't you see? Nothing good can come of it. I don't
want to...to reconcile with you. It's over for me. And

even if it wasn't, how can you possibly imagine that forcing me to go away with you would somehow make me change my mind?"

"Answer me this. Is there *anything* that would make you change your mind?"

"Absolutely not."

"Then this is the only option I've got."

"That's insane. I just told you it can't work."

"Maybe you're wrong. And since you have no other suggestions…"

"Suggestions? You want suggestions? What about keeping your word? What about giving me those papers and going back where you belong?"

He shook his head. "Uh-uh."

"Mack. I don't want to get back together with you. And I do *not* want to spend two weeks alone with you."

"But you will spend two weeks with me. If you want those divorce papers."

"Mack, be reasonable. You have to see that doing this will get you nowhere."

He smiled, a rueful smile. "I'm staying at the Northern Empire Inn. Give me a call when you're ready to agree to my terms."

# Chapter Three

The phone rang at nine. It was Logan, calling from his hotel room in Seattle. He said that he was learning more about the advances in the treatment of childhood infections than his practice could afford. There was a certain very pricey piece of state-of-the-art equipment he wanted to buy.

As he talked, Jenna tried to keep her mind on what he was saying, tried not to think about Mack, about how angry she was, how trapped she felt. About what in the world she was going to do now.

"Jenna? You still with me?"

"Of course. I'm right here. How's the food there—and are you getting enough sleep?"

"The food? I've had worse. And yes, I'm getting plenty of sleep. What about you? Miss me?"

"Desperately."

He chuckled. "Don't overplay it. I'll become suspicious."

Suspicious. Oh, Lord. If he only knew.

And he *should* know. She would have to tell him.

But not now. Not on the phone from seven hundred miles away.

She'd tell him when she could sit down with him, face-to-face, after he returned home.

He asked, "So what are you and Lacey up to tonight?"

"We're not. I came home and there was a note on the fridge. A hot date, it said."

"I didn't know Lacey was seeing someone in Meadow Valley."

"I don't think she is. It's probably just one of her old high school friends, Mira or Maud—or maybe both."

"The terrible twins. Scary." He spoke jokingly. But he wasn't joking, not really. Logan had never approved of Lacey's old friends. He didn't much approve of Lacey, either, though he always treated her kindly, partly for Jenna's sake and also because he liked to think of himself as Lacey's "honorary" older brother.

"The twins are all grown up now," Jenna reminded him. "And they've settled down considerably. They haven't spray-painted obscenities on high school walls or gotten caught breaking and entering for years. Maud's married and a mother—and a darn good one, from what I hear."

"That's reassuring," Logan muttered dryly. "Seriously. Is Lacey all right? She seemed a little…subdued the other day." Logan had been at the house when Lacey had first arrived from L.A.

"She's fine. Just taking a break from the rat race, she

said. A few weeks in her hometown. Some rest and relaxation. Oh, and she also mentioned that a certain gallery owner had been talking about showcasing her work. Evidently the deal fell through somehow."

"A disappointment." His tone was knowing.

"That's what it sounded like to me. So if she seems a little down, that's probably why."

"She'll get over it."

"Of course she will."

"What she ought to do is get a *real* job. She's twenty-five years old, after all. Time to make a few realistic decisions. There's no reason she couldn't move back to Meadow Valley permanently. That house of your mother's is half hers now. As soon as you and I get married, she could have it to herself. Plenty of room to set up a studio and paint in her spare time. She ought to—"

"Logan," Jenna cut in gently.

He was silent, then he chuckled. "I know, I know. None of my business. But she *is* your sister. And I worry about her."

"I know you do. And it's very sweet of you."

"Tell me again how much you miss me." She could picture the loving smile on his handsome face. The image made her feel about two inches tall.

"Jenna? Are you there?"

"I miss you," she said. "A lot. And I…" Her throat closed up. She had to swallow before she could get the words out. "I love you. Very much."

"And I love you, Jenna Bravo. Did you get those papers in the mail from Florida yet?"

"Uh. No. No, I'm afraid that I didn't."

"Well. It's only been a few days. We have to exercise a little patience, I suppose."

"That's right. Logan, I…" But no, she told herself again. Not now. It's not right to tell him something like this over the phone.

"What is it?" Concern threaded his voice. "Is something wrong?"

"No. Nothing. Nothing at all. I just…I'll be glad when you're home."

Softly he agreed, "So will I."

Jenna hung up feeling like a two-timer, a woman of questionable moral character, dishonest and bad. She could have killed Mack McGarrity. She muttered a few choice expletives under her breath.

And then, before reason could reassert itself, she got out the phone book and looked up the number of the Northern Empire Inn.

She dialed it quickly, and when the operator answered, she growled, "Mack McGarrity's room, please."

He picked up after the first ring. "McGarrity here." His voice, so deep and firm and resonant, vibrated along her nerves, sent a shiver moving just beneath the surface of the skin.

She could hear a television in the background, a man talking, then audience laughter. "Hello?" he said, impatient now, sounding like the old Mack, the oh-so-busy Mack, the Mack who'd dragged her to New York City without bothering to get her input on the move— and then hardly had a spare moment for her once he got her there.

She opened her mouth, then shut it without making a sound. What was there to say that she hadn't already said?

She heard him draw in a breath. And then, in tender reproach, he whispered her name.

"Jenna…"

She lowered the handset and laid it oh so carefully back in its cradle.

Jenna didn't sleep well that night. She couldn't get comfortable in her own bed. And then, when she finally did drop off, she had a dream about Mack.

About making love with Mack.

In the dream, their lovemaking was every bit as beautiful, as sensual and sweet and soul shattering, as it had been in real life.

They lay on a white bed—the bed in the window of her shop, as a matter of fact. In the dream, though, the bed drifted in some warm and safe and hazy place. It floated, with Jenna and Mack naked upon it, in a kind of misty void.

Mack touched her, the way he used to touch her—in the beginning, when it was all so new and magical. When what he'd found with her was still enough to make him put aside temporarily the demons of ambition that drove him.

His eyes were the sky, blue turning cloudy. His hands, so warm and strong, moved over her body in a lazy, arousing dance. She moaned, and he kissed her, the deepest, longest, most sensual kiss she had ever known. It went on and on. She pressed herself closer to him and realized that he was already within her. There was that perfect, full sensation of joining.

Her eyes drooped closed. His kiss deepened even more. Impossible, that a kiss already so deep could continue to intensify. But it did. And they were moving together, sighing together, on the wide white bed in the middle of a warm and lovely nowhere.

Then all at once she was standing in the waiting room of a doctor's office, looking through the receptionist's window.

And it was Logan, not a receptionist, who stared back at her. "There's no cure for you, Jenna." His voice was icy cold. "I'm afraid your case is terminal."

She woke with a cry, sitting straight up in bed.

The next day Jenna looked in the phone book for the number of the attorney who had handled her divorce from Mack. It wasn't there. She remembered the address, so she drove by the attorney's office that evening, on the way home from Linen and Lace. But her lawyer had moved. The building was now occupied by a florist's shop.

Logan didn't call that night. Jenna felt guiltily grateful for that. As long as she didn't talk to him, she didn't have to keep asking herself if it was better to tell him the truth right now—or to wait until she could tell him to his face.

Sunday, Linen and Lace opened at one in the afternoon. Jenna went out at a little after ten o'clock and bought bagels and cream cheese. Then she woke Lacey and the two of them sat in the breakfast nook, warm September sunlight pouring in the windows, drinking coffee and sharing an impromptu brunch.

Lacey talked a little about her stalled career dreams. She'd been living in L.A. for five years now. She shared a downtown loft—in a rather rough neighborhood that made Jenna nervous—with a friend, a fellow artist. Lacey painted every chance she got, and she was making connections, building a network of people who knew and liked her work. Every now and then she'd sell a painting. But as yet, her long string of jobs waiting tables and serving at private catered events were what paid the rent.

Jenna really did believe her sister had talent. And Lacey had come a long way from the troubled, rebellious teenager who'd once been known by her teachers as the Scourge of Meadow Valley High. Now Lacey really *cared* about something.

"You work hard," Jenna told her. "And you love what you do. You just keep working. Someday you'll get the recognition you deserve."

Lacey had what Jenna always thought of as a naughty angel's face—wide blue eyes, a lush, full mouth, a delicate nose and beautiful pale skin. She liked to wear tight-fitting tops and flowing, semitransparent skirts. To Jenna, she always seemed a cross between a rock star and a fairy princess.

Now the full mouth was stretched to a grin. "It's obvious why I come home—to hear you tell me that I'm bound to succeed."

"And you are. I *know* you are. Do you need money?"

"No, I do not. I'm managing just fine."

They shared a second bagel and Jenna poured them each more coffee.

Then Lacey asked, "So what's gone wrong in your life lately?"

Jenna tensed, but tried her best not to let Lacey see it. "What do you mean?" She hoped she sounded breezy. "Everything's fine."

Lacey leaned closer. "Come on. It's me. Your bad baby sister. I grew up spying on you, remember? I saw you get your first kiss."

This was news to Jenna. "You did not."

"I did. You kissed that redheaded boy, the one with all the freckles, whose ears stuck out. Chuckie…"

Jenna felt her cheeks coloring. "Oh, God. Chuckie Blevins."

"You were thirteen. And that Chuckie. He was some kisser. He slobbered all over you—and you wiped your mouth after. But in a very Jenna-like way, so considerately, waiting until Chuckie wasn't looking."

"I can't believe you were *watching* that."

"You bet I was. It was probably the most exciting thing I ever saw you do." Lacey shoved a thick hank of curly blond hair back over her shoulder and sipped from her coffee cup. "And I still want an answer to my question. What's going on?"

"I don't—"

"Oh, stop it. *Something* is going on. You try to hide it, but you've got that worried, nervous look in those eyes of yours. It's the way you looked when you ran away from Mack McGarrity."

Jenna stiffened. "I beg your pardon. I did not—"

Lacey didn't even let her finish. "You did, too. Okay, okay. You called it a visit home. But you brought your cat with you, for heaven's sake. And you never did go back to New York. You bustled around here, inventing little cleaning and decorating projects to spiff up the house, acting busy but looking worried and sad, putting on fake smiles and trying to stay upbeat. But I could see. Anyone who cared about you could see. Something was very wrong."

"Well, my marriage was ending. Of course I was worried. And I didn't go back to New York because there was no point in going back. It was over between Mack and me."

"Jenna. I'm saying that you've seemed the same way

for the last couple of days—not sad this time so much, but worried and really preoccupied. And I want to know what's bothering you."

Jenna looked at her sister for a long time, torn between the probable wisdom of keeping her own counsel and the real need to share her problem with someone she could trust.

Need won out. "Mack's in town."

Lacey set down her bagel without taking a bite of it. "You're joking. It's a joke, right?"

"No. It's no joke."

"In town? *Where* in town?"

"He's staying at the Northern Empire Inn."

"And he came to town to see *you?*"

"Yes."

"Does Dr. Do-Right know?"

"Lacey, I really wish you'd stop calling Logan Dr. Do-Right."

Lacey wrinkled her nose. "Sorry." Then she put on a contrite look. "Let me try again. Does *Logan* know?"

"I'm telling him as soon as he gets back from Seattle."

"Translation. You haven't told him yet." Lacey picked up her bagel again, looked at it, then dropped it for the second time. "I can't stand it. Talk. Tell me *everything.*"

"It's awful," Jenna warned. "It's embarrassing and unfair and just plain wrong. And if I thought I could get away with it, I'd do something life-threatening to Mack McGarrity."

"Just tell me what's going on."

So Jenna explained the whole mess to her sister.

At the end, Lacey asked, "Have you called your lawyer about it?"

Jenna sighed. "I don't have a lawyer, not as of this

moment. The lawyer I did have has apparently closed up shop and moved away. He's not in the phone book anymore. And yesterday I drove by the address where he used to have his office. There's a florist shop there now."

"Great," Lacey remarked, in a tone that said it was anything but. "So you need a new lawyer."

"That's right. And I'll need a good one, I think. If I do end up having to divorce that man for the second time, he's promised me he'll think of a thousand ways to drag things out all over again."

"You know, he's always been kind of an S.O.B."

"You said it, I didn't."

"Maybe if you just hang tough, he'll give up."

"I keep hoping the same thing. But…" Jenna let a weary shrug finish the thought.

Lacey nodded. "Mack McGarrity is not the type who gives up."

"Exactly."

Lacey picked up her coffee mug and sipped. Then she set the mug down. "Can I ask you something?"

"Go ahead."

"Didn't you *notice* that you never got the final papers for your divorce?"

Jenna braced her elbows on the table and rubbed at her eyes. "It crossed my mind now and then. But you have to understand, it was *over.* We'd made an agreement. The rest felt like formalities. And I wasn't thinking about marrying anyone else then, so…"

Lacey was watching her way too closely. "Don't hate me, but are you *really* sure it's over between you and Mack?"

Jenna's answer was immediate. "Of course I am. Why?"

"Well, there was just something so… powerful, between the two of you. It's not the same with Dr. Do— er, Logan."

Jenna knew she shouldn't ask, but she couldn't seem to stop herself. "What do you mean, not the same?"

"Well, you and Logan are just perfect for each other, on the surface. A couple of straight arrows who want to raise a bunch of cute, happy kids. But there's something a little bit…" Lacey let the sentence trail off unfinished.

Jenna shifted in her chair impatiently. "What? A little bit what?"

"I don't know. Lukewarm, I guess. Something kind of tepid about the whole thing."

Jenna felt defensive—and tried not to let it show. "Logan and I are both mature adults now. We know what we want. If that seems lukewarm to you—"

Lacey put up a hand, palm out. "Look. Sorry. I'm talking out of turn. Logan adores you. He always has."

Jenna easily read between the lines of what Lacey had just said. When Lacey used words like *tepid* and *lukewarm,* it wasn't Logan she was talking about.

Jenna shifted in her chair again. "There is a lot more to making a marriage work than how much heat is generated."

"I realize that," Lacey said gently. "Honestly I do." She reached across the table and wiggled her fingers. "Come on. Put 'er there."

Jenna slid her hand into her sister's.

"So," Lacey said. "What do you plan to do now?"

Jenna groaned. "Leave the country?"

Lacey gave Jenna's hand a squeeze. "Come on. Seriously. What next?"

"Well, I'll see a lawyer on Monday, just to make certain of my options."

"And then?"

"If it turns out there's nothing I can do but give Mack his two weeks or divorce him all over again, I'm going to wait a while. Hang tough, as you put it. See if, just maybe, I can outlast him. I mean, eventually he has to get tired of hanging around here…doesn't he?"

"Hey, don't ask me. I'm only the little sister—and if he won't give up and give you the papers, then what?"

"What choice do I have? I'll start divorce proceedings. Again."

Lacey looked down at their joined hands. "What will you tell Logan?"

"The truth."

"When?"

Now Jenna was squeezing Lacey's hand. She teased, "For someone who has never liked Logan, you seem awfully worried about him all of a sudden."

Lacey pulled away. "What do you mean, I never liked Logan? Of course I like Logan. Just because he drives me insane with his endless and irritating advice on how I should run my life doesn't mean I don't care about him—and you haven't answered my question. When will you tell him?"

"As soon as he gets back from Seattle."

Jenna went to see a new lawyer on Monday and heard what she already knew. She could turn in the old papers, signed by both parties, and be eligible to remarry in about six months. Or she could start the whole process all over again.

After she talked to the lawyer, she did nothing. After

all, she told herself, that was what she had planned to do, see if she could wait Mack out.

Logan had arrived home too late on Sunday for them to get together. But Monday night they went out to dinner. Jenna planned to tell him about Mack then. But she didn't. She said nothing. She spent the meal asking him a thousand unnecessary questions about his trip and trying her best not to let him see how on edge she was.

Logan stopped in at the house for a while when he took her home. Lacey was there. Logan mentioned that he'd noticed an ad in the *Meadow Valley Sun.* The local art supply store needed a sales representative.

"Thanks, Doc," Lacey replied. "But I think I'd rather enter a convent. Or maybe hire myself out to a medical research lab somewhere. You know, as a human guinea pig for important experiments that could mean the end of cancer in our lifetime."

Logan let out a weary sigh. "Lacey, I'm not joking. It might turn out to be a good thing for you."

Lacey opened her mouth to utter more wisecracks, but Jenna caught her eye. Lacey smiled sweetly. "No, thanks, Doc. Really." A moment later she slipped from the room.

She reappeared as soon as Logan left.

"You didn't tell him, did you?" She was shaking her head.

"I just couldn't bear to."

"You'll have to. Eventually."

"I know. And I will. Eventually."

But not right now.

For right now, Jenna waited. Though she couldn't sleep at night and she was distracted in the daytime, she waited. And felt frustration and misery and a kind of righteous fury that Mack had put her in this untenable position in the first place.

She waited, hoping against hope that Mack would see how unreasonable and outlandish his ultimatum was. That she'd check the mailbox one evening and find the signed papers there—along with a short note of apology from Mack saying he regretted any pain he'd caused her and he was headed back to Key West.

She waited.

And she thought too much about Mack—so much that she found herself wishing more than anything that she could make herself *stop* thinking about him. She wished she could stop thinking about the ways he was the same as he used to be—and the ways he was different. Wished she could stop wondering about what he might be doing with himself, hanging out at the Northern Empire Inn with nothing to do but wait for her to call. She wished she could stop thinking about how she shouldn't be thinking about him and she was going to *stop* thinking about him—which only led her to think about him some more.

On Wednesday she and Logan met for lunch. He frowned at her across the table and said she seemed distracted lately. He wanted to know what was wrong.

She evaded. She thought, this *will* all blow over. Mack will come to his senses and send me the papers and then Logan and I can laugh about how silly the whole thing was.

Logan said, "Those papers haven't come from Florida yet, have they? Is that what's been on your mind?"

She gulped and admitted that the divorce papers *had* been on her mind, and that no, she didn't have them yet.

"Maybe you should call Mack McGarrity again."

Before she was forced to come up with a reply to that suggestion, the waiter miraculously appeared with their food. Once the waiter left, she exercised great care to move the conversation onto safer ground.

On Wednesday evening, as she was closing up the shop, Jenna thought she saw Mack across the street, just going into a store called Furniture By Hand. She stood at her own shop window for several minutes, waiting to see him come out of the other shop's door. He never emerged, at least not while she watched for him.

She wondered, was it really Mack? Or just someone who looked like him? Or worse, could it be her imagination working scarily overtime? It occurred to her that she couldn't even be sure that he was still in town.

That night she called the Northern Empire Inn for the second time. She asked for Mack McGarrity's room. And the clerk put her through.

He answered on the second ring that time. "McGarrity here."

She said, "I was hoping you might have come to your senses and gone home."

"No. I'm still here."

"This isn't right, Mack. It isn't fair."

She heard him draw in a breath. "It's only two weeks, Jenna."

"Give me those papers and go back to Florida where you belong."

"Not until you come with me."

She knew that the next thing she said would be shouted. So she hung up the phone, her nerves disgustingly aflutter.

She thought of those words her sister had used. *Lukewarm*. And *tepid*.

There was certainly nothing tepid about her response to Mack McGarrity.

But what about Logan? *Was* she lukewarm and tepid when it came to him?

Well, what if she was—just a little?

Maybe she liked it that way. Maybe she was mature enough now to appreciate a kinder, gentler sort of love.

Except…

Well, it *had* been beautiful with Mack. In bed. Beautiful and astonishing and utterly right.

And the truth was, she and Logan had never actually made love. Not in the complete sense of the word. Not in the consummated sense.

They'd agreed to wait until after the wedding.

And waiting had seemed good and right, up till now.

Up till Mack McGarrity had appeared in town.

Up until those dreams Jenna kept having now about the way it used to be with Mack. How Mack couldn't keep his hands off her and how she couldn't stay away from him.

How they *didn't* wait.

Maybe, she thought Wednesday night, after she hung up on Mack for the second time that week, she and Logan needed *not* to wait. Maybe she and Logan needed a night in each other's arms. A night to seal their bond in the most elemental of ways.

Yes. That might just be it. She needed to make love with Logan in order to wipe out the memory of Mack's touch.

She shared her insight with Lacey on Thursday night.

Lacey blinked those big blue eyes. "Wait a minute. You're saying you and Dr. Do-Right have never…?"

"We were waiting." Jenna hated how prim she sounded. "Until the wedding. And stop calling him Dr. Do-Right."

Lacey nodded, a very unconvinced sort of nod. "Waiting. Right."

"People do wait, you know."

"I know."

"You're not acting as if you know."

"Well, I mean, it just took me by surprise, that's all. The thought of it, of you and—"

"Do not call him—"

"I won't. The thought of you and *Logan...*" Lacey's face was red.

"The thought of Logan and me what?"

"Well, you know. In bed. Making love. I never thought about that. But I guess that makes sense—that it would be hard for me to picture." Lacey laughed, a thoroughly irritating little titter of a laugh. "Because you've never done it, right?"

Jenna felt vaguely insulted. "You are not helping me out one bit here."

"I'm trying."

"Try harder."

"I will."

"Good. So?"

"So, in my humble opinion, if you really want to seal your bond with Logan, the first thing you ought to do is to tell him the truth. That Mack's taken a room at the Northern Empire Inn and he intends to stay there until you agree to go away with him."

"I am *not* going to go away with Mack."

"Don't tell me that, tell Logan."

"I will."

"When?"

"Tomorrow night, all right? Is that good enough for you?"

"Now is better. And don't look at me like that. You asked."

"Well, fine. All right. I'll call him right now, tell him I need to talk with him."

Lacey turned around and snared the phone off the breakfast nook wall. "Here you go."

Jenna took it—and then just sat there, holding it.

"What?" Lacey groaned. "All of a sudden you've forgotten his number?"

"Of course I haven't forgotten his number. I know his number."

"Hey. Look here. You've got him on auto dial."

"Lacey—"

But it was too late. Lacey had punched the button and Logan's phone was ringing.

"This is Dr. Severance."

"Uh. Hello."

"Jenna. Hello." As always, he sounded so happy to hear her voice. "What's up?"

"I wonder…" She hesitated.

Lacey mouthed the words, "Do it!"

Jenna made a face at her sister and then forced herself to go on. "Do you think you could come over here? There are a few things I need to talk to you about." Lacey gave her the high sign and a big, congratulatory grin.

Logan said, "Are you all right?"

"I'm fine. I just…really need to talk to you."

"I'll be over right away."

# Chapter Four

Lacey decided to make herself scarce. As she went out the door, she advised, "Don't wait up—and don't you dare chicken out this time."

"I won't," Jenna replied, sounding a lot more confident than she felt.

Logan arrived five minutes later. Jenna led him to the back parlor, the big, comfortable room off the kitchen, where the family had always gathered. He sat on the roomy dark green convertible sofa and looked up at her, a worried frown creasing his brow. "This is about whatever's been bothering you for the past week, isn't it?"

She sat down beside him. "Yes."

He turned toward her, still frowning. In his somber expression she saw his concern for her. And his love. "You know that whatever it is, you can tell me, don't you?"

"I know. I just…"

"You know that I love you?"

"I do. And I love you." It was true. She did love him. But not in the way she had loved Mack McGarrity. And that did bother her. It bothered her terribly.

"Logan, I wonder…?"

"Yes?"

"Would you…kiss me? Really kiss me?"

He sat back from her a little. "Kiss you? I thought you were going to tell me—"

She put three fingers lightly against his lips, to silence him. "I will. I'll tell you. I'll explain everything. Just…would you please kiss me first?"

His dark gaze scanned her face. "Kiss you."

"Yes. Please."

His expression softened a little, the worried frown fading. He slid an arm around her shoulder and gently, with the tip of a finger, tipped her mouth up to his.

Light as a breath, his lips met hers. His mouth was warm and soft and his big arms cradled her cherishingly.

She closed her eyes and tried to give herself fully to the act of kissing him, sliding her hands up his broad chest, allowing her lips to part, inviting him to deepen the kiss. His tongue slid into her mouth.

Jenna sighed. But she knew as the small, tender sound escaped her that it was a fake sigh, a forced sigh, an effort to convince herself—and Logan, too—that she was an eager participant in this.

Jenna closed her eyes tighter, kissed him back harder, tried to call up memories of when they'd been teenagers.

Teenagers necking in the front seat of his car.

It had been exciting then, hadn't it? She was certain it had.

But now wasn't then.

Between now and then, there had been Mack.

Mack.

That did it. Just the thought of his name.

Jenna shoved at Logan's chest.

Startled, Logan pulled away enough to look down at her. "What is it? What's wrong?"

He still had his arms around her. She felt trapped there, all wrong there. "Please. Let go."

He released her and sat back. "Jenna. What the hell is going on here?"

"I…I don't think I can marry you, Logan." She didn't know she was going to say it until after the words were out. And then, once she *had* said it, she stared at him, stunned at what she herself had just uttered.

Logan stared back at her, bewildered. And hurt. "Why not?"

She took his hand and looked into his face, right into his eyes. "You are such a good man. A *kind* man. A man who wants just what I want. A man I could always count on to be there when I needed him…"

"Then why can't you marry me?"

"Because this…you and me…it just isn't right for me."

His dark eyes were shining, a shine that very well might have come from unshed tears. Jenna watched his Adam's apple move as he swallowed, forcing down the emotions a man hesitates to reveal.

When he spoke, as always, he strove for calm and reason. "And how did you come to this realization?"

She looked away, and then back. And then, finally, she made herself say it. "Mack's in town. He's refused to sign the divorce papers unless I spend two weeks with him first."

Logan swore under his breath. Then he asked, carefully, "How long has he been here?"

"A week."

"And you…didn't feel you could tell me?"

"I kept hoping he'd give up and go away. I'm furious with him, and I can't believe he's doing this and…I just wanted it to all be over before I said anything to you."

"But it's not over."

Jenna hitched in a tight breath. "No. It's not."

"You're talking about more than just the divorce papers, aren't you? You're talking about you and him."

Jenna wished with all her heart that she didn't have to answer that. But she knew that she did.

"I believed it was over, between Mack and me," she said. "I swear I did, or I never would have said yes when you asked me to marry you."

"But…?"

"But the minute I saw him again…" She shook her head. "I *don't* want to get back together with him. It could never work out. But there *is* unfinished business between Mack McGarrity and me. And I think I'm going to have to take care of it."

"Wait a minute. Don't tell me that you'll do what he wants you to do, that you'll actually go away with him!"

Jenna swallowed. "I…it's possible. I just might."

Logan held her hand more tightly, squeezing the fingers hard enough that she winced. "Jenna. Look what's going on here, look at the way he's maneuvering you. He's a manipulative S.O.B."

Gently Jenna pulled her hand free. "Lacey more or less called him the same thing."

"It looks like this is one situation where Lacey and I actually agree."

"You don't understand. You don't know him. He lost his parents when he was very young. He never had a real family. He grew up in foster homes. He had to scratch and scuffle for everything he ever got. When he wants something, he goes after it, any way he has to."

"And he's decided, after all this time, that he wants you?"

"I can't read his mind. But I do know there was a time when he and I shared something very special. He told me last Friday that he was trying to come to grips with what went wrong."

"He's chosen a hell of a way to go about it."

"As I said, it's the only way he knows."

Logan made a low noise in his throat. "Listen to you. Defending him."

She put her hand against the side of his face, longing to make him understand. "Logan. I have to do this."

Scowling, he ducked away from her touch. "I think it's time I had a nice long talk with that—"

"Please. Don't."

"Jenna. He's forced you into this."

"No. No, he hasn't. I don't *have* to go with him. I could divorce him all over again. It might take time, but it wouldn't take forever. If I go away with him, it will be because I choose to do it. For myself."

Logan looked at her piercingly. "You're sure?"

"I am." She slid the ring off her finger and held it out.

"Keep it," Logan said.

"No. That wouldn't be right."

Reluctantly he took it. A few minutes later, she walked him to the door.

And ten minutes after that, she was walking out herself. She got into her car and headed straight for the Northern Empire Inn. She knew the way. The inn was a Meadow Valley landmark, built over a century before.

She was lucky. She found a parking space near the front entrance. The fine old wood floors creaked a little under her feet as she strode through the foyer and up to the front desk.

"Mack McGarrity's room, please."

The desk clerk, who looked about twenty and had big brown eyes, smiled at her sweetly. "I'll ring his room and tell him he has a visitor. Your name, please?"

"Just tell me where his room is. I'll find it myself."

"Oh, I can't do that." The clerk's brown eyes had gone wider than before.

"And why not?"

"Well, I mean, it's…" Her smooth brow furrowed as she tried to think why. And then she remembered. She announced, with great pride, probably quoting from a training manual, "Because all of our guests have a reasonable expectation of privacy."

*Mack McGarrity has no expectation of privacy at all,* Jenna thought, *not right now, not when it comes to me….*

But of course, she didn't say that. The clerk was only following orders. "My name is Jenna Bravo. Tell him I'd like to come to his room."

"One moment, please."

The clerk turned to the antique switchboard behind her and rang Mack's room. When she turned back, she was all smiles again. "Mr. McGarrity is expecting you."

"I'll bet he is," Jenna muttered to herself.

"Excuse me?"

"I said, I'll be so glad to see him. Which room is he in?"

"He's taken the East Bungalow. Go out that door there, across the back patio and take the trail that winds to your right."

The East Bungalow, nestled among the oaks well away from the main building, was a wood frame structure, blue with white trim. It had a cute little white porch, complete with a rocker, a swing and planters under the front windows. The lights were on inside, spilling a golden glow out into the mild September night.

The door was wide open and Mack was standing in the doorway—lounging, really, looking lazy and insolent and quite pleased with himself. As Jenna marched up the porch steps to confront him, he gave her a slow once-over with hooded eyes.

Her body responded to his glance as if he had touched her. A hot little shiver slid over her skin, a shiver of awareness, of sensual recognition.

He straightened from his slouch and folded his arms over his chest. "It's about time you showed up."

She paused on the threshold. He was blocking the doorway. "May I come in?"

"By all means." He stepped aside.

She entered warily, into a front sitting room decorated in Victorian style, with lace curtains at the windows, glass-shaded lamps and a sofa and love seat with carved claw-footed legs. Most of the furniture had been pushed against the wall to make room for two desks, set at right angles to each other. One desk had a laptop, a fax machine and telephone on it, the other a full-size computer, complete with mammoth monitor. At the moment, the monitor was running a screensaver of planets, stars and moons hurtling endlessly through deep space.

"Well," Jenna said. "I see you've been keeping busy this week."

He closed the door. "I like to keep an eye on how my stocks are performing."

"Oh. That's right. You take big chances. And they pay off."

He grinned. "Do you remember *everything* I said the other night?"

"I remember all the important parts. Like what I have to do to get those divorce papers out of you."

He went to where all the furniture was crammed against the wall and pulled the coffee table out enough that there was room to slide onto the sofa behind it. "Have a seat."

"No, thank you. I'm here to ask if, just maybe, you might have come to your senses and decided to behave like a decent human being."

He shrugged and sat down himself, plunking his long legs on top of the coffee table and laying his arms along the sofa's carved back. "Come on, Jenna. You know I can't do that. I'm a *lawyer,* after all."

She glared down at him, determined to communicate her cold contempt for him and the havoc he'd wreaked on her nice, well-ordered life.

But truthfully, she didn't feel cold. She felt…energized. After days of confusion and misery, she was taking charge of this situation. And it felt good.

"All right," she announced. "You can have your two weeks."

He gave her a quick salute by briefly dipping his golden head. "I'm pleased to hear you've come to see things my way."

"No. No, I have not come to see things your way. Not

at all. I've just agreed to *do* things your way—up to a point."

"Up to what point?"

"I want to make a few of the decisions."

He studied the toes of the expensive hand-tooled boots he was wearing and asked in a suspicious tone, "What kind of decisions are you talking about?"

"The major kind. You know, the kind I somehow never got to make when we were together. Such as where we'll go and what we'll do."

He swung his feet to the floor, shoved the coffee table a little farther from the sofa and braced his elbows on his knees. "I thought we could—"

"Save it. You can tell me what *you* want to do later, because we'll do what *I* want to do first. That's fair, isn't it?"

"Fair?" He looked at her as if he didn't know the meaning of the word—which, of course, shouldn't have surprised her.

"Yes, fair. I get to decide where we go and what we do during the first week. The second week will be yours."

He leaned back into the couch cushions. "How generous of you."

"I'm glad you think so. You will pay for all of it."

He didn't seem terribly upset by that news, but he did remark, "Let me get this straight. *You* get to decide where we'll go—and *I* have to pay for it all?"

"I'm only deciding half of the time. And you're the one who started this, remember? You're the one who camped out here and wouldn't leave until I did what you wanted. Well, I'm doing what you wanted. And you can darn well pay for it. Besides, you can afford it."

He muttered something under his breath.

"What's that?"

"Nothing. All right, all right. I'll pay."

"And we will have separate rooms."

He grunted. "Why did I know you were going to say that?"

"Separate rooms, Mack."

He let out a big, fake sigh. "All right. Separate rooms." He was grinning again, a very irritating grin. "But nothing says you can't change your mind."

"I will not change my mind." She was truly proud of how firm she sounded.

He looked wistful. "We did have a great sex life. Remember?"

She did remember, all too well. She repeated, "I won't change my mind."

"Never say never."

"Do you understand? Separate rooms."

"Yeah. Right. I hear you loud and clear." He chuckled. "You've changed, Jenna. You're not the same sweet, gentle-natured girl I married."

"You're right. I'm not. And maybe you're having second thoughts about this. It's okay with me. Really. Just sign those papers and—"

"Not a chance. We're doing this."

"Then I'll need a few days, to take care of things at my store and make our travel reservations."

He shrugged. "Fine. Can you have it all handled by Monday?"

"Yes, I can."

"And where are we going on Monday, anyway?"

She hadn't decided yet. But if she told him that, he'd only start in about where *he* thought they should go. "Let me surprise you."

"I never much liked surprises."

"Too bad. I'll make all the arrangements for my week. You can reimburse me later."

"The arrangements for *what?*"

"Uh-uh. I told you. It's a surprise."

He gave her an oblique look. "Am I allowed one request?"

"That depends on what it is."

"I'd really prefer we didn't stay here in your home-town."

She was tempted to tell him that it was her week and if she decided to remain here, they would. But that would only have been pure orneriness. Truthfully, she didn't want to stay in Meadow Valley any more than Mack did. In Meadow Valley they'd constantly have to worry about running into familiar faces—like Logan, for instance.

"Don't worry," she said. "We're not staying here."

The slight crease between his brows smoothed out—and he came right back with more demands. "If we're flying, be damn sure you at least book first-class seats."

"First class it is."

He leaned an elbow on the sofa arm and rested his fist against his mouth.

She did not like the way he was looking at her. "What?"

He let the fist drop. "I see you gave the good doctor back his engagement ring."

She glanced down at her left hand, thought of Logan again, felt a stab of mingled guilt and sadness. "Wasn't that what you wanted?"

"I wanted you to go away with me. Is that really so bad?" His eyes were softer now, more gray than blue.

That softness did it, made her answer him honestly. "Mack, it's not what you wanted, it's how you went about getting it."

He sat forward again. "If I'd come to you and asked you to give me two weeks before making our divorce final, what would you have said?"

There was only one answer to that question, and they both knew it. "No."

His eyes had that gleam in them, the one that said he'd made his point. "So. What choice did I have?"

"You had the choice of asking me, and then accepting my answer."

"The way I asked you to come back to me seven years ago?"

She looked at him and shook her head.

"What?" he said. "I did. I asked."

"You did not ask, Mack. You never asked. You *told.*"

"I flew here from New York just to try to talk to you. To get you to see that I—"

"Oh, please. You fit in a flight between meetings. You took a cab from Sacramento International and when you got here, you made the cabby wait. You pounded on the door of my mother's house at nine-thirty at night, in a hurry as always, and ready with your demands. When I opened the door, you didn't *ask* me anything. You *told* me to get my things together and get out to that cab. You had a midnight flight back to LaGuardia for both of us. And an important meeting the next afternoon at two."

"I was trying to make a future for us, damn it."

"Mack. By then, there was no 'us' to make a future for."

"I realize that now. I should have spent more time with you. But as I remember, that meeting I had to get back for *was* an important one."

She gave a weary little laugh. "You know, Mack, in the entire time we were married, I don't think you ever had a meeting that wasn't important."

"I came to get you. I wanted you with me. *You* were always the most important thing in my damn life."

"Thing, Mack? *Thing?* I think you just hit on the operative word."

"You know what I mean. You *were* important to me."

"You had a very strange way of showing it—and the point is, when you came to get me then, you did not ask. You told."

"And you said no."

"That's right. I did. It was a major breakthrough for me."

He wasn't all that interested in her breakthrough. "You said no," he reiterated. "The same as you would have said no this time around, if I'd asked. Or if I'd told. So I didn't ask *or* tell. I used a little leverage."

"And now, for some reason, you're trying to convince me, or maybe yourself, that using 'leverage' is okay. And I'm telling you it's not. It's what you did. And we'll make the best of it. But it is not okay. Got that?"

"Yeah. I'd say you've hammered it in pretty good." He leaned against the sofa arm and gave her the same kind of slow once-over he'd given her when she came up the porch steps. "And you really are meaner."

"I warned you."

"It's okay. I can take meaner. Now."

She didn't trust the warmth in his eyes, or the sudden velvety sweetness in his deep voice. She moved back a step. "I should go."

"Why?"

Her knees had started doing that ridiculous wobbly

thing—and her heart kept up a steady, rapid boom-boom-boom inside her chest. "I said I'd spend two weeks with you. Beginning on Monday, and it's not Monday yet."

"Nothing like a head start, I always say." He stood slowly, not making any sudden moves. "Have you eaten? We could—"

"I ate hours ago."

He stepped around from behind the coffee table. "A drink, then. The bar is right there." He gestured at an armoire against the wall to her right. Then he started toward her.

"No." She backed up a second step. And a third. "No drink. No, thanks."

He kept on coming. "Jenna. Are you afraid of me?"

"I am not."

"I never hurt you, did I?"

"Of course not—not physically, anyway. But..."

He knew what she meant. "There are other kinds of hurt."

"That's right."

"You hurt me, too."

"Then we're even."

"Yeah. Sure. We're even." He backed her right up against the section of wall next to the door. "Your upper lip is quivering, just like it used to do whenever something really got to you."

"It's not a quiver. It's a nervous twitch."

"It's twitching, then. I really like your mouth. Did I ever tell you that?"

"Yes." She cleared her throat. "You did. Way back when." She was thinking, *Tell him to step aside. To move back. To get out of the way so that you can go.*

"It's not a full mouth, but it's so nice and wide and friendly—and then, there are those dimples on either side when you smile."

"I am not smiling now."

"I know." He sighed. She felt his breath, sweet and warm, across her cheek. "And you want me to get back, right?"

"That's right."

"Because you're leaving."

"I am."

"Because you already ate and you don't want a drink."

"Yes."

"Because the two weeks don't begin till Monday."

She nodded.

"And you don't believe in head starts."

His mouth was very close. She was staring at it, remembering what it felt like on hers, remembering, all at once, their first kiss.

They'd been standing by a door then, too. The door to his apartment in L.A. It was after they'd gone out to eat Italian food, and then returned to his place for that last cup of coffee.

She'd told him she did have to go. And he had walked her the few steps to the door. And she'd said something about taking Byron with her.

And he had touched her then, cradling her face in both of his warm hands, raising her chin so she had to look right at him. "I don't want you to go," he whispered.

And then he kissed her. She cried out at the first touch of his lips on hers, not a loud cry, but an urgent one. Her mouth opened beneath his. To her, it felt like the opening of her very soul. From that instant, she knew: this was the man for her.

"Stay," he whispered against her parted lips….

Jenna blinked.

She was not in Mack's old L.A. apartment. She was in the East Bungalow at the Northern Empire Inn. And she was leaving.

Mack said, very softly, "Are you sure you don't want to—?"

"I am sure."

He took the crystal doorknob and gave it a turn. The chirping of crickets from outside grew louder and the cool evening air came in around them.

She said, "I'll call you, as soon as I make the reservations."

He was still looking at her mouth. "I'll be here."

The three words sent a dangerous thrill zinging through her. *I'll be here.* Oh, what she would have given to have heard him say those words years ago. To have heard him say them then—and mean them. To have had him truly with her when he said he would be, instead of always working, always busy, always preoccupied, far away from her even when he seemed to be close.

Mack saw the wishful look on her face. It gave him hope—enough that he suggested one last time, "Change your mind? Stay?"

She shook her head and went out into the night, through the grove of oaks, along the trail that led to the glowing lanterns strung along the back patio of the Northern Empire Inn.

## Chapter Five

Saturday, Jenna decided where she and Mack would be going. She booked their flights and made a few other calls. She also briefed her clerks on their upgraded responsibilities while she would be gone.

Lacey agreed to stay in town for the two weeks. She'd keep an eye on the shop, look after the house and take care of Byron. She said she wasn't quite ready for the L.A. rat race yet, anyway.

She also said she could not believe that Jenna had agreed to run off with Mack McGarrity.

"I try not to think of it as 'running off,' Lace."

Lacey heaved a big sigh. "Poor Logan—but I do think it's the best thing, whatever happens with Mack. You were the right woman for Logan, but he was never quite the right man for you. I just hope he gets over it.

And I wish he had more friends—a brother or something, someone he could really *talk* to about it."

Jenna, who felt terrible about Logan herself, couldn't resist remarking, "It would have been nice if you'd shown him this much sympathy when he and I were engaged."

"Why? He didn't need it then. He really is such an irritating man. But now, well, I just worry about him, you know? I guess I have to admit, I've developed a certain…fondness for him, over the years."

Jenna was worried about him, too. Which was why she suggested, "Maybe you could stop by and see him, in a few days. You know, just to make sure he's doing all right."

"Oh, great idea. That's exactly what he needs. Your bad baby sister showing up at his door."

"I think it would mean a lot to him. I think he cares about you, too."

That seemed to give Lacey pause. "You do?"

"Yes. I know he got on your nerves, always pushing you to move back to town and 'settle down.' But he did it because you matter to him, I'm sure of that."

"Well," Lacey said. "I'll think about it. Visiting him, I mean."

Jenna called Mack Saturday evening to tell him they were booked on a flight from Sacramento to Denver. Their plane would leave at ten on Monday morning.

"What's in Denver?" he demanded.

She considered dragging out the "surprise," since she didn't really want to listen to him groan over where she'd decided they were going. But then again, he might as well groan now as later.

She said, "Denver is where my cousin Cash is picking us up. He has a small plane. He'll fly us to Medicine Creek, Wyoming. We're staying at the Rising Sun, which you just may remember is the Bravo family ranch."

Mack was still stuck back there with her first sentence. "Wait a minute. You have a cousin named *Cash?*"

"I'm sure I mentioned him, when we were married." Not that he would have been listening.

He said, "We're still married."

"Let's not get into that right now, please. Back to Cash. His real name is John, but everyone calls him Cash. He's my second cousin, actually. His grandfather was my grandfather's brother, on my father's side."

"Right."

Jenna knew what Mack's face would look like right then. His eyes would have that glazed-over look they always got when she started talking about the various members of her extended family.

"I've wanted to go to Wyoming for a long time, Mack. I even asked you once or twice to go with me, way back when."

It had been a dream of hers, a visit to Wyoming, ever since that awful second year of their marriage, after the move to New York City. She'd felt so lonely, so far away from home, a small-town girl in a very big city with a husband who had no time for her.

She'd learned from her mother that she had family right there in New York: Austin Bravo, a first cousin once removed. His children were grown. He and his wife, Elaine, lived on the Upper East Side.

Mack was supposed to have met Elaine and Austin. But as usual, at the last minute some problem at the firm came up and he backed out of the dinner engagement that Jenna had arranged with them. Jenna went alone. And Austin and Elaine had told her all about the ranch in Wyoming, which had been in the Bravo family for five generations.

Mack started grumbling. "What's it like in Wyoming in September, anyway? I'll bet it's damn cold. And it's windy there, too, did you know? Nothing but wind and prairie and cattle, from what I've heard."

"Mack, we are going to spend *my* week at the foot of the rugged Bighorn Mountains, getting to know the Wyoming branch of my family. Another second cousin of mine, Zach Bravo, whose father, by the way, is Austin Bravo, the one you were supposed to have met when we—"

"Can we skip what I was supposed to have done all those years ago? Please?"

"Certainly. As I was saying, Zach runs the ranch. He's married, has two daughters and a new baby due about three months from now. They're looking forward to our visit."

"Jenna, the whole point of this two weeks is that we're spending some time alone. That's a-l-o-n-e. Meaning just you and me. As in, *No one else around.* How are we going to be alone with your second cousin and his wife and the kids and the—"

"We will have time alone. I promise you."

He asked, "How big is this house where your cousin and his family live?"

"Not quite big enough for us to have separate rooms, I'm afraid."

"How sad," he said smugly. "So you're saying we'll be sharing a room, after all?"

"No, I'm not saying that at all. As it turns out, there's

a smaller house a little way from the main house. The woman who lives there is away on some kind of trip, so that's where we'll be staying. Tess—that's Zach's wife, the one who's having a baby—said that house had more than one bedroom. So we're in luck."

He muttered something that was probably an expletive.

She said, "I've got everything arranged."

"Yeah. I can see that—and I guess I'd better pick you up at eight Monday morning, all right? That'll get us to the airport in Sacramento in plenty of time."

"Eight sounds perfect."

Jenna hung up feeling really good. She was in charge and she and Mack were going somewhere she'd always wanted to go.

But by Monday morning at eight-thirty, as she paced back and forth in the foyer with her suitcases waiting a few feet away, she was not feeling good. Not feeling good at all.

As she paced, Byron appeared, tiptoeing along the hall between the back parlor and the front door. He strolled up to her, sat down in her path and looked up expectantly. She bent and took him into her arms.

He purred. She vented.

"Déjà vu," she muttered. "That's French for 'I've been here before,' and I have, Byron. You know that I have." She scratched the cat behind an ear. "'Eight o'clock,' he said. 'I'll pick you up at eight.' Well, as usual with Mack McGarrity, eight o'clock has been and gone and Mack McGarrity is nowhere in sight."

Right then, the phone rang. "Great. Now we get the excuses." She put Byron over her shoulder and stalked to the extension in the front parlor.

"What?" she barked into the mouthpiece.

"You're mad."

"You're right."

"Look. Something's come up, something completely unexpected and I—"

"Unexpected?" She tried not to shriek at him. "It's an hour's drive to the airport. Our plane takes off in—" she glanced at her watch "—eighty-three minutes. We don't have *time* for the unexpected right now."

"Listen. I'm on my way."

"You had to call to say you're on your way?"

"I know I'm late. I'm sorry. I wanted to let you know that I *am* coming over there. In fact, I'm here. Look out the window."

She did, and saw a silver-gray Lexus pulling up to the curb. Mack was behind the wheel, a cell phone at his ear. He waved at her.

She set down the phone and marched to the foyer, where Byron began to squirm to be let down. She bent and set him on the floor. He ran off down the hall. Then she turned to pull open the door.

Mack strode swiftly up the steps toward her, wearing faded blue jeans, a black T-shirt and a dark leather bomber jacket, looking like Steve McQueen in *The Great Escape,* ready for anything and so handsome it hurt. Funny, she thought, he never used to wear blue jeans, back when. Then, he wore expensive suits and designer ties—even at first, when he couldn't afford them. Apparently now that success was his, he no longer felt the pressing need to dress for it.

She stepped back and gestured him over the threshold, turning immediately for her suitcases. "Come on. Let's get these out to the car and—"

"Jenna."

She did not like the way he said her name. Slowly, she turned back to him. He had both hands stuck in the pockets of that gorgeous leather jacket and a very guilty expression on his face. That was when she knew what he was going to say next.

She said it for him. "You're backing out."

"Jenna, I—"

She went to the door and shut it. Then she planted both fists on her hips. "Just say it. You're not going."

"There's a…crisis. I'm sorry. I don't like it. But I'm going to have to put off our two weeks together."

"A crisis."

"Yes." He spoke very quietly, too quietly, in fact. "A crisis. Something I just can't put off dealing with."

"A meeting, right? A really terribly unavoidably *important* meeting. Am I right?"

"No. You're not." His voice rose in volume. "It's not a damn meeting."

"Stop shouting," she said. "You'll wake up my sister."

His mouth became a flat line and he muttered, "Sorry," but not as if he really meant it.

"Well," she said, making no effort at all to mask her sarcasm. "I suppose I should think of this as progress. At least you're telling me in person that you can't do what you said you'd do. The old Mack would have gone ahead and told me over the phone."

"You may not believe me, but this *is* important. I'm flying to Long Beach right away and—"

"Long Beach? Long Beach, California?"

"Right. And—"

"What's in Long Beach?"

He didn't answer, just went on with what he'd been

saying before. "—the minute this situation is handled, I'll call you and we can—"

"What *situation?*"

"*This* situation."

"Mack. I am exerting great effort not to start shouting at you. You could help me a little here. You could tell me what the problem is. You could tell me *why* you're backing out on me."

"I'm not backing out on—"

"What *is* the problem?"

He glared at her, then he sucked in a big breath and raked his hand back over his hair. "It's not a good idea, I think, to go into it now. If you'll just wait until I've—"

"Wait? You want me to *wait?*"

"Yeah, but only until I've taken care of this thing and we have a little time to—"

"Stop. Stop right there." She held up her left hand and wiggled the fingers at him. "Notice. No engagement ring. Because of you, I have broken up with a wonderful man who loved me with all of his heart."

Mack made a low noise in his throat. "What? You expect me to feel guilty about that? Well, I don't. Not one damn bit. It was a wise move on your part. You're not ready to marry the good doctor right now. It wouldn't be good for you, and it certainly wouldn't be good for him to marry another man's wife. You need—"

"Do not tell me what I need, Mack McGarrity. Listen to what *I* am telling *you*. You wanted two weeks. I am giving you two weeks. And those two weeks are starting *right now*."

"Jenna, I'm trying to tell you that I—"

"Stop talking. Listen. If the two weeks do not start now, they are not going to start at all, because I will do what I threatened to do when you first proposed this crazy scheme of yours. I'll divorce you all over again."

"Jenna. That's foolish. You don't want to do that."

"That's another thing I never could stand—the way you always thought you knew what I wanted. Well, you don't know what I want. *I* know what I want. And if you listen, I'll tell you. I want our two weeks to start right now. I'm ready to start right now, ready to get it over with. I don't want to wait around until *you* decide *you're* ready. I've been there and done that back when I lived with you."

"This is hopeless," he said. "You just will not listen. I keep trying to tell you that doing it now is not possible."

"Yes, it is possible. Because I'm willing to compromise a little."

"Compromise. I don't like that word."

"That's only because you have never done it in your life. But you're going to get your chance now. This is my offer. Your week will come first. We can spend it doing whatever it is you just *have* to fly to Southern California to do."

"That's a bad idea."

"Take it or leave it."

"No. Jenna. What I have to do right now isn't what I had in mind for my week at all. I wanted us to get away together, to be alone someplace private, someplace beautiful. I was hoping—"

"Stop trying to soften me up. You can't. I've been through it all with you before. We're going to Long Beach for this emergency of yours—or we aren't going anywhere."

He scraped a hand through his hair again, stared down at his boots and shook his head.

"I mean it, Mack. We start today, or we never start at all."

"Jenna…"

"And right now, before we begin, you are going to tell me what this emergency is."

"Damn it, Jenna."

"Now."

"All right," he said—and then he looked away.

She waited for a count of ten and then demanded, "Mack. Tell me."

He turned to her, glaring. "My mother is sick. They believe that she's dying."

Jenna was certain she hadn't heard him correctly. "Excuse me. I could have sworn you just said—"

"I did." He said it again. "My mother is dying."

"But…how could that be? You don't have a mother. Do you?"

## Chapter Six

Mack felt like an idiot as he was forced to confess, "Yes, Jenna. I do have a mother." He couldn't believe she'd kept after him until she'd made him tell her. The old Jenna would never have been so determined.

Oh, where had the old Jenna gone?

The new Jenna was shaking her head. "But you always said…you always led me to believe that you had no family, that you'd been raised in foster homes."

"I *was* raised in foster homes—mostly, anyway." Damn, he did not want to go into all this now. "Look. It's complicated. It's one of the things I thought we'd be talking about during our two weeks."

"Well. I guess you thought right. We will be talking about this mother you never said you had during our two weeks—which are starting now. I assume you've already set up a flight?"

"I have a plane waiting at Sacramento Executive Airport. And we need to get on it ASAP." He picked up her two suitcases, leaving the small overnight case for her to deal with.

She followed behind him, not arguing for once, as he went out the door and down the porch steps.

On the drive to Sacramento, Jenna used Mack's cell phone to call her family in Wyoming and tell them that their visit had been postponed. She also called the airline to say they wouldn't be making the Denver flight.

The private plane, a twelve-seater, was ready for takeoff when they got to the airport. The pilot loaded their baggage as Jenna and Mack settled into the passenger cabin, which was empty save for the two of them.

As soon as they were in the air, she turned to Mack. "Okay. Tell me about the mother you never said you had."

Mack had taken the window seat. He stared out over the wing at Sacramento's considerable urban sprawl. "Do you know that one in eight Americans lives in the state of California? Pretty incredible, huh?"

"Mack." Her voice was gentle.

It hurt, somehow. That gentleness. Hurt much more than all the hard accusations she'd hurled at him just about every time they'd spoken over the past week and a half. It hurt because it reminded him of the old Jenna. And of all he'd lost when he lost her.

Of all it was very possible he could never get back.

She wasn't the same.

But then, neither was he.

And the attraction was still there. That, he was sure

of. For him and for her, too, no matter how hard she tried to hide it.

In the end, it hadn't worked the way they were. Maybe it would turn out that they were both different enough in the right kind of way. Maybe a new beginning would be possible.

Then again, maybe he was whistling in the dark.

"Mack?"

He turned to look into the face that he'd never been able to forget, the face that had, on more occasions than he would ever be willing to admit, appeared in his dreams. "I didn't lie to you, not exactly."

The dimples he'd always loved showed faintly at the sides of that wide mouth of hers. "You lied only by omission."

"That's right."

"So. Now's the time to tell me what you left out."

He didn't know quite where to begin.

In that gentle, old-Jenna voice, she prompted, "You told me that your father died when you were six."

"That's right. And that was the truth."

"Somehow, I got the idea that your mother died shortly after."

"Maybe because that was what I wanted you to think. But my mother didn't die. She is alive—or she was a few hours ago. And I…have two sisters." Hazel eyes widened, the tiniest bit, in shock, at that news. He added, feeling just a little guilty, "I never told you that, either, about my sisters, did I?"

"No, Mack. You never did."

"Bridget and Claire. They were eight and four when my father died."

"You also never told me…how your father died."

"He was killed in a convenience-store holdup. He was the poor chump behind the counter. They were young, my parents. They didn't have much."

"That must have been tough on your mother."

"That's right. She didn't know what to do. She couldn't support us by herself. She put the three of us into foster care and got a job as a secretary in a small employment agency. For a while, she would come and visit us all the time."

Jenna touched the back of his hand. Mack felt that touch to the center of himself. But it must have been an unconscious gesture, one she instantly regretted, because she jerked her hand back within seconds after she made contact.

She asked, "What do you mean, she visited for a while?"

"I mean that the visits tapered off. Bridget and Claire and I were all in different foster homes by the time I was seven. And it was around that time that my mother started coming less and less often to see me. She came on my eighth birthday, I remember that. It was the last time."

"You mean, after that you never saw her again?"

The disbelief on Jenna's face made him smile. He remembered her mother, Margaret, who had been tall and capable, with a wide smile a lot like Jenna's. Jenna's father had died when Jenna was—what?—fifteen or sixteen, Mack was pretty sure. He was also sure that it had never occurred to Jenna's mom to put her children in foster care, let alone to relinquish all claim to them.

But then again, Jenna's father had been a successful insurance salesman and Jenna's mother had run the office for a title company. No doubt there had been a big life insurance policy and sufficient money coming in that Jenna's mother never had to worry all that much about where her family's next meal would come from.

Mack shrugged. "My mother came to see me on my eighth birthday, and that was it."

"But why? Why would she do that, desert you like that?"

"It turned out that she wanted to marry her boss— and she never managed to tell him about the kids she'd farmed out. When he proposed, she put us up for adoption, giving up all claim to us, along with any responsibility for our care."

"They told you that, when you were a child?"

"No. They only said, as gently as they could, that my mother couldn't take care of me anymore and I had become a ward of the court. I found out why later, after the class-action suit."

"Why not until then?"

Mack looked out the window again. The steady drone of the engines filled the cabin, and high white clouds rose up like towers of cotton in the distance.

"Mack."

He looked at her again then. "All those years when I was growing up in other people's houses, and later, when I was slaving away at college, when I met you…I just wanted to forget about her. Even though I didn't have the facts then, I knew that she had dumped me, that she had tossed me and my sisters overboard like so much extra baggage in a sinking boat."

Right then, Jenna ached for him. And maybe she understood him a little better than before. Was that a good thing? She wasn't sure. She felt such conflicting urges when it came to Mack, not the least among them the compelling need to guard her heart against the kind of damage he had inflicted on it before.

He said, "All my life I wanted money. Lots of it. I guess it's a classic situation. I thought money would protect me against the kinds of losses I suffered as a kid. Then I got what I wanted. I had money. And not much else."

Jenna's heart contracted. *Not much else.* She supposed that was true, in a way. He didn't have his family—his mother, or his sisters. And he no longer had a wife.

He went on, "So I hired investigators, to help me find out what had happened to my past."

"They tracked down your mother?"

He nodded. "I went to Long Beach, where she lives now, and I contacted her. She agreed to meet me in the lobby of my hotel."

"How long ago was this?"

"Two years. She was…she looked so small to me. And kind of faded and tired. And so damn sad. She cried, and she smoked cigarette after cigarette. And I kept thinking I should put my arm around her or something, but I couldn't quite make myself touch her. She said that she never had managed to tell her husband about us—Bridget and Claire and me—and she just didn't know how she was going to be able to bring herself to tell him then, either."

Mack let out a long breath. "It's strange. In my mind, over the years, I had made her into a kind of monster, a damn evil bitch who had dumped her own children. But looking at her then, I only felt sorry for her. She said she knew it was terrible of her, that if I didn't hate her already, I would when she asked what she was going to ask of me."

Jenna had a good idea what that must have been. "She still didn't want to tell her husband about you."

"That's right."

"And what did you say when she asked you not to tell him?"

"I said all right."

Jenna knew then, if she'd ever really forgotten, why she had loved this man. "Oh, Mack."

"Well." His voice was gruff. "What the hell else was I going to say? That I hated her guts and never wanted to see her again?"

"Some men might have said exactly that."

"No," he said. "No sense in that. I pretty much knew where I stood with her when I went looking for her."

"And since then?"

His mouth curved in a half smile. "I've kept in touch with her. I set her up with a P.O. box, so I could write to her and she wouldn't have to worry about her husband finding out. And she sends me stuff."

"Stuff?"

He looked embarrassed. "Stuff. You know, ugly ties for my birthday. Socks at Christmas. She's got a thing for those cheese-and-salami gift packs. You know, they come in a wooden box with a trademark branded into the lid. Inside, there's lots of fake green Easter-basket grass and different kinds of cheddar and smoked sausage—I get a lot of those."

Jenna's throat burned a little with the sudden pressure of tears. But she knew that Mack McGarrity had never been a man to accept a woman's pity. She swallowed the tears down and tried to speak lightly. "Oh, Mack. Cheddar and smoked sausage?"

"That's right. I tried to…help her out a little."

"Give her money, you mean?"

He nodded. "She wouldn't take it. She said that she

and her husband were doing fine. She didn't need anything from me. She just wanted a letter now and then, and a place to send the salami and cheese."

Jenna had more questions. "Has she been ill for a while now?"

"Not that she told me about."

"But you said she was sick."

"A heart attack, pretty much out of the blue. She's only fifty-two. I picked up my messages this morning and there was one from her husband. I managed to reach him at the hospital. He told me that the prognosis isn't good and that she's asked to see me."

There was a positive note here. Jenna pounced on it. "Her husband, you said? Her husband was the one who called?"

"That's right. His name is Alec. Alec Telford. Seemed like a decent enough guy."

Jenna repeated the name. "Alec. And your mother… her name is Doreen, right?"

He looked vaguely surprised. "You remembered."

How could I forget? she thought. He had told her so little about his family. Every detail she'd squeezed out of him had been information to treasure. "I believe that you also told me her maiden name was Henderson."

He chuckled, but without much humor. "It looks like you've got all the facts."

She grunted at that one. "Hardly. And what I'm getting at here is that, since Alec was the one who called you, it looks as if Doreen did finally tell him the truth, right?"

"I guess we could logically assume that." He turned toward the window again. She knew he was hoping he'd answered enough questions for a while.

But she had one more she just couldn't hold back.

"What about your sisters, Bridget and Claire? Did you find them, too?"

He turned to her with obvious reluctance and gave her his best lawyer's look. "And if I did?"

"Mack. Don't be like that. Just tell me. Did you find them?"

"Yes, I found them."

"And?"

"Jenna. Enough."

"No. Come on. I want to know about them."

"Oh, all right. Bridget's married. She and her husband have three kids. She lives in Oregon. And Claire is married, too. No kids yet, though. She teaches high school in Sacramento. From what my sources told me, both women are doing just fine."

"Sacramento? Did you stop in to see Claire, then, on your way to Meadow Valley?"

"No."

"But why not?"

"Jenna…"

"Oh, Mack, come on. I just want to know what your sisters are like."

"From the reports I got, they're nice, middle-class women with ordinary lives. But I can't say for sure. I've never talked to them."

She frowned, confused. "But why not? You went to all the trouble of finding them. It seems to me that meeting them would be the next logical step."

"After what happened with my mother, it occurred to me that maybe they wouldn't appreciate my popping into their lives out of nowhere."

That was a phony excuse if Jenna had ever heard one. "But—"

"Jenna. Let it go, all right? I haven't contacted my sisters, and I won't be contacting them. I know they're okay and that's enough for me." He turned to the window once more and stared out, as if the sight of rearing clouds and the rolling, dry mountains far below utterly fascinated him.

At the hospital they asked at the front desk for Doreen Telford's room. The clerk gave them some mumbo jumbo about critical care and asked them to take a seat. Someone would be down to speak with them shortly.

Mack didn't like the sound of that. "What's wrong? Is she worse?"

"Sir, if you'll just have a seat, as I said, someone will—"

"I know what you said. And I asked if my mother's gotten worse."

"Sir, I—"

Jenna cut in then, taking Mack by the arm. "All right. We'll be right over there." She tugged on Mack's arm. "Come on. We can wait a few minutes. It's not the end of the world."

Mack glared down at her, but he did allow her to lead him over to a black leather bench against the adjacent wall. When they reached the seat, she pulled him down beside her.

"Something must be wrong," he said. He felt strange, uncomfortable in his own skin. And his stomach had knotted up. "I didn't like the look on that clerk's face."

Jenna patted his arm. "It's all right. Just relax. She said it would only be a few minutes."

In spite of the dread that tightened his gut, Mack almost smiled. Ever since he'd walked into her shop, ten days ago now, she'd made it painfully clear he was to keep hands off. Never consciously had she touched him. On the plane, when she'd forgotten herself for a moment and reached out, she'd yanked her hand back so fast he could almost have missed the fact that she'd reached out at all.

So maybe this was a step in the right direction. She had her arm in his and she was holding on to him with her other hand.

All right, it was mostly to keep him from jumping up and laying into the admissions clerk. But she *was* holding on. And it felt damn good.

He endured the next ten minutes mostly because she *kept* holding on. He held on right back, even pushing it so far as to twine his fingers with hers—a move she allowed, though she stiffened a little at first and sent him a suspicious glance.

But then she relaxed. She held on to him and let him hold on to her. After all, it was the kind of grim situation when a man most needs a woman's touch.

Staring bleakly out over the reception area, Mack spotted the tall, stoop-shouldered man when he emerged from the hall to the elevators. The man wore a wrinkled short-sleeved dress shirt, dark slacks and black shoes. He had thinning gray hair and a certain look on his face: the glazed, rather numb stare of a man who has just taken a huge, unbearable blow and has yet even to begin dealing with it. A man in those first blank moments of pure shock.

Mack knew. It was his stepfather, Alec Telford. And he knew what the look on his stepfather's face meant.

He'd be getting no more boxes of salami and cheese in the mail. His mother was dead.

# Chapter Seven

The man Mack knew to be Alec Telford went to the admissions desk and spoke briefly with the clerk. The woman said something in reply, her gaze sliding over to where Mack and Jenna sat against the wall.

The tall, dazed fellow turned and came toward them.

Mack heard Jenna's voice, soft and cautious, in his ear. "Do you think that might be—"

"Yes." Mack let go of her hand. "I do." They stood at the same time.

The man stopped a few feet from them. "I…hello, I'm…" He blinked, his kind brown eyes going more vacant than before, as if he couldn't quite manage to call up his own name. "Alec," he said at last. "Call me Alec." He made a brave effort at a smile, one that stretched his mouth into a pained grimace.

Jenna said, "Mr., er, Alec, maybe you ought to sit down."

The brown eyes blinked again. "Sit? No, I don't think so." He turned resolutely toward Mack and held out his hand. "You're Mack. Dory's..." He gulped, his eyes going watery. Then he blinked again. "You're Doreen's boy." He extended a hand.

"Yes. I'm Mack McGarrity." Mack held out his own hand. They shook.

Alec leaned toward Mack. "I'm so sorry to tell you this, but Doreen...she's gone. It happened just..." He blinked some more and then sent his vacant gaze wandering the room.

Finally he found what he sought: a clock, on the wall above the admission desk. "Just an hour ago. An hour and five minutes, actually. I was sitting with her. And she opened her eyes. She said, 'My arm hurts, Al. My arm really hurts.' And then...all those machines they had her hooked up to, those machines started beeping. Nurses and doctors came racing in. They did all they could, but they couldn't save her. She...she's gone now."

"Come on," Jenna said. "Come on, Alec. You sit down right here." She took the older man by the shoulders and guided him to the bench. Mack knew a moment of stark gratitude that she had forced him to bring her here.

Alec Telford let his head drop back against the wall and looked up at Mack and Jenna. "I...I'm sorry." He was frowning at Jenna. "You are...?"

She gave him one of those smiles that haunted Mack's dreams, wide and tender and achingly sweet. "Jenna. Jenna Bravo. I'm Mack's, um, friend."

Mack resisted the urge to jump in, to correct her, to insist, She's Jenna *McGarrity*. And she is my wife. Alec

Telford, who had just lost his own wife, wouldn't give a damn anyway at that point.

"Well," Alec said. "Nice to meet you, Jenna."

Jenna's beautiful smile got even wider. "Nice to meet you, too."

The older man tried to pull himself a little straighter. "I meant to…do better at this. I wanted to…" His sentence wandered off into silence.

"It's all right," said Jenna. "You're doing wonderfully. Really."

Mack took his cue from her. "Yes. Uh. Thank you. For coming down yourself to tell me."

"I…well, it was the least I could do." The older man closed his eyes, licked his dry lips.

Jenna started moving away. Mack sent her a frantic look.

"Back in a jiff," she said, and headed across the room.

"So many…things to deal with," Alec Telford said. "I don't seem to be handling it very well."

"You're doing fine," Mack said automatically, watching Jenna as she went to the water cooler in the corner and filled a paper cup. "It's a big shock."

"You resemble her," Alec Telford said. Mack turned back to the man on the bench, who was staring at him with a sort of musing intensity that Mack found unsettling. "Not in size, of course. She was so small. But…the shape of the face. And the eyes. Those blue-gray eyes…"

My mother, Mack thought. He's saying I look like my mother. What the hell should I say in response? "Yes, I…well, I…" God. Jenna needed to get back here. She needed to get back here right now.

And then miraculously, there she was, the filled paper cup in her hand. "Here, Alec. Some water, maybe…?"

"Oh. Thank you." Alec took the cup and drank it in one swallow—so of course Jenna had to trot right back to the cooler and get him more. Fortunately, while she was gone that time, Alec didn't feel the need to start in again about how much Mack looked like his mother.

Once he'd had his second cup of water, Alec pushed himself from the bench. "Well. I can't sit forever, now, can I? I admit, I've been sitting upstairs, since they… took her away. Just sitting there, thinking that I should get busy. And then they told me you had arrived, Mack. And so I…" He paused, closed his eyes, took in a breath. "I do believe I am babbling," he said.

"Alec." Jenna laid her hand on his thin, heavily veined arm. "Alec, is there anyone here with you, to help you?"

"Help me? No. No, I've…it's always pretty much been just Dory and me. But I'm…quite capable, really. I can manage. No problem." He blinked, turned to Mack. "Tonight. Could you come to the house, do you think? There are a few things Dory wanted you to have. You have the address?"

Mack nodded.

"And the phone number?"

"Yeah."

"About eight?"

"Sure."

"Good, then—oh. Wait. Where are you staying? I probably ought to know, just in case there's something I—"

Jenna cut in then. "Alec, we can deal with all this later. Mack and I aren't going anywhere now. We're staying right here, with you, to help you."

Mack almost said, We are? But he shut his mouth over the words just in time.

Alec blinked some more. "Oh, no. I couldn't ask you. I can manage. Honestly, I—"

"Of course you can manage," Jenna said. "But there's no reason you have to manage, not all alone, anyway."

"You're...you're sure?"

Mack didn't think he'd ever seen anything so heart-breaking as the sheer relief on his stepfather's face when Jenna replied, "We're positive. We're staying with you."

They spent the rest of the day taking care of the thousand and one things that require attention when someone dies.

They found a funeral home. They contacted Alec and Doreen's insurance agent, settled up with the hospital and removed Doreen's few personal items from her room there.

Alec had a widowed sister, Lois Nettleby, who lived in Phoenix.

"I suppose I'd better call her," Alec said absently. "She and Dory weren't real close, but I think she'd want to know."

Jenna encouraged him. "Call her right now."

So he did. Lois promised she'd be on the first flight she could find.

Then they drove to the funeral home in the Lincoln that Mack had rented. There they chose a casket and set the funeral date: Friday, in the afternoon. Alec already had a place to bury his wife.

"We bought our cemetery plot two years ago," he said. "It was mostly for me, of course. She's thirteen years younger than I am..." He paused, swallowed. "Excuse me. I mean, she *was* thirteen years younger. We just...we never imagined that she'd be the first to go."

Jenna put her arm around his narrow shoulders. Mack watched from a few feet away, marveling, as he'd been doing for hours, at the ease and grace with which she soothed a virtual stranger's grief.

She whispered something in Alec's ear, too low for Mack to make out the words. Something reassuring, apparently, because Alec nodded and said, "Thank you, Jenna. I appreciate that."

When they were through at the funeral home, they returned to the hospital, where Alec got his car. Jenna rode with him to his house and Mack followed in the Lincoln.

The house was ranch-style, a reverse floor plan, with the kitchen toward the front. Alec took the mail from the mailbox before he unlocked the door.

Inside, the curtains were drawn and the stale air smelled faintly of cigarettes. Alec trudged to the kitchen and tossed the mail onto the table, adding to the pile already waiting there. The phone on the wall above the counter rang. Alec picked it up, said hello and then, "Yes. All right. Six-fifteen. We'll be there to meet you."

He hung up. "That was Lois. She's coming into John Wayne Airport at six-fifteen." A half-empty carton of cigarettes stood on the counter, near his elbow. Alec shook his head at them. "Dory…" It came out sounding suspiciously like a sob. But then he collected himself, and spoke with strictest self-control. "She never would quit." He grabbed the carton and threw it in the trash.

After that, he didn't seem to know what to do with himself.

But Jenna knew. "We need to make some calls, Alec. People will want to know what's happened, where to send flowers, what time the funeral will be."

At first, Alec protested that there was no one to call. But Jenna had him get out Doreen's address book. As he looked through the names and addresses, he found that there were several people who would want to be notified.

"Would you like me to call them?" Jenna offered.

"No. No, I think it's something that I ought to do myself."

As Alec made the calls, Mack decided he was getting pretty tired of feeling useless. He dug around in the cupboards and came up with stuff to make sandwiches. Standing side by side at the kitchen counter, he and Jenna put them together.

My mother's kitchen, Mack thought as he squirted mustard from a squeeze bottle onto slices of bread. My mother's kitchen. Who would have thought I'd ever be here?

An African violet in a glazed pot sat on the windowsill, surrounded by a large number of small ceramic animals: cats, dogs, horses, frogs…

A stunning flash of memory hit him: the kitchen window, in the house they'd lived in before his father died, the same—or at least, much the same—tiny animals arranged with care along the sill.

*"Mackie…"* His mother's voice. *"See, Mackie? A kitty and a doggy, a pony and parrot…no, no. Very careful. They're fragile, Mackie. They could break…."*

Mack closed his eyes, breathed in through his nose as it struck him. What memories he had of her were all he would ever have.

He wondered why that should hurt so much. It wasn't as if he'd expected there to be more.

Jenna was rinsing lettuce in the sink. He glanced

over at her and she gave him one of her gorgeous smiles. "Okay?" she asked softly.

He realized he did feel better. "Yeah. I'm okay."

They ate the sandwiches. Then it was time to head for the airport in Orange County. Lois Nettleby's flight got in right on time. Alec spotted her and waved as she came down the exit ramp. She waved back, a pleasantly stout woman with a deep tan and friendly wrinkles fanning out from her dark eyes.

They drove Lois and Alec back to the house. By then, it was after eight. Alec mentioned again the mementos he had for Mack, then added, "But I guess there's no rush about them. We can take care of them tomorrow. Could you come by in the morning, do you think? Say, around ten?"

Mack said that he'd be there. He thought that dealing with them tomorrow—whatever "they" were—sounded like a great idea. Alec looked dead on his feet. And Mack himself wanted a stiff drink, a long hot shower and a king-size bed—preferably with Jenna in it.

And all right. Maybe he wouldn't get Jenna in his bed tonight. But there was nothing in the agreement he'd made with her that said he wasn't allowed to hope.

During their flight, he'd called and booked rooms at a good hotel on Ocean Avenue. The fact that it was a Monday in late September worked in his favor. He'd had no problem getting a two-bedroom, two-bath suite with a big living area between.

They entered the suite through the little foyer that opened onto the living-dining room. Jenna stepped over the threshold with great caution and then stood looking at him with narrowed eyes.

He took off his jacket and tossed it over a nearby chair. "That look you're giving me shows a total lack of trust." He did his best to sound injured.

She wasn't buying. "We agreed. Separate rooms."

He marched over and opened a door. "Notice. A bedroom, complete with its own bath. See that door over there? You'll find the same thing if you open it."

Before she could comment, there was a tap on the entry door.

The bellhop. They waited as he distributed bags to their separate rooms, then showed off the wet bar and the refrigerator full of snacks and cold drinks. Finally he drew the curtains, revealing a balcony and a really splendid view of Long Beach Harbor at night. He pointed out Catalina Island, and a spur of land to the west where the *Queen Mary* was forever moored.

"If there's anything else I can get you, just buzz the concierge," he said. Mack produced a generous tip. With a blinding smile, the bellhop departed.

Mack and Jenna were left alone again, regarding each other.

Mack spoke first. "You were terrific today," he said. "Thank you."

She acknowledged his thanks with a slight dip of her head, then went to the glass door that looked out on the dark ocean, on the gleaming harbor lights. "It's important, I think, when you lose someone you love, to have people around you, people to help. I was glad we could do that for Alec." She took her gaze from the night and focused on him. "He's a very nice man."

"Yes," Mack said. It seemed a woefully inadequate response, but he had no better right then.

"Mack?"

"What?"

"I'm sorry. That she's gone."

For some reason, he had to look away.

She came toward him and stopped just a few inches away. Her scent taunted him—sweet, but not too sweet. And never forgotten, not even after seven years.

She said his name once more. "Mack."

Her hand closed on his arm, gently, with care. He covered her hand with his own. She pulled and he followed where she led, back to the balcony door. They stood looking out at the ocean and the night.

"When my mother died," she said, "the very hardest thing, the thing that seemed impossible to me, was that I would never have any more memories of her. What I had up till that point was it. There was no possibility that there would be more between us than there had already been. No more little moments ahead that would later come flashing back when I thought of her—no more things she might say that would stick in my mind, no more hugs, no more smiles. I'd had them. All the hugs and the smiles she would ever give me…"

Mack gave no response. He couldn't. What she had just said was so exactly what he'd felt, back in his mother's house, when he'd looked at that ceramic menagerie in the kitchen window and remembered his mother's soft voice in his ear, calling him Mackie, showing him her treasures, cautioning him of their fragility.

Jenna laid her head against his shoulder. Her cornsilk hair brushed his arm. It felt so warm, her hair. And it tickled a little.

He wanted to turn to her, pull her close and lower his mouth to hers. But he didn't. He knew damn well that right then it was comfort she offered and nothing more.

He wanted it, the comfort. He would spoil it if he made a move on her.

"One thing I don't think I'll ever understand," he heard himself say.

"What?"

"How she could be married to a man for all those years and never tell him the truth."

He felt her hair whisper against his arm as she looked up at him. "You never told me the truth, about her. You led me to believe that she'd died years ago."

He realized he'd forgotten to breathe. So he did. Very carefully, letting out the breath he hadn't known he'd been holding. "I wanted to tell you. You were the only one I ever wanted to tell."

"But you didn't."

"Because I also wanted to forget."

"And did it work? Did you forget?"

They both knew the answer, but he said it anyway. "No. Eventually, I had to deal with it, with her. Hell, I'm still dealing with it."

"You did a good job today—of dealing with it."

"Thanks." He still wanted to kiss her. He wanted it pretty badly. But he didn't try it.

Even for a man who didn't mind taking chances, there were some things too precious to risk—things like how far they'd come toward each other during the bleak day just passed.

She had her arm wrapped in his and her head on his shoulder.

For right then, it was plenty. It was more than enough.

## *Chapter Eight*

When Jenna retired to her own section of the suite, she called Lacey at home. She wanted to see how things were going at the store and to let her sister know where they were staying. She waited as the phone rang, her nerves a little on edge, thinking how far away Meadow Valley seemed right then, wondering what kind of questions Lacey would ask and how she could effectively explain all that had happened since Mack had picked her up that morning.

It turned out she didn't have to explain anything. Lacey wasn't there. Jenna left a brief message, just the address and phone number of the hotel.

The next morning Mack ordered breakfast for them in the suite. It was a little windy to enjoy the balcony, so they ate at the glass-topped table in the living area.

As Jenna spooned up poached eggs and nibbled her toast, she couldn't help thinking of other breakfasts they'd shared.

The very first one, for instance, in his L.A. apartment. He'd gotten up before her and run down to the corner convenience store, bringing back two large coffees and half a dozen chocolate-frosted cake doughnuts with sprinkles on top.

He'd bent over her and kissed her awake. "I've brought breakfast. Breakfast in bed."

She'd sat up among the pillows and wrapped herself in the sheet. He'd passed her one of the coffees, his warm fingers brushing hers, a casual contact that thrilled her to her toes. No coffee before or since had ever tasted so good.

They hadn't been able to stop looking at each other, *grinning* at each other. Her hair was all tangled and her makeup had rubbed off and she felt like the most beautiful woman in the world. It was all very smug and magical and right.

She'd barely enjoyed one doughnut when he was reaching for her and pushing her down among the pillows. Later, when they got up to shower together, he found two little sugar sprinkles pressed into her back, right at the ridge of her shoulder blade. He licked them off.

Perhaps that had been the best breakfast of her life. And she'd shared it with Mack.

The worst one had been with Mack, too. In their New York apartment, about a week before Jenna decided on the visit home—the one from which she would never return.

It was an awful, silent breakfast for the most part. She remembered the clink of their spoons stirring coffee, the way he so carefully spread jam on his toast.

He'd come in very late the night before, from one of those meetings that somehow always managed to go on till all hours. She'd been asleep, but she woke when she heard him enter the bedroom.

She had lain there turned away from him, trying to keep her breathing shallow and slow. It had come to that point with them, the point where she faked sleep when he came home late. Where she avoided his eyes at the table. Where she gave him her cheek to kiss instead of her lips, because she knew that if she looked right at him, all the things she wanted to tell him, all the things he kept refusing to hear, would come spilling out all over again—and to absolutely no avail.

Avoidance was the order of the day by then. So she lay there on her side, measuring her own breathing.

But after he'd taken off his clothes and climbed in beside her, the hopelessness of their life together had struck her like a sudden blow. The tears had come welling up.

He had heard her whimpering as she tried to stifle her sobs. "Damn it, Jenna. It's late. I'm beat. Don't start this now."

They'd ended up shouting at each other—or rather, he had shouted. She had wept and pleaded.

And then, the next morning at breakfast, there had been silence.

Until she had glanced across at him spreading jam on his toast so very carefully and her mouth had opened and there she was, begging him again.

"Mack, please. I just want a baby, Mack. If I only had a baby, I could—"

He stopped her with a look. Then he dropped his toast onto his plate, got up from the table and went out the door.

The worst breakfast of her life. Yes, it had definitely been that one in all its hideous hurtful silence, shared, as the best had been, with the man across the table from her now.

Mack picked up his coffee cup, drank and met her eyes over the rim. He was wearing a polo shirt and chinos, clothing she'd noted with some relief when she emerged from her own room to find him sitting in an easy chair reading the *Los Angeles Times*. She'd worried just a little that she might catch him in a robe, or without his shirt, or in some other distracting state of semiundress.

But no. He'd played it straight.

Mack set his coffee cup in its saucer. "Deep thoughts?"

She had the urge to speak frankly, to admit she'd been thinking about the rough times they'd had. And to say that she believed he'd been right in not wanting children back then. From a more mature perspective she realized that having a baby rarely saved a marriage—or effectively consoled a neglected wife. Now she could see how the demands of a little one would only have made their problems worse. And that when the inevitable breakup did come, an innocent child would have been stuck in the middle.

However, if she admitted that he'd been right to say no to a baby back then, she wouldn't be able to stop herself from asking him how he felt about having children now.

She wasn't sure she ought to do that just yet. The issue had once been a heavily charged one. To bring it up now would only dredge up old hurts.

And it could also be a step toward real intimacy with him. Not long ago she would have sworn she would never take such a step.

Now she had to admit she felt differently. She'd reached the point where she couldn't swear to anything.

He was watching her. Waiting to hear whatever she might reveal.

"It's nothing," she lied.

She knew by the smile he gave her that he didn't believe her. But he didn't press her.

"More coffee?" He picked up the pot from the warmer.

"I'd love some." She held out her cup.

When they got to Alec's house, Lois had left for the supermarket.

"She's got a list a mile long," Alec said. "She's a dynamo. She's always been like that, the type who takes charge. Ordinarily, it irritates me. But right now, I'm grateful. I need someone taking charge."

Jenna glanced around the kitchen. It did indeed look as if Lois had been busy. The stack of unopened mail had vanished from the table and the air smelled more of cleaning products than of cigarettes. It appeared that the floor had been mopped. Also, the sink was free of dirty dishes.

"Coffee?" Alec offered. He gestured toward the coffeemaker. The pot was half full. "It's made."

Both Jenna and Mack declined.

"Well, then." Alec pointed toward the living room, down the short hall perpendicular to the front door. "Go on in and sit down. I'll get you those things I mentioned."

Jenna and Mack filed into the living room, but neither of them felt like sitting. They stood side by side in the center of the room, between the television and the maple coffee table, which bore a basket arrangement of dried flowers and a neat fan of *National Geographic*s.

"Sit down, sit down." It was Alec, appearing from the hall that led to the back of the house. He was toting a big cardboard box and had a pair of half-lensed reading glasses perched on his nose. "Mack, would you shove those magazines out of the way?"

Mack didn't move. Jenna shot him a glance. He had a look in his eyes that she couldn't quite read. "Alec. Listen. We don't have to open it now. I'll just take it with me and—"

"Please." The older man's voice wasn't much more than a croak. He coughed. "There's so much I don't know, so much I wish I could understand. I would be so grateful, if you'd only let me…" He fell silent. Then he sighed. "I'm sorry. Of course I have no right to ask such a thing. This box is yours, not mine." He made a move to hand Mack the box.

Mack hesitated, but only for a fraction of a second. Then he turned, picked up the magazines and tossed them under the coffee table. "Put it down here, Alec."

Alec held on to the box. "Are you certain?"

"Yeah. Come on."

So Alec set the box on the table. Then he and Mack sat on opposite ends of the sofa. Jenna took a side chair.

The box was taped securely shut. Alec produced a utility knife, which he handed to Mack. Jenna realized her heart had started beating a little faster as Mack slit the tape and turned back the flaps.

Mack pulled out photo albums first. There were three of them. They were numbered, the numbers written by hand on cards tucked into plastic pockets on the spines. Mack opened the first one.

Jenna couldn't really see from her seat across the table. She stood and craned forward. Mack saw her problem and slid toward the center of the sofa, leaving a space for her on his right. She took the seat he offered. He gave her a smile. Without even thinking about it, she moved a little closer to him.

They spent an hour just turning pages. Mack was able to pick out Bridget and Claire. And his own very young self. He recognized his parents, too. His mother, tiny and pretty, stood in front of a slightly run-down California bungalow-style house, holding on to his father's arm and smiling bravely into the sun.

Once they had looked through all the albums, they found school progress reports, three of them for Bridget and one for Mack. Instead of A's and B's, Mack's report showed S's and O's, for "Satisfactory" and "Outstanding." N.I. meant "Needs Improvement." He had only one of those, in the category of "Follows Instructions."

Beyond the albums and the report cards, they discovered a number of drawings made by very young hands. There were also little swatches of baby hair and three tiny first teeth wrapped in squares of white silk. They found three sets of knit booties, one blue and two pink. And birth announcements, birthday party invitations, other small articles of clothing: tiny knit hats and a yellow bib. There were rattles and two small dolls, a tattered brown teddy bear and a dog-eared Little Golden Book of a Christmas story titled *Noel.*

"All those years we were together..." Alec shook his head. "She never said a word. But she had what we used to call her sad times, when she would hardly smile, when she'd have a certain miles-away look in her eyes. At first I would ask her what was wrong. But she would only pat my cheek, tell me, 'It's one of my sad times, Al, that's all....'"

Alec readjusted his glasses on the end of his nose. "After our first few years together, I just accepted that the sad times were a part of who she was. I knew they would come, and that eventually they would pass. But I never knew why. Not until a few hours before she died. I…" Alec seemed to catch himself. He looked from Mack to Jenna. "Maybe you'd rather not hear all this."

Jenna waited for Mack to answer, but the silence stretched out too long. She couldn't bear it. "No," she said, "Really. Please…"

To her relief, Mack spoke up then. "Yeah. It's okay. Go ahead."

"All right. I…well, isn't that strange? I can't remember exactly what I was—"

Jenna suggested softly, "You said you never understood your wife's sad times, until a few hours before she died."

"Oh. Yes, of course. That's right. All those years. I never knew the cause of them. And then, the day she died, I was sitting by her bed, holding her hand and…she told me." He looked at Mack. "About you. About the girls. She said she knew almost nothing about Bridget and Claire. That she hadn't seen them, hadn't heard from them, or about them, in all the years since she'd given them up. But that you had come looking for her. That you had grown into a fine man. You were wealthy and successful, a lawyer. She spoke of you with such pride. She said you had told her that her daughters were doing all right. She asked me to call you, said she needed to see you. She explained about this box then. She said that whatever happened, I had to make sure you got it. I promised her I'd take care of it."

Alec picked up a folded square of yellowed con-

struction paper. Carefully he unfolded it to reveal a
stick-figure family beneath a big yellow sun. In the
lower right-hand corner, the name Bridget was written
in red crayon.

One by one Alec touched the smiling stick-figure
faces: father, mother, daughters, son. "She was telling
me this impossible, incredible thing. That she'd had a
whole family I never knew about. I should have had a
thousand questions. I *do* have a thousand questions.
Now. But then…nothing. Then, I was just plain scared.
I only wanted to give her whatever she needed, make
any promises she had to hear. I knew the worst was
coming, that I was losing her.

"And *she* knew, too, didn't she?" Alec looked to
Mack for an answer, but Mack said nothing. So the
older man looked beyond Mack, at Jenna. "Don't you
think she must have known that she didn't have long?"

Jenna had no answer either. She gave what she could,
a sad look and a shrug.

Alec refolded the stick-figure family and gently set
them next to the stack of albums. Then, with great care,
he took a swatch of silk in his hand. He peeled it open
and stared at the tiny tooth inside. "I told her from the
first that I didn't want children. I told her I was set in
my ways. That I wanted us to have our freedom, I
wanted her all to myself."

He swallowed, shook his head. "Later, after a few
years, I started to see things differently. I told her that
maybe it would be nice…a little boy, or a little girl."

He slid a finger and thumb up under the dark frames
of his glasses and rubbed at his eyes. "But she never got
pregnant. Now I'll always wonder…was it on purpose?
Because I had said once that I didn't want children? Or

because she couldn't forgive herself, couldn't let her-self have another baby after the ones she'd given up? It's so sad. She didn't understand, how much I loved her, how much I could have accepted, the longer and longer I loved her. How I would have wanted to go looking, to find you. If she'd only told me. If I'd only known…"

It was after two when Jenna and Mack stowed the box of keepsakes in the trunk of the Lincoln and headed for the hotel. Mack had been ready to leave much ear-lier, but Lois had returned and insisted that he and Jenna stay for lunch. So they'd all sat around the kitchen table for a while as Lois bustled about getting the food ready. Then they ate. After the meal, there were cookies and coffee.

Lois kept the conversation going. She chattered away about how things had changed in Long Beach since her last visit and how much she enjoyed her life in Arizona. Jenna asked questions and made interested noises. The men were mostly silent.

Mack didn't have much to say during the drive to the hotel, either, which was all right with Jenna. Looking through Doreen's secret box of keepsakes had been dif-ficult even for her—and she wasn't the husband from whom Doreen's secret had been kept, or the son Doreen had given away.

When they got to the suite, Jenna checked the hotel phone. The message light was dark: no calls. Mack pulled out his cell phone and punched up a number.

Jenna dropped her shoulder bag on a side table and wandered over to the chair where Mack had laid his news-paper earlier that morning. She sat down and began glanc-ing through it, tuning out Mack's phone conversation.

But then she heard him say, "Yes. To Miami, the next flight you can find me."

Jenna set down the paper and listened, bewildered and beginning to get angry, as he made reservations for two to Florida.

By the time he hung up, she was on her feet. He started to punch up another number, but got only halfway through it before she commanded, "Wait a minute, Mack."

He punched the off button and looked at her impatiently. "What?"

"What are you doing?"

He made one of those noises that always used to drive her crazy in the old days—a low, intolerant, utterly contemptuous sound. "What does it look like?"

"It looks like you're making arrangements to leave."

"Very perceptive."

Her irritation was increasing. "I don't like this, Mack. It feels way too much like old times."

Now he was glaring at her.

Thank God she was a thirty-year-old woman now, much too mature to be intimidated by a man's facial expression. "Yes," she said, "just like old times. You've got the phone in your hand. You're making reservations. You think you're flying to Florida right away and you also think that I'm going with you. Is that correct?"

He made a growling sound that she decided to consider an answer in the affirmative.

She continued, "You think we're flying to Florida. And have you discussed this with me at all? Have you asked me what I think about it, if I want to go, if I'm even *willing* to go? No. You have not. As I said, it's just like old times, when you thought nothing of taking a job in New York City and then informing me that we were moving." She gave him her sourest smile. "You know, Mack, if I didn't mind being kept in the dark about major decisions, I might have stayed married to you."

"You *are* married to me."

"You keep saying that."

"Because it's true."

"When you behave in this manner, it only reminds me that if I can just get through the next twelve days, you'll never be able to say that again."

He tossed the phone on a low table a few feet away from him. Jenna winced when it hit. "It's my damn week, remember? It's supposed to be my choice where we go."

That gave her pause. He did have a point. She'd hardly consulted him when she'd chosen Wyoming for *her* week.

And now, looking more closely at him, into those gray-blue eyes, she could see the pain he imagined he could outrun.

"I'm finished here, Jenna. I've got that damn box my mother left me and I'm sorry I didn't get here in time to hear whatever she had to say to me. We spent yesterday doing what we could for Alec. Now his sister is here. He'll manage all right. I've got five days left in my week. And I want to spend them *my* way. I want to show you my house, take you out on my boat. I want what I asked for in the first place. Time together, just you and me."

At that moment, she actually wished she could give him what he said he wanted. But she knew it wouldn't be right. "Well, I'm sorry." She put real effort into making her voice gentler than before. "We have to stay for the funeral."

"My mother is dead, Jenna. She's not going to care if I miss her funeral."

"Oh, Mack. Haven't you heard? Funerals aren't for the dead. They're for the rest of us. And your stepfather needs you to be there for this one."

"Damn it, I only met the man yesterday. I can call him right now and tell him we've got to leave. It's not going to kill him if I don't stick it out to the end."

"Maybe it's not. But it will hurt him, and he has been hurt enough. And Mack, I think it would mean so much to him, I honestly do, to have you there at her funeral. It would show him that you're able to do what has to be done, that you turned out all right, you turned out to be the kind of man who knows how to forgive."

"Hell. I forgive her. I think Alec knows that."

"Then you'll reinforce that knowledge. Because that man really likes you, Mack, that man wants a connection with you. In a way, if you think about it, you're the closest he'll ever come to having a child."

His lips made a flat line. "It's too late for that. I'm nobody's child."

"Of course you're not. But you know what I'm getting at. You know what you have to do. I'm sorry that it hurts you. But there's no getting away from it. You talk about how you've forgiven your mother. Do you think you'll be able to forgive yourself if we run off to Florida right now?"

He didn't answer immediately, but when he did, her heart rose. "All right, damn it. We'll stay."

They stood near the glass door to the balcony. Beyond the glass, it was a gorgeous Southern California day. The sky was the softest, palest of blues, dotted here and there with white cotton-puff clouds. Gulls wheeled above the golden stretch of beach below them and a few young mothers with toddlers sat beneath bright umbrellas in the sand. The sea looked calm as glass.

Jenna wanted to touch the man beside her, so she went ahead and did it. She took his arm, the way she had the night before, and, as she had then, she rested her head on his shoulder. "This is a lovely hotel. And look at that beach. Key West might be fabulous, but this isn't half bad. Long Beach has become a real resort area. See those islands out there, with all those cute small hotels on them?"

He chuckled. "Jenna. Those are dressed-up oil derricks."

"You are kidding me."

"Nope. They've been there for years. The Disney people came up with the look. They put a false front on them and light them at night. Very attractive."

"You could have fooled me."

"I think I heard somewhere that they're named after dead astronauts. Island Chaffee, Island Grissom. The oil industry here is nothing if not innovative."

A thought came to her—a way to make their stay a little more bearable to him. She lifted her head and their eyes met. "I'll tell you what, since you're being so gracious about this—"

He pretended to scoff. "Gracious? Now, there's a word I'll bet you never thought you'd use in conjunction with me."

She laughed. It felt good, standing there at his side, overlooking the Pacific, her arm in his and a feeling of real accomplishment spreading through her.

In the old days, at this point, she would have been crying and Mack would have been packing their suitcases to go.

But this wasn't the old days. She was stronger than she had been then. And he was…gentler, more willing to let her have her say.

"That's right," she said. "Gracious was never a word I would have used to describe you. But I'm using it now. And since you *are* being gracious, I can be gracious, too."

The grin he gave her sent a shiver racing along the surface of her skin. "Does this mean you're giving up on those damn separate rooms?"

She clucked her tongue. "Dream on."

"Excuse me. I don't consider making love with you a dream. I consider it a very real possibility."

"Consider it whatever you want. I said separate rooms and I meant what I said."

He had stopped grinning. The look in his eyes melted her midsection and did that embarrassing wobbly thing to her knees.

He turned, so quickly that it startled her. She might have backed up, but he gave her no chance. He reached for her and hauled her close. With a sharp gasp of surprise, she splayed her hands against his chest.

"Mack." It was a warning, one he didn't heed.

Before she could order him to let go, his mouth came down and covered hers.

# Chapter Nine

Apparently, some things never changed.

It was that moment at the door to Mack's L.A. apartment all over again, even all these years later.

Jenna heard her own small cry as Mack's mouth opened over hers. She stopped pushing him away and slid her hands upward, over his big, solid shoulders. His tongue found hers and danced with it.

She couldn't help herself. She stroked the back of his neck. She had always loved that, the feel of his skin at the nape, the texture of the hair that his barber cut with electric clippers, silky and stubbly at the same time. She pulled him closer. And he did the same to her, nestling her hips along his thighs, so that she could feel his desire for her, there against her lower belly.

Oh, she was melting. Yes, all softness. All willingness.

Though she shouldn't.

Shouldn't do this.

Shouldn't give in to this.

This wonder…

This glory…

His hands roamed her back, sliding over her hips one minute, cupping her the next and pulling her even closer—and then moving upward, so that he could tangle his fingers in the strands of her hair.

His tongue went on playing with hers.

And she played back.

Oh, how lovely. Playing back. She and Mack played so well together. They had from the first.

And oh, how easy it would be to fall right into playing again…

How delicious and lovely…

But she couldn't.

She really couldn't.

With a sigh that was part regret and part determination, she put her hands flat against his chest again and broke the kiss. "No, Mack."

He opened his eyes and stared down at her. He didn't look happy. She moved in his arms, signaling clearly that she wanted him to let her go.

He did, but he also asked, "Why not?"

She longed to fling out a quick and flippant response. But they both deserved better. They deserved—and they needed—as much honesty as they could bear, wherever this two weeks together ended up taking them.

She said, "Because making love was always so good with us. Sometimes I think it was too good. Sometimes I wonder if it was all we had, really. A great sex life, as you said the other day."

He was shaking his head. "No. There was more. You know there was."

"Do I? You were on your way to make it big at any cost. And I was getting a business degree, getting a little taste of the larger world before I went home and opened my store and married Logan and raised a family. We…intersected over Byron. And there was this attraction. Maybe it was only physical, did you ever think about that? Maybe all that was good was the sex and that's why it didn't last."

"Jenna." He made her name into a tender rebuke. "How can you say it didn't last? We're both here now, aren't we?"

She held her ground on that one. "It *was* ended. We agreed on the terms of a divorce."

"But we didn't go through with it."

"*I* went through with it. You were the one who didn't sign the papers."

"And you never came looking for me to find out where they were."

"I did come looking for you. I came looking for you two weeks ago. I asked you—"

"Wait a minute."

She folded her arms across her middle and let out a small sound of irritation. "What?"

"Do we really need to go into all this again?"

She caught her lower lip between her teeth, worried it a little, then let it go. "No. You're right. We don't. All I'm trying to say is that I'm not allowing the sexual part of our relationship to take over everything again. I want a little balance. I want to be sure we've got more in common than how good it feels making love together."

"So. You're admitting we do have *something,* then?"

"Yes. I am. And as I was trying to tell you before you distracted me, I'm willing to give a little ground here."

He looked doubtful. "You're kidding me. You? Giving ground?"

"Yes. Since you've been so gracious about staying for your mother's funeral, once the funeral's over, we can go to Key West—and stay until the two weeks are up."

A smile lit his eyes. He teased, "What about Wyoming and all those Bravos you want to get to know?"

"I guess Wyoming and my Bravo cousins will just have to wait. I'll get there. Someday." She looked out past the balcony again. "And I am thinking it might be nice to take a walk on the beach."

"Right now?"

"You have something better to do?"

"I did. But you turned me down."

"So?"

"So, let's go."

The red light on the hotel phone was blinking when they returned to the room an hour later. A message from Alec. Mack called him back.

Alec invited them to his house for dinner that night.

Mack wanted to decline. They'd spent last night taking care of Alec. Tonight, he'd imagined a long, intimate evening, just him and Jenna.

But before he could make their excuses, Jenna spoke up. "It's Alec? What's up?"

And he had to ask Alec to hold on while he told her about the invitation. And naturally, she thought they should go.

And hell. So did he.

He told Alec they'd be there.

He hung up and turned to Jenna. She was standing a few feet away, in front of the gilt-framed mirror near the door, brushing out the tangles the wind had put in her hair. He went to her, stopping just behind her. Their eyes met in the mirror.

"Six-thirty," he said. "For cocktails. For dinner, Lois is whipping up something called Chicken Fiesta."

"Sounds interesting." She touched the tip of the brush to her pretty, slightly pointed chin. "But somehow, I didn't picture Alec as the type to serve cocktails—and on Tuesday night, too."

"Maybe it's just to impress us."

He'd meant the remark jokingly, but she actually considered it. "Maybe. But my bet is that he wants to make you feel at home. Your mother told him you were wealthy and successful. He probably thinks you drink cocktails every night. Isn't that what all millionaires do?"

He shrugged. His mind wasn't really on Alec. He could smell the salt air on her skin. Her cheeks shone pink, from the wind and the sun. She looked so clean and fresh and… wholesome.

Yes. That was the word for Jenna: wholesome. He'd never imagined until he'd first set eyes on her how utterly erotic wholesomeness could be. She parted that silky yellow hair of hers in the middle and it fell straight to her shoulders in a simple, classic style.

With a finger, very slowly, he lifted a section of that shining hair away from the side of her neck.

Hazel eyes darkened. "Mack…"

"Shh."

He lowered his head and put his lips against her neck, tasted the sweetness of her skin and the tang the sea

wind had left there. She allowed the caress, even surrendered so much as to let out a soft sigh.

But he played fair. He didn't linger. He would keep
their agreement on the issue of lovemaking.

For the moment, anyway.

He met her eyes in the mirror again. "So. We've got
what? Maybe an hour to kill?"

"I've got sand in my shoes. I was just thinking I'd
take a shower and change my clothes."

"I'd offer to wash your back for you, but unfortunately…"

"I'd have to say no."

"You wouldn't *have* to say no."

"Oh, yes, I would."

She left him, disappearing into her private section of
the suite. He called and changed the plane reservations
from tomorrow to late Saturday morning. Then he
prowled the main room for a while, trying not to picture Jenna in the shower, the water cascading over her,
running between her full breasts, tracing glittery rivu-
lets along her smooth belly and slithering down into the
golden curls between her slim legs.

Finally he went to his own room and took a shower
of his own—a quick, cold one.

Alec had made a giant pitcher of margaritas. They sat
on the back patio around a glass-topped table in chairs
with floral-patterned cushions.

"Dory always loved it back here," Alec said.

Jenna could understand why. The yard was cozy and
well cared for, with a green stretch of lawn and a bou-
gainvillea spilling over the tall redwood fence.

Alec talked about his employment agency, Telford

Temporaries, where he and Doreen had met. He'd sold the business just last year. He and Doreen had planned to do some serious traveling.

"We took a cruise, last winter." His eyes had a faraway look. "The Mediterranean. From Lisbon to Barcelona in ten days. We strolled the Casbah in Tangier, went to the Central Market in Casablanca, visited that medieval cathedral in Palma de Mallorca and…" He seemed to shake himself. "Well. Let me just say, we had a wonderful time."

He asked about Mack's life. "Dory mentioned you live in Florida. Are you with some big law firm there?"

Mack said that he didn't practice law anymore and explained how he was able to live on his investments.

Lois spoke up then. "So Jenna, do you live in Florida, too?"

"No. I live up north. Meadow Valley. It's a little town in the—"

"Oh, yes. In the foothills. One of the gold rush towns, right? I hear it's lovely there."

"I like it."

"My brother tells me that you and Mack are… friends?"

Jenna began to feel a bit uncomfortable at that point. "Yes. That's right."

Her discomfort increased when Lois asked, "So then, how did you two meet?"

Jenna cast a quick glance Mack's way. No help there. He was sipping his margarita with one eyebrow annoyingly raised. She knew just what he was thinking: Go ahead. Tell her.

And why shouldn't she? There was nothing to be ashamed of.

Jenna sipped from her own drink, gathering a little false courage and her thoughts as well. Finally she said, "Mack and I were married once. We divorced, but it turned out the divorce was never finalized. So now we're…"

"Trying again," Lois provided, her tanned face lighting up and the wrinkles around her eyes deepening as she grinned.

No, not exactly, Jenna almost said. But then she reconsidered. "Trying again" didn't sound bad at all. Why muddy things up with confusing details neither Alec nor Lois needed to know?

Lois had turned to her brother, who sat to her left. "See? Didn't I tell you that they had to be much more than just friends?"

Alec nodded. "You did, Lois. That's exactly what you said."

Jenna sipped more of her margarita and resisted the urge to glance at Mack. She knew what she would see if she looked at him, anyway: humor in his eyes and a big grin on his sexy mouth. She didn't need that.

"A refill?" Alec asked.

Well, what do you know? Her glass was empty. And such nice big glasses they were, too. "Yes, please. These margaritas are excellent."

By the time Lois served the chicken, Jenna was starting to feel just a bit tipsy. When Alec offered another refill, she politely turned it down.

She wished she'd never had that second one, because during the meal Alec said something about the possibility of Mack approaching his sisters with the news that their mother had died.

Mack managed to avoid giving the older man an answer. He did it quite skillfully, saying he'd think about it, but that right now they should just concentrate on getting through the funeral.

Alec, the dear old sweetheart, backed right off. And Lois patted his hand and told him Mack was probably right.

The whole exchange was over before Jenna, in her pleasant margarita haze, could put her two cents in. She would have brought the subject up again, but the moment never seemed quite right. And besides, dangerous subjects were always best raised when a woman had her wits fully about her—especially dangerous subjects that concerned Mack McGarrity.

They left for the hotel at a little after ten. The big car had a very smooth and quiet ride. Jenna couldn't resist leaning back and closing her eyes.

She woke to the feel of Mack's lips brushing her ear. "You planning to sleep in the car tonight?"

It seemed so natural, to make a sleepy sound, to turn her mouth to his and—

She stopped herself just in time. "Let's go in."

His lips were only an inch from hers. And his eyes looked dark and full of sensual secrets that he just might be willing to share with her.

His mouth brushed hers, once, then he whispered, "Did we ever make love in a car? I don't remember it. I doubt that it's something I would have forgotten."

They hadn't, but she didn't tell him that. He would probably only take it as an invitation to try it now.

All she said was "Mack," and she shook her head.

He mimicked her movement, his head going back and forth in time with her own.

Then he turned to his door and leaned on the handle.

\* \* \*

The next day, over breakfast, Jenna told Mack that he really ought to consider getting in touch with his sisters.

He said, "I think that's my decision to make."

"But—"

"Let it go, Jenna. It's not for you to decide."

Though she pressed her lips together in obvious disapproval, she did let the subject drop.

Then, after breakfast, she suggested that she and Mack should take Alec and Lois out that night.

Mack tried to demur. It was about time they had a damn evening alone, he thought.

But Jenna wouldn't let it go. "Call him. He had us over to his house last night and I'm sure it'll be good for him, to get out for a while."

"Did it ever occur to you that maybe he's not in the mood to get out?"

She picked up the phone and shoved it in his direction. "Ask him. Let him answer for himself. And let him choose the restaurant. Someplace he feels comfortable."

Mack let her stand there for a count of five, holding out the phone and glaring at him. As he made her wait, he indulged in a moment of nostalgia, recalling how sweet and malleable she'd been when she was younger.

Then, with a heavy sigh, he gave in and made the damn call. Alec said that he and his sister would love to go out to dinner with them.

"Now what?" Mack asked, after he'd called the restaurant Alec had chosen and learned that reservations would not be required. "I suppose you have something really constructive planned for today."

She pinched up her mouth at him. "You have some problem with constructive activities?"

"Hell, no. But I'd rather take it easy, enjoy ourselves, just you and me."

"Well, actually, I was thinking…"

"Stand back."

"Very funny. Remember that day we drove down to Seal Beach?"

He did. "It was a Sunday, I think. In June. We had a day off and no money and we got in the car and headed south. We had our swimsuits with us. We changed on a side street, right in that old Chrysler I had. Remember? You made me stand guard while you were changing, though you never did explain to me what the hell I was supposed to do if someone dared to peek in."

She laughed. "Lord. I remember that."

It had been a good day, one of the last of the good days, as a matter of fact. Not long after, Mack had taken the job in New York.

Mack said, "Seal Beach is damn easy to get to from here."

"That's just what I was thinking."

The drive took less than half an hour. They found parking on a side street, then strolled down tree-shaded, brick-lined Main, wandering in and out of any shops that caught their eye. Jenna picked up a few souvenirs, among them a melon-colored T-shirt for Lacey and a fur-covered toy mouse for Byron. When they tired of shopping, they sat for a while in grassy Eisenhower Park, then chose one of the restaurants near the pier for lunch.

They even wandered over to Surfside Beach to watch the surfers floating on their bright-colored boards, waiting for the perfect wave—which, at least during the half hour that Jenna and Mack observed them, never seemed to come along.

When they returned to the hotel to get ready for dinner, Jenna detoured straight to the phone. No message light.

Mack had carried in the bags of souvenirs. He dropped them onto a chair. "You're expecting an important call?"

"No. I'm just beginning to worry a little about Lacey. I called her and left the number here on Monday. I thought that she'd at least check in, let me know she got the message."

"You think she might be up to her old tricks?"

She sent him a look. "What old tricks?"

"The way I remember it, during the time you and I were married, she ran away from home about a half dozen times."

Jenna jumped to her sister's defense. "She was a teenager then. And she had problems."

"That doesn't answer my question."

"All right. No, I do not think she's run away from home. She's very responsible now. She keeps her agreements. And besides, what good would it do her to run away from Meadow Valley? She doesn't even live there anymore."

Mack muttered something about feminine logic, then added, "If you're worried about her, call her again."

She picked up the phone, dialed—and got her own voice on the answering machine. This time she left a message asking Lacey to please call the hotel right away. She hung up picturing Byron wandering the rooms of her mother's house, starved for both Fancy Feast and companionship.

She dialed Linen and Lace. Marla, her head clerk, said that yes, Lacey had been in both yesterday and the day before to take care of the receipts. Jenna hung up from that call feeling moderately relieved.

Then Mack said, "We've got to pick up Alec and Lois at seven. If you want one of those half-hour showers of yours, you'd better get moving."

"I do not take half-hour showers."

He smiled. Very slowly. "How much do you want to bet?"

"Oh. Right. And then you'd have to time me, wouldn't you? I don't think so."

"You have a suspicious mind."

"Only where you're concerned."

They stared each other down for a minute, then he commanded gruffly, "Take your damn shower."

He looked so…huggable right then, those gold eyebrows scrunched together and the corners of his mouth drawn low. If she hadn't been exercising such care to avoid physical contact with him, she would have kissed him hard and possessively, right on the mouth.

Lacey did call, just as Mack and Jenna were leaving for Alec's house.

"Hi." Lacey laughed, a breathless sound. "Listen, I promise you, the cat is fine and the store is fine. And I know I should have gotten back to you sooner, but every time I thought of it, it was either midnight or four in the morning or some other totally inappropriate time."

Jenna thought Lacey sounded nervous, even a little bit manic. "Lace, are you okay?"

"Of course. So what's going on? I thought you were supposed to be riding the range in Wyoming this week."

Mack was standing by the door. He lifted an eyebrow at her. Jenna gave him a nod, mouthed, "Just a minute."

Then she spoke to her sister again. "Mack's mother died. We're here in Southern California until the funeral on Friday. Then we'll go to Mack's house in Key West. We're skipping Wyoming, after all. But I'll call you from Florida as soon as we get there."

"Wait a minute. I thought you told me that Mack McGarrity was an orphan."

Jenna glanced at Mack again. He was leaning against the door—waiting with reasonable patience, actually. "It's a long story. I'll explain it all when I get home."

"Is it…going well, between you two?"

Jenna smiled. "You know, all in all, I do believe it is."

"Well. Good." Now, what was she hearing in Lacey's voice? Relief? Satisfaction?

Unfortunately, she had no time right then to ask. "Listen, we're just going out the door, taking Mack's stepfather out to dinner."

Lacey showed no inclination to linger, either. "Okay. Have fun. Call me from Florida."

"I will."

They went to a restaurant Alec liked in Huntington Beach, where the menu offered a dozen varieties of fresh fish each day. Alec seemed very quiet through the meal. He admitted on the way home that maybe he hadn't been ready yet to go back to one of the places he used to visit with Doreen.

Mack glanced significantly at Jenna. She read his look. *I told you he wasn't ready for a night on the town.*

When they got to the house, Alec asked if they'd like to come in for coffee. Jenna would have said yes, but Mack clamped a hand over her arm. A shiver of excite-

ment sizzled through her, distracting her enough that she
didn't object when Mack said, "Thanks Alec. But I think
we'll just go on back to the hotel."

In the suite, Mack found two miniature brandy bottles in the well-stocked bar. He poured one for each of
them. Then, brandy in hand, he sat on one of the sofas
and put his feet up on a hassock. Jenna wandered to the
glass door that led to the balcony and looked out on the
harbor lights. She sipped, and couldn't help smiling to
herself as she thought that those lovely little island hotels were actually oil derricks.

Then Alec came to mind and she felt her smile
fade away.

"Why the frown?"

She turned. Mack was watching her.

He patted the space beside him on the sofa. She
started to move toward him, then reconsidered. They
probably shouldn't be getting too cozy. She shook her
head and murmured ruefully, "Better not."

Mack's jaw tightened. He glanced past her, his fine
mouth a hard line. She knew what he was doing: calling himself away from the brink of saying something
he might regret. Finally he laid his arm along the sofa
back and looked right at her again.

She decided to go on as if the uncomfortable moment
hadn't occurred. "I was just… thinking of Alec. How
hard it must be for him. They had a lot of years together, he and your mother. And it seems that they were
happy years, for the most part."

Mack said nothing.

She could feel his irritation with her and she tried

again to brush it off, this time with an offhand shrug. Still, he said nothing. She turned to look out over the harbor again.

That was when he deigned to speak. "Do you want me to agree with you, that Alec has it rough right now?"

She looked at him once more. "You don't have to agree with me, Mack. It's a fact."

"Yes, it is. A fact. And I think we've done about all we can personally do about it."

"I wasn't implying that we should do anything more."

"Oh, come on." He knocked back a gulp of brandy and winced as it went down. "Give yourself a minute or two. You'll come up with five or six ways that we can help to ease the poor man's pain—ways that will give us more very good reasons not to be alone together." He studied her face for several seconds before adding, "You have so many creative methods of avoiding me."

She wanted to argue, but she couldn't. She *was* avoiding him—avoiding getting too close to him, either physically or emotionally. And why shouldn't she? She had carefully specified separate rooms when they'd set up this little two-week adventure. He'd agreed to her terms. There was no reason she should feel defensive about sticking to them.

But she did feel defensive. "You're irritated because I didn't sit beside you just now? Is that it?"

"Partly. You're constantly putting physical space between us. And you don't limit yourself to space. You put Alec between us. And my sisters, too."

"How?" she demanded, feeling suddenly self-righteous. Physical space, certainly. Alec, maybe. But his sisters? No way.

"If you could only get me to agree to it, we'd be spending the second half of our two weeks enjoying a little family reunion with Bridget and Claire." He swirled his brandy around in his glass, then sipped again. "Go ahead. Tell me that isn't true."

She couldn't. Because it was. She cleared her throat. "Well, Mack, I do think that you should—"

"Jenna. I know what you think. You've made it painfully clear. Will you give it a rest now?"

"But I just—"

He set his glass on the table, and not gently. "Damn it, Jenna. I am not going to hunt down my sisters. Look what happened when I found my mother. She asked me not to tell her husband that I existed. And then she died."

"Oh, please. As if she died just to spite you."

"That's not what I meant. My point is, she's gone. I found her only to lose her again. This time, for good— and I can see in those eyes of yours what you're thinking. Yes, she did tell Alec about me in the end. And I'm here, sticking it out right through her funeral because you insisted. But after this, I'm finished. I've had enough of family reunions to last me a lifetime." He picked up his brandy again and drank the last of it. Then he set down the empty glass once more.

"And as for Alec," he said, "the man lost his wife. It hurts. And you personally are not going to be able to make it stop hurting. Only time will do that. If he's lucky." He stood. "I'm going to bed."

She let him get halfway across the room before she stopped him. "Mack."

He turned. "What?"

She admitted, "You're right. About Alec, anyway."

He didn't smile, but at least his expression relaxed a little. "I know I am. Good night." He went into his bedroom.

She whispered, "Good night, Mack," after he had shut the door.

The next day they drove up into the greater Los Angeles area. They visited Westwood Village, even drove by the apartment where they had met and been so happy together.

"It looks a little run-down."

"Mack. It looked a little run-down when we lived there."

"I guess. Maybe I just remember it through a kind of rosy haze."

His words pleased her, inordinately so. "You do?"

"It *was* a good time, Jenna."

"Yes. It was."

That little Italian place where they'd eaten that first night was still there. They couldn't resist going inside, where the light was dim and dusty plastic grapes hung from fake trellises overhead and between each of the booths.

They decided to go all out and order the meal they'd shared that first night: salads and linguini with white clam sauce and a glass each of the house Chianti.

When the linguini came, Mack tasted it and shook his head. "It's not as good as I remember it."

She answered lightly, "Nothing ever is."

He looked at her across the table, his gaze tender and seeking as a caress. "I disagree. Some things are every bit as good. In fact, they're even better—or they could be, if you'd give them a chance."

"I think I am. Giving them a chance."

He grudgingly admitted that yes, she was. But he wished that she'd give them even more of a chance.

She twirled her fork in her linguini and decided it would be wiser not to reply.

After lunch they cruised east along Sunset, checking out the latest Rock and Roll billboards. And then they drove down Hollywood Boulevard, which was still just as tacky as both of them remembered.

It was after three when they headed back to Long Beach. Traffic was terrible. It took them an hour and a half to get to the hotel. They listened to an oldies station and sang along, inventing their own lyrics when the real words escaped them.

Mack caught her looking for a message light when they entered the suite.

"Uh-oh," he said. "No messages. No one calling us. No one we have to call. It's just you and me tonight."

She thought of dear, sweet Alec, and hoped he was all right. And she remembered her sister, that strange breathless quality to her voice. But she didn't mention either Doreen's husband or Lacey. It didn't seem the time for that, somehow.

Tomorrow there would be Doreen's funeral to get through. They would call early, to ask Alec if there was anything he needed, anything he'd like them to do.

But today was just for her and Mack. And the time had come when she had to admit to herself that she wanted it that way.

"A swim?" Mack said.

It sounded like a wonderful idea to her.

The temperature was in the low eighties. More than warm enough to sunbathe on deck chairs after a dip in the Olympic-size pool. They put two banana-style lounges head to head, lay down on their stomachs and whispered to each other as the water dried on their skin. After a while, Mack laid his cheek on his crossed arms and closed his eyes.

Jenna rested her chin on her hands and thought how really good he looked, so tanned and fit. She tried not to let her gaze linger on his strong arms, with their dusting of golden hair. She had always loved the feel of that hair. She used to put her hand on his arm, very lightly, not even really touching the skin, to feel that wonderful feathery silkiness against her palm.

She stared at the top of his golden head, at his strong shoulders and powerful back. The longing inside her was so strong right then—to reach out a hand, to touch. To say yes when he looked up with a certain question in his eyes.

Every day, every hour, every moment they spent together, Jenna found it a little more difficult to resist the pull between them.

He lifted his head. Her heart caught.

But then he only laid his other cheek against his arm without ever actually looking up. She heard him sigh.

And something inside her shifted.

Or maybe something fell away—an obstacle, an obstruction. An old, deep pain giving up, letting go, stepping aside so she could see the truth.

She was glad that he had come to find her. And glad that they were sharing this time together.

Did she still love him?

Oh, Lord. Probably. Most likely, she had never stopped.

But at this point, it didn't really matter what kind of

label she put on it. If she called it love, or just desire, or the longing to try again.

What mattered was that up till now, she'd invested a lot of effort into keeping certain barriers between them.

From now on, that would change.

From now on, she intended to put heart, body and soul into tearing the barriers down.

# Chapter Ten

Mack could feel her watching him. He lifted his head.

One look into those shining hazel eyes and he knew.

So much for the damn separate rooms.

She gave him a quivery smile. "Let's go in the water again."

He couldn't right then. Everyone would have known exactly what was on his mind. "You go ahead."

"Sure?"

He nodded. He watched her walk toward the pool's edge, thinking she still looked every bit as good to him in the flesh as she'd looked in his dreams. She was slim and tall and she carried herself with a kind of quiet dignity he'd always admired. She wore a simple two-piece white suit that didn't reveal any more than it should. Wholesome. Yes. And achingly sexy at the same time.

But it wasn't only the way she looked. It was something else. Something indefinable. Some sweetness he'd never encountered before or since. Some…openness to him.

There had been other women. In the years without her.

Some had been kind and warm and funny, like Jenna. Some hadn't. None had lasted very long. After a while they had only reminded him of how much he missed what he'd once had with her.

She dived from the pool's edge, very neatly, cleaving the water with hardly a splash. Her crawl was as tidy as her dive, across the width of the pool and then back. She stopped near the edge, treading water, to trade a few words with a matronly woman in a flowered swim cap.

By then, Mack had his arousal under control enough to push himself off the banana lounge and onto his feet.

She looked his way and waved.

He went to join her in the water.

They got back to the room at a little after seven, both still wet from a final dip in the pool. They had closed the curtains earlier against the afternoon glare, so the main room of the suite was shadowed and cool. Maybe too cool. Jenna had her towel wrapped around her shoulders. She gathered it tighter.

"Why do they always think they have to keep it sub-zero in hotel rooms?" she asked through chattering teeth.

"There is a way to deal with that."

Her eyes widened. He knew what she thought he had meant.

And maybe he had. But just to be contrary, he turned and fiddled with the thermostat. "It should warm up in a minute or two." He turned back to find that she had closed the small distance between them.

She was still shivering. He did the natural thing and pulled her close. It felt good. Right, as it always had. Her hair was wet silk against his cheek. She smelled of chlorine, a smell about as far from erotic as any smell could get—or at least, he'd always thought so until now.

"Brr." She scrunched her shoulders, trying to get closer. He wrapped his arms a little tighter around her, enjoying the softness of her slim body beneath the towel, and waited for her shivers to subside.

He felt no need to try to tempt her anymore. No impulse to seduce.

Seduction, if there had actually been one, had already occurred. It had happened all by itself somehow, outside, by the pool, when they lay on those banana lounges, under the good, dry heat of the California sun.

She was his now.

No need to rush.

The shivering stopped. He pulled back, rubbed his hands up and down her arms, over the nubby fabric of the towel. "Better?"

"Mmm-hmm."

Her mouth was too tempting, tipped up to him like that. He lowered his own, and hesitated, on the brink of the kiss they both hungered for.

She said his name, "Mack," so softly. With such yearning.

He kissed her.

Her mouth was cold, turning warm, and warmer still. The sweetness beyond her lips was as it had been the other day, as he'd remembered for all these years. Incomparable. Perfect. Exactly suited to him.

He slipped his hands under the towel to touch her.

Moist and cool. Like satin, her skin. She sighed, and kissed him harder.

They stood there by the door, between the thermostat and the gilt-framed mirror, kissing.

It went on forever, that kiss.

He was the one who pulled away. Gently. Reluctantly. He cupped her chin in both hands and his fingers tangled in the wet strands of her hair. He watched her eyelids open. She looked at him, a dazed and dreamy, utterly relaxed kind of look.

He brought his mouth to hers again. "Are we done with separate rooms, then?" He murmured the words against her soft lips, so that saying them became another kiss.

She smiled, and he felt that smile, her lips moving against his own. "Do you really have to ask?"

"Maybe not. But I'd like to hear you say it."

"It would please you—" each word was a kiss "—to hear me say it?"

"It would please me. Very much."

"Then, yes," she said. "We're done with separate rooms."

She let out a moan that heated the very air around them as he put his mouth against her neck, tangling his fingers in her hair at the same time and pulling her head back to expose her white throat.

He kissed his way down, over the twin points of her collarbone, stopping there briefly to put out his tongue and taste the chlorine and the wonderful smooth sweetness that was her skin.

He took the towel in both hands, peeling it over her shoulders. It dropped with a soft thud to the carpet at their feet. And then he went on, moving down, between the lush curves of her breasts. He pushed at the straps of her suit.

She took his meaning, reaching behind herself, wriggling a little, until she had the top of that white suit unhooked. It fell away and he had her breasts in his hands. They were cool and damp, little goose bumps all over them. He buried his face between them, breathing deeply, remembering….

All the times, their times together. His hands on her body, touching her, kissing her, thinking that she belonged to him, that he could never lose her, that it would always, always be that way.

That they would be together.

Forever.

Together.

He took her nipple into his mouth, drew on it. She surged up toward him, cradling his head in her hands, pulling him nearer, making little hungry, needful sounds, the sounds he remembered.

The sounds he had longed for.

For way too many years.

He let his hands follow her tender curves, down over her torso, under the white waistband of her suit. She shuddered. And then her hands were there, too, helping him to push the thing off and away.

At last she was naked.

Naked in his arms.

He traced a circle around her navel with a lazy finger. She moaned and ground her hips against him. His finger dipped lower, into the soft curls at the apex of her thighs. She lifted herself toward him. He touched her, intimately, feeling the heat and the wetness grow hotter and wetter still at the command of his stroking hand.

She moved against him eagerly as he caressed her. He kissed her other breast, tasted the nipple as it hardened and bloomed. Then he went lower, his mouth sliding down. She put her hands on his shoulders, to brace herself—to brace them both—as he sank to his knees before her.

"Mack."

He looked up. And she was looking down, her eyes so dark, the pupils wide open, her mouth red and full from the kisses they had shared. Her still-wet hair fell in thick coils against her cheeks. She lifted both hands, a languorous movement, swaying on her feet a little, as she smoothed the wet strands back, behind her ears. Her full, sweet breasts rose and then settled with the action.

"Mack…" She was still looking down at him.

"Shh…"

"No. No, listen. Mack, outside, by the pool. It was when I realized…"

He laid his hands on the sleek swell of her hips, then slid them inward, so his thumbs met in the warm cove between her thighs.

She gasped. He parted her slowly, gently, sliding his thumbs along the feminine crease beneath those golden curls.

"Glad you came back…" She sighed. "So good…to be with you…" She gasped. "Mack. I did think it was over. I didn't think…there was a chance for us anymore…."

"There's still a chance, Jenna."

"I…I think so, too. Now."

"Good." He leaned closer, scenting her. She moaned, gave up the effort to talk. She closed her eyes and clutched his shoulders harder.

And he tasted her.

It was something he had feared he might never know again…the taste of her.

He kissed her deeply, using his fingers to part her. She cried out, and then began moving, her hips working, finding the rhythm that would give her the most pleasure. He held her steady as he went on kissing her, drawing on her with his mouth and stroking with his fingers as well.

"Mack," she groaned, "Oh, Mack…I can't…" She stepped backward. He followed, not letting her go. She found the wall, beside the mirror, to brace herself.

He kept tasting, kissing, stroking. And she surrendered completely at last, with the wall to hold her upright and her hands clutching his head, her body moving of its own volition, seeking the sweet explosion that would give her release.

She cried out again, her head thrown back, as she went over the edge. And he tasted that, too. Felt the tiny nub of her sex pulsing hot against his tongue.

She stiffened, her hips thrust toward him.

And then, slowly, with a low purr of a laugh deep in her throat, she let her knees give way.

Rising, he caught her before she reached the floor. She fell into his arms, soft and limp, no longer shivering, totally his. He turned her without effort, put an arm at her back and one under her knees and lifted her against his chest.

She draped her long slim arms around his neck and nuzzled his ear. "Where are you taking me?"

"To my bed."

# Chapter Eleven

The walls of Mack's room had been painted a deep maroon. The bed was king-size, with a lush black-and-gold-patterned spread. He had a west-facing window like the one in the main room, looking out on the beach and the harbor beyond. The black-and-gold curtains were open wide and the setting sun hovered, a ball of red fire, above the calm blue sea. The room seemed to burn with light.

Mack laid Jenna on the bed and turned to shut the curtains.

She caught his wrist. "No. Leave it. I like it. It's like being inside a fire."

He looked down at her, his gaze sweeping from her tangled damp hair all the way to her toes. Jenna felt her skin flushing, her nipples tightening, her whole body responding to the heat in that look.

"Inside a fire…" he repeated, as if he found the words arousing.

She rose on the bed, still holding his wrist, until she was kneeling there before him, on the black-and-gold coverlet.

She brought his hand to her mouth and kissed the knuckles. Then she ran her own fingers slowly up his arm, as she'd longed to do out by the pool, barely touching the skin, brushing the fine silky hair, making it rise.

He bent forward, kissed her, their lips meeting so lightly, a butterfly of a kiss.

She continued to caress him, sliding her hand past his elbow, over the hard swell of his biceps, to his shoulder—and then trailing the pads of her fingers down his side. She smiled when she touched the sensitive skin of his belly and he couldn't manage to hold back a gasp. Slowly, taking all the time in the world about it, she slid a finger under the waistband of his swim trunks. He gasped again.

She pushed her hand farther under and made contact.

A third gasp from him as her hand closed around him. He was so silky, so thick and hard. She smiled to herself. It made her feel powerful to hold him like that, in the palm of her hand.

He muttered a low oath and dispensed with the swim trunks, ruthlessly shoving them down and away.

Now she could touch him freely. And she did, curling her hand more firmly around him, stroking slowly, loving the feel of him, loving the way he closed his eyes and threw his head back, a deep moan escaping his parted lips.

She bent closer, lowered her mouth to him and took him inside. He shuddered. She loved that, had always loved that, the feel of his big body shaking at her touch.

He allowed her a few minutes of that kind of play. Then he caught her face in his hands and made her look up at him.

"No more." His voice was ragged. "I'll lose it."

She couldn't resist. She bent one more time, gave him one last, lingering kiss, one he bore in a breath-held, agonized silence.

Then she raised her gaze to his again. "Come down to me."

He didn't move, only looked at her, a look that burned like the light from the slowly sinking sun, a look that claimed her. She shivered a little, but not with cold.

She took his right hand, tugged on it. "Mack…"

With his left hand, he reached for the drawer in the nightstand and came out with a small foil-wrapped pouch.

Jenna stared at the pouch and remembered.

Mack had always used protection.

Because he did not want to make a baby.

She closed her eyes, old hurts rising.

"Jenna." He said her name so gently.

She kept her eyes closed, despising herself a little for her own reaction. She was not the lost and confused young woman she had once been, the woman who had begged for a baby to fill the emptiness in her life.

It was totally appropriate that he'd have protection. Totally appropriate and right.

And really, what would she have done if he hadn't shown a little forethought here, since she wasn't on the Pill and she'd failed to pack a diaphragm? Would she have pushed him away at the last minute? Or worse, taken a foolish, thoughtless chance and possibly ended up pregnant, when nothing between them was settled or sure?

She opened her eyes, gave him a smile. A real smile,

though perhaps it did quiver a little at the corners. "I see you're prepared."

"Did you think I wouldn't be?"

"I guess I didn't think about it either way. Until now."

"I made no secret of wanting you, Jenna."

"No. No, of course you didn't. You did the right thing, to be ready when the moment came. This is just…old stuff I'm reacting to, that's all."

His eyes narrowed briefly. She knew that he understood exactly what "old stuff" she meant. But he didn't speak of it.

She sighed.

He was staring down at her. Waiting, still clearly aroused, but holding himself tightly in check. The light in the room was redder, deeper, as the sun touched the ocean at the edge of the world.

"Do you want to stop?" he asked, his voice rough, dangerous—yet at the same time rigidly controlled.

She pressed her lips together, drew in a breath and shook her head.

Another surge of heat flared in his eyes. And then his face changed, the look of strain passing, leaving his hard features softer.

He tore open the foil pouch.

She held out her hand. "Let me."

He said her name then, softly, hungrily, with a needful tenderness that brought tears to shimmer in her eyes and made everything suddenly all right again.

He set the torn pouch in her palm. She peeled it open to reveal the condom inside. Then slowly, lovingly, she rolled it down over him.

She set the empty pouch on the nightstand and held out her hand again. This time he took it, coming down onto the bed with her, straddling her, reaching for her other arm and raising them both above her head.

He held her there, in that vulnerable position, rising up enough to slip his legs between hers and then kneeling at the juncture of her open thighs.

He bent close, kissed the soft whiteness at the underside of each upraised arm. She moaned, lifting her torso. After a moment of sweetest agony, he gave her what she wanted, his mouth closing hot and strong over a nipple. She moaned again, and pushed herself toward his suckling kiss.

He drew deep. She felt the pull, down in the female heart of her. She wanted to reach for him, to drag him down and take him inside her.

But he continued to hold her arms helpless over her head, as he went on kissing her breast, drawing so deeply that she thought she might faint from the sheer erotic pull.

She couldn't bear it.

Yet she did bear it.

And bore it some more when he turned his attention to the other breast.

At last, long after the point when she felt absolutely certain she could bear it no longer, his mouth went roaming. He trailed one endless wet kiss over the top swell of her breast, up to her neck, her throat, her jaw, her cheek…

He sank down upon her as his mouth covered hers.

She opened for him, rising toward him as he filled her. They cried out together.

Perfect, yes. Exactly right.

Even after all these years.

They began to move together, finding the old

rhythms instinctively, with no thought or effort required. She wrapped her legs around him and they were one, in the red, burning light of the slowly setting sun.

She felt his pleasure cresting. Her completion rose to meet it. They hit the peak together on an endless, seeking kiss.

Jenna realized she must have slept.

The sun had set long ago, the red glow slowly fading to darkness. Now the room was silver and shadows. She lifted her head. Out the window, the night sky looked hazy, the stars bled away in the gleam of harbor lights.

Mack lay almost on top of her, his cheek against her breast and an arm across her waist. She looked down at his head, dark in the half-light, and she smiled a woman's knowing smile.

He stirred, as if he felt her looking at him. She wanted to touch him. Maybe she should have let him sleep some more. But the reality of having him here, where she could put her hand on him, was too tempting to resist.

So she ran a finger around the whorling shape of his ear.

He lifted his head and opened droopy eyes.

Then he smiled. And she smiled right back—just the kind of smiles they had given each other nine years before, the first night they met, when they'd ended up right where they were now: in bed together. That night, she remembered, Byron had jumped on the mattress between them, settled himself in and purred so loudly that they had both laughed.

Mack touched her cheek with a finger and guided a swatch of hair back behind her ear. "You're frowning. Why?"

"I miss Byron. I wish he were here."

He chuckled. "I don't know. The way I remember it, he always took up more than his fair share of the bed."

She idly traced a figure eight on the hard bulge of muscle at his shoulder. "I hope he's doing all right. He needs companionship, and I have this feeling that Lacey might be leaving him alone too much."

"I'm sure he's fine." He kissed her chin.

A question occurred to her. And now that she'd truly given herself to this two-week endeavor, she felt perfectly easy in her mind about asking it.

"Mack?"

He rolled to his back, then turned his head to lift an eyebrow at her. "What?"

"Why did you fight me so hard over Byron—and then all of a sudden just decide to let it go?"

He turned his face to the ceiling and put his arm across his eyes. Unease tightened her stomach. Was he going to evade, or maybe become angry with her for bringing up an unpleasant part of their past?

He dropped his arm and met her eyes again. He didn't look angry at all. The tightness in her stomach faded away. "Hey. I had a real soft spot for that damn cat. And I considered him mine as much as he was yours."

"I know. But those aren't the real reasons you tried to take him from me, are they?"

He was watching the shadows on the ceiling again. A silent moment passed before he answered. "The 'real' reasons aren't so simple. They're angry reasons, and they're vengeful. I'm not proud to admit to them."

"Please. I just want to understand."

His chest rose and fell as he drew a deep breath. "I

don't know. Sometimes I think that honesty between the sexes has been highly overrated."

She realized he was teasing her. She nudged him in the side. "Come on. Tell me."

He rolled over, lifted himself up on his elbows and stared at the headboard, which was an interesting creation of dark wood and wrought iron. "I didn't want to let you go," he said, "but I knew you weren't coming back to me. And I was damn insulted that you wouldn't take any alimony. I'd worked my tail off to make a decent living—and the price, I was beginning to realize, had been losing you. It seemed to me that the least you could do was take some of the money, ease my pride a little. That way I could have told myself that at least I'd been good to you financially. But you wouldn't take any money. All you wanted was the cat."

She touched his back, starting at the swell of his shoulder and running her hand downward, over hard muscle and tight skin. "So you decided you wouldn't let me have him."

"That's right. But after a year of the old back-and-forth, demands and counterdemands from your lawyer and then mine, I started to see it a little bit differently."

She suggested, "You mean you realized you were acting like an ass?"

He leaned closer, kissed the tip of her nose. "Exactly. And I told my lawyer to get it over with, that you could have the cat."

She dared to ask the next meaningful question. "So then, if you wanted to get it over with, why didn't you sign the papers?"

He let out a long breath. "I thought we'd been through that one. I didn't sign the papers because I didn't really want a divorce from you, not subconsciously, anyway. Your lawyer worked up the settlement and sent it to my lawyer—who was a colleague of mine, by the way, someone who worked in the firm, which I left shortly after you and I came to terms."

"Because of the class-action suit?"

"Right. The firm wouldn't touch it. But I knew I could win it and that it would pay off big. So I left the firm. And when the divorce papers came through, my lawyer got hold of me and told me to come in and sign them. I never got around to it. I was too busy with the lawsuit, getting what I'd always wanted, making myself into a millionaire—or that's what I told myself. I paid my lawyer off and, periodically, his assistant would call me to remind me to come in. In the end, I went and got those papers, thinking that I'd take care of them myself. But I didn't. I stuck them in a drawer and told myself I'd forgotten about them."

He glanced directly at her, saw her disbelieving expression and added, "Just as I'm sure you told yourself you didn't notice that the final decree never happened to come through. But, as I have pointed out before, I think you did notice. And you didn't do anything about it, either. Not for all these years."

She acquiesced. "Maybe you're right."

"Whew." He pretended to wipe his brow. "I think we're making progress here."

"So do I. And I want us to continue to make progress." She touched the side of his face, which was slightly rough now with evening stubble. "I have another question. A request, really. And before I ask it, I want to say that I promise you, I do intend to stay with you for the remainder of our two weeks. I *want* these two weeks now. I hope you believe me."

She saw in his eyes that he knew what was coming. He moved back to his own pillow. "Damn it, Jenna."

She didn't allow his retreat, but canted up on an elbow, so that she could wrap her hand around the back of his neck. She rubbed, gently but insistently. "Mack…"

He gave her a measuring, wary look. "You want the divorce papers, don't you?"

She leaned closer and kissed his rough cheek. "I do, Mack. And I want them now."

## *Chapter Twelve*

He rolled away from her, brought his feet to the floor and rose to loom over her. "Why?"

She sat and plumped her pillow against the headboard. Then she reached for the sheet and pulled it over herself. "I want us to start fresh, Mack. You don't need to hold those papers over my head anymore to get me to be with you. Please. Just give them up."

He stared down at her. He had on his lawyer look now. Calculating. Distant. "You don't need them until our two weeks are over."

She ached for him then, for that part of him that still couldn't quite trust her good intentions, the part of him, she realized now, that always expected to be abandoned in the end.

"You're right," she said. "I don't need the papers right now. But I do need for you to *give* them to me now."

He asked again, "Why?"

She phrased her answer with care. "You agreed to certain things, Mack. First, that you would sign those papers five and half years ago. And then, a few weeks ago, that you would sign them and send them to me. Those were…promises, Mack. Promises you broke. I think you owe it to me to do what you can now to make good on those promises. I think you owe it to yourself."

A muscle worked in his jaw. "What about the first promise? The one we made to each other. *To have and to hold,* damn it. What about that?"

"The time came when we both agreed we couldn't keep that promise anymore."

"Not for me it didn't. You were the one who left."

Patience, she thought. She raked her tangled hair away from her face and kept her voice calm and low. "Yes, Mack. I did leave. And you may be right that we both knew we weren't…finished with each other. But I also believe there was a time when we both accepted that our marriage had ended."

"I didn't," he said. "I never accepted that, not really."

She reached out and caught his hand. He didn't pull away. She decided to consider that a good sign. "Come back to bed. I didn't want this to end up a battle. I honestly didn't." She lifted the sheet with her free hand. "Please?"

His jaw remained set, his eyes cool and wary—but he allowed her to pull him back to the bed. Using the hand that wasn't holding his, she propped his pillow against the headboard for him and then settled the sheet over them both.

"It was over, Mack. You know it was."

He looked down at their joined hands. "What is this? You just have to be right about this, is that it?"

"No. I'm only trying to convince you to do what you know in your heart is the fair and best thing."

He squeezed her hand—and not gently. "Don't try to tell me what's in my own damn heart."

"Mack. Let's look at this another way."

He slid her a suspicious glance. "What other way?"

She sucked in a breath and took another big leap into even more dangerous territory. "Tell me this. Have you made love with any other women since we've been apart?"

He turned toward her then. His eyes gleamed through the dark, feral and a little frightening. "Your point being?"

"My point being that I know you took your wedding vows seriously. You would not have slept with someone else unless you believed at the time that you weren't married to me anymore."

They stared at each other. Jenna's heart drummed in her own ears. She felt like a woman who'd decided to stroll across a swamp—using alligator backs as stepping-stones.

Mack asked softly, "Did *you?* Make love with anyone else?"

She knew for certain then that there had been other women. Strangely, the knowledge caused her no more than a twinge of sad regret. Whom he'd slept with in the time they'd been apart was his business. Jenna truly believed what she was trying to make him see: they *had* been divorced—in their hearts, anyway. She only hoped that his lovers had been good to him, and that he had treated them well in return.

"No, Mack. I didn't make love with anyone else, but

not because I felt I was still married. I *was* divorced from you. I just…never found anyone else I wanted that way."

"Not even the good doctor?"

"No. Not even Logan." She waited, almost wishing she hadn't taken the argument in that particular direction.

He looked straight ahead, toward the door to the main room. "You make me ashamed."

"I swear to you, that was not my intention."

He gave her hand another quick, hard squeeze. She squeezed back.

He said, "You'll have to let go—if you want me to get those damn papers from my suitcase."

She did let go. And he went into the walk-in closet in the corner of the room. When he came out again, he was carrying a large manila envelope. He sat on the edge of the bed and opened it, then pulled the papers out. "Look them over. They're signed and notarized."

"I trust you," she said.

He chuckled at that, and ruefully shook his head. Then he shoved everything back into the envelope and handed it to her.

"Go on," he said. "Put it away."

She canted forward and kissed him. "Thank you."

"Go ahead. Do it."

She pushed back the sheet and left the bed, strolling nude to the door, through the main room, and into her part of the suite. There, she tucked the envelope into a side pocket of one of her suitcases.

When she returned to him, he had slid beneath the sheet and leaned up against the headboard again. He watched her walk toward him.

"You look good, Jenna."

She smiled her pleasure at the compliment as she pulled back the sheet and got in beside him.

"Are you hungry?" he asked. "It's after nine."

She shook her head. "Not right now. You?"

"Not really."

She felt his hand brush her thigh. She cuddled up closer, rested her head against his chest. "It's been a long time."

"Too damn long." He put his hand beneath her chin and guided it up so that their lips could meet.

The small funeral chapel was filled with flowers.

There were arrangements on stands, in tall vases, in baskets and in urns. Doreen's especial favorite had been white roses, so two giant vases of them flanked the open casket. Unlike most hothouse blooms, they actually gave off a scent.

"Lovely," Lois said. "The smell of those roses…"

"Dory would be pleased," Alec added in a tight voice.

Inside the open casket, Doreen Henderson McGarrity Telford lay in a bed of white satin, her tiny, thin hands resting on her stomach. She wore a trim blue suit with a slim knee-length skirt. The short jacket had three-quarter sleeves and a round collar. A little round hat with a half veil sat daintily atop her graying chestnut-brown hair.

During the viewing, which preceded the funeral ceremony, Jenna stared down at Doreen's small, serene face, thinking that she looked like a nice, aging housewife from an earlier era, a nice housewife who had lain down for a nap in her favorite suit.

Jenna sat with Mack and Alec and Lois, in the front row. The chapel was small, and only about a third full.

"Mostly people from the agency," Alec whispered. "The people we worked with. And a few neighbors, of course…"

During the viewing and before the service began, the others approached and offered their sympathies. Alec nodded and thanked them and told them how grateful he was that they could come.

The service was brief, a few hymns and hopeful verses from the Bible and some kind words from a robust, florid-faced minister. Once the last prayer had been said, the minister invited them all to proceed to the cemetery.

In the cemetery, the pallbearers carried the casket from the long limousine to the place that had been prepared for it, beneath the feathery green leaves of a jacaranda tree. Come June and July, the branches would be weighted with soft violet blooms. Jenna closed her eyes and pictured that, the masses of purple flowers arching over the cool, grassy spot. She found the image soothing.

Once the pallbearers had set the casket in place, the minister quoted more scripture and said another prayer. Alec placed a single white rose on the closed lid of the coffin.

And then it was over.

Lois whispered, "We're all going to the house."

Jenna nodded. Mack took her hand and they turned for the car.

At Alec's house there were cookies and cake and punch on the table. People stood in little groups and talked quietly, of what a nice service it had been, so simple and moving. They said fond things about Doreen, how quiet she'd always been, and so good at heart. Alec made a point of introducing Mack around, and of explaining how pleased and grateful he was that Dory's son had come to help him through this difficult time.

If people were surprised to find that Doreen had a son, they didn't show it. Watching their faces, Jenna thought that they really *weren't* surprised. It seemed to her that they simply hadn't known Doreen well enough to feel that her son was someone they should have been told about.

And why was that? Jenna wondered. Had Doreen kept people at a distance in order to minimize the possibility that the question of whether she had children would ever come up? Or was it, perhaps, just that Doreen was a very private sort of person?

Jenna wished it might be the latter, but feared the former.

How many different ways, she wondered, had Doreen paid for the choice she'd made to give her children away?

Jenna looked for Mack and found him across the room, talking quietly to Lois. He glanced up and their gazes met. Jenna let the wonderful jolt of awareness sizzle through her, watching as a smile teased the corners of his mouth.

She thought of the night before and felt acutely alive, all her nerves humming, her skin prickling. Was it wrong, to feel so wonderful on the day they laid Mack's mother in the ground?

She didn't think so. And she didn't think that Doreen would have minded at all—though of course, she'd never know.

People began leaving around six. Jenna and Mack stayed until everyone else had left. Then they, too, said their goodbyes. Mack explained that the two of them had a morning flight to Miami.

Lois said she was staying for another week or two,

and then she would try to talk Alec into coming and visiting her in Phoenix for a while.

Alec said, "Mack, when you talk to your sisters, please tell them I hope someday to meet them."

Mack glanced away, then back. "It might be a while, Alec."

Alec squeezed his arm. "Whenever you get around to it, then."

"Fair enough. You know how to reach me, if you ever need me for anything."

"Yes, of course. I have that address and phone number you gave Dory."

"That should do it."

"Mack?"

"Yeah?"

"It's meant so much—that you were here."

Mack cleared his throat and nodded. The two men looked at each other, each seeming to have something more to say, but neither actually getting the words out.

"Go on." Lois elbowed her brother in the ribs. "Give him a hug. You know you want to."

Lois's prompting was all Alec needed. He reached out and put his thin arms around Mack. Mack returned the embrace, but awkwardly, as if a hug was something he wasn't quite sure he ought to be participating in.

Finally Alec took Mack by the arms and stepped back. "You're a fine man, son. Dory was so proud of you…and so am I."

Mack mumbled something. It might have been "Thank you."

Alec's eyes gleamed with held-back tears as he turned to Jenna. She grabbed him and hugged him hard. He whispered, "I hope things work out between you two."

She pulled back, gave him a nod and a smile, then turned to Lois to get one more hug.

"Don't be strangers. Stay in touch," Lois commanded as she let them out the door.

"You okay?" Jenna asked softly when she and Mack were in the Lincoln, headed back to the hotel.

He felt for her hand, found it. "I'm okay. Ready to get out of here, ready to hang out under the banyan trees, to watch a Key West sunset from the deck of *The Shady Deal.*"

"That's the name of your boat? *The Shady Deal?*"

"That's right."

She lifted their joined hands and kissed the back of his. "I never pictured you living in a place like Key West."

He gave her a quick grin, then focused on the street ahead of them again. "I love it. It's tropical. And it's seedy. It has very little dignity. But it has style. It's the perfect place for me."

"Mack McGarrity. You are never seedy. No way."

"Hah. But you admit I lack dignity."

"I didn't say that."

"But you thought it."

"I did not."

He had to pull his hand away to make a turn. She watched his profile, saw his expression grow serious.

"What are you thinking?"

"So strange," he said. "Those people today, coming up to me, offering their condolences. Condolences for what? I never really knew her."

"It's what people do at funerals, Mack. A show of support, letting you know that they care."

"I understand that. I only meant that it felt strange. I

kept thinking, Who *was* she, anyway? What in the hell went on in her mind?"

"I think…she was a good woman, at heart. That she made a tough choice, told a big lie to someone she loved and then never knew how to tell the one she loved the truth."

Mack laughed, a sound without humor. "I guess we can think whatever the hell we want now, can't we? She won't be around to tell us we're wrong."

"She was a good woman, Mack, I just know she was. After all, Alec loved her. A man like Alec could only love someone good…and I know that she loved you. I'm positive of it."

He sent her another glance, a glance with doubt in it, and the shadow of a lifelong hurt. But he didn't say anything. Not much later, they reached the hotel.

The minute they got inside the suite, Mack pulled her close and buried his head against the curve of her neck. She wrapped her arms around him, held him as tightly as he was holding her.

His lips moved against her neck as his hands fumbled at the few pins she'd used to hold up her hair. He found the pins, dropped them.

Her hair fell around her shoulders. "There," he whispered. "Yeah…"

She tipped her head back, offering her lips. His mouth covered hers.

Jenna gave herself up to his kiss, understanding his need right then—to touch, to feel, to reach out for life. She moaned as his tongue mated with hers.

He began to undress her, sustaining the kiss as he walked her toward his room. They left a trail of clothing through the main room, into his room, to the edge of the bed. They had to break apart to remove the rest: his shoes and socks and boxer briefs, her panty hose and bra.

He reached for the drawer in the nightstand and took out the condom. She rolled it down over him. They fell across the bed together.

Jenna ended up on top. When she took him inside her, they both kept their eyes open. The curtains were closed then, the room dim and cool. She moved above him, looking down, wishing she could take all his old hurts into herself and turn them to pure joy.

He surged up inside her. She felt him pulsing, finding release. She didn't try to reach a climax of her own, but simply let herself relax on top of him, cuddling her head into the crook of his shoulder, smiling to herself as his arms came around her.

She turned her head, pressed her lips against the side of his neck. "It was a tough day."

He made a low, lazy sound of agreement. His hand was stroking her hair.

"And we'll be in Florida tomorrow…" she reminded him tenderly. "We'll spend the rest of our two weeks doing whatever you want to do."

"Hmm. Whatever I want?"

She nipped the place she'd kissed a moment before. "Don't push your luck."

They were still in bed an hour later when the phone rang. Mack answered it, then handed the phone to Jenna.

"It's your sister."

Jenna took it. "Lacey?"

"Oh, God, Jenna." Lacey sounded as if she might burst into tears. "Please don't hate me…."

"Hate you? Lacey, what are you talking about?"

"It's Byron," her sister said. "He ran away. I don't have a clue where he's gone."

## Chapter Thirteen

"Byron's missing?" Jenna held back her own cry of dismay. She thought of the strange way her sister had sounded the last time they had spoken. "How long has it been since you saw him?"

"Wednesday. He was here then, I swear to you."

"So he disappeared…?"

"Yesterday. I came back to the house to feed him and I couldn't find him."

"Have you checked all the closets? And the cupboards in the kitchen? Sometimes he—"

"I swear to you, Jenna. I've looked everywhere, into every cupboard, every closet, every nook and cranny. He must have gotten out somehow, though I can't figure out how he managed it. None of the screens are unhooked, and I never left any of the doors open." Lacey let out a moan. "I know what you're thinking. And you're right. I didn't pay enough attention to him. I've been having…well, the last few days have been… Let's just say I haven't been around the house much."

"What's going on? Where have you been?"

"Oh, Jen. It's…I think we'd better talk about that later. Right now, there's more you have to know."

Jenna slumped against the headboard, "There is?"

"Mmm-hmm. You see, today I…I thought I heard him, in the attic…." Lacey paused long enough to let out another small moan of misery.

Jenna sat up a little straighter. "You thought you heard Byron in the attic?"

"Yes."

"And?"

"I went up there."

"And?"

"I thought I heard him again, way over in the corner, under the eaves—you know, above the upstairs bedroom in the front of the house?"

"Yes. I know the place you mean."

"There's no attic floor there, just those big beams and the ceiling of the bedroom below and—"

Jenna was getting the picture. "You didn't…"

"I did. I put my foot through the bedroom ceiling. I smashed up the bone in my heel, 'mushroomed' it. That's what the doctor said. And I also left a big, ragged hole in the ceiling. You should see it. What a mess."

"Forget about the ceiling for now. What about you? How did you get back down out of the attic?"

"It wasn't pretty. But I managed it."

"And then?"

"I called 911 and they came and they carted me over

to Meadow Valley Memorial. When I got there, they took X rays, wrapped up my foot and gave me some crutches. They sent me home for the night, but I have to be back tomorrow by two in the afternoon. For surgery." Lacey moaned some more. "Oh, I didn't want to call you. But I figured I'd better. I'm going to have trouble getting over to the shop to check on the money. And then there's Byron…"

"You say you're at home now?"

"Yes. Until tomorrow."

"Is someone there to help you?"

"Mira and Maud were here." Lacey spoke of the "terrible twins," her friends from high school. "They made me some dinner and a bed downstairs. Mira said she'd be back tomorrow, to take me to the hospital."

"So you're all right. For tonight?"

"Yes, yes, I'm fine. I can get around on the crutches if I have to, and they gave me some painkillers, so it doesn't hurt too much."

"I'll be there tomorrow, as soon as I can get a flight."

"Oh, God. I've ruined everything. Jenna, I'm so sorry for messing up like this. And poor Byron… He *has* to turn up soon. I just know it. He's probably off somewhere sulking, don't you think? Oh, I feel so guilty. I feel like a real jerk…."

"Don't worry. I'll see you tomorrow, I promise."

"Mack McGarrity will probably hire a hit man to do me in."

Jenna glanced at Mack, who was lying on his side facing her, his head propped on his hand. He'd been frowning since he'd heard that Byron was missing—and he'd started scowling at the point where Jenna mentioned getting a flight.

Now he demanded, "What the hell is going on?"

Jenna waved at him for silence and spoke to her sister again. "I mean it. Stop worrying. I'll be there. Probably not tonight. It's too late. But tomorrow, as early as I can."

"All right. I am so sorry."

"Relax. I'll see you soon."

Lacey murmured a pitiful goodbye and Jenna hung up.

Mack pulled himself to a sitting position and folded his arms across his chest. "Well?"

She hit him with it. "Byron's missing and Lacey broke her foot. I have to go back to Meadow Valley right away."

Mack said nothing.

He was thinking that the damn cat would eventually come back on his own. Bub knew how to take care of himself. He'd been a stray when he'd suckered Jenna and Mack into adopting him.

And didn't Lacey have a few friends in her hometown who could help her through the next few days?

But he could tell by the look in Jenna's eyes and the set of her soft, very kissable mouth that she was going. No sense getting on her bad side trying to talk her out of it. He'd worked damn hard, after all, to get himself on her good side. And he really liked it there.

"Mack." She looked adorably contrite. "I'm so sorry. Your two weeks in paradise don't seem to be turning out the way you planned."

"I'm going with you."

"Are you sure? We could—"

He didn't let her even suggest an alternative. "I said I'm going with you."

"All right. If you're positive that's what you want to do."

* * *

They arrived at Sacramento Executive Airport at 10:00 a.m. the next morning. Mack had a rental car, another Lexus, waiting and ready to go.

It was a little after eleven when they reached the house at the top of West Broad Street in Meadow Valley. Mack pulled in behind a dark blue Cadillac.

He turned to Jenna. "Looks like your sister's got company."

Jenna gulped. "Yes. That's Logan's car."

Mack turned off the engine. "What's he doing here?"

"I don't know. I suppose he heard that Lacey was hurt. He's always thought of himself as a kind of big brother to her. I'd imagine he just wanted to check on her, to see that she's all right."

Mack didn't look the least satisfied with her suggested explanation. "You think he knows you're coming back today?"

Jenna let out a long, exasperated sigh. "I don't have the faintest idea what Logan knows about all this."

"I don't like it."

"Can we just go in, please? We can't learn anything sitting out here."

"Fine."

Jenna met Mack at the rear of the car and took the two bags he handed her. They trooped up the front walk, Jenna in the lead.

On the porch, Jenna set down her bags, anchored her purse strap more securely on her shoulder and unlocked the door. Then she stuck her head in and called out good and loud, "Hello? Lacey?"

After an unnerving three beats of silence, Lacey answered, "We're back here!"

Jenna turned to Mack, who stood on the porch behind her, holding a suitcase in one hand and a garment
bag slung over the opposite shoulder. "They're in the
back parlor."

He shrugged.

She thought of Logan, of the way the unshed tears
had gleamed in his dark eyes the last time they'd spoken. Guilt gave her a sharp, very unpleasant little poke.

"Jenna. Are we going in?"

"Of course."

"Well?"

"All right." She pushed the door open all the way,
picked up the bags again and entered the house. "Just,
um, set everything down here."

They lined the suitcases up to the left of the door and
Mack draped the garment bag over them. Then there
was nothing else to do but seek out her sister and Logan
in the back of the house. "This way."

Mack followed behind her, along the central hall to
the back parlor.

They found Lacey sitting in the old velvet easy chair,
her injured foot propped on an ottoman in front of her,
with pillows stacked up to keep the foot high. A set of
crutches lay on the hardwood floor beside the chair.
And a TV tray sat on the other side, laden with tissues
and a water glass, a thick paperback novel, the remote
telephone and a bottle of some kind of prescription
medicine.

Logan stood by the fireplace. He was a long way
from tears right then. His strong jaw was set and his dark
eyes glittered with what looked like anger. Lacey
seemed upset, as well. Two vivid spots of color stained
her pale cheeks.

No one spoke for an agonizing three or four seconds. The silence seemed to bounce off the cream-colored walls. Jenna cast a glance at Mack, watched him eyeing both her sister and Logan.

Then Lacey declared way too brightly, "You're early!"

Jenna frowned. "Not really." She had called Lacey from the airport and told her that they'd be about an hour.

"Well, I mean, I didn't expect... It's just that I..." Lacey waved a hand. "Oh, never mind. Um, hello, Mack. How have you been?"

"Just fine."

"You remember...each other?" Lacey put out a hand palm up and gestured from Mack to Logan.

The two men exchanged curt, unsmiling nods.

Lacey looked at her outstretched hand as if she didn't remember how it had gotten extended. She brought it back and made a pretense of smoothing her hair. "Um, Logan heard I had hurt myself. He just came to check on me." Her big smile got bigger and her cheeks colored even more deeply. "Didn't you, Logan?"

Logan hesitated, but then said gruffly, "That's right." He turned and spoke to Jenna. "She's got Jeb Leventhal as her surgeon. He's the best. She'll be fine."

Jenna gave him a smile that was probably as false as Lacey's. "That's good to hear."

Logan cleared his throat. "Well. I think it's time I was going."

"Yes." Lacey's eagerness was painful to see. "You'd better go."

Logan nodded at Mack again. And for the second time, Mack nodded back. Logan smiled at Jenna. She smiled in return.

Lord, this was awful. All four of them, smiling and nodding, their sentences trailing off into harrowing silences.

At last Logan turned and left them.

No one said a word until they heard the front door close. By then, Lacey's smile had slipped. She sighed.

Jenna went to her, brushed the soft, wild curls away from her face and placed a kiss at her temple. "Are you in pain? Is there anything I can get you?"

"No. I'm fine. I mean, it hurts, but I just took a codeine half an hour ago. I'm all right." She bit her lower lip. "Byron hasn't shown up yet."

"He will. Soon. I'm sure."

"I'm such a—"

"Lace. Ease up on yourself, will you?"

"I went ahead and slept down here." She indicated the convertible sofa a few feet away, which was folded out into a bed, the covers all tangled, testimony to an uneasy night. "It's just too hard to get up and down the stairs."

"We might as well move you into my room." Jenna had the master suite, on the ground floor at the front of the house.

"No. I'm okay here. I'll only feel more rotten if I kick you out of your own bed."

"Lacey, it's all right, really. There are three bedrooms upstairs. I can take one of them, no problem."

"Right. Maybe the one with the gaping, ragged hole in the ceiling."

"Stop it. A hole in the ceiling is not that big a deal."

"Keep your room. I mean it. And will you just quit fussing over me? Please?" Lacey cast a glance at Mack, who waited, arms folded across his chest, near the stairs that led to the upper floor. "Are you staying, Mack?"

"I am."

"Then tell my sister that she should help you bring in your suitcases or something, will you?"

One side of his mouth kicked up. "Jenna. You should help me bring in our suitcases. Or something."

Jenna sent an exasperated glance from her sister to Mack and then back to Lacey.

Lacey waved her hand again. "Go on. You two get your stuff inside. I'm fine." She picked up the phone from the TV tray at her side. "I'll just call Mira and tell her she won't have to ferry me to the hospital, after all."

"Give a yell if you—"

Lacey was already punching up numbers. "I will, I will. Now, go on. Please."

Jenna led Mack back to the front door. But once she had both bags in her hands, she just stood there, undecided.

Mack read her easily. "I'll share your room," he said. "And your bed. I doubt that your sister is going to be shocked if she finds out."

She turned and led him where he wanted to go, to the door halfway back down the central hall that opened onto her bed-sitting room and adjoining bath.

"I like this," he said, setting the suitcase down on the russet-and-saffron-colored rug and laying the garment bag over a chair. He glanced around approvingly at the dark furniture, the pale walls and the red velvet comforter on the wide four-poster bed.

Her heart was beating way too fast, knocking itself painfully against the wall of her chest.

Somehow, she felt so terribly…vulnerable, here, with him, in this particular room, the room that had once been her parents' room and later her mother's alone. The room that, for the past few years, had become her own private retreat.

Strange. She'd paraded before him in their Long Beach hotel suite without a stitch to cover herself and found it as easy and natural as breathing. But standing here with him now, fully clothed, their suitcases between them, she felt utterly naked and extremely uncomfortable about it.

"I'll...clear out a couple of drawers for you. And there's room in the closet, for whatever you need to hang up. Why don't you go on out and bring the rest of the bags in and I'll—"

"Jenna." His voice was like velvet. His eyes knew too much.

"I...what?"

He stepped around the suitcases and came up close. Too close. He lifted a hand and touched her, his finger burning a caress into the tender skin of her cheek. "Your upper lip is quivering."

"Twitching, you mean."

"Twitching. Right. Nervous?"

"I...yes. For some reason I am."

"You never thought I'd be in this room with you, did you?"

That was true. She hadn't. Not ever.

But she had dreamed of him often while she slept beneath the red comforter. Dreams like the one where they floated on the white bed, naked without ever removing their clothes...

His hand trailed downward, over her jaw, tracing a heated line along the side of her throat.

"Mack..."

"What? Afraid I'll push you back on that nice, big bed and have my way with you right now?"

She caught his hand before it could go any farther, and then kissed it, a gesture they both recognized as placating. "It's just…it is strange. Having you here. You only came here with me that one other time, remember?"

"Our first Christmas together. We slept in that room upstairs, in the back."

"My room. Or it was until my mother died." She let go of his hand. "You hated Meadow Valley."

He didn't try to deny it. "I was afraid you were going to try to trap me here—and don't get that look. For me, at that time, moving here would have been a trap. And you kept dropping hints, remember? About how I could start my first law practice here, hang out a shingle over on Commercial Street. It wasn't what I had in mind for myself."

"I know. You were headed for a partnership in a major big-city firm."

"And all you wanted was to come back to your hometown."

"That's right."

"And in the end, you did come back, didn't you?"

"Yes. I did."

"And something else is bothering you, beyond my being here in this room with you, beyond unhappy memories of the way we were. What is it?"

She leaned on the end of the bed and rested her cheek against one of the tall, carved posts. "I just feel strange about this whole thing, I guess. Coming back here, instead of going to Key West. Running into Logan again. And something's going on with Lacey, did you notice? Something other than her broken foot and Byron's disappearance."

He gave her a shrug and the slightest hint of a smile.

She frowned at him. "What? You know something I don't?"

"It's only a guess."

"Tell me."

"It looks to me like your ex-fiancé has moved beyond the big-brother role with your little sister."

"Moved beyond the...?" Her mouth dropped open. She shut it. "You mean...? No. Not those two. Never in a million years. Lacey said she might check on him, you know, to see that he was all right, after you and I left town, but..."

"Looks to me like she checked on him but good. And I have to tell you, I think it's great. Whatever distracts the good doctor from his lifelong devotion to you is A-okay with me."

Jenna could not get her mind around such an idea. "But Mack...Logan and Lacey? I just can't see it."

Mack shrugged. "My other suitcase and your overnight case are still in the trunk. I'll get them."

Jenna stared rather blindly after him as he went out the door into the hall.

Imagine that. Logan and Lacey. Could it be true?

She'd have to ask Lacey...when the right opportunity presented itself, of course. After Lacey had made it through her surgery, sometime when the two of them were alone.

Jenna was still standing in the same spot when Mack returned with the rest of their bags. The sight of him got her moving. She went to the big bureau to empty a couple of drawers.

Lacey's surgery went well. She had to stay in the hospital that night, but Dr. Leventhal promised she could go home Sunday morning.

Mack and Jenna left the hospital at a little after seven. At the house, Jenna found enough in the cupboards and refrigerator to fix them a simple meal of pasta and salad. She even had a nice bottle of red wine she'd been saving.

They cleaned up the kitchen together. And then they went to her bedroom.

By then, the feeling of strangeness at having Mack with her in the house where she'd grown up had passed. She found it all felt very natural between them again. Natural and right and more beautiful than ever. They made love slowly, making the pleasure last.

Afterward, they soaked in the claw-footed tub in her bathroom. She sat between his legs and leaned back against his chest.

"This is heaven." She sighed.

He murmured his agreement, his hands busy below the surface of the water, doing things that very soon had her moaning and calling his name.

Eventually they retired to the four-poster bed again and dropped off to sleep around midnight.

It was after two when Jenna woke. She lay staring at the ceiling, certain she had heard the low, rusty sound of Byron's peculiar meow.

No other cat meowed like her cat. He did it so seldom. It always came out rough and raspy, as if his vocal cords had forgotten how to make the right sound.

There it was again.

Jenna sat up in bed.

Mack turned over and squinted at her through the darkness. "Huh?"

"I thought I heard Byron. You know that meow he has? Kind of raspy and rough?"

He sat up beside her, instantly awake. "Where?"

She was already pushing back the covers. "I'm not sure. Outside the bedroom door, I think. In the hall."

The shirt Mack had been wearing the day before lay over a chair. She scooped it up and pulled it on. It covered her to the tops of her thighs. Hardly modest, but it *was* just the two of them—and maybe, if they were lucky, one raspy-voiced black cat.

Mack took a minute to yank on his boxer shorts. Then he followed her out into the hall.

Jenna switched on the light. Nothing.

"Could we just look around?" she asked.

He shrugged. "Why not?"

They searched the two parlors, the kitchen and laundry room, even the bathroom under the stairs.

"Let's go ahead and check upstairs," she suggested when they'd exhausted all the possibilities on the lower floor. Mack didn't argue, so she turned on the light at the foot of stairs and they started up. At the top, she crossed the landing and entered the front bedroom, Mack right behind her.

Jenna switched on the overhead light and they stood for a moment, looking up at the ragged hole in the ceiling where Lacey's poor foot had gone through. Jenna made a mental note to call around on Monday, see if she could find someone to fix the thing for her. The drywall would have to be patched and then retextured. She could manage the painting herself.

"Well?" Mack said.

"Just considering the repair bills. Let's look around."

They checked under the bed, in the closet, beneath the bureau and bed tables. Even in the bureau drawers. Nothing.

Mack stood in the middle of the room and looked up

at the hole again. "Do you think he could be up there? Maybe Lacey really did hear him."

They decided to give it a shot. Jenna got a flashlight, then they climbed the small, dark set of stairs that went up from the landing. They scoured the cramped, low attic, pushing boxes and old furniture out of the way so they could see behind it, but they found no sign of Byron.

When they got back to the second floor, they went through the rest of the rooms there just in case—the other two bedrooms, the two bathrooms and the big closet on the landing.

When there was nowhere else to look, they trudged back down the stairs and into Jenna's bathroom. Jenna sat on the edge of the tub and rinsed the attic dust from her feet and hands, ending by splashing the clear, warm water on her face. Mack waited until she was finished, then rinsed the dust off himself, as well.

They returned to the bedroom and settled back down in bed. Mack pulled her close.

She laid her head on his chest. He stroked her arm tenderly and she listened to the strong, steady beating of his heart.

After a while, she whispered a confession. "I don't think I really heard him. I think I only *wanted* to." She felt Mack's lips against her hair and asked, "Do you think we'll ever find him?"

"Hell, Jenna. How would I know?"

She lifted her head, found his eyes through the darkness. "It doesn't matter if you know. Just say yes."

"All right. Yes." With his thumb he wiped away the two tears that had somehow managed to get away from her and trail down her cheeks.

She sniffed and laid her head back down. "I guess I can probably go to sleep now."

He spoke once more, his voice low and infinitely soft. "I love you, Jenna. I've always loved you."

"I know, Mack. I love you, too."

"Love wasn't enough before, was it?"

"No, Mack. It wasn't."

"Will it be enough now?" Something in his voice made her certain that he smiled then, though she still lay against his chest and could not see his face. "Now it's your turn to say yes, whether you really know the answer or not."

She lifted her head again. "Yes." He kissed the end of her nose. Then she asked cautiously, "Are you... ready to talk about it now? About the things each of us wants? About whether we could make our lives fit together again?"

He looked at her deeply. Then he settled her head back onto his chest. "Not now. We have a week and a day left of our original agreement. Let's make the most of it. We can work everything out at the end."

## Chapter Fourteen

They brought Lacey home the next day, Sunday. The doctor said it would be several weeks before she could walk without the aid of a crutch.

Mack carried her into the house from the car. She was groggy from the painkillers she'd been given and fell asleep shortly after Mack laid her on the sofa bed. Jenna and Mack tiptoed out, closing both sets of louvered doors, the one to the kitchen and the one to the central hall.

Lacey slept a lot the next couple of days. Jenna checked on her frequently, making sure she was comfortable, that she had everything she needed.

But Lacey had no use for coddling. She kept shooing Jenna away, insisting that she was fine. She knew how to use her crutches if she needed them. She could hobble to the bathroom and the kitchen well enough.

She tried to be upbeat, but Jenna could see the worry in her eyes. She'd planned to take a few weeks off, and then go back to Southern California and find herself another job. A few weeks now looked as if it might stretch into a few months. She'd had to call her L.A. roommate and tell her she'd better find someone else to help with the rent.

Also, Lacey had let her health insurance lapse after she'd lost her most recent waitress job. To pay for her surgery she'd had to dip into the money their mother had left her. Jenna offered to help out, but Lacey only shook her head and said she could and would pay her own bills.

Jenna tried not to worry about her. But the cheerful facade was such a very thin veneer. Lacey's blue eyes had circles under them. And she didn't put much effort into personal hygiene. Her gorgeous golden hair hung lank around her shoulders.

Twice, Jenna tried to bring up the subject of Logan. Both times, Lacey shook her head. "Let it be, Jenna," she said. "Just…leave it alone."

"If you ever want to talk about it, you know I'm here."

"Thanks, but there's nothing to talk about."

So Jenna left it alone. She fussed over her sister as much as Lacey would allow. And she checked on the shop daily, but let her clerks keep the schedules she had set for them during the time she was supposed to have been away. She had the ceiling of the upstairs room repaired and retextured and even bought the paint she needed to finish the job.

Mack had business of his own to tend to. He went out Monday and returned with a carful of computer equipment. He set it all up in one of the spare rooms on the second floor. He spent a few hours a day in there, on the Internet, presumably trading stocks.

The majority of the time, though, Jenna and Mack managed to be together. They devoted a portion of that time to hunting for Byron.

Jenna called the local animal shelter and reported the cat missing. The woman at the shelter assured her that since the cat wore an identifying tag on his collar, Jenna would be notified immediately should the cat be brought in.

They had flyers made, with a picture of Byron, Jenna's name, address and phone number, the number on Byron's tag, and an offer of a reward. They tacked the flyers up all over the neighborhood, and even went around knocking on doors, asking people if they'd seen a short-haired black cat with some gray around the neck and a blue studded collar. No one had.

After they'd put up the flyers and talked to the neighbors, they told each other that Byron would show up some time soon.

And they focused on enjoying themselves, on making the most of every moment they had. They drove down to Sacramento for a couple of evenings out, where they ate at good restaurants, went to a play one night and a movie the other. Then they rode back up to the foothills after midnight to enjoy what was left of the darkness in Jenna's bed.

Closer to home, they explored the local tourist attractions, climbing down into the cool, moist caves of hardrock gold mines together, wandering the rooms of a couple of gingerbread-decked historic Victorian houses. On Wednesday they took a long drive up into the mountains, where the fall colors were already in full show.

They kept to the agreement they'd made, to work everything out when the two weeks were over. Sometimes

Jenna wondered at their mutual reticence when it came to discussing the future. But she didn't allow herself to wonder too long or too deeply. This lovely time they shared was finite. She didn't want to waste a minute of it stewing over the differences that could push them apart.

On Thursday Lacey asked Jenna if she'd pick up a few art supplies for her, a couple of big sketch pads and some charcoals and pastels. Jenna took this as a good sign, that Lacey was ready to do more than read and watch TV and worry about the money she didn't have. Jenna and Mack drove down to Sacramento to the store Lacey had recommended.

On the way, Mack quizzed Jenna. He found out that Lacey painted in oils and in water colors, as well. He grabbed a clerk the minute they got to the store and drilled the man on what kinds of equipment Lacey might need.

Besides the items Lacey had asked for, Mack ended up buying an easel, a number of blank canvases already stretched across wood frames and a set each of oil and watercolor paints. He also chose a worktable that could be folded up into an easy-to-carry suitcase, as well as several high-quality brushes.

As he strolled the aisles of the art supply store, grabbing things the clerk had suggested and throwing them into the cart, Jenna tried to explain to him that Lacey would probably be upset when she saw all he'd bought. He'd spent so much more than she could afford.

"I'm not letting her pay for it," Mack said. "So don't worry about that."

"But Mack. Her self-esteem right now is at an all-time low. And she has a lot of pride. She'll insist on paying for it."

"So? She can insist all she wants. As far as I'm concerned, she needs to be doing something she loves, something worthwhile. I'm just making sure she has the materials for it."

"But—"

"Save the buts, Jenna. I'm doing this."

When they returned to Meadow Valley and Mack and Jenna began lugging all their purchases into the back parlor, Lacey didn't say a word. At first. She sat in the easy chair, watching them troop in and out, her lips a thin line and her arms crossed under her breasts.

"Is that all of it?" she asked at last with pained civility.

"You bet." Mack set the folded easel against the fireplace. He was grinning. "I talked to the clerk at that store where you sent us. He told me the kinds of things you might need, so I bought 'em."

"I asked for some sketch pads, and something to draw with. Period."

"Yeah, well. You need all this other stuff if you're going to really get some work done."

"Who said I planned to 'really get some work done'?" She quoted him directly, with a sneer twisting her lips. "You can just pack all this stuff up and take it back where you got it. I didn't ask for it and I don't want it."

Mack wasn't grinning anymore. "Oh. Sorry. I guess I misunderstood. Your sister told me that you were an *artist.*"

Lacey's white skin had flushed a deep red. "I *am* an artist, thank you very much."

"Well, then. If you're an artist, you need all this stuff."

"I cannot afford all this stuff." Lacey cast an outraged glance at Jenna, who was standing near the doors to the hall, wondering if she should say something or just let the two of them duke it out. "Jenna, tell him he has no right to—"

"Leave Jenna out of this," Mack commanded. "She already told me not to buy what you need. I did it anyway. So she's in the clear here."

"She is not. She brought you into this house and—"

He let out a groan. "Oh, come on. Let's get back to the real issue. I can afford all this stuff. Believe me. It's less than nothing to me. And you need it. You need it very badly."

"You have no idea what I need."

"Sure I do. You need to paint. Right? Because you're an artist and that's what you do. And you also have several weeks where you won't be able to do much else. If you look at it that way, this could be the perfect opportunity for you."

Lacey actually rolled her eyes—but the hot color was fading from her cheeks. "'The perfect opportunity.' Oh, brother."

"Think about it," Mack said. "Give it twenty-four hours. I'll just leave all this equipment right where it is until then. If you decide that maybe you can use it, then it stays. Otherwise, Jenna and I will take it all back."

Lacey looked more pensive now than furious. "I suppose it would be pretty inconvenient for you, to have to drive all the way back down to the valley just to return everything."

"Yeah," Mack said. "It would."

Jenna hid a smile. The inconvenience would be minimal, and they all knew it. She and Mack had driven down to Sacramento and back three times already. They'd probably go again, for dinner and a

show. They could easily cart all the art supplies along
with them.

But she had a feeling that wouldn't be necessary.
She had a feeling Lacey was going to give in and let
Mack provide what she needed.

And she felt such pride—pride and the tender sweetness of her love. Yes, pride and love. The two emotions
mingled together, making her chest tight and her eyes
a little bit misty.

She wondered if Mack even knew how much he had
changed in the past seven years. The old Mack would
never have done such a thing for her sister—not from
any smallness of spirit, but because it never would have
occurred to him.

The old Mack had no time for other people's needs.
He'd been too busy trying to fill the bottomless need inside himself.

Mack added, "I mean it. We'll take it all back tomorrow. That is, if you decide you're not going to use it…"

The next morning, when Jenna and Mack were tiptoeing around the kitchen trying to get themselves some
breakfast without waking the night owl, Lacey called to
them from the other side of the louvered doors.

"You can stop whispering and giggling in there. I'm
awake."

Mack called back, "Real men don't giggle."

"Sorry. Whispering and laughing, then."

"That's better. Want coffee?"

"Yes. Black."

Jenna carried it in to her.

Lacey was sitting up against the backrest of the sofa
bed, and smiling sleepily. "Thanks. I can use that."

Jenna handed over the hot drink and Lacey sipped. "Mmm." She wrapped both hands around the mug. "I had an idea…."

Jenna slipped off her shoes and sat down on the bed, scooting up against the backrest so that she and her sister sat shoulder-to-shoulder. "Tell me."

"You know those old floor screens up in the attic, the ones with the teak frames and the rice paper botanical prints down the center of each panel?"

"What about them?"

Lacey sipped more coffee. "Do you think you and Mack could bring them down here for me?"

"What are you planning to do with those old things?"

Lacey glanced at the northeast corner of the room, where sunlight streamed in the double-hung window next to the fireplace. "The light's not too bad in that corner. I want to set up a sort of studio over there. Put up that easel Mack bought me, and get a couple of straight chairs, one for me to sit on, one for my foot. I'll use the screens to divide off the space." Lacey fiddled with the hem of the melon-colored T-shirt she'd worn to sleep in, the T-shirt Jenna had brought her from Seal Beach. "You know how I am when I'm working on something. I don't like anyone peeking over my shoulder."

Jenna laid her hand on her sister's. "We'll get those screens down here right after breakfast."

Lacey set the mug on the little table to the left of the bed and leaned her head on Jenna's shoulder. "Mack's right. I have all this time. I should put it to good use."

"Yes. That was good advice."

"He's changed," Lacey said softly. "When he was here all those years ago, I don't think he said more than two words to me. Hello. Goodbye. That was it. He wasn't…interested in some messed-up kid with a chip on her shoulder, even if that kid was your little sister. But now, well, he's just not the same S.O.B. I remember so fondly."

Jenna chuckled. "Yes. He *has* changed."

Lacey lifted her head. "So. Will you get married— or stay married…or whatever?"

"I don't know yet."

"When *will* you know?"

"Sunday or Monday. We're going to talk it all over then. And until then, we're just going to be together and love every minute of it."

"People should do that more often—just be together and love every minute of it." Lacey looked away. Then she sighed and rested her head on Jenna's shoulder again. "You smell good." She pulled back, lifted a lock of her own limp hair off her shoulder and looked at it critically. "Haven't washed this in a couple of days, have I?"

"Has it really been that long?" Jenna made her voice light.

Lacey pulled a face. "You are disgustingly tactful."

"Was that a compliment?"

"Yeah. I guess it was."

After breakfast, Lacey disappeared into the bathroom under the stairs. When she came out, she smelled of bath powder and her hair had regained its old luster. Meanwhile Jenna and Mack brought down the screens. They dusted them off and set them up to divide off the area Lacey would use as her studio.

Once the screens were in place, Lacey told them where to put the chairs she needed as well as her new worktable, the easel, the various supplies and the stack of blank canvases. Then she told them to get lost.

"And no peeking behind these screens." She spoke to both of them, but she was looking at Mack. She knew that Jenna already understood how she felt about privacy when she worked. "I want to feel confident that no one will see what I'm doing until I'm ready to let them see."

Mack grunted. "What do you want, an oath signed in blood?"

Lacey let out a groan. "Go on, get out of here, both of you. Give me some peace and quiet."

Jenna and Mack were only too happy to oblige.

Friday went by way too fast. Lacey sat in the easy chair and sketched—and then disappeared behind her screens for hours at a time. Mack and Jenna painted the ceiling of the room upstairs. By the time they were finished, Jenna said it was impossible to tell there had ever been a hole in it.

Saturday dawned warm and bright. It almost might have been summer again, the day was so mild.

Jenna packed a picnic lunch. She and Mack put on jeans and sturdy shoes and drove up into the mountains again. They found a side road and followed it until the pavement gave out and the ruts got too deep to make it safe to go on. Then they took their lunch and a big old blue-and-red quilt and they started walking through the tall pines. The trail they chose wound up the side of a hill.

They found what they sought when they crested the hill: a small glen, with a grassy plot of ground, trees all around and a stream bubbling cheerfully over a rocky outcropping a few feet away.

They spread their blanket and ate their lunch. Jenna had packed sugar cookies for dessert.

"You've got sugar on your mouth," Mack said when

she had finished her cookie and brushed the crumbs from her hands.

She gave him a teasing smile, one that had him scooting close and guiding her down onto the blanket.

He kissed her, running his tongue over her lips first, licking the sugar away.

He chuckled. "Sweetest kiss I ever had."

She lay looking up at him, into those eyes that were like a cloudy sky. Overhead, the pine branches moved and sighed together in the warm autumn wind.

He kissed her again and she closed her eyes. She felt as if she floated, so much like the way it had been in her dream of him. The two of them, floating in this little glen on the faded blue-and-red squares of the quilt.

If only they could float like this forever....

After a time, he pulled back. He put his hand on the side of her face. His skin was warm, slightly rough. She turned her head, pressed her lips against his palm.

"One more day," he whispered.

She sighed, and the sound seemed to come not only from inside her, but from the wind in the trees, from all around. "Yes. Just one more..." She touched his face, as he was touching hers, and she wondered why she felt so sad at the thought that their two weeks were almost past.

After all, they knew now that they had love. And for the past few glorious days, love *had* been enough.

And they had both changed over the years. They'd changed in positive ways. Surely they could make it work now.

Mack kissed her some more. She lifted her arms and wrapped them around him. He sank down upon her, on the blue-and-red quilt, in the private little glen at the crest of the hill with the warm wind sighing around them. She pulled Mack tighter, kissed him harder, to make her silly doubts go away.

Not much later, the wind turned cooler. Clouds began to gather. They straightened their clothing and packed away what was left of the lunch they had shared. Then they rolled up the quilt and started down the hill.

The rain began just as they reached the car—and ended right after they got to the house. They found Lacey's doors closed, which meant she was probably working and didn't want to be disturbed. They retreated to Jenna's bedroom, kicked off their shoes and lay down on the bed to continue what the short storm had interrupted.

Mack kissed her and she kissed him back and wished that tomorrow would never have to come. That this could go on forever, the two of them, spending long, lazy days just being together, talking and laughing and making slow, tender love.

When the doorbell rang, they still had most of their clothes on.

Mack lifted his head. "Who's that?"

"I don't know. Maybe Lacey's expecting someone."

Jenna sat up and reached for her shirt, which Mack had tossed to the foot of the bed. She stuck her arms in the sleeves and began buttoning up. Mack rolled to his back and lay there, watching her in that special way that spread warmth in her belly and made her fingers awkward and slow.

He raised his arms and laced them behind his head. She stared dreamily at his bare chest, at the powerful muscles of his flexed arms.

He grinned. "Hurry back."

"You know I will." She managed to button that last button, then tucked the shirt into the waistband of her jeans. She bent close to give him one more kiss before she rose and padded on bare feet to the front door.

The visitor was a boy. A boy she'd never seen before.

He looked about ten and he carried a battered skateboard tucked under one scrawny arm. He wore a grimy baseball cap turned sideways and pants five sizes too big, chopped off at the knees. His dingy white T-shirt, also way too big for him, had a rip at the shoulder and the name of some rock-and-roll band emblazoned on the front. His sockless feet were stuck into a pair of unlaced and totally disreputable black sneakers.

Jenna glanced past him, out to the street. No one else waited there. The boy appeared to be alone.

"Yes?" she asked cautiously.

He was clutching a sheet of paper in his free hand. He held it up and Jenna saw that it was one of the flyers she and Mack had plastered all over the neighborhood.

The boy said, "It says here that there's a reward for this cat."

## *Chapter Fifteen*

Hope made Jenna's heart beat faster. "You have my cat?"

"First I wanna know. How much is the reward?"

"But do you have him?"

"Maybe."

Jenna sucked in a calming breath and told her heart to slow down. She didn't know this boy. He hardly looked reliable. "Either you have him, or you don't. Which is it?"

"It depends." The boy was folding up the flyer. "How much is the reward?"

"What's going on?" It was Mack. He'd pulled his shirt on, but his feet, like Jenna's, were still bare. "You have the cat?" He pinned the boy with an accusing glare.

The boy slid the flyer into a pocket and started backing up.

Jenna said, "Wait. We just want to know—"

But the sight of Mack had spooked him. The boy whirled and raced down the walk.

"Stop him!" Jenna cried. "He's got Byron!"

Mack didn't hesitate. He sprinted around her and down the front steps. Jenna took off right behind him. The boy had already leapt the low front gate.

Mack jumped the fence just as the boy was scrambling onto his skateboard. Before the boy could roll out of reach, Mack managed to catch hold of his too-big T-shirt. He gave a hard tug and the boy lost his footing. The skateboard went flying and the boy dropped backward, right into Mack's arms.

"Hey, leggo! Lemmego!" The skateboard shot away down the steep sidewalk. "You better lemmego right now!"

Mack tucked the boy under his arm and started to turn for the gate as the skateboard veered off into the grass several houses away.

"My skateboard!" the boy shouted, flailing wildly with his skinny arms and legs. "Leggo. I've gotta get my skateboard!"

By then, Jenna had begun to reconsider the wisdom of sending Mack after the child. "Mack. Maybe you'd better let him go. I don't think—"

"Help!" The boy shouted. "Kidnappers! Rapers! Somebody help!"

Jenna winced. "Mack. I think you'd better—"

"They've got me! They're killin' me!"

Mack muttered a curse. But he did lower the boy to the ground. The second his feet touched the sidewalk, the kid took off.

Mack called after him. "About the reward? It's ten thousand dollars!"

Jenna gasped. It was a lot of money. Even for a cat as wonderful as Byron.

The dirty tennis shoes skidded to a stop. Slowly the boy turned.

"The reward," Mack said again. "For the cat. Ten thousand dollars."

The boy stared for a full count of five. Then he turned again and trotted down to where his skateboard had veered off the sidewalk.

Once he had the skateboard tucked safely under his arm, he faced Mack once more. "Nobody pays that much money for an old black cat."

"I do," Mack said.

"Why?"

"Because I can afford it. And I want the cat back."

"You rich?"

"Yeah. I'm rich."

The boy looked down at his dirty sneakers, then back up at Mack. "Listen. I didn't *steal* him or anything. He just showed up. He wanted to hang around. Okay, yeah, I fed him. But I didn't feed him much. He stayed anyway. It's not like he's a *prisoner.* He could go any time he wanted to."

"Ten thousand," Mack said again. "Where is the cat?"

The boy took off his hat, looked into it, and then plunked it back on his head. "This better be for real."

"It's for real," Mack said. "But tell me. Is this cat a talker? Meows all the time?"

The kid looked down again, shifted his skateboard from one hand to the other, and shook his head. "Naw. He does nothin' but purr all the time. He purrs real loud." The boy reached into his back pocket and pulled out the folded flyer. "But he's got on a blue collar and a tag with the number you gave on this paper."

Mack looked at Jenna then. "Sounds like Bub to me."

She nodded and drew in a deep breath to slow her racing pulse. Joy was shimmering through her. Byron was all right.

Mack turned to the boy again. "What's your name?"

The boy said nothing, only glared in defiance as he stuffed the flyer back into his pocket.

"Come on. Your name."

The boy gave in and muttered, "Riley."

"Okay, Riley. You get ten thousand dollars if you give us back the cat."

Riley considered, trying hard to look un im pressed, though excitement made his black eyes shine. At last, he nodded. "Okay. Deal."

Mack gestured at Jenna. "This is Jenna. I'm Mack. Why don't you come inside while we put our shoes on?"

Riley's mouth twisted with disdain. "Fuggetaboutit. I don't go inside a stranger's house. I'll wait on the porch."

"Fair enough."

Jenna saved her second thoughts until she and Mack were alone in her bedroom, yanking on their shoes and tying up the laces. "You're not really going to give ten thousand dollars to that boy, are you? He can't be more than ten or eleven years old."

"What? You want me to cheat him?"

"Of course not. But that's a lot of money to just hand to a child."

He finished tying his second shoe. "I assume he's got parents, or someone who looks after him. We can give the money to them—and hurry up. Who knows how long that kid will wait out there?"

Jenna grabbed her purse and Mack grabbed his keys, wallet and checkbook and they hurried out the door.

Riley refused to get into the Lexus. "Get in a stranger's car? You think I'm outta my mind? You follow me, I'll lead you there. I can move pretty fast on my skateboard."

He wasn't exaggerating. He flew down West Broad Street, his stringy hair blowing out from under his cap, and turned the corner at Hill Street so swiftly and sharply that Jenna couldn't hold back a gasp.

He kept going, never breaking stride, down steep streets and around tight corners. Mack and Jenna, in the Lexus, did manage to keep up, but came close to losing sight of him more than once when he suddenly spun around a corner and zipped off in another direction.

They ended up on the outskirts of town where small, run-down houses were tucked among the trees. Battered old cars stood on blocks in dirt driveways. And broken toys littered overgrown yards, yards surrounded by rusting chain-link fences.

Riley turned into one of the narrowest driveways, where an aged Day-Glo-green hatchback with a bashed-in driver's door huddled under a listing carport. Mack pulled in behind the green car. Riley was already at the side door of the dilapidated clapboard house, skateboard under his arm, holding open the sagging screen.

Mack and Jenna got out of the car and went to join him.

"You have to be quiet," Riley said. "If the baby's sleeping, my mom won't like you waking her up."

A long wail from the house put an end to that concern.

Riley winced. "Never mind. She's awake."

The boy led them into a small, dingy kitchen, where ancient linoleum, worn through to black in spots, covered the floor, and a yowling baby sat in a high chair, pounding tiny angry fists on the tray. A thin woman with lank dark hair was trying to feed the baby some kind of cereal, but the child kept yowling and spitting out the food.

The woman turned when they entered, her dark eyes first widening in surprise, then quickly narrowing down to slits. "Riley. What's this?"

"They're here for Blackie, Mom," the boy announced. "And they're paying a big reward."

The baby continued to scream.

The woman's eyes narrowed farther. "What reward?"

"Money, Mom. Lots of it." The boy raised his voice to compete with the screams of the baby and the drone of the television that reached them from the open doorway to the next room. He pulled the flyer from the back pocket of his ragged pants and held it out. His mother took it and peered at it doubtfully.

"Ten thousand dollars," Riley said with unmistakable pride. "They're gonna pay us ten thousand dollars for that cat, Mom."

The woman's mouth dropped open. Then she shut it tight. She wadded up the flyer and tossed it on the table.

Shaking her head, she stood, went to the sink, grabbed a soggy washcloth and returned to gently wipe the screaming baby's mouth. That accomplished, she dropped the washcloth next to the flyer and pulled the baby from the chair. She laid the child over her shoulder and patted her on the back.

"There, there, Lissa, don't you cry. It's okay. It's okay, now…."

The baby let out one more long wail—and then quieted, hiccuping a few times and grabbing on to the woman with tiny pink hands. "Better?" asked the woman tenderly. "You feel better now?"

The baby hiccuped again and the woman patted her back some more, sending a scathing glance first at Mack, then at Jenna. "What is this? Ten thousand dollars for an old stray cat? Who you think you're trying to fool?"

"We're not fooling anyone." Mack's deep voice was flat. "Mrs…."

"You from Child Welfare, is that it? Some new trick you people are pulling now? Telling crazy lies to an eleven-year-old boy? We are doing the best we can here, mister. We don't need any tricks played on us, you hear?"

Jenna stepped forward then. "Please. I'm Jenna Bravo and this is Mack McGarrity. We are not from Child Welfare. That black cat means a lot to us. We just want him back."

The baby was starting to fuss again. The woman rocked from side to side trying to soothe her. "Honey, honey, it's okay…." She scowled straight at Jenna. "That cat's in the other room. You take it and go."

Riley grabbed his mother's arm. "Mom! We can have the money, can't we? They said they'd pay, Mom. We got a right to the money."

The woman shook him off and went on rocking the baby. "Hush, you're scaring Lissa. No one pays that kind of money for a cat. Just give those folks what they came for and let them go."

"But—"

"Riley Kettleman, I don't want to have to tell you again."

Riley stared at his mother, mutiny in his eyes. But she looked straight back at him over the downy head of the baby girl. The boy was the one who looked away first. His thin shoulders slumped.

He turned to Mack and Jenna. "Come on. He's in here."

Riley led them into a cramped living room, where two other children, a boy and a girl, were sprawled on the threadbare brown carpet, watching cartoons. Byron lay between them. The cat looked up at them and yawned.

Jenna's heart lifted. "Oh. Glad to see us, are you?"

As usual, Byron said nothing.

Riley scooped him up and scratched him behind the ear. "Gonna miss you, Blackie." He handed the cat to Jenna. Byron was purring quite loudly by then. Jenna grinned at the familiar sound.

The girl on the floor, who was probably about six, blinked and tore her gaze away from the images on the television screen. "Hey. They're takin' Blackie?"

"He's theirs," Riley said. "They got the right."

"I love Blackie!" The little girl's eyes filled with tears.

"Don't be a jerk, Tina," Riley instructed. "It's their cat and they're takin' him."

Tina sniffed. "I'm not a jerk. I just don't want Blackie to go away."

"Maybe we'll get another cat," Riley bargained, "like a kitten, or something."

"Did Mom say?"

"I'll talk to her. But right now, just say bye to Blackie."

The little girl stood and buried her face in Byron's sleek coat. Then she turned soulful eyes up to Jenna. "Maybe we could come visit him sometimes?"

Riley didn't give Jenna a chance to answer. "He's their cat, Tina. Mom says we have to turn him over and let them go."

Tina poked at the other boy with her bare foot. "Blackie's leaving."

The boy waved a hand, but kept his eyes glued to the TV screen. "Bye...."

Jenna raised Byron to her shoulder. His steady purr droned in her ear as Riley led them back through the kitchen where the baby sat in the high chair again, quiet and contented now as her mother spooned cereal into her mouth. The woman didn't spare them so much as a glance as they went by.

Jenna paused at the door, letting Riley and Mack go out ahead of her. "Mrs. Kettleman?"

The woman granted her a cool look.

"I really appreciate your taking care of my cat."

The woman straightened her shoulders. Her eyes had changed from cold to accusing. "You shouldn't have lied, shouldn't have gotten my boy's hopes up like that. That's maybe the worst thing in the world, hope. It lifts you up and then you end up crashing down."

"It wasn't a lie. Mack is willing to pay the money he offered."

The woman blew out a disgusted breath, then turned back to her baby. She dipped up a spoon of cereal and patiently poked it into Lissa's tiny pink mouth.

Jenna hesitated, thinking she ought to say more. But what? Riley Kettleman's mother had clearly heard enough. She pulled open the door and left the kitchen.

Outside, Mack was leaning against the Lexus, writing a check.

Riley stood a few feet away, his head tipped to the side, watching Mack warily. "My mom said not to take your—"

Mack looked straight into Riley's dark eyes. "Do you want the money or not?"

Riley chewed his lower lip. "I thought it would be cash money. Checks bounce. I know that."

"This one won't."

"Yeah. Right."

"Listen. This check is drawn on a national bank. There's a branch of that bank right here in Meadow Valley. You get your mother to take this check to that branch. They'll cash it for her."

Riley gulped. And then he nodded.

Mack asked, "You think you can get her to take it in and cash it?"

Riley bit his lower lip, considering, then nodded again. "I'll say, what have we got to lose? Either things will still be the same as they are now, or we'll have ten thousand dollars we didn't have before."

"Good thinking." Mack bent to the checkbook again. "Her last name is Kettleman, right?"

"Yeah."

"How do you spell it?"

Slowly Riley spelled the name.

"I need her first name, too."

"Erin. *E-r-i-n.*"

Mack glanced up. "Or maybe I should make it out to your father?"

Riley lifted his head high. "Like that'll do anybody any good. My dad is dead."

Byron purred all the way home. The sound filled up the quiet car. Jenna petted her cat and felt so grateful to have him back—grateful and sad at the same time.

Sad for Erin Kettleman and her four children. Sad for

Erin's husband, who had died and left a struggling family behind. She closed her eyes and said a little prayer that Riley's mother wouldn't tear up Mack's check. That she'd take a chance on hope one more time.

Jenna glanced over at Mack. He was staring straight ahead and didn't see the tender smile she gave him.

She almost spoke, but what was there to say? Some comfortable platitude? Some cliché? *That poor woman...those poor children...?*

No. Better just to ride in silence, with Byron purring on her lap and Mack in the driver's seat, taking them home.

Lacey was almost as happy as Jenna to have Byron home again. She hugged him and he allowed her to fuss over him, purring contentedly for her as he did for everyone else.

She scolded him. "Oh, I just felt so terrible, you naughty boy. And here you are, look at you, back home again and none the worse for wear." She beamed up at Jenna. "He looks great."

"He sure does."

Lacey gazed down at the cat again and pretended to scowl. "Don't you ever do that again, you bad boy."

Byron looked up at her, yawned and went on purring.

"We should celebrate," Lacey said.

"Absolutely," Jenna agreed, pleased to see the happy color in her sister's cheeks.

Mack spoke up then. "I'll go out and get some steaks and a couple of bottles of wine."

Jenna volunteered, "I'll come with you."

"No. Stay here with your sister. I won't be long."

Something in his tone bothered her. Something distant, something withdrawn.

"Mack? Are you sure you don't want me to—?"

But he was already on his way down the hall.

Jenna shrugged and let him go. She and Lacey fussed over Byron some more and Jenna told Lacey about the small house on the outskirts of town where Riley Kettleman lived.

Lacey said what Jenna kept thinking. "I just hope that woman takes a chance and cashes that check."

When Mack returned, they opened the wine. They proposed several toasts: to Byron, to Riley, to the mysteries of fate. Later, Jenna stuck three potatoes in the oven to bake and tossed a big green salad. Mack grilled the steaks to medium rare perfection on the old gas grill out in the backyard.

They ate in the dining room, on the good china.

More than once during the evening, Jenna noticed that Mack seemed preoccupied. But the minute she'd catch his eye or ask him a question, his distant expression would vanish. He would smile and answer her warmly. She'd tell herself that she was just imagining that faraway look in his eyes.

Later, when Jenna and Mack retired to her room, they made slow, perfect love, which neither inclement weather nor a knock at the door interrupted. Jenna thought it was the best kind of ending to a very special day. She fell asleep smiling, with Mack's arms around her and Byron purring steadily from the foot of the bed.

Her dreams, however, were disturbing ones.

In one, Riley Kettleman flew down a busy street on his skateboard, sliding in and around large, threatening vehicles. The drivers honked at him, and slammed on their brakes. Some of the drivers even leaned out their windows and shook their fists and swore. Riley ignored them. He rolled on down the street, fearless and fleet as the wind.

The street faded away. And Riley's mother stood in her small, run-down kitchen and tore up Mack's check. The walls of the rickety house fell in and the pieces of the check blew away in the autumn wind.

And then Jenna and Mack drifted by on the white bed. Mist curled around them. They were in that floating, hazy void again. But now they weren't making love. They were just…sitting there, looking at each other. Jenna reached out her hand to him. But some invisible barrier stood between them. She couldn't touch him.

She called to him, her cries getting louder and more frantic as she saw that he didn't hear her. He only sat there, looking at her so sadly, a few inches…and a thousand miles away.

She began to cry.

The tears were trailing down her face, into her hair, as she opened her eyes.

She was lying on her back, staring at the ceiling. It was still dark.

Jenna sniffed and swiped at her cheeks, turning to her side where she could see the bedside clock.

"Jenna?" The sound of his voice, so tender and deep.

Her heart twisted. He touched her shoulder. She rolled to her back again and he canted up on an elbow to look down at her. His eyes gleamed at her through the shadows.

"Our last day," she said.

He saw her tears, gently rubbed them away. "Not yet. It's still night."

"It's 3:00 a.m. Technically, it's tomorrow."

White teeth flashed as he smiled. "Just like technically, we're still married."

"Yes, Mack. We are. And we have to talk."

"We will."

"When?"

"After breakfast. Will that do?"

"Okay." She sighed. "I had bad dreams. I couldn't reach you. You were right there…but I couldn't touch you. And that boy, Riley—"

"Shh." He turned her on her side again, pulled her in against him, so that they lay spoon fashion, his body cradling hers.

"Do you think they'll be all right? That boy. His mother…the other three children?"

He smoothed her hair away from her cheek and brushed a kiss against her ear. "Go to sleep, Jenna. Just go to sleep."

"Oh, Mack. Why is the world so cruel?"

He kissed her again. But he didn't answer.

"Mack? Whatever happens, I want you to know that this has been the best two weeks of my life."

He chuckled then. "Right. We went to a funeral in Long Beach. Bub ran away and your sister broke her foot."

"We met Alec and Lois. And my sister is going to be okay, and Byron is home again now. And I think we did something really important. I think we…found out why we got married in the first place. We found out that there *was* love between us, that it never really died. Now, no matter what, when I think of you, I'll think of the good things."

"So," he whispered softly. "No regrets?"

For some reason she chose not to examine, tears filled her eyes again. She blinked them way. "Absolutely none."

"Good. Now go back to sleep."

He pulled her closer. Byron tiptoed from the foot of the bed to stretch out beside them.

It wasn't long at all before sleep came to claim her again.

## Chapter Sixteen

They woke together, with the dawn. In the kitchen they moved about quietly, brewing coffee, poaching eggs, buttering toast. Lacey didn't call to them from behind the louvered doors, so it was just the two of them at the table, with Byron sitting on the little rag rug in the corner, purring and giving himself a thorough morning bath.

"Let's get out of the house," Jenna said once they'd scraped the plates and put them in the dishwasher. "Away from the possibility that the phone will ring or someone will knock on the door."

"All right."

Outside, the air was brisk and the wind had a bite to it. Mack wore his leather jacket and Jenna had pulled on her old red plaid mackinaw coat. They got in the Lexus.

Mack asked, "Where to?"

"How about where we had our picnic yesterday? I don't think anyone will bother us there."

Mack parked the car in the same place that they'd left it the day before. They got out and he went around to the trunk for the blue-and-red quilt.

He tossed the quilt over his shoulder. "Let's go."

They started into the trees.

It was much cooler in the little glen at the crest of the hill than it had been the day before. But since they both had their jackets, it was bearable. They spread the quilt and Jenna found four smooth rocks to hold the corners down. Then she sat, tucking her legs to the side and shivering a little as the chilly wind found its way under the warm wool of her mackinaw.

Mack stood above her, at the edge of the blanket, his hands in his pockets.

She looked up at him and forced a smile, though she felt terribly nervous all of a sudden. "Sit with me." She patted the blanket beside her.

He let her suggestion pass without response. He was looking at her mouth. "Your lip is twitching."

She pressed both lips together in an effort to make the twitching stop. It didn't help. "I know."

"I don't…know where to start."

Neither did she, really. She pulled at a loose thread on the quilt and tried to organize her thoughts, which suddenly seemed to be spinning off in a thousand different directions at once.

"We could start at the beginning," he said.

She nodded. "That sounds right."

Mack dropped to a crouch, picked up a twig from the yellowing grass and broke it in two. "When you called me and told me you were going to marry the doctor, at first I was stunned. Just at the idea that you could even think of marrying someone else…" He paused then, to toss both bits of twig away, one and then the other. "It seemed impossible to me." He laughed, a dry sound. "That's my ego for you. Here we'd been apart for seven years, should have been divorced for five. I hadn't seen you in all that time. And yet…" He sat then, on the edge of the blanket, and wrapped his arms around his knees. "I couldn't just let it go. I had to see you again, had to try…" He seemed not to know how to go on. He looked up at the pine branches swaying overhead, then down at the blanket, then across the glen, where the clear water of the little stream burbled cheerfully over the rocks.

Finally he tried again. "What I'm saying is, I didn't really think it through all that well. I just knew I had to get myself some time with you, one way or another, to find out if maybe you felt the same as I did, to see if there was still anything there for you, when you thought about me."

The wind blew Jenna's hair against her mouth. She brushed it away. "And so now you know. There's still something there."

"Yes. Now I know."

"And the question is…what do we do about it?"

He nodded.

She wanted to touch him, wanted to reach out and put her hand against his cheek. She wanted to feel his lips against her palm. And then she wanted his mouth touching her own, his body covering hers, shielding her against the chill of the wind.

When they touched, it always seemed as if there was

no need for words. When they touched, she could forget the future, and put aside the past. When they touched, there was only the moment, only right now.

But they couldn't put off discussing the future forever. The time *had* come to deal with what would happen next.

She kept her hands to herself. "I love Meadow Valley, Mack. You know I do. But I don't…I don't *need* to live here the way I did once. I don't feel that a place defines who I am anymore. I realize now that I could have done better, when we lived in New York. I could have tried harder to make a new life there."

He scanned her face, his gaze intent. "You're saying you'd move to Florida with me now?"

"I would. Yes. I'd give it a try. And a *real* try this time. We could fix up that house of yours—you did say it needs fixing up?"

"Yes, I did."

"And you could teach me to fish. Isn't that what you do on that boat of yours—fish?"

"Yeah. I fish. And sometimes I just drift."

"I could do that. Drift. Up to a point."

He shifted, looked away again. "Up to what point?"

And she said, as clearly and firmly as her suddenly tight throat would allow, "I want children, Mack. I always have. I think you know that. I want…an ordinary, everyday, garden-variety family. I want a husband who's around a reasonable amount of time."

He turned to face her again. "A husband who's around. That, I can do now. I can be there, with you, whenever you need me."

"Yes. I know. And it's…" She swallowed, took a breath, and said, "It's almost enough."

"Almost?"

"Yes. Oh, Mack…" There it was again. That over-powering urge to reach out. But she didn't do it. She laced her hands together in her lap and chose her words with utmost care. "I want kids we can love and raise to-gether. Our own babies, if that's possible. But if for some reason we couldn't have children, then I'd want to adopt. I just want to do that, to help some little ones grow up and start their own life. To me, that's the most important thing there is. I wouldn't feel I'd really lived if I didn't raise a child or two."

He said nothing. His eyes were tender and sad.

"Would you…do that with me, have a family with me, Mack? Do you think that you could?"

He spoke then, but only to say her name soft and low. "Jenna…"

She bit her lip to keep from begging him. All those years ago she had begged him. It had done no good.

She doubted that it would do much good now.

Her nose was starting to run. And a few pointless tears had gotten away from her. She felt in the pocket of her mackinaw and found a tissue. Carefully she smoothed it out. Then she blew her nose and wiped the tears from her cheeks.

Mack rose to his full height as she slid the soggy tis-sue back into her pocket. He walked a few feet away and stood staring down the trail they had climbed up the side of the hill.

She thought he looked so tall and strong standing there—tall and strong and utterly alone. She ached for him, for the lost little boy he had been long ago, for the driven young man who couldn't slow down enough to be a husband to her—and for the drifting, footloose millionaire he was now, the man who still hadn't found real meaning in his life.

Finally he turned to her again. He came back to the blanket, but stopped at the edge. "I keep thinking about that kid, Jenna. About Riley Kettleman. About that baby, little Lissa—and those two other kids, Tina and whatever the other boy's name was. I keep thinking that those kids haven't got a prayer. That their father is gone and their mother can't provide for them. That it's the same old story, over and over. People start out with the best damn intentions. They get together and they have children. And then something happens. Divorce. Death. Lost jobs, lost hopes..." His voice had gone rough, as if something inside him were tearing. He paused, stuck his hands into his jacket pockets, pulled them out again. "Jenna, I just don't think I can do that. Bring some kid into the world, into my life. Kids...they don't understand. They trust. They believe that you will take care of them. But that doesn't always happen. Things go wrong, things you can never anticipate. And children are left with less than nothing. I couldn't do that to another human being."

She really hadn't meant to touch him. But she couldn't stop herself. She reached up, took his hand. "Mack..."

He didn't pull away, but he didn't come down to her, either. He only looked at her through bleak and lonely eyes. "I know," he said. "It's not rational, that I feel that way. You're not Erin Kettleman. You've got a business, you own a house. You're a woman with your own resources.

"And I've got money now. I could protect the ones I loved, no matter what happened to me. I could see to it that you never ended up like Riley's mother, living in a run-down shack with four children and no way out, or like my own mother, feeling you had to make a choice between your children and a man." His fingers tightened over hers, hard enough that her bones ground together. But she did not wince, and she didn't pull away.

"In my mind, I understand," he said. "In my mind, I realize that the chances my children will end up like I did are minimal, that even if we both got hit by a truck, they could still be provided for. But then I think of what it was like for me. To have a family, and then to have nothing. My father dead. My mother just…gone. And my gut knots up and I can't get air. I've even lied to myself that someday I'm going to change, someday I'll let go of all this irrational, faulty reasoning. I'll realize that I'm like just about everyone else. I'll want children.

"But Jenna. It hasn't happened. And the truth is, I don't think it's ever going to happen." He tugged on her hand. "Come up here. Come on."

She let him pull her to her feet.

He wrapped his arms around her, but held himself away enough that he could meet her eyes. "I'm sorry, Jenna. I don't know what the hell I was thinking, to force you into this two weeks with me, when I knew how you felt about having a family—and I also knew that on that issue I hadn't really changed. I'm just a selfish S.O.B. to the end, I guess, and I—"

"Shh." She wrapped her hand around the back of his neck and pulled his head down close to her. With a low sound he buried his face in her hair. The cold wind blew around them. The pine branches swayed and rubbed together, making a sound like a long, drawn-out moan.

"I told you last night," she whispered. "I have no regrets."

And she didn't. Not a one.

Except perhaps regret that she was losing him. Losing him all over again...

Oh, Lord. She couldn't bear it. She *wouldn't* bear it.

Yes, she did long for children. But she didn't want to have them with anyone but Mack. She had learned that the hard way, and she'd hurt her dear friend Logan deeply in the process.

She pulled back enough to swipe the stubborn tears away with her hand. "Mack. Listen. If you feel that you just can't—"

He took her by the shoulders, his fingers digging in. "Don't say it."

She didn't understand. "What?"

"Don't give away your children for me."

"What children? I don't have any children."

"But you will. And you should. You'll make a hell of a mother."

"No. Not without you."

He cupped her face. His palms were warm. "It's not going to work with us, Jenna."

"Don't say that. That's not so. It will work. We'll make it work. This time, we are not going to throw what we have away. Oh, Mack. Please. Just stay here with me, in Meadow Valley, for a few more weeks. Let me get my sister on her feet again, and put my shop up for sale. Then I'll go with you to Florida. We'll make a life together. A good life. Just say that you'll stay married to me, that you want me as your wife."

Instead of answering, he kissed her, his mouth covering hers with a yearning so powerful, it stole her breath away. She kissed him back, pressing close, warmed by his body against the coldness of the wind, tasting the salt of her own tears on his lips.

We will be all right, she thought. We'll make it. Somehow.

If he couldn't let himself have children, so be it. She would have no children, either. Half a dream, after all, was better than no dream at all. She would focus on what they *did* have and let what might have been alone.

Mack was the one who ended the kiss.

And her hopes, as well.

He pulled away and stared into her eyes.

He said, "It won't work, Jenna. I'm leaving today."

Nothing she could say would dissuade him.

When they got back to the house, he went straight upstairs to unhook his computer equipment and take it out to the car. Jenna couldn't bear to watch him getting ready to leave her. She glanced at the door to the back parlor: still shut. And it sounded quiet in there. Lacey might still be sleeping—or she could be hard at work.

Of course, she wouldn't mind the interruption once she learned that Mack was going.

But Jenna turned from the louvered doors without knocking. Mack was leaving. There was nothing Lacey could do about it. No reason to drag her into the final goodbyes.

Jenna trudged to the front parlor and sat on the sofa. She stared blindly out the window at the Boston fern hanging from the eaves above the porch rail, thinking rather numbly that it was getting too cold out there for the fern now. She would have to remember to bring it in tonight.

And tomorrow…

Her mind skittered away from tomorrow.

From all the tomorrows.

Without Mack.

In her side vision she noted a flicker of movement: Byron, tail held high, strutting her way from the arch to the dining room. He came and sat at her feet and looked up at her expectantly.

She patted her knees. He jumped and landed lightly on her lap. She stroked him, long strokes, from the top of his head to the end of his tail. He arched his back and purred his pleasure, then walked in a circle and curled up in a ball. She stared out the window and absently petted his silky head.

She heard Mack come down the stairs and go back up twice, heard the front door opening and closing as he carried the equipment out. Then he went to the bedroom to gather up his things in there.

Too soon, he appeared in the doorway to the hall. He had his garment bag slung over his shoulder and he carried a suitcase in either hand.

Jenna set Byron on the floor and stood. "I'll help you carry that stuff out."

"I can manage."

"No, really. I don't mind." She walked toward him on legs that felt numb. All of her felt numb, actually. A puppet on a string, moving at the commands of her mind, which felt distant from the rest of her, far away. Disconnected.

"Lacey's door is closed," he said. "I don't want to bother her. Will you tell her goodbye for me?"

How considerate, she thought. He's broken my heart, but he won't disturb my sister.

She said, "All right. I'll tell her."

Byron approached him. Mack set down the suitcases, laid the garment bag over them. "Hey, Bub…" He bent and scooped up the cat. "You stick close to home now, don't go running off again." The cat dipped his head, to get under Mack's hand. Mack stroked him a few times, and scratched him behind the ears. "Bye, Bub." He bent and set the cat down.

He handed her the garment bag and he took the two suitcases. She followed him out.

He'd loaded his computer equipment into the back seat of the Lexus. The red-and-blue blanket and yesterday's empty picnic basket were still in the trunk. Mack set down the suitcases and took the garment bag from her, laying it over them as he had in the house. Then he took out the quilt and the basket and passed them to her. She stood there, shivering a little without her coat, her arms full of the things he had handed her, waiting as he loaded up the trunk. She watched him tuck the suitcases in with the box of mementos his mother had left him. He laid the garment bag over everything and closed the trunk lid.

And then there was nothing more for him to do but get in the car and drive away from her.

A barrage of questions rose to her lips.

Where are you going now? You don't have a flight to Florida yet, do you? Won't it take a while to arrange one? Why don't you just stay here until then?

Why don't you stay here with me?

Why don't you stay here…forever?

She held the questions back. She already knew the answers to most of them, anyway. And the others hardly mattered.

They stood on the curb, facing each other, her bundle of blanket and basket between them—well, much more than that between them, really: the children she longed for.

And the children he could not bring himself to have.

She saw in his eyes that he wanted to kiss her.

She didn't think she could bear that right then, though she knew that later, in the long, lonely time to come, without him, she would yearn for every kiss that they hadn't shared.

But now was not later. Now she could not bear one more kiss. Now one more kiss would be the difference between numb dignity and senseless, tearful pleading.

She needed her dignity.

Right then, it was all she had left.

She clutched the blanket tighter, and the handle of the basket, too, holding them close and high in front of her, a barrier to his touch.

She hitched in a breath. "Goodbye, Mack."

"Goodbye, Jenna."

He walked around to the driver's-side door. She found herself following him, standing there, waiting, as he slid in behind the wheel, shut the door, started up the engine, then rolled his window down.

"File the damn papers right away," he said. "Understand?"

She stared at him, wondering what he meant. And then she remembered. The divorce papers.

"Yes. I will. I understand."

He saluted her with a quick wave of his hand. Then she stepped back and he pulled away from the curb.

She stood there, staring after him, clutching her blanket and her empty picnic basket to her heart, long after the Lexus had turned the corner and disappeared from view.

## Chapter Seventeen

Lacey hobbled out of the back parlor and into the kitchen about half an hour after Mack left. Jenna was sitting at the table, her head bent over a sheet of lined paper. She looked up and pasted on a smile.

Lacey saw the pain behind the smile. "What's happened? Are you all right?"

Jenna licked her lips. They felt very dry, for some reason. "Mack's gone. He said to tell you goodbye."

Lacey maneuvered herself the rest of the way to the table, and lowered herself into a chair. She set her crutches on the floor beside her as Jenna pushed another chair her way. Carefully Lacey lifted her injured foot onto the second chair.

"Coffee or something?" Jenna offered. "Breakfast, maybe?"

Lacey waved at the air. "Forget about that right now. Are you serious? Mack just left?"

Jenna swallowed convulsively. Then she coughed. "He didn't *just* leave. He…we…" She had to swallow again before she could finish. "It didn't work out, between us. So yes, now he's gone." She bent over the sheet of paper again.

Her sister's hand came down and covered the paper.

Jenna sighed and looked up.

"Talk to me," Lacey said.

"Lacey, I—"

"Come on." Lacey's voice was so gentle. She lifted her hand off the paper. "What's this?"

"I…I was making a list. I was thinking that it would help, for the next few days. To know just where I'm going and what I need to do. There's a lot to do, really. I've got to get back to the shop full-time. I have been neglecting it, these past few weeks. And this house…" She looked around the bright, old-fashioned kitchen. "This house really could use a good top-to-bottom cleaning."

Lacey made a small, tender noise and held out her arms.

"And then there's the divorce," Jenna said. "Mack gave me the papers. I have to take care of that. Can't have it dragging out forever this time. It's best if I cut it clean."

Lacey just looked at her, arms still outstretched.

Jenna stared back, defiant—and aware of her own foolishness. Was there really anything to be gained by rejecting an offer of comfort and love?

Jenna rose from her chair and went to kneel beside her sister. She rested her head in Lacey's lap and felt Lacey's gentle hand stroking her hair.

"You still love him?" Lacey asked.

"Mmm-hmm."

"And he still loves you?"

"Yes."

"So why did he leave?"

Jenna sighed again. "Can we just…let it go? I don't really want to go into it now."

"You're acting as if it's pretty much final."

"It is." Jenna lifted her head and looked into her sister's eyes. "It's absolutely final. He's gone and he's not coming back."

The small blue box, tied with a white bow, was waiting on her pillow when Jenna went to her room a few minutes later.

She sat on the edge of the bed, picked up the box and turned it over in her hands.

There was a card attached.

Jenna,

I bought this years ago. In New York. Right after I won the lawsuit and I had the money I'd always wanted, but I didn't have you. I went into a certain store on Fifth Avenue, and I saw this and I wanted it for you. I could damn well afford it. So I bought it. And I've kept it. And I've thought that I would probably never give it to you.

But somehow, this seems the right time.

The note ended there. She turned the card over, hungry for some final word of love, of endearment, of sweet tenderness. There was none. Not even his name.

She tugged on the end of the white ribbon. It fell away into her lap. She lifted the lid.

Inside, on a bed of white satin, sat a small, perfect pin in the shape of a cat. A cat made of diamonds. With twin emeralds for eyes.

She lifted the little cat free of the box and went to the mirror above the big bureau. With great care, she pinned it over her heart.

It wasn't the kind of thing that looked right with the T-shirt and khaki skirt she was wearing. But she admired it anyway, turning it slightly, back and forth, so the stones caught the light and winked at her.

Then she took it off and laid it back in the box. She wrapped the box in the white ribbon and tied the ribbon in a bow. After a little pulling and smoothing, it looked just as it had before she had opened it.

She took the card and the blue box and put them in the bottom drawer of the bureau. The drawer also contained the silver rattle her great-aunt Matty Riordan Bravo had sent from Wyoming when Jenna was born. And a garnet ring Jenna had prized as a child. And also the little velvet case that held her wedding band.

Jenna treasured every item in that drawer, though they were all things she wouldn't wear or use again.

Five days later, on Friday at seven in the evening, Erin Kettleman came knocking on Jenna's door. Her hair was neatly combed, held back with two butterfly clips at her temples. She wore a faded brown jacket and carried a small tan purse.

"Is he here?" she asked. "Mr. McGarrity?"

Jenna's heart gave a little lurch at the sound of his name. "No, he left on Sunday. For Florida, I believe."

Erin Kettleman put her hand, palm flat, against her chest. "I've left Riley with the children. He's very responsible. And Lissa's asleep." Her thin lips tipped upward in a wobbly smile. "I don't know how long she'll stay that way, though. I—"

"Mrs. Kettleman, please. Come in." Jenna reached out and took the other woman by the arm.

Erin Kettleman allowed herself to be led inside, to the front parlor.

"Have a seat." Jenna offered the Chippendale-style chair near the sofa.

"Thank you." Erin Kettleman took the chair.

Jenna went to the sofa and perched on the end, close to her guest. "Something to drink?"

"Um. No. I really can't stay long."

"Your jacket?"

"I'll just keep it on." The dark eyes scanned the room. "This is a beautiful old house."

"It was my mother's."

"Your mother's." Erin Kettleman folded her hands over the tan purse that lay in her lap. "Well. That's real nice."

The two women stared at each other. Silence yawned, then both began speaking at the same time.

"I don't know how to—"

"Did you cash the—?"

They both stopped, smiled, apologized.

Then Erin Kettleman said, "Yes. I cashed Mr. McGarrity's check. Riley talked me into it. He can be very convincing, that boy." A wistful gleam came into her eyes. "He's a lot like his daddy, to tell you the truth."

Jenna took in a breath, then released it in a rush. "I'm so glad. That you cashed it."

"And *I'm* so grateful. And sorry for how rude I was last Saturday. I didn't believe it. I couldn't let myself believe it. Lately I've had the feeling that one more disappointment would finish me off. My husband, Riley senior, he died just six months ago. We…we never had much, but when Riley was alive, somehow we always got by. Since he's been gone, though, things have just seemed to go from bad to worse. I've been real scared. Scared we just weren't gonna make it. Scared that…" Erin Kettleman decided against finishing that thought. She pressed her mouth tightly closed and looked away.

Jenna leaned closer and brushed a hand against Erin's worn coat sleeve. "But you weren't disappointed this time, were you?"

"No. No, I was not." There was that quavering smile again. "Let me tell you, that was some moment. I was shaking when I signed the back of that check. And then the teller took it, along with my ID, and punched up some numbers on her computer. *Then* she said, 'How would you like that, Mrs. Kettleman? In hundreds?'" Erin Kettleman let out a short, high-pitched laugh. "My heart just stopped, I'm not kidding you. Just stopped dead right there in my chest. I thought there would never be another moment quite like that one. But I was wrong."

Jenna frowned. "Wrong? How so?"

Erin Kettleman unsnapped the clasp on her purse. She reached in and pulled out a single sheet of paper. She held it out. Jenna took it.

It was a letter from Mack, a curt, straight-to-the-point letter on plain stationery with no return address. Jenna scanned it quickly.

Dear Mrs. Kettleman,

I have decided to establish a trust fund in your name. For the next twenty years you will receive five thousand dollars per month to help cover living expenses for yourself and your family. Also, since the cost of education continues to rise, I have set up college funds for each of your four children.

Please contact the Meadow Valley office of Dennis Archer, attorney-at-law, at your earliest convenience to receive your first payment from the trust. Mr. Archer will be happy to answer any questions you may have concerning this bequest.

All my best to you and your family,

M. McGarrity

"It came today," Erin said, her voice hushed, hollow with something very close to awe. "I called that attorney. He said…" Erin closed her eyes, breathed deeply and opened them again. "He said that he'd been waiting for my call. I have an appointment, for ten o'clock Monday morning. I can hardly believe it. Why? Why would he do such a thing? He doesn't even know us. We're strangers to him."

"Strangers?" Jenna smiled. Oh, Mack, she was thinking. Oh, Mack. What a lovely, perfect thing to do….

Erin Kettleman was staring at her, waiting for her to go on.

Jenna tried to explain. "I think that, in a certain way, Mack feels…very close to you and your family."

"In what way? Please tell me. Please help me to understand. It's so hard to believe that this is really happening. I keep thinking I'm gonna wake up in a few minutes and find out it's all just a crazy, impossible dream. Maybe if I knew *why* he did it…please, Ms. Bravo. You've got to tell me."

There was no resisting such a plea. Jenna didn't even

try. She told Erin Kettleman of Mack's childhood, of the father he'd lost and the mother who had given him and his sisters into the care of the state. Of the funeral the two of them had attended recently in Southern California.

Erin's eyes were misty by the time the tale had been told. "How sad," she murmured. "How awful for him and his sisters—and for his mother. That poor woman. There was a time I would have judged her for what she did. But after the past six months…I think it's the worst thing that can happen to a mother, to wonder if you're going to be able to take care of your own. To find yourself thinking that maybe they'd be better off without you. Oh, that is painful. That is the worst thing in the world."

Jenna nodded. "I think he wants your family to have a better chance than his did."

"Well." Erin stood. "Thanks to him, we will."

Jenna rose and handed her the letter. Erin tucked it back into her purse. "I plan to write to him. To thank him. I suppose I can just…give the letter to the lawyer?"

Jenna understood Erin's unspoken question: *Should I give it to you?* "Yes, give it to the attorney," Jenna said firmly. "He'll know where to send it so that Mack will be sure to get it."

"Well. All right, then. I suppose I'd better get on home." Erin turned for the front door.

Jenna followed behind her, then moved past her in the foyer to open the door. The night air outside was cold. Erin shivered and wrapped her jacket closer around her.

And Jenna went ahead and asked the question she'd been wanting to ask since she'd answered the door and found Riley's mother standing on the porch. "Do you think you might bring the children by now and then? I'd love to see Riley again—and maybe hold little Lissa…."

It was Erin's turn to touch. She clasped Jenna's shoulder. "I'd love that, too." She grinned. Jenna thought she looked very young at that moment. "But I've got to warn you. They can be a handful."

"That's all right with me."

"Then I'll call you. In a week or two. We'll drop on by."

"That would be wonderful."

"Maybe Mr. McGarrity could come by too and—"

Jenna shook her head. "I'm afraid he's not coming back."

"Oh?" Erin let go of Jenna's shoulder. "But Riley said he thought the two of you—" Erin cut herself off, blushing a little. "Well. What does an eleven-year-old boy know, anyway?"

Jenna smiled. "He knows enough. Unfortunately, it didn't work out, between me and Mr. McGarrity."

Erin sighed. "I'm sorry."

"So am I."

There was a silence. The two women regarded each other. Then Erin wrapped both arms around herself again. "You're standing here in just that light sweater. I should let you go."

"Come any time. I mean it."

Shyly, Erin promised that she would.

Jenna waited until Erin had climbed into the battered green hatchback before she closed the door. Then she leaned against the door frame, wrapped her own arms around her middle and stared down at her shoes.

She felt joy, she realized, for the Kettleman family. And pride. It was a truly fine thing that Mack had done.

She also felt sadness. Always, she felt sadness lately.

She did miss him so.

And the house seemed so quiet. She could use a lit-

tle company. But the door to the back parlor was shut.
It had been shut when Jenna came home from her store.
Apparently Lacey was hard at work and didn't want to
be disturbed.

With a sigh, Jenna pushed herself away from the wall
and turned for the kitchen. She would brew herself a nice
pot of tea to cut through the evening chill. And maybe in
a little while Lacey would emerge from behind the louvered doors. They could share the tea and Jenna could tell
her sister what Mack had done for Erin and her children.

But an hour later, Lacey's door remained firmly shut.
Jenna rinsed out the teapot and went to her own room.

The next morning when Jenna entered the kitchen to
fix herself some breakfast, she found the coffee brewed
and her sister fully dressed, leaning on a crutch and fry-
ing eggs at the stove.

"Lace? It's seven in the morning. Are you feeling all
right?"

Lacey turned her head and looked at Jenna over her
shoulder. Her eyes were shining, her face flooded with
excited color.

Jenna stared. "You look…terrific."

"I'm fixing breakfast," Lacey said in a strange,
hushed tone. "We'll eat. And then I think it's time you
saw what I've been working on." Lacey pushed a heavy
lock of hair back off her face and added, "I think it's
pretty good, but—" She cut herself off with a nervous
shrug. "Well. Whatever you think of it, you're bound to
see it sometime. Might as well get it over with."

Twenty minutes later, Jenna followed behind as her
sister stumped into the back parlor.

The painting was waiting where Lacey had somehow managed to prop it, against the side of the sofa bed. Lacey gestured at it with a toss of her bright head.

"There it is," she said grimly. Then she stepped to the side and waited for Jenna's reaction.

At first, Jenna could do no more than stare.

"Well," her sister demanded after a minute. "Hit me with it. What do you think?"

Jenna didn't know what to think. It was a nude, a male figure, and it was utterly breathtaking in its sensuality and power. A mask covered the face—a stark, simple mask that seemed carved from dark stone. In spite of the mask, Jenna knew who her sister's model had been. There was something in the tilt of the head, the shape of the shoulders—though of course, Jenna herself had never seen Lacey's subject in the nude. And she had certainly never perceived the stunning sensuality that her sister must see when she looked at him.

"You hate it," said Lacey flatly.

"No," said Jenna. "No. It is…incredible. Beautiful. Perfect."

"Oh." Lacey sucked in a breath, let it out slowly. "You think so? You honestly do?"

Jenna nodded. "Words fail me. But it's good, Lace. It's more than good."

Lacey let out another long rush of air. "You cannot know how terrific it feels to hear it from someone else— even if that someone *is* my sister who thinks everything I do is just fabulous."

"This is more than a sister's loyalty talking here, Lace. I swear to you."

"I think you mean that."

"You know I do—but I have to ask…"

Lacey closed her eyes. "I wish you wouldn't."

"Lace," Jenna said softly. "Please. Look at me."

The sisters stared at each other. Then Lacey announced, "I need to sit down."

Jenna waited as her sister hobbled to the easy chair. Once Lacey was settled, Jenna asked tentatively, "The painting...it's Logan, isn't it?"

Lacey nodded, then let out a short, slightly wild laugh. "I warned you I might check on him, to see how he was doing, after you left."

"And I, um, take it you did."

"Did I ever. I still don't really know how it happened. I thought I was going to *comfort* him, I guess. I knew his poor heart was broken at losing you for the second time. How we ended up in bed together...well, stranger things have happened, I suppose, but not to me. It was crazy. Totally insane. It lasted for five incredible days, until I lost poor Byron and put my foot through the ceiling, which made it necessary for you and Mack to come home."

"Lace. Do you love him?"

Lacey closed her eyes again, let her head fall back against the chair. "I think I do," she said in a whisper. "Can you believe it? I think I love Logan Severance. Sometimes it seems that I might have always loved him. I just didn't realize it." Lacey opened her eyes and looked at Jenna. "He was the last person I ever thought I'd love, I swear that to you. I never had any...designs on him. Until I knocked on his door after you and Mack left town together, it never even occurred to me that maybe the animosity I'd always felt toward him was based on something else altogether. I hope you don't think that I—"

Jenna put up both hands, palm out. "Hey. It's okay. You don't have to convince me. I believe you. And you're both honorable people. Nothing would have happened between you if Logan and I had stayed together. I know that."

Byron appeared then, from the door to the central hall. He strutted up to Lacey and jumped into her lap. Lacey waited until he settled down and then scratched him behind the ears.

"Logan still loves you, Jenna."

Jenna opened her mouth to protest, but Lacey only shook her head. "It was a classic rebound situation for him, that's all."

Jenna knelt beside her sister. "No, Lacey. Listen. It's honestly over, between Logan and me. And it never could have worked between us, anyway."

"Tell that to Logan."

"I will. If you want me to."

"No."

"But I—"

"No. I didn't really mean that, about talking to him. Please don't say anything to him. Please just leave it alone."

"But if you love him—"

"If I love him, what?" Lacey had stiffened. Her eyes sparked with blue fire.

"Well, then you can…work things out." Jenna knew that sounded lame.

Apparently Lacey thought so, too. "Work things out?" she scoffed. "Like you and Mack did?"

Jenna had no answer for that. She stood and backed away a step. Byron, clearly uncomfortable with Lacey's sudden agitation, jumped from her lap.

"I just told you. Logan doesn't love me. He loves you—and you love Mack McGarrity, don't you?"

"Lacey, I—"

Her sister looked up at her, pure challenge in her eyes. "Don't you?"

"I…"

"For heaven's sake, will you just say it?"

"All right. Yes. I love Mack."

"And Mack loves you? Is that right?"

"Yes. He does. He loves me."

Lacey made an impatient sound. "I have to tell you, Jenna. If I thought Logan loved me, no one—and nothing—could keep me away from him. So I have to ask, what's *your* excuse?"

"Well, I…we…"

"You, we, what?"

Jenna blurted it out. "I want children. He doesn't."

Lacey frowned. "He doesn't want children…ever?"

"That's what he says."

Lacey said nothing for a count of three, then admitted grudgingly, "Well. Okay. That is a tough one."

"But I—"

"Yeah?"

"I'm willing to do without children. I do love him, Lacey. I think I'll always love him. And since last night, I've started to see that there are other ways to contribute to the raising of children than to have them yourself."

"What happened last night?"

"Remember that boy who found Byron?"

"I remember."

"Well, last night, while you were working, his mother dropped by. She told me that Mack has set up a trust fund for her, five thousand a month for the next twenty years—as well as college funds for each of her children."

Lacey gave a low whistle. "What did I say? Not the same S.O.B. he used to be. Not the same S.O.B. at all."

"That's right. And it's got me thinking. He's contributing to those children's lives, contributing in a very big way. And that's… important. It's, well, it could be enough for me, what we might do, together, to help other people's children grow up. And…I still love him. I'll always love him. And I miss him. And I don't want to live without him."

"Then don't. Track him down and tell him. Tell him again and again. Until he finally gives up and admits that you're the only woman in the world for him. Until he comes to his senses and confesses that he can't wait to start spending the rest of his life at your side."

Jenna stared at her sister. "You know," she said. "That's good advice."

"So take it."

Jenna dropped to the end of the sofa bed. "All right," she said. "I believe that I will."

## Chapter Eighteen

Jenna and Lacey did a lot of talking that weekend.

Lacey confessed that if Jenna wanted to sell the house their mother had left them, she would be more than glad for the extra cash. As soon as she could walk again, she intended to return to L.A. Maybe love had not worked out for her. But she was more determined than ever to fulfill her career dreams.

So they agreed. They would sell the house. They settled on a fairly low asking price, reasoning that neither of them wanted to wait forever to get on with the next phase of their lives.

Monday, Jenna visited a Realtor. She also placed an ad in the *Meadow Valley Sun*, putting her store up for sale.

Five weeks later, they got a solid offer on the house. By then it had been seven weeks since Lacey's surgery.

She got a clean bill of health from her orthopedic surgeon and immediately called a friend in L.A., who invited her to stay there until she found something of her own. The next day she made arrangements to ship the painting of Logan to the artist friend with whom she'd previously shared the downtown L.A. loft.

And on Thursday, November 19, Jenna drove her sister to Sacramento International Airport.

"You don't have me to worry about anymore," Lacey said before she boarded the plane. "The house is sold and Marla can manage the store for a while. I think you'd better take a little trip to Florida. Time's passing. You need to start breaking down Mack's defenses so you can get going on the rest of your lives."

"You're absolutely right." Jenna hugged her sister.

"So? When are you leaving?"

"I'm making a plane reservation as soon as I get home."

"I'll call you the minute I get a new place—and you'd better call me and keep me posted on your love life."

"You know that I will."

"Did I tell you that you're the best sister this ex-juvenile delinquent ever had?"

"You did. So keep painting and making me proud, will you?"

"I will, I promise. I love you."

"Oh, Lace. I love you, too…."

That evening Erin Kettleman brought the kids over. They cooked hot dogs on the grill in the backyard in the rain and ate them at the breakfast nook table. Little Lissa fussed through most of the visit and Tina and the younger boy, Will, got into a spat or two. But Riley declared the meal the best he'd ever had, and all the children were thrilled to see Byron again. The cat sat in one small lap after another, purring loudly the whole time.

Before they left, Jenna told Erin that she and her cat were headed for Florida on Monday.

Erin's smile was one of pure delight. "You're getting back together with Mr. McGarrity?"

"Yes, I am," Jenna answered without a second's hesitation.

The next day, Jenna let both Marla and her other clerk have the morning off. Business was brisk, but she could handle it. In a couple of days, they'd be on their own for a while. They might as well have it a little easy until then.

At a quarter to twelve she was showing a regular customer a set of café curtains and the linens to match when she heard the bleat of the door buzzer.

She turned with her best smile ready.

And the whole world stood still.

It was Mack.

Mack.

In chinos and that sexy brown leather jacket, hands in his pockets, looking at her as if he'd like to grab her and hold her and never in a million years let her go.

"Hon?" said her customer, a thin redhead with a penchant for crinkle skirts and silver jewelry. "Hon? Are you feeling all right?"

Jenna reached out and put her hand on a nearby display rack to steady herself. "I'm just fine. Would you... excuse me?"

"Sure enough. You take your time," her customer said, though Jenna hardly heard her. She was already walking along the towel aisle toward the man who stood a few feet from the door.

"Mack," she said when she reached him. The name had everything in it. Her love. Her longing. Her joy at the sight of him. "Hello."

He took her left hand, on which her plain wedding band gleamed, and then gently touched the cat-shaped diamond pin she wore near her heart. He smiled. Lord, how had she lived without his smile? "You're glad to see me," he said.

"Glad doesn't cover it. There isn't a word big enough to cover it." She drew her shoulders back. "I was coming to get you, Mack."

The light in his eyes was beautiful to see. "You were?"

"Yes. On Monday. I'm still your wife, Mack. I never took those papers in. Because I intend to remain your wife."

He said her name then, "Jenna," in a whisper, from the heart. And then he reached for her.

There were two other customers in the store besides the redhead with the silver jewelry. One of them gasped, the other said, "Ahh…" And the redhead murmured, "How sweet."

Neither Mack nor Jenna cared what her customers thought. They kissed for a long time, a kiss of true reunion, a kiss between man and wife.

At last he lifted his head, but he still held her close, right against his heart.

He said, "I did it, Jenna. I went to see both of my sisters."

"Oh, Mack…"

"And they are two very nice women. Bridget has three happy, loud, normal kids. And Claire is pregnant with her first baby. It's going to be a girl. I…well, I think if they can do it, maybe I can do it, too."

"Mack. Are you saying…?"

He nodded. "I'm terrified, scared out of my wits. But yes. I'll do it. I'll have a family with you. It feels like the biggest damn chance I'll ever take in my life. But I'm good at taking risks…right?"

"You are, Mack. You take chances. And those chances pay off."

"You really didn't file the papers?"

"No."

"And you really want to stay my wife?"

"Yes."

"I don't even have to beg you or get down on my knees?"

"Well, a little begging *would* be nice…."

He yanked her close again and called her a naughty name. Then he kissed her for the second time.

And he said, "I love you."

And she said, "I love you, too. So much. So very much…"

And right then the buzzer rang again. It was Marla, ready for work.

"Do you think you could handle things here on your own for a while?" Jenna asked.

Marla said that she could. So Jenna grabbed her purse and her coat and she and Mack left the store. They walked hand in hand to the Queen Anne Victorian at the top of West Broad Street.

Byron was waiting just inside the front door. Mack scooped Jenna up and carried her straight to the master bedroom on the first floor. The cat followed behind them, purring quite loudly, his long black tail held high and proud.

* * *

A few weeks later, Mack and Jenna renewed their vows, in Florida, aboard Mack's boat, *The Shady Deal*. Mack flew the guests in. Lacey was there, and Mack's sisters and their families, and Alec and Lois, and the entire Kettleman clan.

After the ceremony Jenna and Mack left for a second honeymoon. They went to Wyoming. Jenna met the children of her grandfather's brother. And in the years to come, she always insisted that they conceived their first child there, on the ranch that had been in the Bravo family for five generations.

# THE M.D. SHE
*HAD* TO MARRY

For Auralee Smith, my mom,
who's already had one or two dedicated to her.
But such a terrific mom should get grateful
dedications on a regular basis.
I love you, Mom.
Here's to you...again.

# *Chapter One*

On a sunny afternoon at the end of June, Lacey Bravo returned to the old homesteader's cabin behind the horse pasture at the Rising Sun Ranch to find Dr. Logan Severance waiting for her.

She had known he would come. Still, the sight of him, there in the shade of the rough-shingled overhang that served as the cabin's front porch, sent her pulse racing. Her palms on the steering wheel went clammy with sweat. She felt pulled in two directions at once. Her foolish heart urged her to rush into his arms. And something else, some contrary creature inside her, wanted only to spin her new SUV around and speed away, leaving nothing but a high trail of Wyoming dust in her wake.

Neither action was really an option. Throwing herself into his arms would only embarrass them both. And as for running, well, Lacey had done plenty of that before she was even out of her teens. Eventually, she'd given it up. It never solved anything.

With a weary sigh, Lacey pushed the door open and maneuvered herself out from behind the wheel and down to the ground. She shut the door. Then, with as much dignity as she could muster, given that lately she tended to waddle like a duck, she plodded to the rear of the vehicle to get the two bags of groceries she had picked up in town.

She barely got the back door up before Logan was at her side. "I'll take those for you."

Her initial reaction was to object, to lift her chin high and announce haughtily, "I can carry my own groceries, thank you."

But she stifled the impulse. There would be dissension enough between them. There always had been. And now, with the baby coming, the opportunities for argument would no doubt be endless. Better to keep her mouth shut whenever possible.

His dark gaze swept over her. She wore a tent-like denim jumper, a pink T-shirt and blue canvas ballerina flats.

Ballerina. Hah. An image from an old Disney movie, of a hippo in ballet shoes and a tutu, flitted through her mind.

No, she was not at her best. And he looked great. Terrific. Fit and tanned, in khaki pants and a cream-colored polo shirt. He looked like a model on the cover of a Brooks Brothers catalog—and she looked like someone who'd eaten a beach ball for lunch. She knew she shouldn't let that bother her. But it did.

"Hasn't your doctor told you that at this point in your pregnancy, you shouldn't be driving?"

She gritted her teeth and granted him the tiniest of shrugs.

"Is that a 'yes'?"

Lacey exerted superhuman effort and did not roll her eyes. "Yes, Doctor. That is a 'yes'."

He made a low, exasperated sound. "Then what are you doing behind the wheel of a car?"

"I treasure my independence."

The words may have sounded flippant, but Lacey did mean them. Doc Pruitt, who ran the clinic in the small nearby town of Medicine Creek, *had* been nagging her to avoid driving. And Tess, her cousin's wife, who lived in the main ranch house not a half a mile away, would have been glad to take Lacey wherever she needed to go. But to Lacey, a car—and the possession of the keys to it—meant self-determination. Never would she willingly give that up.

Except, perhaps, for the love of this man.

But not to worry. Her independence was safe. Logan's heart was otherwise engaged.

"Lacey," he said, in the thoroughly superior tone that had always made her want to throw something at him. "There are times in life when independence has to take a back seat to necessity. It's not good for you, or the baby, for you to—"

"Logan, can we at least get inside before you start telling me everything I'm doing wrong?"

He blinked. Maybe it actually occurred to him that he'd started criticizing her before he'd even bothered to say hello. Whatever. Without another word, he scooped her grocery bags into his big arms and turned toward the cabin. Lacey was left to shut the rear door and trudge along in his wake, across the bare dirt yard, past the dusty midnight-blue luxury car he had driven there and up the two rickety steps to the cabin's front entrance. On the porch, he stood aside for her to open the door. Then she moved out of his way to let him go first.

They entered the main living area, which was small and dark and simply furnished. Lacey loved the cabin— *had* loved it on sight. Though the light was never good enough to paint by, the rough plank walls pleased her artist's eye. And the layers of shadow were interesting, dark and intense in the corners, fading out to a pleasant dimness in the center of the room. Beyond the main room, there was a small sleeping nook in the northeast corner and a bathroom in a lean-to outside the back door.

Logan didn't seem to share her admiration for her rustic surroundings. His dismissing glance flicked over the stained sink, the old iron daybed bolstered to double as a sofa, and the faded curtain that served as a door to the sleeping nook.

He dipped his head at the grocery bags. "Where do you want these?"

Lacey moved to clear a space on the old pine table, shifting a stack of books, a sketch pad, a box of pastels and some pencils to one of the four ladderback chairs. "Right here." She pulled the chain on the bulb suspended over the table. The resulting wash of light was harsh, but functional.

Logan moved forward and slid the groceries onto the table, then stepped back. They regarded each other. She saw that there were circles under those fine dark eyes of his.

Was it only the severity of the light? No. Now that she stared directly at him, she could see more than irritated disapproval in the sculpted planes of his face. She saw weariness. Reproach and concern were there, too.

She cleared her throat and spoke gently. "Did you drive all the way from California?"

He shook his head. "I flew out of Reno. To Denver, where I transferred to a smaller plane, which got me to Sheridan. Then I rented a car for the rest of the trip."

"You must be tired."

His mouth tightened. She read the hidden meaning in his expression. He'd come to take care of her, whether she liked it or not. His own comfort was nothing. "I'm fine."

"Well. I'm glad to hear it."

The silence stretched out again. Maybe he was thirsty. "Do you want something to drink?"

He shrugged, then answered with a formality that tugged at her heart. "Yes. Thank you. Something cold would be good."

"Ginger ale?"

"That's fine."

. She went to the refrigerator, which was probably a collector's item—it stood on legs and had a coil on top. She took out a can, then turned to the cabinet over the one tiny section of counter.

"Never mind a glass," he said. "Just the can is fine."

She handed it to him across the table, absurdly conscious of the possibility that their fingers might brush in passing. They didn't.

She gestured at the chair in front of him. "Have a seat."

He ignored that suggestion, popped the top on the can and took a long drink.

She stared at his Adam's apple as it bobbed up and down on his strong, tanned throat and tried to ignore the yearning that flooded through her in a warm, tempting wave.

She wanted him.

Even big as a cow with the baby they had created together, she'd have happily sashayed right over to him and put her mouth against that brown throat. With delight, she would have teasingly scraped the skin with her teeth, stuck out her tongue and tasted—

Lacey cut off the dangerous erotic thought before it could get too good a hold on her very healthy imagination. As if she even *could* sashay, big as she'd grown in the last month or so.

Logan set the ginger ale can on the table. "How long have you been here?"

"Seven weeks."

He waited, clearly expecting her to elaborate. When she didn't, he asked, softly, "Why?"

She looked away, realized she'd done it, and made herself face him again. "Why not? This ranch has been in my family for five generations. My second cousin, Zach, runs the place now."

"That doesn't answer my question. What made you choose to come here?"

"Jenna suggested it." As Lacey said her sister's name, it became clear to her that she'd been avoiding saying it. For her own sake or for Logan's, she couldn't be sure. But the name was out now. And the world hadn't stopped. "She and Mack stayed here for a few weeks last year."

There. She had said *both* of the dangerous names.

Jenna and Mack. The woman Logan loved. And the man who had taken her from him.

Lacey watched for his reaction. If he had one, he wasn't sharing it. His face remained composed. He didn't even blink.

"Jenna knows—about you and me?" His voice was cautious, but resigned.

"Yes."

"She knows that the baby is mine?"

Lacey nodded. "I told her about you and me not too long after it happened—and about the baby a few months ago. She wanted me to go and stay with her and Mack in Florida for the birth."

"Why didn't you?"

Lacey stared at him. Did he really want to hear the answer to that one? Apparently he did, or he would not have been so foolish as to ask.

She shrugged. "I didn't want to intrude on their happiness." Jenna and Mack were like newlyweds, having recently reunited after years apart. "And Jenna is pregnant, too. Her baby is due in September."

Logan glanced down at the table between them. He might have been looking at the bags of groceries, or the empty soda can—or simply *not* looking at her. "Well," he said, "Jenna always did want lots of kids."

"Yes. She did."

Logan raised that dark gaze once more. "So you came here."

Lacey nodded. "It's peaceful and it's beautiful. And I have family around, ready to help if I need it. It was the perfect place to come and have my baby."

He let a moment of charged silence elapse before announcing, "You should have come to me."

Well, she thought. We're into it now, aren't we? She knew where he was headed, of course. She'd known from the moment she saw him on the front step. And even before that. She'd known what Logan Severance would do from the first day she admitted to herself that she was pregnant—because she knew *him.*

And she had her refusal, complete with excellent reasons for it, all ready to give to him.

But the thought of hashing through it all made her feel about as tired as he looked. And her back was aching.

If he wanted to stand up for this, fine. He could stand. She'd rather take it sitting down.

Lacey pulled out a chair and lowered herself into it.

Logan waited to speak again until she was settled— and until it became clear that she wasn't going to respond to his last remark. "The baby's due in a week or so, right?"

"Yes." Her shoulders kept wanting to droop. She pulled them back and met his eyes. "Everything's fine. Normal. I got an appointment with the doctor here as soon as I arrived. He's been taking good care of me."

Logan looked irritatingly skeptical. "You've been watching your diet, taking it easy?"

Oh, why did he so often manage to make her feel like some incompetent, irresponsible child? Apparently, old behavior patterns did die hard. In spite of the dramatic shift in their relationship last fall, right that moment the years seemed to peel away. She was the bratty kid with a chip on her shoulder and he was the annoyingly straight-arrow boyfriend of her big sister.

"Lacey. Answer me. Have you been taking care of yourself?"

"Honestly, everything is fine."

That gained her a disbelieving glare. "Why didn't you contact me earlier?"

"I contacted you as soon as I could bear to. And if we're into 'why didn't you,' then why didn't you call the number I gave you and let me know that you were on your way here?"

"And have you tell me not to come? I don't think so."

Her mouth felt so dry all of a sudden. It was one of the many bothersome things about pregnancy. Cravings came on out of nowhere. She wanted water. She could already taste its silky coldness on her tongue. She started to push herself to her feet again.

Logan frowned. "What is it?"

"Nothing. I just want a drink of water, that's all."

"I'll get it."

"No, don't bother. I can—"

But he was already striding to the sink. He took a glass from the corner of the counter, rinsed it, and filled it from the tap. Then he carried it to her and held it out.

She looked at the glass and then up, into his eyes. His kindness and concern did touch her. He was a good man, always had been. Much too good for the likes of her. She felt a smile flirting with the corners of her mouth. "You know, until a few years ago, there was no running water or electricity here in the cabin. It cost a bundle, apparently, to run electrical lines and water pipes out here. But my cousin Zach had it done last summer. Pretty convenient, huh? Otherwise, you'd have had to head for the well out back to fill that glass for me."

"Just drink." His voice was gruff.

This time, as he passed her the glass, his fingers did

brush hers. His fingers were warm. She wondered if hers felt cold to him.

"Thank you." She drank. It was just what she'd wanted, clear and cool and satisfying as it slid down her throat.

"More?"

She shook her head, set down the glass.

Logan pulled out the chair nearest hers and dropped into it. He braced his elbows on his knees and leaned toward her. The light caught and gleamed in his dark hair.

His eyes were softer now. "I didn't call when I got your letter because I knew you would only try to talk me into staying away."

Her smile started to quiver. She bit the corner of her lip to make it stop. "That's true. I would have."

"It wouldn't have worked."

"I know. You'll do what you think is right. You always have." Except during those five days last September, a voice in her mind whispered tauntingly. *Then you did things you didn't approve of. And you did them with me.*

He looked down at the rough boards between his feet, then back up at her. "This baby changes everything, Lace."

She wanted to touch him. The slight brushing of their fingers a moment before had whetted her appetite for the feel of him. Oh, to simply reach out and run her fingers through that shining dark hair, to trace his brows, to learn again the shape of his mouth.

Tenderness welled in her. He had traveled such a long way and he wasn't going to get what he came for—what he would say he wanted, what he would call the right thing.

He said it then, as if he had plucked the words right out of her mind. "We have to do the right thing now."

She sat back in her chair and clasped her hands beneath the hard swell of her belly. "Your idea of the right thing and mine are not the same, Logan."

He answered her with measured care. "The right thing is the right thing, period."

"Fine. Whatever. The point is, I'm not going to marry you."

## *Chapter Two*

Logan had pretty much expected this. He straightened in the chair and kept his voice level and reasonable. "Before you turn me down flat, let's discuss this a little. You're in no position to raise a child on your own, and I'm willing to—"

"Logan, I told you. No. It's a two-letter word meaning negative, out of the question. Uh-uh. Forgetaboutit." She pushed herself to her feet. "We are not getting married."

"Why not?"

She stared at him for a moment, then made a show of hitting her forehead with the heel of her hand. "What? You can't figure that one out for yourself?"

"Spare me the theatrics. Just answer the question. Why not?"

Muttering under her breath, she turned to her groceries, grabbed a box of Wheat Thins in one hand and a can of cocoa mix in the other and started toward the ancient wood-burning stove that crouched against the wall by the front door.

His frustration with her got the better of him. "Sit down," he commanded.

It was the wrong thing to say, and he knew it. But something about Lacey Bravo tended to bring out the tyrant in him.

Why was that? He had no idea. He considered himself a reasonable, gentle man, as a rule. He *was* a reasonable, gentle man as a rule. Ask just about anyone who knew him.

Lacey ignored his command. She reached the stove and put the crackers and cocoa mix on the open shelf above it. Then she turned for the table again and shuffled his way, her abdomen heavy and low in front of her—low enough, in fact, to make him suspect that the baby inside her had already dropped toward the birth canal.

It could be *less* than a week before she brought his child into the world.

They needed to get married.

She reached into the bag again. He stood. "Lace. Stop. You know we have to talk about this."

She took her hand out of the bag and raked that thick gold hair of hers back from her forehead. "Not about marriage, we don't."

"I disagree. I think marriage is exactly what we do need to talk about. I think that—"

She put up both hands, palms out. "Wait. Listen. You're the baby's father. And of course, you'll want to see him or her, to be a part of his life. I understand that and I can accept that. But it really isn't necessary for you to—"

"It damn well *is* necessary. You're having my baby and a baby needs a mother *and* a father."

"I told you. The baby *will* have a mother and a father. They just won't be married to each other, that's all."

"A two-parent home is important to a child."

"Sometimes a two-parent home isn't possible."

"In our case, it's entirely possible. I want to marry you. We're both single. I make a good living and I do care for you. I believe that, deep in your heart, you also care for me. I know I'm rough on you sometimes, rougher than I have a right to be. But I'll work on that, I promise you."

She said nothing, only looked at him, shaking her head.

He thought of more arguments in his favor. "We have…history together. I feel I really *know* you, that you really know me. We could build a good life together, I'm sure of it."

Still, she didn't speak.

A grotesque thought occurred to him. "Is there another man? Is that it?"

She closed her eyes and sucked in a breath.

He realized that, if there was another man, he didn't want to know. Which was irrational. Of course, if there was someone else, he needed to know.

He asked again. "Lace? Is there another man?"

"No," she said in a tiny, soft voice. "No one. There hasn't been anyone. Since you. Since quite a while before you, if you want to know the truth."

Relief shimmered through him. "Good. Then there's nothing to stop you from marrying me."

She backed up and let herself down into the chair again. "How can you say that?"

"Lace—"

"No, Logan. I am not going to marry you." She looked up at him, blue eyes glittering in defiance, mulishly determined to do exactly the wrong thing.

Impatience rose in him again. "Why not?"

She glared at him. "You keep asking that. Do you really want an answer? Do you really want me to say it right out?"

He didn't.

But he wasn't about to tell her that. She'd only look at him as if he'd just proved her point.

"Let me put it this way," she said with heavy irony. "If I ever do get married, it won't be to a man who's in love with my big sister."

He tried not to flinch as the words came at him.

And he did realize the opportunity they presented. Now was his chance to tell her firmly that he was not in love with Jenna. But somehow, he couldn't quite get the denial out of his mouth.

Lacey smiled sadly, shook her head some more, and murmured his name in a knowing way that made him want to grab her and flip her over his knee and paddle her behind until she admitted he was right and accepted his proposal. Until she confessed how glad she was that he had come at last, that he was ready, willing and able to make everything right.

Lacey wasn't confessing anything. She said, "I have my own plans. I'm staying here in Wyoming until the baby's born and I'm back on my feet. Then I'll return to L.A."

Absurd, he thought. Impossible. And harebrained, as

well. "You can't be serious. There is no way you can
support both yourself and a child on what you make
working odd jobs and selling a painting every now and
then."

"We'll get by. Jenna and I sold our mother's house.
I have money put aside from that, and a new car, so the
baby and I will be able to get around. In fact, I have everything I need." Her full, soft mouth stretched into a
smile—a rather forced one this time. "And besides, I
know you'll help out."

He reminded himself that he would not lose his patience again. She had always been like this. Impetuous
and wild. Running away whenever things didn't go her
way. A virtual delinquent as a teenager, hanging out
with all the troublemakers at Meadow Valley High. And
then, at twenty, taking off for Los Angeles to study
under some famous painter, sure she would "make it"
as an artist. Six years had gone by since then. She hadn't
made it yet.

Now she proposed to drag his baby to Southern California to scrape and starve right along with her.

It wasn't going to happen. "I'll help out, all right,"
he said. "We'll get married. You'll live with me. You can
paint your paintings in Meadow Valley just as well as
in L.A."

"I said no, Logan. And I meant it."

He folded his arms across his chest—mostly to keep
himself from reaching out and strangling her. "This
isn't last September. You can't just explain to me how
I don't love you and I'm only on the rebound from your
sister and it's time we both moved on."

"You happened to agree with me last September, in
case you've forgotten."

Had he agreed with her? Maybe. He'd been confused as hell last September. Hard to remember now *what* he had felt then.

Jenna had left with Mack McGarrity.

And then, out of nowhere, her little sister, who had always irritated the hell out of him, showed up on his doorstep, real concern for him in her gorgeous blue eyes and a big chocolate cake in her hands.

"You need chocolate, Dr. Do-Right," she had said. "Lots of chocolate. And you need it now."

Dr. Do-Right. He hated it when she called him that. He had opened his mouth to tell her so—and also to tell her to please go away.

But she just pushed past him and kept walking, straight to his kitchen. She put the cake on the counter and began rifling the drawers. It didn't take her long to find the one with the silverware in it.

"Ah," she said. "Here we go." She grabbed a fork, shoved the drawer shut and thrust the fork at him, catching him off guard, so that he took it automatically. "Eat."

He looked at the fork and he looked at the cake.

Damned if she didn't know just what he was thinking. "No," she said. "No plate. No nice little slice cut with a knife. Just stick that fork right in there, just tear off a big, gooey bite."

He stared at her, stared at her full mouth, at her flushed face, her wide eyes…

And he realized that he was aroused.

Aroused by Jenna's troublemaking little sister, damned if he wasn't.

He had set down the fork, backed her up against the counter and spoken right into that deceptively angelic face of hers. "Shouldn't you be back in L.A. by now?"

Her breathing was agitated, though she tried to play it cool. "I told Jenna I'd take care of things here."

"I don't need taking care of."

She didn't say anything, just looked at him through those blue, blue eyes.

"You'd better go," he had warned.

She made a small, tender sound.

And she shook her head.

They ate the cake sometime after midnight, both of them nude, standing in the kitchen, tearing into it with a pair of forks, then feeding each other big, sloppy bites.

Lacey shifted in her chair. Logan's eyes looked far away. She wondered what he was thinking.

He blinked and came back to himself. "I don't want to analyze last September. It happened. We weren't as careful as we should have been and now you're having my baby. You know damn well how I feel about that."

Yes, she did know. He was just like Jenna. He wanted children. Several children. He also wanted a nice, settled, stay-at-home wife to take care of those children while he was out healing the ills of the world. A wife like Jenna would have been.

In almost every way, Logan and Jenna had been just right for each other. Too bad Jenna had always loved Mack McGarrity.

Logan held out his hand.

Lacey knew that she shouldn't, but she took it anyway. He pulled her out of the chair. He would have taken her into his arms, but she resisted that.

Her belly brushed him. They both hitched in a quick

breath at the contact and Lacey pulled her hand from his.

She turned toward the table, toward the grocery bags still waiting there, thinking that the move might gain her a little much-needed distance from him.

It didn't. He stepped up behind her, so that she could feel him, feel the warmth of him, close at her back.

He spoke into her ear, his voice barely a whisper. "You need me now, Lace. Don't turn me away. Give me a chance. I want to marry you and take care of you…of both of you."

Oh, those *were* lovely words. And, yes, they did tempt her.

But it wouldn't work. She had to remember that. It couldn't work.

He did not love her. He couldn't even say that he no longer loved her sister. He'd marry her out of duty, in order to claim his child.

And she would spend her life with him feeling like second best, wondering when he kissed her if he was imagining her sister in his arms. She didn't want that. They had too many differences as it was. Without love on both sides, they wouldn't stand a chance.

Gently, he took her shoulder, the touch burning a path of longing down inside of her, making her sigh. He turned her to face him.

And he smiled. "I'm feeling pretty determined, Lace."

She smiled right back at him. "So am I."

"We'll see who's *more* determined of the two of us. I'm not going away until you come with me."

"Then you're in for a long stay in Wyoming."

"I can stay as long as I have to."

"You couldn't stay long enough."

"Watch me."

"What about your practice? How will your patients get along without you?"

"Don't worry about my patients. I have partners to cover for me. I can stick it out here for as long as it takes."

"Oh? And where will you be staying? Have you made reservations at the motel in town?"

"No. I'll stay here with you."

He looked so certain, so set on his goal. She couldn't stop herself. She touched the side of his face. The stubble-rough skin felt wonderful—*too* wonderful.

She jerked her hand back, thinking how much one thoughtless touch could do. In a moment, she'd have no backbone left. Whatever he wanted, she'd just go along.

"You can't stay here," she said in a breathless tone that convinced neither Logan nor herself. "It's out of the question."

He pressed his advantage. "Look. You're alone here. The baby's due any day now. I don't even see a phone in this cabin. How will you call for help if there's an emergency?"

She tipped her chin higher. "I'm in no danger. The main ranch house is nearby—you must have driven past it to get here."

He nodded. "I stopped in there for directions, as a matter of fact. And it's too far away. You could have trouble reaching it, if something went really wrong."

"I have a cell phone. I can call for help if I need to."

"You're telling me that a cell phone actually works out here?"

"Yes."

He made a small chiding noise. "Not very dependably, though. I can see it in your eyes."

"It doesn't matter. I'm perfectly safe here."

"Not in your condition. You know you shouldn't be alone."

He was starting to sound way too much like her cousin. Zach—and Tess, too—had been nagging her constantly of late, trying to get her to move to the main house now that her due date was so close. She kept putting them off.

She did plan on moving, as soon as the baby came. Tess already had a room ready for the two of them, with a nice big bed for her, and a bassinet and a changing table and everything else that the baby would need.

But right now, Lacey felt she was managing well enough. And the cabin did please her. She had music— a boom box and a pile of CDs in the sleeping nook. She read a lot and she sketched all the time. Lately, since just before she'd come to Wyoming, she'd discovered that she no longer had the kind of total concentration it took to work seriously on a painting. But that was all right. She sensed that it would come back to her, after the baby arrived—no matter what Xavier Hockland, her former teacher and mentor, chose to believe.

And certainly she could manage to make it to the main house when her labor began. Tess could take her to the hospital from there.

Logan began prowling around the room. He stopped by the big stove. "What do you use to heat this place?"

"Wood. Lately, the weather's so mild, I hardly need heat, though. And if I do, I only have to build one fire, in the morning. By the time it burns down, it's warm outside."

"How do you cook?"

"Same thing. I build a fire."

"You're chopping wood in your condition?"

She made a face at him. "No. Zach takes care of it. He keeps the wood bin out in back nice and full."

"But you have to haul it in here and build the fire yourself?"

"It's not that difficult, Logan."

"Heavy lifting is a bad idea at this point. Your doctor should have told you that."

"Logan. Come on. Stop picking on sweet old Doc Pruitt. I only carry in a few pieces of wood at a time. There honestly is no heavy lifting involved."

He marched over to her again. "You need help around here. And even if you won't marry me, I think I have a right to be here when my baby is born."

She opened her mouth to rebut that—and then shut it without making a sound. He was right. If he wanted to be here for the birth of their child, who was she to deny him?

"Who knows?" he added. "You might even need a doctor in a hurry. Then you'd be doubly glad that I stuck around."

Score one more for his side. She could go into labor any time now. If, God forbid, anything should go wrong before she reached the hospital in Buffalo, it wouldn't hurt to have a doctor at her side.

And who was she kidding, anyway?

Beyond the issues of her isolation in the cabin, of a father's rights and Logan's skills as a physician, there was her foolish heart, beating too hard under her breastbone, just waiting for any excuse to keep him near for a while.

It astonished her now, to look back on all those years growing up, when the name Logan Severance had inspired in her a feeling of profound irritation at best. Logan Severance, her sister's perfect, straight-A boyfriend, who played halfback on the high school football team, took honors in debate and went to University of California in Davis on full scholarship. Logan Severance, who seemed to think it was his duty to whip his sweetheart's messed-up little sister into shape. He was always after her to stand up straight, carping at her about her grades, lecturing her when she ran away or got caught stealing bubble gum from Mr. Kretchmeir's corner store.

Sometimes, she had actually thought that she hated him.

But not anymore.

Now she knew that she loved him. She had figured that out last September, on the fifth glorious day of their crazy, impossible affair. It turned out to be the last day. As soon as she admitted the grim truth to herself, she had seen the self-defeating hopelessness of what she was doing. She had told him she couldn't see him anymore.

He had called her three times after she returned to L.A. She'd found his messages on her answering machine and played each of them back over and over, until they had burned themselves a permanent place in her brain. She had memorized each word, each breath, each nuance of sound…

*"Hello, Lacey. It's Logan. I was just—listen. Why don't you give me a call?"*

*"Lacey. Logan. I left a message a month ago. Did you get it? Are you all right? Sometimes I… Never mind. I suppose I should just leave you alone."*

*"Lace. It's Logan. If you don't call me back this time, I won't try again."*

She had started to call him a hundred times. And she had always put the phone down before she went through with it, though she had known by his second call that she was carrying his baby, known that eventually she would make herself tell him.

Known he would come to her as soon as she did.

And that once he came, it would be harder than ever to send him away.

He smoothed a coil of hair back from her cheek. She savored the lovely, light caress.

He murmured so tenderly, "Say I can stay."

She put off giving in. "I don't want to hear any more talk about marriage. It's out of the question, Logan. Do you understand?"

His eyes gleamed in satisfaction. "That's a yes, right?"

"Not to marriage."

"But you'll let me stay here with you."

"Just until the baby's born. After that, you have to go. We can make arrangements for you to see the baby on a regular basis, and we can—"

He put a finger against her lips. "Shh. There's no need to worry about all that now."

She pulled her head back, away from the touch of that finger of his. It was too tempting by half, that finger. She might just get foolish and suck it right inside her mouth.

His grin seemed terribly smug.

She told him so. "I do not like the look on your face."

"What look?" He reached for one of the grocery bags. "Come on. I'll help you put this stuff away."

## Chapter Three

As soon as the shopping bags were emptied, Logan went out and got his things from the car. There was only one bureau in the dark little cabin. A scarred mahogany monstrosity with a streaked mirror on top. It loomed against the wall by the rear door, sandwiched between a pair of crammed-full pine bookcases. Lacey gave him three of the eight drawers. He'd traveled light, so everything fit in the space she assigned him.

As he unpacked, Lacey sat in the old rocker in the corner, watching him, rocking slowly, her abdomen a hard mound taking up most of her lap, her head resting back, those blue eyes drooping a little.

When he finished, he shoved his empty bag and extra shoes under the daybed. Then he dropped onto the mattress, which was covered with a patchwork quilt. "That's that."

"Umm," she said softly. The rocker creaked as she idly moved it back and forth.

He leaned an elbow on the ironwork bedstead and allowed himself the luxury of just looking at her.

She looked good. Her skin glowed with health and her golden hair still possessed the glossy sheen he remembered. Pregnancy seemed to agree with her. That pleased him. He wanted more children, after this one. A whole house full. It wouldn't be the way it had been when he was a boy, just him and his father and the endless string of housekeepers who had never managed to take the place that should have been filled by a wife and mother.

His kids would have more than that. His kids would have brothers and sisters—and both of their parents. There would be noise and laughter and a feeling of belonging.

Lacey went on rocking—and she smiled.

He wanted to touch her, to put his hand on the fine, smooth skin of her cheek, to run it down over her throat and then over her breasts, which looked sweet and firm and full, even beneath the shapeless denim dress she wore. He wanted to spread both hands on her belly, test the hardness of it now, when she was so close to term, maybe even get lucky and feel his baby kick.

But he knew she wouldn't allow such intimate explorations of her body. Not now. Not so soon after he'd forced himself back into her life.

He was going to have to wait to have his hands on her. Probably until after he had managed to convince her to marry him.

Well, fair enough. He'd waited nine months, telling himself most of the time that this physical yearning he felt for Jenna's little sister would eventually pass.

It hadn't. And recently he'd allowed himself to accept the fact that it was only Mother Nature playing at irony.

Lacey Bravo, of all people, was his sexual ideal.

Explain it? He couldn't, didn't really even care to. Human beings were primates, after all, aroused by things they didn't consciously understand. By certain scents and secretions. Desire had nothing at all to do with logic. It was a chemical reaction, the natural attraction of one healthy specimen for another, designed to perpetuate the species.

Now that Lacey was having his baby and he meant to marry her, he found it a real bonus that he wanted her so much. They might have their problems in a lot of different areas, but he didn't think sex was going to be one of them.

She stopped rocking and lifted her head off the backrest. "Are you tired?"

He almost said no. But then he reconsidered. He could use a nap, as a matter of fact. He'd been up well before dawn. And he hadn't been getting much sleep in the last week anyway, not since her letter had arrived.

"A little," he said. "I'll lie down for a while if you will, too." He wanted to make certain she got plenty of rest.

"It's a deal." She put both hands on the rocker arms and levered herself to a standing position.

He asked, in a tone as offhand as he could make it, "Is there a double bed behind that curtain?"

She gave him a lazy grin. "Nice try. You get the day-bed." She shuffled out the back door. After a few minutes, he heard the toilet flush. She came back in, only to disappear behind the curtain in the corner.

He paid a short visit to the bathroom himself, then took off his shoes and lay down. Like every other piece of furniture in the cabin, the bed appeared to be something salvaged from an earlier era. It had creaky springs and a lumpy mattress and it wasn't long enough to fully accommodate his six-foot-three-inch frame. But he stretched out as best he could, letting his stocking feet hang over the edge and pulling one of the long sausage-shaped bolster pillows under his head.

A strange kind of peace settled over him, a deep relaxation, a sense of well-being. It was a state he hadn't experienced in a long time. He dropped off to sleep like a rock falling down a well.

The next thing he knew, someone was knocking on the door.

Logan bolted to a sitting position, blinking and staring around him, wondering where the hell he was.

Then it all fell into place. The long trip from California. To this cabin. In Wyoming. Lacey. Pregnant with his baby. She was resting now, on the other side of that curtain over there. He glanced at his Rolex. She'd been in there for less than an hour.

And whatever idiot had dropped in for a visit would probably wake her with the next knock.

He jumped to his feet and padded swiftly to the door. When he pulled it open, he found a cowboy on the other side. Behind the cowboy, hitched to one of the poles that held up the porch, a handsome horse with a reddish-brown coat let out a low snort and flicked his shiny tail at a couple of flies.

The cowboy lifted his hat in greeting, then settled it

back on his head. "I'm Zach Bravo." His gaze shifted down, paused on Logan's stocking feet, then quickly shifted up again. "Just thought I'd stop by and check on things out here."

"Logan?" It was Lacey's voice, sounding slow and sleepy, from the other end of the room. "Who is it?" She stood just beyond the curtain in the corner, her feet bare, her face soft and her hair mussed from sleep.

"It's Zach," said the cowboy, craning to see around Logan, who had positioned himself squarely in the open doorway.

Lacey grinned and started toward them. "Come on in. I can probably scare up a beer if you want one."

Zach Bravo stayed where he was. "No. Got to get a move on. Never enough hours in a day around here. But Tess asked me to see if you wanted to come over to the house for dinner tonight. Around six?"

Logan stepped aside a little as Lacey came up next to him. "Zach, this is Dr. Logan Severance, a...dear friend." Logan didn't miss her slight hesitation over what to call him. He'd bet his license to practice medicine that Zach Bravo didn't miss it either.

"Pleased to meet you." The rancher held out a tough brown hand.

Logan took it, gave it a firm shake. "The pleasure is mine."

"You'll come for dinner then...both of you?"

Lacey lifted an eyebrow at Logan. He nodded and she smiled at her cousin. "We'll be there. Six o'clock."

"So I'm your dear friend," Logan challenged the minute Zach Bravo had mounted his horse and trotted away down the dirt road that led to the cluster of ranch buildings just over the next rise.

Lacey made a noise in her throat. "What should I have said? Former lover? The father of my child?"

"How about husband?"

"But that wouldn't be true, now, would it?"

"We could make it true."

She looked at him for a long, cool moment, then announced defiantly, "Zach comes out to check on me two or three times a day, which is just another reason why I'm perfectly safe on my own here."

"I'd say he came to check on *me* this time."

"Right. He's protective. More proof that I'm in no danger at all, as I've constantly tried to make you realize. You simply do not have to stay in this cabin with me. If you want to be here when the baby's born, you could take a room in the motel in town and—"

"I'm not leaving, Lacey—and your cousin strikes me as a conservative man, the kind of man who would feel a lot better if you were married to the father of your child."

She put her hands on her hips. "You are truly relentless. Now we should get married so as not to offend Zach's conservative sensibilities?"

"I'm only pointing out that—"

"Logan. You said you would drop it."

Lacey gave him her best unwavering stare. She was wondering, as she had more than once in the past nine months, how she could love such an obnoxious man.

He stared right back, which forced her to demand, "Are you dropping it, Logan?"

He made a growling sound. "All right, all right. I'm dropping it."

"Good."

His handsome face had settled into a scowl. She

watched him rearrange it to something more gentle. "We've got another hour and a half before we have to make our appearance at your cousin's house. Why don't you go on back behind that curtain and lie down again?"

She blew a tangled curl out of her eye. "No, thanks. I'm wide awake now." She marched to the sleeping nook, ducked inside and came out with her lace-up hiking boots.

His eyes narrowed with suspicion. "What are you doing?"

She sat in the rocker and pulled on one of the boots. It wasn't easy, working around the bulge of her stomach, but she'd had a lot of practice in the past few weeks. Huffing and puffing, she tied the boot, pulled on the other one, tied it up, too.

"Lacey."

She stood, turned to the bureau, picked up the brush lying on top and went to work on her hair. Their eyes met in the mirror. "I'm going out behind the cabin a ways. There's a creek that runs by back there. Very picturesque. I've been doing a few sketches. Willows and cottonwoods, a few cows and their calves…" He was scowling again. She pretended not to notice. "I'll be back in an hour or so, in plenty of time for dinner with Zach and Tess and the family."

"Are you sure that you should—?"

She turned and pointed the brush at him. "Don't, all right? Just…don't. Nothing's going to happen to me down by the creek. It's barely a hundred yards from the back door, for heaven's sake."

"What if some big bull comes at you?"

"It's not an issue."

"This is a cattle ranch, isn't it? If I'm not mistaken, bulls live on cattle ranches."

She struggled to contain her building exasperation. "There's a barbed-wire fence that runs between this particular spot on the creek and those cattle I mentioned. If there are any bulls nearby, they would most likely be on the other side of that fence."

"But—"

"Read my lips. I'll be fine."

"I'll come with—"

"Logan. Stop. If you insist on staying here, in a twenty-by-twenty-foot space with me, we're going to have to give each other a little breathing room. I am going alone."

He shut his mouth, made another growling sound and then dropped to the side of the daybed. "Great. Fine. Do what you want to do. You never in your life did anything else." He braced his elbows on his spread knees and shook his head at his stocking feet.

Tenderness washed through her. She set down the brush. "You're the one who needs more rest. Come on. Stretch out and sleep for an hour. You'll have the cabin all to yourself. Forget all your cares and I'll wake you up when I get back."

He didn't say anything, just went on staring at his socks.

"Logan…"

"All right. I'll take a damn nap." He lay down on his back with his feet over the edge, turned his face to the wall and shut his eyes.

Smiling to herself, Lacey collected her sketch pad and a couple of nice, soft pencils from the chair where she'd set them earlier. Before she went out, she couldn't resist whispering, "Sleep well."

"Thanks," he grumbled, neither turning his head nor opening his eyes. "Be careful, for God's sake."

"I will, Logan. I promise you."

He was sound asleep when she returned, lying in almost the same position she'd left him in, his hands folded on his chest. His head, however, was turned toward the room now.

Lacey stood over him, admiring the beauty of his body in repose, thinking that maybe she could do a few sketches of him sleeping—nothing too challenging right now. She wasn't up for it. But she could certainly line out a few ideas in pencil.

Then, later, after the baby came, she could go back to what she'd started, delve more deeply. She loved the softness of his face when he was sleeping. And something else. Some…determined vulnerability. Some aspect of his will that came through even when he was unconscious, some sense that he distrusted the necessity of surrendering to sleep.

He had a wonderful face, handsome in a classic way. And very masculine—she'd always thought so, even before she realized she was in love with him. A broad forehead, a strongly defined supraorbital arch, so the eyes were set deep, shadowed in their sockets. Cheekbones and jawline were clean and clear-cut and his finely shaped mouth possessed just enough softness to betray the sensuality she'd discovered with such delight during their five incredible days together last fall.

Though he didn't know it, she had painted him. A number of nudes, from memory, in the first months after their affair. She believed they were her best work so far. And she had exercised great ingenuity, in all of them, so as not to reveal his face.

Had she been wrong to paint him without his knowledge? After all, Logan Severance was not the kind of man who posed for nude studies—let alone the kind who would allow them to be hung in an art gallery for all the world to see. Those paintings weren't in any gallery yet. But someday they would be. Lacey had told herself that she'd protected his privacy by obscuring his face. But sometimes she felt just a little bit guilty about them, wondered what his reaction would be if he ever saw them—which he would probably have to. Someday.

She wasn't particularly looking forward to that day.

"What are you staring at?"

Caught thoroughly off guard, Lacey gasped and stepped back. She could have sworn he was sound asleep just seconds ago. But those eyes looking into hers now were clear and alert.

"Well?"

The truth slipped out—or at least, some of it. "I was thinking that I'd like to sketch you while you're sleeping."

"Why?"

"Something in your face. Something… unguarded, but unwillingly so. It's very appealing."

He grinned. "You like me best unconscious, is that what you're telling me?"

She'd regained her composure enough to reply smartly, "I wouldn't have put it that way, but now that you've done it yourself…"

"Marry me. You can watch me sleep for the rest of our lives."

She resolutely did not respond to that. "We should go. It's quarter of six."

At the big side-gabled wood frame ranch house, Zach introduced his family to Logan.

"This is Tess." He put his arm around his wife. "And our daughters, Starr and Jobeth."

The older of the two girls, a beauty of about eighteen, with black hair and Elizabeth Taylor eyes, gave him a polite "Hello." The younger one, Jobeth, who looked ten or eleven, smiled shyly and nodded.

Next, Logan shook Edna Heller's slim, fine-boned hand and learned that she had once been the ranch's housekeeper but now was one of the family; her only daughter had married a Bravo cousin, Cash. She lived in the foreman's cottage, which was just across the drive from the main house.

"And this is Ethan John," Tess said. She held up a big, healthy blue-eyed baby. "Ethan is just six months old today." The baby gurgled out something that sounded almost like a greeting.

They ate at the long table in the Bravos' formal dining room. Ethan John sat in his high chair and chewed on a teething ring and occasionally let out a happy, crowing laugh.

"Ethan's already had his dinner," Tess explained. "We enjoy having him with us during meals, but we don't enjoy watching the food fly. So I feed him early and he sits with us and everybody's happy." Tess turned her smile on Logan. "Do you have children, Mr. Severance?"

Logan answered that one carefully. "Not yet."

"You plan to, then?"

He sent a significant glance at Lacey, who was sitting directly to his left. She smiled at him, an innocent, what-are-you-looking-at-me-for? smile. Apparently, he was on his own here.

"Yes," he said. "I plan to have children…very soon."

Now it was Zach and Tess's turn to trade glances. And the two girls, as well. They looked at their parents first, then swapped a glance of their own. Edna Heller somehow managed to make eye contact with all four of the others. She shared knowing looks with Zach and Tess, and right after that flashed a "mind your business, girls," expression at their daughters.

Lacey was grinning. Apparently she thought the whole exchange of meaningful looks rather amusing.

Logan didn't. As far as he was concerned, those flying glances were just more proof that Lacey needed to come to her senses and marry him immediately. It was an embarrassment to sit here with this nice family and have them all wonder what the hell was going on between their unmarried pregnant cousin and the strange man who'd shown up out of nowhere this afternoon—and appeared to have set up housekeeping with her.

He wanted to get the truth out in the open. He wanted to say bluntly, That's my baby Lacey's carrying and I've come to marry her and take her home with me where she belongs.

But he couldn't do that. Not here at the Bravo dinner table, with a girl of Jobeth's age listening in.

"How do you and Lacey know each other?" asked Edna Heller. She was a small, slender woman, probably in her fifties, and very feminine—though in her eyes Logan could see a glint of steel. Not much would get by her.

She was smiling at him in the most polite way and waiting for an answer. Unfortunately, the truth wouldn't sound good at all. *I've been in love with Lacey's sister since I was eighteen years old. Jenna was going to marry me—until she decided to run off with Mack McGarrity instead.*

Lacey came to his rescue on that one. "Logan and Jenna went to school together. Logan's been sort of a big brother figure to me over the years."

Edna Heller's eyebrows rose daintily toward her hairline. "Ah. A big brother figure."

"He's always felt he has to take care of me. He still feels that way. Don't you Logan?"

"That's right."

"That's…admirable of you, Mr. Severance."

"Thank you, Mrs. Heller."

"You know, for years my son-in-law, Cash, imagined himself a big brother to my Abigail. But then he married her and found out he was deeply in love with her. Abigail, of course, always worshipped him."

"Oh, really?" Logan said, for lack of something better to say.

Lacey couldn't let Edna's observation go unchallenged. "Are we supposed to be noting similarities between Cash and Abby—and Logan and me?"

"Well," said Edna airily. "Only if the shoe fits, as they say."

"The shoe does not fit. Logan and I are not getting married. And if you ask him, he'll tell you he never got any worship from me."

Edna might give the Bravo daughters stern looks admonishing them to stay out of others' affairs, but she clearly thought of herself as someone who had a right to be in the know. She turned to Logan. "Well, Mr. Severance?"

*Lacey hasn't fully accepted the idea yet, but we are getting married,* he thought. He said, "No. Worship is not the word I would use to describe Lacey's feelings for me."

"What word would you use, then?"

He shrugged. "Let's just say it wouldn't be worship and leave it at that."

There was a silence, which was quickly filled with nonsense syllables from the baby and the clink of silver against china plates.

Zach said, "More potatoes, Logan?"

"Yes, please. This is a terrific meal, Tess."

Tess colored prettily at the compliment. "Well, I must confess. Edna always does the potatoes around here. I swear she has a way of making them light enough that they could get right up and float off your plate."

Edna smiled graciously—and went back to her velvet-gloved interrogation. "And how long will you be staying on the Rising Sun, Mr. Severance?"

He shot a look at Lacey. She'd had a lot to say a minute ago. Maybe she'd want to put her two cents in on this one.

But not this time. She only looked back at him, thoroughly annoying in her pretended innocence.

He shrugged. "I'll be here a week or two. At least until the baby's born."

"You're a doctor, you said?"

"That's right. I'm in family practice."

"This is…a vacation then?"

"Not really. I'm here to…help Lacey out, in any way I can."

Glances went flying again. He almost wished they would all just say what they were thinking. Then he could answer them. He could explain his position and enlist their aid in convincing Lacey to see things his way.

"Well," said Tess, taking pains to remain neutral. "We hope you'll enjoy your stay."

He was neutral right back at her. "I'm sure I will."

The baby dropped his teething ring. Tess picked it up, wiped it off, and handed it to him, then suggested casually, "We've been trying to talk Lacey into moving to the house."

Lacey reached down the table to brush Tess's arm. "Stop worrying. I told you, I'm just fine at the cabin for right now."

Tess sighed. "I disagree. And I wish Dr. Severance would help me to change your mind."

Fat chance, Logan thought. He said, "I've known Lacey for fifteen years. In all that time, I haven't changed her mind about a single thing."

Lacey laughed. The musical sound tingled along his nerves and warmed something down inside him. "That can't be true, Logan. You must have changed my mind about something in a decade and a half. It's not as if you haven't tried."

He turned his head and looked right at her. The reaction was instantaneous—that chemical thing between them, which unscientific men called desire. It heated his blood, made him glad his lap was covered by Tess Bravo's lace tablecloth.

He should not allow her to do this to him. She was nine months' pregnant, for pity's sake. He ought to be ashamed of himself.

He arched an eyebrow at her. "You're right." To his relief, his voice sounded fine, level and calm. It gave no inkling of what had just happened under the table. "It's incredible when you think about it. But it's true. I have never changed your mind about a single thing."

"Yes. Yes, you have."

"Oh, come on, Lacey."

"I remember distinctly—"

She didn't either, and they both knew she didn't. "What?" he demanded. "You remember what?"

The baby, in his highchair, chortled to himself as a slow smile curved Lacey's eminently kissable mouth. For a moment, Logan thought she would actually say something about the two of them, about how she'd never in her life imagined him as a lover—but that was one thing he had definitely changed her mind about. He had to resist the urge to clap his hand over her mouth.

And then she said, "Broccoli."

He didn't think he'd heard her correctly. "Broccoli?"

Lacey nodded. "You convinced me to give it a try. You said I would like it raw. With ranch dressing."

He stared at her, thinking, Liar. You never ate any broccoli for me—raw or otherwise.

"Yes." That smile of hers was too innocent by half. "Broccoli. Remember?" She was blatantly teasing him, pouring on the innuendo.

But it could be worse, he reminded himself. At least she hadn't said what he'd feared she might.

He forced a smile to answer hers and let her have her silly lie. "I don't know how I could have let myself forget."

"More string beans?" Tess asked him.

He thanked her and spooned a second helping onto his plate.

The talk turned to safer subjects.

Zach asked Jobeth about a calf she had chosen to raise herself as a 4-H project.

Jobeth explained how she planned to experiment with different varieties of feed.

Then Tess wanted to know how things were going for Starr. Evidently, the older girl had a job at a local shop called Cotes's Clothing and Gift.

"A summer job is a summer job," Starr said. "It gets a little boring, but it's not that bad. Mr. Cotes offered me four more hours on Saturdays. I'm going to take them. Might as well make use of my free time this summer. When school starts, I want to keep my focus on studying, where it belongs."

"Our Starr is a straight-A student," Edna declared with pride.

A contrary glint came into the girl's impossibly beautiful violet eyes. "At least I am now."

Zach frowned. "We are proud of you. Very, very proud."

Starr lifted her lovely chin. "Thanks."

Evidently, the girl had had some problems in the past. Logan wondered what, but the subject had already shifted again.

Zach was suggesting that Logan might want to saddle up and ride with him and Jobeth and the men sometime in the next few days. He could see how things were done on a working cattle ranch.

Logan confessed, "I think I've been on a horse about three times in my life. And they weren't very lively horses, if you know what I mean."

Zach chuckled. "We'll find you something sweet-natured and easy-going—or you can ride in one of the pickups. Your choice."

"Then I'd enjoy a tour, Zach. Thanks."

Beside him, Lacey slid back her chair and stood. "Excuse me."

Apprehension pulling a thread of tightness across his chest, Logan looked up over the ripe curve of her belly and into her eyes. "What is it? Are you feeling all right?"

She laughed and put her hand on his shoulder. It felt good there. Damn good. "Relax. I'm fine. I need to…make use of the facilities, that's all."

"You're sure. If something's—"

She lifted her hand and stroked the hair at his temple. "Logan. Eat." Her hand was cool and her eyes were a summer sky—clear, stunningly blue. A smile quivered across that soft mouth of hers. He had to remind himself that they were not alone, or he would have laid his palm on her belly, a possessive touch, which would have felt totally appropriate then. At that moment, she was all softness, all openness. And all for him.

But then she seemed to catch herself. She jerked her glance away. Her smile vanished.

She dropped her hand. "I'll be right back." She slid around the chair and headed for the hall.

He watched her until she'd disappeared from view, reluctant to relinquish the sight of her, wondering at her swift change of mood. For a moment, she had been so damn… tender.

Just as she'd been when he woke and found her standing over him in the cabin an hour before. He'd seen the softness in her eyes then, too. And something else. Worry, maybe.

But softness, definitely.

And even earlier, while he unpacked his few things. She had sat in that rocker and watched him, a dreamy, contented expression on her face.

As if she…

It came to him. Right then, at the Bravo family's dinner table, as he watched her waddle away through the living room, then disappear beyond a door that led to the front hall. It all snapped into place.

For Lacey, this was more than a matter of sexual attraction. More than affection, more than the commonality of a shared past. More even than the most important issue of the child she was about to have.

She was in love with him.

It made perfect sense. The abrupt way she had broken it off in September—that must have been when she had realized.

And what about the times he had called her and she'd never called back? That hadn't been like her. Before, she would have called, if only to insist that she was fine, that he was not to worry about her, that he needed to get on with his life and let her get on with hers.

Yes. She was in love with him—and she feared, because of Jenna, that he would only hurt her.

He wouldn't. Never. Jenna was gone for good now, living in Florida with Mack McGarrity, a baby on the way. She was no threat to what Logan and Lacey might share.

Damn. Lacey loved him.

True, he didn't have a lot of faith in love lately. He'd loved Jenna for all those years and in the end, his love had not been enough to hold her.

But this situation was different. He was already committed to making a life with Lacey. He had been from the moment he'd learned that she carried his child. If Lacey thought herself in love with him—whatever the hell that really meant—it could only work in his favor.

A lightness seemed to move through him. A feeling of rightness, of ease.

And of power, too.

She loved him.

He knew now, with absolute certainty, that she would say yes to him. She had that wild streak. And she was willful. She might not be the wife that Jenna would have been. But she would be his in a way that Jenna never had.

She was already his.

Because she loved him. Lacey Bravo loved him.

He hadn't realized that doubt had been eating at him, eroding his self-confidence, setting his nerves on edge. He hadn't realized it until now, when doubt was gone.

He turned back to the table, a grin pulling at his mouth—and found six pairs of eyes focused on him. Even the baby was watching him.

"That girl's a pistol," Edna muttered under her breath.

"She's independent," said Tess warmly, speaking right up in Lacey's defense. "I admire independence."

Edna gave Tess a fond smile. "Of course you do. So do I. But the fact remains. She needs a husband."

Zach Bravo was still staring at Logan. "You're here to marry her," he said. It wasn't a question.

Logan felt satisfaction, to have it out in the open, to be able to answer simply, "I am."

Zach nodded. "Better not waste any time about it. That baby is likely to show up any minute now."

# Chapter Four

It was barely eight-thirty when they got back to the cabin.

Logan suggested that they sit outside for a while and watch the sun set behind the mountains.

Lacey vetoed that idea. "I'm tired," she said.

It was a lie. She wasn't tired. She simply had to get away from him. Having him so near, having to be so very careful, was making her crazy.

She was no good at carefulness. She had never taught herself how to hide what was in her heart. She wore her emotions on the surface. And she liked it that way, felt comfortable in her own skin because she could always be honest about what was going on inside her. And it translated into her work, gave her a freedom to create whatever came to her, to follow her own ideas wherever they wanted to take her.

But she couldn't afford to let her emotions show now. If she did, Logan would only use her poor heart against her. Her love would become his ally in his relentless quest to do the right thing—the Logan Severance version of the right thing, which included marrying the mother of his child whether he loved her or not.

She had to watch herself every minute. And still, she kept messing up, kept slipping into ridiculous moments of pure adoration. Kept snapping to attention to find herself staring at him dreamy-eyed, mooning over him as he slept, caressing the side of his face at the dinner table while Zach and his family looked on.

He was watching her strangely now, one corner of that sexy mouth tipped up, a musing, thoroughly nerve-racking look in his eyes. "Tired? You? The original night owl?"

He had her dead to rights, of course. Even far advanced in pregnancy, Lacey Bravo *was* a night owl. She went to bed late and if she got up by noon, she felt she'd started the day good and early.

She stuck with her lie. "Tonight, I *am* tired. I'm taking a shower and I'm going to bed."

Of course, once she got there, she knew she wasn't going to be able to sleep.

She decided to do a few exercises. She practiced her Kegels—contracting and relaxing the muscles she would use in childbirth. She sat up and rolled her neck and did a few simple stretches. She got on her hands and knees and flexed her back, then relaxed it, remaining aware of her breathing the whole time.

When she ran out of exercises, she tried to concentrate on a novel, sitting up among the pillows, the book propped on her big stomach. But her attention wandered. The baby seemed restless. The little sweetheart kept surprising her with nudges and pokes. And her back was aching. It was hard to get comfortable.

She heard Logan go out to the bathroom, heard the water pipes sighing as he took his shower. When he came back in, she heard him moving around in the main room and wondered just what he was doing out there.

Then she heard the click as he turned off the light over the table. The springs of the daybed creaked. And then silence.

From outside, faintly, came the far-off howling of lonely coyotes and the hooting of an owl. But there was no sound at all from the main room. She continued her attempt at reading until ten, then gave up and turned off her own light.

As the hours crawled by and she couldn't sleep, she silently called Logan Severance a hundred nasty names. She practiced more Kegels—hundreds of them. She sat up and rolled her neck, stretched her arms, closed her eyes, breathed slowly and evenly in and out, seeking relaxation and inner peace.

Hah.

By midnight, her poor bladder could no longer be denied. She pulled on her robe and tiptoed out to the back door. With agonizing care, she turned the latch, then tried to pull the door open slowly enough that the old hinges wouldn't creak.

They didn't. Or if they did, it was just barely.

Still, he heard them. "Lacey?" His voice was thick with the groggy remnants of sleep.

If she hadn't loved him so blasted much, she could have hated him for that, for his ability to drop right off to sleep while she lay staring wide-eyed into the shadows, counting her Kegels—not to mention the seconds, the minutes, the *hours*.

He sat up. She could see the shape of him, outlined in the moonlight that streamed in, pale and silvery, through the window above the daybed. "What's wrong?"

"Nothing." She pushed the door open the rest of the way and lumbered out into the night.

When she came back, the light was on and he was standing by the rocker, wearing a pair of navy blue sweats and nothing else that she could detect. He had his bare arms folded over his chest.

"Are you in labor?"

She let loose an unladylike grunt. "Is that an accusation?"

He dropped his arms. Lord, that chest of his was beautiful. Planes and angles, power and the readiness for motion. Da Vinci would have drooled. "Come on, Lace. Are you having contractions? That's all I want to know."

"No." She gathered her robe closer around the barrel of her belly. "I am not having contractions. And honestly, there is no need to ask me that. I can assure you, when I *am* in labor, I will have no hesitation at all about sharing the news with you."

"Believe it or not, sometimes a woman won't even know when she's in labor." He was grinning.

"You know, Doctor. You are way too cheerful about all of this."

"It just occurred to me. You haven't called me Dr. Do-Right once since I arrived here."

"I guess I must be slipping—and I'm sure you mean,

a woman might not know when she's in the *early stages* of labor. After a certain point, it's got to become pretty obvious."

"True." He frowned. "Did you ever get a chance to take a childbirth class?"

"No. But I bought a few books and I've been studying them, getting to…understand what will happen."

"Well. Good." There it was again—that musing look in his eye, that half-smile on his lips.

"What is that?"

He lifted a dark brow. "What?"

"That…look."

"Look?"

"Yes, Logan. That look. That look that says you know something I don't."

He lifted both big, sculpted shoulders. "Beats me."

She wanted to slug him. Or kiss him. She said, "I'm going back to bed. And if I get up again, could you pretend not to notice? It's bad enough that I spend my nights going in and out of the back door. I don't need you hovering nearby ready to check my vital signs every time I come in."

"Will do."

"What does that mean?"

"Unless you call for me, I won't get up."

"Thank you."

"You are very welcome."

She peered at him. "What is going on?"

"Nothing. Go on back to bed."

It was good advice, and she knew it. She ducked into the sleeping nook, dragged her poor ungainly body onto the bed and curled on her side. The light in the main room went out.

The next time she got up, about two hours later, Logan didn't even stir.

Daylight came as it always did: earlier than Lacey would have liked.

Not that she noticed. By then, as always, she was finally sound asleep. If Logan went outside, she didn't hear it, and she didn't hear him come back in, either.

But she did hear him fiddling with the stove.

She turned over and grumbled to herself and drifted back into a pleasant, floating state of slumber, thinking as sleep claimed her that at least he was trying to be quiet.

Not much later, she found herself awake again. She sighed, breathed deeply, told herself to relax and let go.

But there was a problem.

She could swear she heard every move he made. The clink of a bowl as he set it on the table, the rustle of cereal spilling out of a box. The muffled click—twice—as he carefully opened, then closed the refrigerator door, the pad of his stocking feet across the plank floor, the glug-glug-glug of milk poured from a carton.

She tried putting her pillow over her head, then even yanked the blankets over that. It did no good.

She was awake—at eight thirty-three in the morning, after having slept fewer than four measly hours.

She knew that Logan usually woke around six. Which meant that in all likelihood, he'd been lying there for at least a couple of hours, actively restraining himself from getting up and starting in with his annoying morning-person activities. The only reason he would do such a thing was to give her a chance to sleep undisturbed.

It was thoughtful of him. And she should have been grateful.

But she wasn't grateful.

She was nine months pregnant and she was tired and Logan Severance was driving her crazy with his will of iron and his musing I-know-something-you-don't-know smiles and his absolute refusal to accept that she was never, ever going to say "I do."

Lacey pulled the pillow closer around her face and muttered a few choice naughty words.

Couldn't he see that it would never work? Even if he returned her love, what possible chance did they have of making it as a couple? They didn't even get up at the same time.

He went back to the refrigerator—did he actually imagine she couldn't hear every move he made?—and put the milk away. Then back to the table again. He didn't scrape the floor with the chair, but it creaked when he sat down. His spoon clinked against the bowl.

When she found herself straining to hear him chew, she knew it was no use.

With another low oath, she shoved back the covers and reached for the tent of the day, a scoop-necked, ankle-length, teal-blue creation, which she'd left hanging on a wall peg along with her bra the night before. Her ballerina flats were right there, too, in the tiny space to the right of the bed. She tore off her sleep shirt and put on the clothes, shivering a little with cold, realizing that he must not have built a fire after all, even though she'd distinctly heard him fooling around with the stove.

When she entered the main room, he looked up in mid-crunch. She didn't say a word, just went out the door and into the bathroom, where she relieved her overworked bladder and splashed icy water on her face and grumbled to herself in the mirror as she raked a brush through her hair.

Logan was over at the stove, clattering the iron covers, when she reentered the cabin. He sent a smile over his shoulder. "Now you're up, I'll make a fire."

He rumpled a newspaper and fed it into the belly of the stove as she went to the old electric percolator on the counter by the sink, filled it with water and plugged it in.

"You're drinking coffee?" A frown of doctorly concern creased his brow.

She unplugged the pot, took the lid off and tipped it so that he could see inside. "Just water. I'm heating water. For tea. *Herbal* tea. Does that meet with your approval?"

"Yes," he said gently. "As a matter of fact, it does." He turned back to the stove. She took a tea bag from the canister and dropped it into a mug. Then, since it never took the water that long to boil, she just stood there at the counter, waiting for it.

"Are you hungry?" he asked, once he'd lit the fire and was carefully putting the cover back in place.

"I'll get myself some cereal."

"Are you sure? Maybe an egg—"

She looked at him. The look must have said exactly what she was thinking.

"Not an egg person, huh?"

"Not in the last, oh, eight months or so."

"I understand."

She doubted it, but she decided not to comment. Soon enough, the water was hot. "There's some instant coffee, if you want it," she muttered grudgingly as she poured the boiling water over her tea bag.

"No, thanks. The cereal's fine."

She carried a bowl and spoon to the table with her. The cereal was already there. He went to the refrigerator and got her the milk. Soon enough, they were sitting across the table from each other, crunching away.

Lacey tried to concentrate on her cereal. She took slow bites and she chewed thoroughly. She'd discovered, especially over the past month, when her entire digestive system seemed to have been crammed into a tiny space between her swollen uterus and her lungs, that if she didn't eat slowly, either hiccups or heartburn would be the result.

"I tried not to wake you," he said with regret, after a few moments of mutual chewing and swallowing.

She sent him a glance. "But you did."

"You're angry."

"No." She had to chew some more. He waited. Once she'd swallowed, she told him, "I was angry when you woke me up. Now I'm..." She sought the word. It came to her. "...philosophical."

He set down his spoon. He looked much too amused. "You? Philosophical?"

She scooped up more cereal, poked it into her mouth. "Uh-huh."

He watched her as she chewed. When she swallowed, he said, "I assume you intend to elaborate."

As a matter of fact, she did. She nodded. "It's just come to me. In a blinding flash of insight."

He muttered, "I'll bet."

"I mean it." She left her spoon in her bowl, braced her elbow on the table and leaned her chin on her hand. "It has. It really has."

"All right. I'll bite. What has come to you?"

Her stomach felt squashed. She arched her back, rubbed at the base of her spine, then settled into her earlier pose, chin in hand. "Our basic natures are at odds."

"Meaning?"

"The fact that you love my sister aside, there really is no hope for us—as a couple, I mean."

His jaw twitched. "That's your opinion."

She sighed. "Remember that old story—the ant and the grasshopper?"

He dared to groan. "You're kidding."

"Nope. You're the ant. Up at first light. Diligent and hardworking, upwardly mobile, always getting ready for a rainy day."

"I'm an ant." He did not look pleased.

She gave him a lazy grin. "That's right. I, on the other hand, am all grasshopper." She gestured at the small, dim room around them. "I take everything—each day—as it comes. I live for the joy of the moment. You don't understand me and I don't understand you. We're just…much too different by nature to have a prayer of making a go of it together."

He studied her for a long moment, looking irritatingly amused. "Correct me if I'm wrong, but as I recall the story, when winter came, the grasshopper died."

She hit the table with the heel of her hand. "See? Total ant logic. Focusing on the very things you can least control."

"I assume you mean death."

"Yes. Exactly. Death. And bad weather, too." She picked up her spoon again and went back to work on the cereal.

"I thought that was the moral of the story," Logan

said. "The ant worked hard and scrimped and saved and lasted the winter. The grasshopper partied. And when the cold weather came…" He shook his head and pretended to look mournful. "Too bad, so sad."

She pointed her spoon at him. "I live in L.A. Bad weather is not a problem."

"We're discussing a fable, Lace. In a fable, bad weather stands for any of a number of possible difficult periods in life."

She'd started out this little discussion feeling pleasantly superior—now she felt just plain disgruntled. "Oh, never mind. You're determined to miss my point and make your own."

"I got your point."

"Right." She bent her head over her bowl and finished her cereal, aware of his eyes on her the whole time.

When she looked up, sure enough, he was watching her.

He said, "Maybe having my baby is the best thing that ever happened to you. As my wife, you know you'll always have a roof over your head when winter closes in."

She reached for the bottle of prenatal vitamins in the center of the table, screwed off the lid and shook one into her hand. "Listen to me, Logan. I'm not going to be your wife. And as far as that roof you mentioned, I don't *need* to know it'll be there. I don't think that far ahead. As I keep trying to explain to you, I'm a grasshopper to the core."

"Fine. So I'll think ahead for you. You *do* need that. Especially now, with the baby coming."

She picked up her bowl and stood. "I can see I'm getting nowhere."

"I wouldn't say that. This has been an enlightening discussion."

"Enlightening for you, maybe."

There it was again, that musing, knowing look in his eyes. "Seriously. I think we have a lot to offer each other."

"Dream on."

"I'll scrimp and save for a rainy day. You'll see that we make the most of every moment. We're the perfect couple."

Something scathing rose to her lips. She bit it back and turned for the sink, where she washed her vitamin down with water, cleaned her bowl and spoon and set them in the wooden rack to dry.

"He seems a fine man," Tess said. "And so handsome, too."

They were sitting in a pair of rockers on the porch of the main house, just Tess and Lacey, enjoying the shade in the heat of the afternoon. Zach and Jobeth had taken Logan out for a look around the ranch, Starr had driven off that morning to her summer job and Edna had settled in with the baby at her own house for a short nap.

"Lacey, did you hear what I said?"

Lacey made a noncommittal sound. She had her sketch pad perched on what was left of her lap and she was busy stroking in shadows with the side of her pencil.

Tess took a few more tiny, perfect stitches on the thick wool sock she was darning. "I hope he got everything worked out all right with the other doctors at his office."

Logan had tried calling his office via cell phone earlier. When the cell phone cut out on him, he'd ended up using the phone at the main house.

"Yes," Lacey said. "His partners have agreed to cover for him."

"Well. That's good."

Was it? Lacey wasn't so sure. But she felt no urge to remark on the fact. She focused on her drawing, her hand moving swiftly and surely over the paper.

Tess cleared her throat. "Maybe I have no right to ask, but I'm going to ask anyway…"

Lacey made a series of quick, deft strokes, cross-hatching more shadows, then looked up from her sketch pad. "Yes," she said, "Logan is the baby's father."

Those big dark eyes of Tess's didn't waver. "He says he's here to marry you."

"When did he say that?"

"Last night. You had left the table for a moment." Tess snipped with her scissors and tied off her thread. "Will you marry him?"

"No." Lacey flipped the cover over her drawing and set the pad on the short bench between them.

"Why not?"

Lacey's back was aching, as it had been for the past few days. She pushed herself from the chair and indulged in a nice, protracted stretch. Tess watched her, saying nothing.

Lacey wandered to the railing and managed to hoist herself up onto it. She put one hand under her belly to support it a little and leaned her cheek against the porch post.

Then she said it. "He doesn't love me. He's always loved Jenna."

Tess bent to her basket, dropped in the sock, and

brought out a plaid shirt with a tear at the shoulder seam. "How do you know that?"

"They were high school sweethearts. And they were even engaged, last year, before Mack McGarrity came back into the picture."

"That was last year. What about now?"

"I've…confronted him with it. Yesterday, when he first arrived and started insisting that we had to get married."

"And?"

"He didn't come right out and say, 'I love Jenna,' but he never denied it, either."

Tess looked over the rows of thread spools in her sewing box, seeking the right color. "Your sister is no threat to your relationship with Logan. Jenna loves her husband."

"Unfortunately, that hasn't stopped Logan from loving *her.*"

"Or so you assume, though he's never actually said as much."

"He doesn't have to say it. I know. And he certainly hasn't said he loves me."

"Have you said you love him?"

"No, and I don't intend to."

"Why not?"

Lacey considered that question—and decided against answering it. Tess didn't seem to mind. She got to work threading her needle, rolling a knot into the end of the thread. She took her first stitch.

Her head still bent over her mending, Tess spoke again. "Whatever Dr. Severance feels for your sister, it's obvious he cares for you. And he also feels…what a man feels when he looks at a certain woman."

Lacey sat a little straighter on the railing. "Sex, you mean?"

"Yes. I mean sex."

"Oh, come on. He did…want me. Nine months ago. But now…"

"He wants you," said Tess patiently. "And I am not talking about nine months ago. I am talking about what I saw on his face last night."

"You imagined it."

"No, I didn't." Tess glanced up in mid-stitch. "And you *do* love *him.*"

Lacey considered a lie of denial and rejected the idea. Tess would know a lie when she heard one. Lacey looked out, over the yard, past the silvery foliage of the Russian olive tree growing in the center of the driveway, to the rolling green land that would soon parch to gold beneath the summer sun. "I'm not going to marry him." She said it very softly.

"Excuse me?"

Lacey turned back to the shade of the porch. A fly buzzed near her ear. She waved it away. "I said, I'm not going to marry him."

Tess kept her gaze on her mending, but a smile curved her mouth. "He's a fine man. And he cares for you. He wants you as a man wants a woman. And you love him. It's enough."

"Enough for what?"

"Enough for a start. Enough to build on. That's all that's really needed at the first in a marriage, if the two people are honorable. If they're willing to persist."

Lacey peered more closely at her cousin's wife. "You sound as though you're talking from experience."

"I am. Zach and I started out with a strictly practical arrangement. He needed a wife. And I needed…a place like this ranch. Somewhere to call home."

Lacey let out a short laugh of pure disbelief. "You and Zach? You're kidding. I can see when he looks at you how he feels. And when you look at him…"

A sweet pink blush crept upward over Tess's soft cheeks. "Yes. But it wasn't always that way."

Bracing her hand more firmly beneath her heavy stomach, Lacey lowered her feet to the porch boards. "Well. Call me a fool. Call me a romantic. But I want to have my husband's love when I marry him."

"Ah, but not just *any* husband. You want Logan Severance's love."

Right then, as if the forces of nature had some vested interest in proving Tess's point, a gust of wind blew down the porch. It ruffled back the cover on Lacey's sketch pad. The drawing Lacey had just been working on—of Logan napping in the cabin—was right there for Tess to see. She glanced at it.

"Very nice," she said.

Lacey stepped forward, flipped the cover in place and turned the pad over so the cardboard backing would hold it shut. "All right. So it's Logan's love I want. So what? Sometimes people can't have what they want."

"That's true. And they certainly will never get what they want if they don't even try."

"And just how do you suggest that I 'try'?"

Tess took a few more perfect stitches, her head tipped thoughtfully to the side. When she pulled the thread through for the third time, she spoke. "Marry him. Build a life with him. Raise that baby together. Give love a place to grow."

*Give love a place to grow.* What a captivating idea.

Too captivating. "That might work for some couples. But not for Logan and me. There are just a hundred ways we don't mesh."

"And those ways are?"

"Well, for starters, at least with me, he can be unbelievably overbearing."

"And you're a born rebel. Your lives will never be dull."

"You don't understand, Tess. You don't know. He is a fine man, just as you said. But I'm not…wife material. Not the kind of wife Logan's always wanted, anyway."

"You will be an excellent wife. You're strong and good-hearted and full of life. Logan Severance is a lucky man to have your love."

Lacey shook her head. "Tess, you're not listening. It simply can't work."

"Shall I tell you what my wise old Aunt Matilda used to say?"

"I'll pass."

Tess chuckled. "Listen up."

"Oh, all right. Go ahead."

"Whether you think you can or you think you *can't*—you're right."

Logan, Zach and Jobeth returned about half an hour later. Tess went in and brought out a pitcher of lemonade and five tall iced glasses. For a while, they all sat together on the porch. Logan asked questions about what he'd seen on his afternoon tour and Zach answered him in that low, pleasant drawl of his.

Lacey sat in the rocker, sipping lemonade and sometimes sketching, listening to the others talk. Now and then Logan would glance her way. Their eyes would meet and she'd find herself thinking about what Tess had said.

*Marry him. Raise that baby together. Give love a place to grow....*

Somehow, right then, in the shade of her cousin's porch on a hot summer afternoon, Tess's lovely, impossible words sounded like excellent advice. Lacey felt good, lazy and content and happy with the world and her own rather insecure place in it.

Even the ache in her back wasn't that bad, though sometimes it did seem to reach around, feeling like thin yet powerful fingers, and squeeze at her distended abdomen. She wondered, as she sat there idly rocking, if she might be having contractions—and then decided that if she was, there was nothing urgent about them. They came irregularly and were never less than ten or fifteen minutes apart.

Edna strolled across the yard with the baby at a little after five and Starr came spinning down the driveway in a dusty sports car a few minutes later.

Tess picked up her mending and her cloth-covered sewing box and stood. "I think it's time I started thinking about getting some food on the table. Lacey? Logan? I hope you'll join us."

"Yes," said Edna. "Please stay. There is plenty."

So they stayed. They walked back to the cabin together at twilight. Logan insisted on carrying her big shoulder tote, which Lacey took everywhere so she'd always have her sketchpads and pencils with her if she needed them.

He reached for her hand halfway down the dirt road and she gave it to him. In fact, she wrapped the fingers of her other hand around his arm and leaned in close. He felt so solid and good, someone she could always lean against and know that he could take the weight.

She chuckled to herself.

He turned, smiled. "What?"

"I was just thinking that you're great for leaning on."

She regretted the words as soon as they were out of her mouth, certain that he would consider them nothing short of an invitation to start in about marriage again.

But he surprised her. He only squeezed her hand, murmured, "Lean all you want," and kept walking.

When they got to the cabin, he made the same suggestion he had the night before, that they sit outside for a while. And this time she accepted his invitation.

They sat on the step and listened to the coyotes howl at the risen moon and hardly talked at all. Talking didn't seem necessary, somehow.

When they went in, Lacey showered first, standing under the arching shower pipe that had been added on to the claw-footed tub. As the water cascaded over her swollen body, it occurred to her that never once since breakfast had he used the dreaded "M" word.

Was that progress?

She didn't know. And she didn't really even care. The day had been a good one, all in all. And she *was* a born grasshopper, someone who knew how to take each day as it came.

She was in bed by ten, listening to Logan's movements in the main part of the cabin, practicing her pregnant-lady exercises, and wishing that the pain in her back would go away. She felt a little keyed up, and her legs were cramping just a bit. She expected another mostly sleepless night.

But surprisingly, she dropped off around eleven.

She woke at one in the morning. She sat straight up in bed as a powerful contraction gripped her. She groaned, a loud, animal sound, one she couldn't have held back if she'd tried.

The light went on in the main room.

Lacey hardly noticed. The contraction lasted forever, a vise of pressure, gripping, holding, not letting go. She went on groaning and tried to breathe, to relax, to go with the pain.

"Lace?"

A strong hand pushed back the curtain to the main room. Lacey found herself staring into Logan's midnight eyes.

He didn't speak. She was grateful for that. She closed her eyes and moaned some more until the contraction finally loosed its grip on her.

Then she realized that the bed was wet. She pushed back the covers. The sweet smell of amniotic fluid drifted up to her nostrils.

She met Logan's eyes again. "The baby's coming," she said. "The baby's coming right now."

# *Chapter Five*

Logan was so calm.

He led her out to the bathroom and gently took away her sodden sleep shirt. She had another contraction right then, standing there naked on the bathroom rug. She sank to her knees.

Logan knelt beside her and gave her his hand. She gripped it as hard as she could while he whispered to her, "Relax, now. Breathe…and relax…"

She let out another of those animal groans. "I have to push, Logan. I have to—"

"No. Don't push. We need to see what's really going on first. Don't push yet. Pant. Come on, short, fast breaths."

She panted. "It was only…" Another groan escaped. "Only two or three minutes, since the last one…"

"It's all right. Everything's fine. Everything's all right."

She panted. She groaned. Great, deep, rumbling, animal groans. When finally the huge invisible hands on her belly relaxed a little, Logan said very gently, "Come on. Let's rinse you off. You'll feel better…"

There were two sets of taps in the old claw-footed tub, one to the tub itself and another for the shower. He turned on the lower ones and helped her climb in over the tub's high, curved sides. She shot him a look of alarm as she noted the red streaks on the inside of her thighs. "There's some blood…"

"It's only bloody show. Perfectly normal. I saw it in the bed, too. But no meconium staining that I can see." He tested the water. "Damn. Still cold. Wait just a minute, sweetheart."

Sweetheart. Even now, naked and huge in front of the man she loved, sweating and confused and expecting the next unbearable contraction to descend any second now, *sweetheart* sounded so good.

"Meconium?" Her befuddled mind tried to place the word.

"Greenish-brown fluid. From the baby's digestive tract. It can sometimes indicate fetal distress."

"But there isn't any, right?"

"No. No meconium. And that's good." He tested the water again. "Okay. The water's running warm enough. Come on." They cupped water in their hands and splashed it over her, together rinsing the sticky fluid from her belly and her thighs.

Then Logan said, "I think we should use soap, just in case…"

She stared at him and it hit her all over again. Her baby was coming and it was coming fast.

She picked up the soap and washed herself thoroughly. Logan soaped his hands as well. Then together, they splashed on more water, rinsing her clean—and it happened again. Another contraction. She squatted right there in the tub, threw back her head and howled.

It lasted a lifetime, but when it finally eased a little and she came back to herself, Logan had found the rubbing alcohol and was dousing his hands with it. He rinsed again and gave her a reassuring smile. "Lie back. Let's have a look…"

He examined her, right there in the tub. And when he was done, he asked, "How far is the hospital?"

"Uh…I don't know. Twenty miles or so."

He swore, but very gently.

"What?"

"I'm not sure you can make it."

"Oh, Logan…" She wanted to be braver, but it was a cry of distress.

"Listen." His voice was a soothing caress. "Everything is normal. The baby's in the right position. You are completely effaced. And you are fully dilated. Do you know what that means?"

"Ready to push, right? But how is that possible?"

"When it comes to having babies, almost anything is possible. And I don't think it's a good idea to ask you to try and hold back for the time it will take to get you to the hospital." He picked up the soap again and began scrubbing his hands for the second time. "You might succeed, but you could slow things down and only make it more difficult in the end. Or you might *not* succeed. And you'd end up having the baby on the side of the road. It's better, I think, if we stay here—at least till help arrives."

She'd been sweating a moment ago, now she was shivering all of a sudden, shaking all over.

Logan grabbed a towel, dried his hands and turned on the space heater in the corner by the door. Then he came back and began pulling towels off the shelf. He knelt, wrapped them around her, and rubbed at her shoulders to get the circulation going. "Better?"

"A little."

"Where's the phone number for your doctor—and the one for the main house?"

She told him.

He turned for the door.

Absolute terror gripped her. "Oh, God. Logan. Don't go…"

"I'll be right back. It won't be three minutes, I swear to you. And maybe I'll get lucky and get through on the cell phone."

She bit her lip and tasted blood—but she kept her mouth shut when he left her.

A minute passed. She knew because she counted the seconds. And then she didn't count anymore because the next contraction claimed her. She rose onto her haunches, grabbed the sides of the tub again and rode it as it crested and finally waned.

Then Logan was kneeling beside her, wrapping a blanket around her. "I got through. They're sending an ambulance. Forty-five minutes tops, they said. And Tess will be here in ten with the things we're going to need." He bent over her. "Do you want to get out of the tub?"

She stared at his lips, wondering why he was asking her that. "I don't…"

He smiled at her reassuringly and stroked the side of her face. His hand felt so good, so solid, warm and real.

"This·is a pretty big tub. You could just stay here, if you want, until Tess arrives with the things to get the bed ready."

She shivered some more, but not as badly as before. The little room was getting warmer. "I'd like…to walk for a bit."

"Sounds good." He helped her from the tub.

Lacey clutched the blanket around her and they trudged back and forth in the short space between the tub and the door—until another contraction doubled her over.

Logan went down to the floor with her again. He whispered to her to breathe, not to push yet, just to wait a little while. She groaned and tried to do what he said, to hold back. At the same time, she wanted to shove him away, to shout at him that she was the one doing this and she'd push if she wanted to.

By the time the contraction passed, she was sweating again. She threw off the blanket and asked for a clean sleep shirt.

"Where?"

"Top bureau drawer."

He left her for the second time. She didn't mind as much as before. Some change had come over her. Some strange, calm feeling. She would do this. She would get through this. She—and her baby—would be fine.

"Tess is here," Logan said when he came back. Lacey was kneeling on the rug again then, her forehead against the rim of the sink basin. The only response she could give him right then was a groan.

He waited for the contraction to ease, then helped her up. "Here." He settled the shirt over her head and she put her arms through the sleeves. "Tess is getting the bed ready and making the fire."

"Don't need…the fire. I'm sweating. Can't you see?"

He smiled and got a washcloth and wet it with cool water.

She sighed when he wiped her face with it. "Heaven…"

Or it was, for a few too-brief moments. Then another contraction struck. She got through it, and then two more after that, relaxing into them as if they were waves—waves that rolled in, rolled through her, then rolled away. They didn't seem to hurt so much as before, though in a way they felt stronger, more focused, more purposeful, somehow.

Finally, Tess stuck her head in the bathroom door. "All ready."

"Then let's go," Logan said.

They went into the cabin, where Tess had removed the curtain that separated the sleeping nook from the rest of the room. The bed had only a white sheet on it, and a number of pillows. There was a stack of towels and one of the receiving blankets on the edge of the bed and a basin of water on a chair.

When Lacey crawled onto the bed, the sheet crackled. Tess had thought to put plastic—a tablecloth or a shower curtain, probably—between the mattress and the sheet. She helped Lacey to arrange the pillows against the headboard, so she could lie in a semi-sitting position, as Logan went to wash his hands again.

"Thirsty?" Tess smiled at her.

Lacey nodded. Tess had a full pitcher of water right by the bed. She filled a glass and Lacey sipped. Then Logan came back and examined her again.

She looked at his dark head between her spread

thighs and couldn't help remarking, "I feel so utterly demure."

He glanced up and winked at her. "Always have been."

She thought, I have never loved you so much as I do at this moment.

"Ready to push," he said.

Lacey grunted. "This is news?"

He and Tess both chuckled, but Lacey hardly noticed. She felt the contraction coming. And she wrapped her hands around her thighs and bore down.

"Do what you feel," Logan said softly. "Bear down until you can't hold your breath any longer. Then take in another one…and bear down again. Let it go, let it happen."

She let out a loud moan. "Logan, I can do this. Just let me…"

He said something gentle in reply. But she didn't really hear it. She had a job to do and, miraculously, she knew how to do it. She sucked in a giant breath and bore down, groaning without shame. When she ran out of breath, she sucked in more and bore down again.

She felt strong, and sure. It wasn't that bad. It wasn't bad at all. And between contractions, she actually rested, with Logan and Tess attending her, letting her wet her lips with cool water, rubbing her back and neck when she would allow that, pressing damp cloths to her sweating brow and the back of her neck.

When the contractions came, she heard them talking, heard it when Tess cried, "There it is. The baby's head. I can see it."

But Tess—and Logan, too—seemed far away to her. The world to her was the hard fist of her contractions, the rising of her uterus and then the bearing down.

"Scoot down now," Logan said, during one of the blessed moments when her body allowed her to rest.

They had put a pair of chairs at the end of the bed. Lacey moved down to them. Logan instructed her to brace her feet, one on each chair. Tess set a basin between the chairs and tucked pillows at Lacey's back and shoulders to help her stay in the most effective position to push the baby out.

When the next contraction hit, Logan said, "This is it. Easy. Pant. Blow. Don't push too hard…"

Lacey made a deep, growling sound. The pressure became almost unbearably intense as her body gave to let the head emerge. Tess said, "Oh!" in a voice full of wonder.

Logan had his hands down there, applying a gentle counter-pressure. "Slow," he said, "careful, not too fast…"

Seconds later, the intense pressure eased.

"The head is out," Logan said.

Lacey looked down at the red, smashed-looking thing between her legs. "Oh, dear Lord. Is it all right?"

"It's fine," Logan said. "The baby's fine. And you are fine. We have no tearing. No tearing at all." His hands worked at the sides of the squashed nose and downward, gently stroking, over the tiny, ugly chin, and the wrinkled throat. Fluid dribbled from the baby's mouth and nose.

"There," Logan said.

"There what?" Lacey demanded.

"That should clear out any mucus that might be obstructing the airways. Now we're ready to let those shoulders out. Are you ready to push again?"

Lacey panted and nodded.

He cradled the baby's head, oh so gently, in his two strong hands. "Okay, push now, push…" She pushed and he lifted the head. "There," he said, "Yes. The lower shoulder is free…"

After that, it was over in less than a minute. Baby and fluids gushed out in a rush. She heard a cry—her baby's cry.

"It's a girl," Logan said. "A beautiful, little girl."

Logan didn't cut the umbilical cord. He said he would leave that for the EMTs, who would have the proper equipment. He wiped most of the blood and fluids from the body of the squirming baby, examining her as he did it, and then pronounced her "a perfect ten."

Tess helped Lacey to scoot back up onto the bed, where she could rest, at last, fully on her back. Lacey pulled up her sleep shirt and Logan gave her the ugly, wonderful baby to lay on her bare breast.

Lacey looked down at the tiny, whining creature with the slightly pointy head, still connected to her body by the pulsing cord, and knew that her life was unutterably changed.

Logan was bending over them both.

And Tess had made herself scarce, somewhere over by the sink.

Lacey spent a moment touching her baby, whispering to her, stroking her warm, mottled skin. Then from the little one, she reached up and touched the side of Logan's face.

At her breast, her baby rooted fitfully. Lacey tried to help her find the nipple, but she didn't quite manage to latch on and stay there.

"She'll learn," Logan said.

"I want to call her Margaret," Lacey told him. "For my mother." She laughed, and then groaned a little, as a mild contraction squeezed her tired abdomen. "My mother was a wonderful woman. And I know that for a few years there, I made her life a living hell. Maybe she'll look down from heaven and see this little angel and be glad she had me, after all."

"I think she's glad," Logan said. "In fact, I know it." Then he murmured, "Margaret," in a musing tone. He nodded. "I like it."

"And *your* mother…?" she asked. "What was her name?" Logan's mother had died when he was six months old. His father, lost to a first heart attack about five years ago, had raised him alone.

"Rose," Logan said. "Her name was Rose."

Lacey stroked her baby's slightly sticky head. "Margaret Rose, then. What do you think?"

She had never seen his eyes look so soft—or so very dark. "Yes," he said. "All right. Margaret Rose."

"Rosie, for short."

"Rosie it is." He put down his index finger. It brushed Lacey's bare breast and then Rosie's wrinkled red fist. Tiny perfect fingers opened—and closed, holding on.

"She's strong," Logan said in a voice low with emotion. "Strong and healthy. Lace, you did a hell of a job."

"Praise? From you—directed at me? Are you feeling all right?"

"I don't think I've ever felt better in my life."

The words were there, in her heart, rising up, undeniable.

She didn't know why she'd ever cared to deny them. Why she'd ever thought it wise to hide the truth from him.

All her old fears and hesitations, her need to guard her independence and protect her woman's pride, seemed foolish now. She didn't need to deny her love anymore, not after what she'd just been through—what all three of them had been through: she and Logan and this tiny miracle who lay rooting at her breast, clutching Logan's index finger, making soft, mewling sounds.

"I love you, Logan," she whispered.

His eyes grew softer still. He started to speak. She put her hand to his lips. "Shh. It's okay. It's just… I wanted you to know. I've known for nine months. It's been my big secret. But it seems kind of silly now, after this, to go on keeping it. It seems like the best thing just to let you know."

He nodded, and pressed his lips to her temple. They sighed together and their daughter gave a small, impatient cry.

A few minutes later, the ambulance pulled up in the yard.

# Chapter Six

Dr. Pruitt arrived with the ambulance. He clamped and cut the umbilical cord. Then he supervised as Lacey pushed out the afterbirth. He performed a formal post-natal exam and weighed the baby: seven pounds, two ounces. He also examined Lacey.

When he was done, he confirmed what everyone already knew: mother and daughter were doing just fine. He said he saw no need for a hospital visit, especially when he learned that the baby's father was a doctor and would be in close attendance over the next twenty-four hours.

The ambulance drove away less than an hour after it had arrived, at a little after three in the morning. Tess suggested a move to the main house, but Lacey vetoed that. She had Logan to look after her and Rosie. And the little cabin somehow seemed like home now. She wanted to stay there, for the next few days at least, just the three of them.

And then…well, she'd worry about that when the time came.

Tess called Zach on the cell phone and instructed him to pile all the baby equipment into the pickup and bring it on over.

"We're keeping everyone awake tonight," Lacey said ruefully, after Tess had hung up.

Tess waved a hand. "We are ranchers," she said. "We're used to being up all hours of the night."

Lacey and Logan took Rosie to the bathroom. Logan held the baby while Lacey showered and changed into a nightgown that buttoned down the front. Then Lacey rested, sitting on the rug with the commode to lean against, as Logan gave Rosie her first bath—which amounted to a few gentle strokes with a warm wash-cloth.

When they got back to the main room, Tess had changed the sheets again and put up the curtain that made the sleeping nook into its own private space. Lacey climbed gratefully onto the bed and drank two glasses of cool water as Logan, over at the daybed, put on Rosie's first diaper. Tess helped Lacey to get com-fortable. Then Logan laid their daughter beside her. The baby rooted at her breast. This time, the little dar-ling actually managed to latch on.

"Let her nurse for five minutes or so on that side," Tess said. "They we'll try the other one."

By the time Logan and Tess tiptoed out, Lacey was as deep in sleep as Rosie. She didn't even hear them bring in all the baby things.

* * *

Lacey woke when Rosie did, about three hours after she'd fallen asleep.

She looked down at the fuzzy, misshapen little head of her daughter and groused, "You aren't going to turn out to be a day person like your father, are you?"

Rosie opened her tiny mouth—first for a big yawn, and right after that, to let out a wail.

The curtain slid back and Logan was there, looking tired and rumpled and absolutely wonderful. "Good morning."

Lacey gave him a smile with all of her newly revealed love in it. "This baby is hungry."

"That's the way babies are. What about you?"

"I'm starved. But I think she's going to insist on eating first. Let's try it in the rocker this time."

It was quite an experience, getting out of that bed. Lacey's body felt as if she'd done something horrible to it—like go through childbirth. Her uterus was still cramping, everything lower down ached from all that pushing—and the last thing she ever wanted to do again was to stand up straight.

Logan chuckled. "I hope you don't feel as bad as you look."

She moaned and muttered under her breath, "Men. And all they'll never have to suffer…"

"I do sympathize."

"Why doesn't that help?"

She left him to comfort the squalling Rosie as she hobbled outside to the bathroom, where she used the facilities, changed her menstrual pad and then forced herself to straighten her spine. Every overworked muscle protested. But she did it. And she stayed upright all the way back to the main room.

Logan built up last night's fire and got started on the breakfast as Lacey and Rosie practiced nursing. By the time she'd changed the baby—on the bureau/changing table that Zach had brought over while she was sleeping—Logan was cracking eggs into a pan.

"How many?" he asked.

"Four."

He laughed. "I see you've gotten over your aversion to eggs."

"And toast, please. And juice and some of that applesauce that's up in the cupboard. And maybe, after that, a big bowl of cereal..."

Tess and Edna arrived at a little after ten. By then, Rosie had been through three diaper changes and two more short nursing sessions. Between the feeding and the changing, Lacey faded in and out of a drowsy half-sleep. She felt sore and tired and utterly content, with her baby in her arms and Logan to take care of them both.

Tess and Edna told Lacey she was not to get up. She ignored them and pulled on her robe. "I need to move around a little." She tried not to groan as she pulled herself straight for the walk across the floor to the rocking chair.

The visitors each held Rosie, cooing over her shamelessly and declaring her the most beautiful child they'd ever seen.

Lacey couldn't help laughing—which hurt her poor tummy. "Why is it people always say that new babies are beautiful? They have rashy red skin and squashed faces and this one even has a point on the top of her head."

Edna was holding Rosie right then. She clucked her tongue and rocked back and forth. "There, there," she told the baby, "don't you listen to Mommy. She knows you're beautiful. She just doesn't want you to become vain about it. And don't you worry about this point on your head. It won't be there for long." She stroked Rosie's fuzzy head. "Of course, Jobeth and Starr can't wait to meet you…"

Tess added, smiling at Lacey, "We told them maybe tomorrow, after you've both had a little more time to recuperate."

When they were through fussing over the baby, they handed her back to Lacey and enlisted Logan's aid in making up a grocery list. "We're going into town this afternoon," Edna said. "We'll pick up whatever you need. Anything else we can do?"

*Jenna,* Lacey thought. She stopped her lazy rocking. Over eight hours since Rosie had come into the world and her Aunt Jenna didn't even know that the momentous event had occurred.

Lacey shot a swift, guilty glance at Logan—and then instantly wondered what was the matter with her. She was not going to put off sharing the wonderful news with her sister just because the mention of Jenna's name might cause Logan a little emotional discomfort.

She spoke firmly. "You can take me over to the main house for a few minutes. I need to make a phone call to Florida, to give Jenna and Mack the news."

Edna frowned in disapproval. "But don't you have one of those portable phones?"

Lacey put Rosie on her shoulder, pushed herself

from the rocker and drew her sore body up tall. "I hate to use a cell phone. When it does work, it tends to cut in and out. And then there's an irritating delay on and off, too. It's no fun trying to talk on it, especially for something like this. Logan, if you'll take the baby, I'll just get into some clothes and then—"

Edna clucked her tongue and bustled over. "You sit back down, young lady. You're in no shape to go traipsing down the road right yet."

Logan and Tess stayed where they were, over by the counter. Neither of them spoke—Logan for reasons Lacey didn't really want to examine. And Tess…well, Lacey had told her about Logan's feelings for Jenna just yesterday. No doubt Tess didn't know what to say.

But Edna was blithely ignorant of the emotional minefield they were forging across here. "Why don't you let Logan or Tess make the call for you right now? Then you can call again yourself in a day or two, when you're feeling up to it."

Tess finally decided to speak up. "Uh, Edna, I think Lacey wants to be the one to give her sister the big news."

Lacey sent Zach's wife a grateful smile. "Yes, I do. I want to tell her myself. And if you'll just drive me over there and then drive me back…please. It won't take long. I'm sure I'm up to it."

She glanced Logan's way again. His face betrayed nothing—not the usual concern for her welfare, and certainly not whatever emotions all this talk about Jenna called up in him. "Logan, do you think you could look after Rosie on your own for a little while?"

He did move then. He strode toward her. "I think I can handle it." His voice, like his expression, gave her nothing. But at least he wasn't trying to talk her out of it. He took Rosie from her, carefully laying a diaper and then the baby on his broad shoulder.

Lacey found herself staring at his fine, large hands, thinking how small—and how safe—their daughter looked cradled in them. Her love was an ache right then. It filled her with warmth—and it hurt, too.

"Great," Lacey said brightly. "I'll be dressed in a flash."

Tess let Lacey use the phone in Zach's office, off the dining room, where she could close the door and enjoy complete privacy.

Her sister answered on the second ring. Just the sound of that soft, clear voice brought tears to Lacey's eyes.

"Hello?"

"Jen. It's me."

"Lace. Hello."

Lacey closed her eyes, picturing her big sister's gorgeous wide-open smile. Nobody smiled quite like Jenna. Nobody in the world.

Lacey said, "So tell me. How are you feeling?"

Jenna laughed. "Great. Considering I'm as big as a house. How about you?"

Lacey breathed deep. "Well, let me put it this way. *I'm* not quite as big today as I was yesterday."

Jenna gasped. "The baby? You had the—"

"Yes. This morning at about two. A baby girl. Seven pounds, two ounces."

"Omigod. I can't believe it. How do you feel? Are you okay? You're calling from the hospital, then? And the baby. How is the baby?"

"We're both fine. I'm at the main ranch house now. Tess brought me over, to call you. We never made it to the hospital. I had the baby in the cabin."

"Oh, dear Lord. You didn't."

"I did. It all happened really fast. I went to sleep at around eleven last night and I woke up when my water broke, two hours later. And an hour after that, I was holding my baby in my arms. And she's perfect. Absolutely beautiful…even if she is the ugliest thing I've ever seen."

Jenna was laughing and sighing at the same time. "Oh, Lace. I…I don't have the words. Hold on. I have to tell Mack."

Lacey heard her sister call her husband, then the excited exchange of information. Then Mack came on the line. "Congratulations, sister-in-law."

She smiled. "Thanks, Mack."

"Take it easy, now. Get lots of rest."

"Yeah. With a newborn. Right."

"Well, get as much rest as you can, at least—and I have to go now. Jenna's trying to rip the phone out of my hands."

"Bye, Mack."

"Take care."

"Tell me you named her after Mother—" it was Jenna again "—that you didn't forget what we agreed."

"How could I forget? If I had a girl, she'd be Margaret. If I didn't and *you* did, then my *niece* would be Margaret. I did. So she's Margaret. Margaret Rose. We're calling her Rosie."

"Rosie. I like it."

It didn't even occur to Lacey to dissemble. Not with Jenna. She could tell Jenna anything. "Maybe you remember. Rose was Logan's mother's name."

"Of course I remember. And I think it's a good choice."

Lacey gulped. "He's here, Jenna."

A pause. "You mean Logan?"

"Uh-huh."

"You finally told him."

"And he came right away."

"Naturally. Oh, Lace. I'm so glad you did it."

"You know what? So am I."

"Will you marry him? He *has* asked you, hasn't he?"

"Demanded is more like it. I told him no. About a hundred times. I finally got him to back off on the subject, as a condition of letting him stick around."

"So what are you saying? You won't marry him? You're firm on that?"

"Oh, Jen. I *was* firm. At first. But he's been...so incredibly supportive. Right with me through everything. True and steady, you know how he is. The kind of man you can lean on, count on, through the toughest times, no matter what."

"Yes. Yes, I do know."

"A total ant."

"What?"

Lacey laughed. "Oh, nothing." And then she felt her smile fade. She clutched the phone tighter. "I...I told him. That I love him."

"That's good."

"You think so?"

"Absolutely."

"He still loves you, Jenna."

"Did he say that?"

"No, but I know he does."

"You're assuming."

"Stop. You sound like Tess."

"You talked with Tess about it? What did she say?"

"She said I should say yes. That Logan and I should get married and I should…give love a place to grow."

Jenna sighed. "Give love a place to grow. I like that."

"So do I. Probably too much. Having a baby has turned me into a sentimental fool."

"You love him. He wants to marry you. He will be good to you, Lacey. I know that he will. And if he doesn't know that he loves you now, he'll figure it out, if you give it time."

"But he *doesn't* love me. He loves—"

"Lace."

"What?"

"I want you to listen to me. Listen to me closely."

Lacey shifted the phone to her other ear and grumbled, "What?"

"I know that man."

"I'm aware of that."

"Don't become defensive. Please."

Lacey shifted the phone back where she'd had it before. "All right. I'm sorry. It's a sensitive subject for me."

"I know. And maybe you don't want to hear this now. Is that it? You had a baby a few hours ago and the last thing you need right now is a lecture from your big sister."

"You know, that's true, I really don't want to hear it. I'll probably never want to hear it. But I probably *should* hear it, for my own good, right?"

"Does that mean you're listening?"

"Yes. Go on. I can take it."

Jenna let a moment of silence elapse. Then she

started over. "I know Logan. And I tried, for so long, to love him the way that you do, because I thought that he and I were right for each other. He thought so, too. And when Logan Severance gets an idea in his head, well, you know what he's like."

Lacey made a noise of agreement. "Do I ever. Certain words come to mind—'relentless' among them."

"Exactly. He never gives up. And he's loyal until death. These are wonderful qualities. But they can also make it so a man can't see the nose in front of his face."

Lacey couldn't help interjecting, "The man is bull-headed."

Her sister thoroughly agreed. "That would be the word. You know how he was in high school. Every girl's dream. Handsome to die for, kind to everyone and her mother, and destined for professional success. Even after he and I started going steady, all the other girls were after him. Some of them were shameless. But I never felt jealous. I knew he had made up his mind to love me and he wouldn't even look twice at any of them. He didn't. In fact, there's only one other woman he ever seemed to pay more attention to than he did to me."

Lacey had been wrapping the phone cord slowly around her finger. She pulled it free. "Logan? Give more than the time of day to a woman who wasn't you? Never."

"Yes, he did."

"Who?"

"You."

Lacey let out a low cry of disbelief. "That's ridiculous."

"No. Think about it. He was always and forever asking about you. Sometimes it used to really get on my nerves." Jenna cleared her throat and imitated Logan's deep voice. "'How's Lacey? Don't tell me she's run away again? When is she going to take her schoolwork more seriously? Don't you think it's about time she stopped getting into trouble? She needs a college education. And I think we ought to talk to her about getting herself a real job…' And on and on and on. I'm telling you, it never stopped."

Lacey couldn't see how that added up to proof of Logan's romantic interest in her. "He was just playing big brother, that's all."

"He took the role a little too seriously, if you ask me. In fact, in retrospect, it seems to me that he took it *way* too seriously. Did it ever occur to you that maybe he's been crazy about you for years now and he's just too obstinate to admit that he chose the wrong sister? After all, he's Logan Severance. And Logan Severance is perfect. He doesn't make mistakes."

"Jen. I always got on his nerves. He wanted to reform me."

"He wanted to do a lot more than reform you—he just wouldn't admit it to himself."

"Wait a minute. I'm starting to see the light here. You're saying all this because you think I should say yes to him."

"I'm saying it because I think it's true."

"You know, I can't help recalling what I told you last September—that if I thought Logan loved me, then nothing could keep me away from him."

"Lace. I have not made all this up to get you to marry him. I honestly haven't. I've been thinking a lot about this and I truly believe there's something to it. *You're* the one Logan really wants."

"And *you* are my big sister, who loves me and thinks I'd be better off if I married the nice, handsome, stable M.D. who is the father of my baby—even if he *is* still in love with you."

Jenna let out a grunt of pure frustration. "I could easily become perturbed with you. He's not in love with me. He only thinks he is."

Lacey wasn't buying. "And what *is* love anyway, but something you think? Where else does it exist…except in a person's mind, in whatever it is we call the 'heart'?"

"No," Jenna said. "I'm sorry. I can't agree with you on that."

"What's not to agree with?"

"Most of all, love is what you *do*. It's a verb. An action word. If you really love, you behave in a loving way."

That hit home. Lacey stared out the window at the side yard, where a few of Tess's chickens pecked the ground. In the distance, off to the northwest, the snowy crests of the Big Horn Mountains reflected back the morning sun.

If love came down to action, she could find no fault with the way that Logan Severance "loved" her. As soon as she'd told him about the baby, he'd put his life and his work on hold to come to her. He'd looked after her from the moment of his arrival here. He'd delivered their baby, and he'd done a beautiful job of it. Now, he was back at the cabin, watching the baby, while she broke the news of the birth to her sister—who also just happened to be the woman who had left him for another man.

"Lace. You still there?"

"I'm here."

"Will you just think about what I said?"

"Yes. I will. I'll think about it."

"I do understand how *you* are, too, Lace. How important your independence is to you, how you've never been one to take the traditional way. Maybe the real issue here is that marriage just isn't for you."

"I never said marriage wasn't for me. I've always thought I *would* marry. Someday. When the right man came along."

"To me it seems pretty obvious that Logan *is* the right man."

"I'm getting that loud and clear."

Jenna took in a long breath and let it out slowly. "Listen. Remember how you told me once that there was something lukewarm between me and Logan?"

"Jenna—"

"Just bear with me for a minute more. Do you remember?"

"Yes. All right. I remember."

"And remember how you laughed when I admitted that Logan and I had never made love?"

"It surprised me, that's all."

"Because you couldn't imagine anyone passing up the chance to be in his arms. Am I right?"

"I didn't think that at the time. I swear."

"I know you didn't, not consciously. Then, he was *my* fiancé, after all. But now. Looking back on it. What do you think now?"

"All right," Lacey conceded reluctantly. "Maybe."

"Maybe what?"

"Jenna, you have made your point. And I really have to—"

"You have to go. I know. But please. Just think about what I've said."

"I will. I promise."

"Great. And kiss my niece for me."

"Will do."

"I can't wait to meet her."

"Soon," Lacey said, and felt a sudden tightness in her chest.

Would it really be soon? She and Jenna lived on opposite sides of the country now. Lacey had a new baby and Jenna was fast approaching her own delivery date. For a while, anyway, life itself would get in the way of their visiting each other.

And if Lacey did marry Logan...

Well, then, it would probably be awkward at best and awful at worst, for her and Logan to get together with Jenna and Mack.

"Soon," Lacey said again, in an effort to convince herself that she meant it.

"Yes," Jenna replied softly. "We'll have to get together soon...."

## *Chapter Seven*

When Tess drove her back to the cabin, Lacey made her cousin's wife let her off in the dusty turnaround out front. "I can walk to the door myself. I'm not an invalid."

Tess shook her head. "You're a wonder, that's what you are. A few hours out of childbed and you're strolling around the yard."

Lacey climbed down from the pickup slowly. "It's only ten yards to the door—and I don't think 'stroll' is exactly the word for it."

"You won't be mad if I just wait here until you get inside?"

"I guess I'll allow that." She *was* feeling a little tired. And the cramping in her uterus had increased a bit. She wanted to lie down and sleep for about a week.

"Edna and I will be back around five, with the groceries. And tell Logan not to cook. We'll bring something over."

"I'll tell him. And thanks. For everything."

"Any time."

Lacey hobbled toward the door. It opened before she got there and Logan came out.

Tess waved and drove off.

"You look beat," Logan said, as he took her arm.

"I'm a little tired, I admit." She leaned on him heavily, grateful for his solid strength, as he led her inside.

Miracle of miracles, Rosie was asleep. She lay on her side in her bassinet, making little sucking motions with her tiny pink mouth.

"I'm just going to go out to the bathroom for a minute," Lacey whispered. "And then I'll lie down."

Dark eyes narrowed. "Is something wrong?"

"I think I'm bleeding a little more than before."

She felt certain that he would reprimand her then, that he'd say she'd been foolish to insist on a visit to the main house just to call Jenna.

But he surprised her. He put his hand on her shoulder, a touch clearly meant to comfort. It had the intended effect. She did feel reassured. She put her hand over his and gave it a squeeze.

"Sometimes the bleeding can be pretty heavy," he said, "especially in the first few days. It's probably nothing to worry about. You can change your pad and put your nightgown back on and come lie down. You'll feel better after you've rested a while."

Logan was right. She did feel better after she'd rested. He brought her the baby about an hour later and he helped her to sit up against the pillows to nurse.

He didn't ask her what she and her sister had said to each other. He didn't mention the call to Jenna at all. Which was all right with her. Lacey didn't really want to discuss the call with him, anyway.

She was quiet as the day wore on.

She had a lot to think about. With Rosie in her arms and Logan by her side, she found herself beginning to see her life in a whole new light.

Perhaps, to an extent, she *had* been irresponsible— living day-to-day, taking things as they came. But now so much had changed.

Through the rest of the morning and into the afternoon, her sister's words stayed with her. She wondered, could they be true? Was she, Lacey, the one Logan *really* loved?

In any case, she certainly did admire Jenna's definition of the word—of it being what people *did* that mattered, not what they said, or even whatever secrets they kept hidden in their hearts.

And Jenna and Tess both thought she should say yes to Logan. Could two such wise and wonderful women be wrong?

That evening, Tess and Edna returned, but only long enough to carry in the groceries and put the dinner on the table. Once they were gone, Logan called to Lacey through the curtain, asking if she'd like him to serve her meal in bed.

"No way," she called back. "I'll eat at the table. This bed rest is getting to me."

"You're sure?"

"Positive. I'll be right out." She wrapped herself in her robe and joined him in the main room.

He was standing at the counter. "Look what I found." He held up two saucers. A plain votive candle was perched on each one. He carried the saucers to the table, set them in the center and produced a wooden match, which he struck with a flourish on the underside of the tabletop.

The sulfur tip hissed as the flame caught. "Dinner by candlelight," he announced as he lit one wick and then the other. He shook out the match. "There."

It was a whimsical gesture, something she never would have expected of him. He *was* a generous man and he knew what women liked. He used to send flowers to Jenna all the time. And during those five glorious days last September, he had taken Lacey out to dinner twice, each time to a fine restaurant, where there were always candles on the snowy linen tablecloth— not to mention champagne chilling in a silver bucket nearby.

But he'd never done a tender thing like this for her— to create a little impromptu romance at a rough pine table with a couple of squat white votives scrounged from a drawer.

It touched her. It touched her deeply.

He pulled out her chair for her and then, when they were seated with the candles glowing between them, he raised his big glass of milk to her in a toast.

"To the mother of my daughter," he said. "A woman with an independent mind and…unquenchable determination."

She laughed. "Independence and determination. I like it."

"I knew that you would."

She raised her glass and they drank at the same time.

Then she thought of a toast of her own. "To the father of my little girl. A man of…unflagging loyalty and truly staggering persistence."

"Loyalty and persistence." He saluted her by dipping his head. "Admirable qualities. Thank you."

She nodded. "You're welcome." They drank again.

When they set down their glasses, Lacey said softly, "Why do I know what's coming?"

He smiled rather ruefully. "You have to admit, I've shown admirable restraint for—what—at least forty-eight hours now?"

"Yes, Logan. You have."

"But my goal hasn't changed. And it does seem to me that maybe you've been rethinking my offer."

"You could be right."

"*Could* be?"

"You'll have to ask to find out."

He studied her face for a moment, then asked gravely, "Would I increase my chances for success if I went down on my knees?"

"Hmm…" She pretended to consider the question, but she didn't pretend for long. "I love to see a man down on his knees."

His expression remained solemn, though humor gleamed in his eyes. "I don't believe I'll comment on that remark."

"A wise decision. One you will not regret."

He set down his napkin and pushed back his chair. In two steps, he was standing beside her. He wore jeans and a dark knit shirt with a banded collar. She thought he had never looked more handsome. But then, every time she looked at him, she found herself thinking that he had never looked more handsome.

He dropped to one knee. "May I have your hand, please?"

She gave it. He bent his dark head. She felt the warm, quick brush of his lips against her knuckles.

Then he was staring up at her again, his eyes so dark, shining with—maybe not love—but something almost as good.

"Ms. Bravo."

She dipped her head and matched his teasingly formal tone, "Dr. Severance."

"Ms. Bravo, much has transpired between us in recent hours. So much, in fact, that my humble hopes have been raised once again."

She arched a brow at him. "Humble? Your hopes are *humble?*"

He gave her a quick, playful scowl—then resumed looking ardent once more. "I would like your hand in marriage, Ms. Bravo."

"No. Really?"

"Yes. Really."

She sucked in a big breath and let it out in a rush. "This is *such* a surprise."

He kissed her hand again. A lovely shiver traveled up her arm. "I can provide for you."

"Ah." She sighed some more, a couple of big, gusty ones. "You're a man with… prospects?"

"Better than that."

"Better?" She fluttered her eyelashes madly. "Do elaborate."

He made a big show of clearing his throat. "Well. All right. If you insist."

"I do. Most definitely. Don't be shy. Enumerate your assets."

"First let me say that my assets are…at your disposal."

"Oh, this is sounding better by the minute. Don't stop now. Go on, go on."

"Well, I own a house. And I've made wise investments."

"What about all that lovely money your father left you?"

"Yes. There's that, too."

"Hmm. This is good. Continue."

"I don't think I'd be exaggerating if I told you that I hold a position of respect in my community."

"Your community." She frowned. "That would be…Meadow Valley, California?"

"Yes. Meadow Valley. In California."

She allowed herself a slow, very significant grin. "I have something of a reputation myself, in Meadow Valley."

His fine mouth twitched, though he kept a straight face. "Yes, I've heard. But I'm willing to overlook that."

"Such a generous fellow you are, Dr. Severance."

"So I've been told…and where was I?"

"You hold a position of respect…"

"Ah, yes. In Meadow Valley. Also gainful employment."

"Always a plus."

"And then there's the fact that you've just had my baby. I don't think we should forget that."

She placed her hand, very delicately, over her stomach. "I promise you. I haven't forgotten."

"And then there are…those tender feelings I bear you."

Now *that* did sound good. "Tender feelings? I find

you are persuading me, Dr. Severance. You are quite wonderfully convincing."

He rose then, in one quick, easy movement. He looked down into her eyes and she watched his expression change, from one of playful devotion to something darker and hungrier.

He said her name. "Lace…"

A shudder ran through her.

"…come up here."

He tugged on her hand, pulling her out of her chair and into his strong arms. She groaned—because it hurt to stand up straight. And also because it felt so absolutely grand to be in his arms again at last.

"Marry me, damn it."

"Oh, Logan…"

He lowered his mouth. It touched hers. He said it again, breathing the words into her mouth. "Marry me."

And then he kissed her.

There was no one—no one—who kissed the way Logan kissed.

She had missed his kisses terribly. Sometimes, in the night, alone, during the months apart from him, she would wake and touch her mouth and remember….

She had thought, for all those long, long months, that she would never feel his kisses again.

But here she was. Feeling them. Taking them into herself, kissing him back.

Her lips felt deliciously bruised when he finally pulled away. She reached up, put her fingers against them.

He commanded for a third time, in a low, very controlled tone, "Marry me."

She opened her mouth to answer.

And from her bassinet in the corner, Rosie started crying.

Lacey moved instinctively toward the sound.

Logan gripped her arms, holding her with him. "Wait," he whispered, "maybe she'll just go back to sleep."

"No. I know that sound. She's hungry."

Heat still burned in his eyes, but one corner of his mouth kicked up in a wry half-smile. "You know that sound? Already?"

"'Fraid so."

"Just wait a minute, though. Just in case?"

"All right."

They waited, staring at each other like a pair of smitten lovers which, Lacey admitted to herself right then, was what they were.

Rosie went on wailing.

Finally, Logan shrugged. "All right." He let her go and she turned for the bassinet.

She waited until she was seated in the rocker with the baby at her breast before she looked up at Logan standing above her and softly whispered, "Yes."

# *Chapter Eight*

The next day, when Tess brought Jobeth and Starr over to see the baby, Lacey and Logan delivered their news.

"Oh, this is wonderful." Tess grabbed Lacey in a hug. "When will the ceremony be?"

"Right away," said Logan. "We'll get the blood tests tomorrow. And as soon as I can coax the results out of whoever runs the local lab, we'll pay a visit to the county courthouse—Wednesday or Thursday, that would be my guess."

But the women had other ideas. Surely Logan could wait a few days at least, until Lacey was recovered enough to enjoy her own wedding? And there really should be some sort of party, something small and simple, understandably, on such short notice. Something with only the family, but a real ceremony nonetheless....

* * *

On Monday morning, Logan drove into Buffalo and came back with a safety seat for Rosie. It took him half an hour to do it, but he finally got the thing properly strapped into the back of Lacey's SUV. Then he loaded mother and daughter into the vehicle and they went to the clinic in Medicine Creek, where Lacey and Logan had their blood tests and Dr. Pruitt produced Rosie's birth certificate, all ready for her parents to sign.

They got back to the cabin two hours after they'd left it. Lacey and the baby took a nap and Logan went to the main house, where he called his office and promised Dan Connery, one of his two overworked partners, that he'd be back in Meadow Valley the following week.

"The problem—whatever it is—is solved, then?" Dan asked, sounding more than a little put out about the whole thing.

Logan took full blame for his partner's frustration. He'd been far from forthcoming about why he'd suddenly found it imperative to fly off to Wyoming for an indefinite stay. He needed to sit down with Dan and Helen Sanderson, the third partner in the practice, and explain what had happened.

He wasn't looking forward to the task. He found the whole situation more than a little embarrassing.

After all, he *was* a doctor. A respected member of his community. A man others rightfully expected to uphold certain standards.

The way Logan saw it, a doctor should never have the bad judgment to become a father *before* he'd managed to marry the mother of his child. Certain…restraint was expected of a physician. And if a physician couldn't exercise restraint, well, he ought at least to know better than to slip up when it came to the use of contraception.

But Logan *had* slipped up. And Dan and Helen had a right to an explanation. There would no doubt be gossip anyway, when Logan returned to town with a new wife *and* a baby.

And then there was the fact that his bride just happened to be his ex-fiancée's younger sister—a younger sister who had once been well-known in Meadow Valley for her exploits as a troubled teen.

Yes, there would be talk. And his partners not only deserved to hear the truth from him, they had a right to hear it from him *first*.

He would see that they did. As soon as he returned.

"I'm…working things out, Dan," Logan said. "I'll explain everything, in detail, as soon as I get back."

"All right. Next Monday, then?"

Monday wouldn't work, and Logan knew it. He and Lacey were getting married on Saturday. There would be a party, which would mean some degree of stress for her. Better to give her Sunday to rest.

And then she had that new SUV of hers. He doubted she'd be willing to leave it in Wyoming. And really, with Rosie so young, it was probably wiser not to try flying anyway. So they'd be driving. That would take two days at least—no, again, he had to consider Rosie. Travelling with a baby could be very slow going. Better give it three.

"Let's say Thursday, to be on the safe side. I'll be driving back and should get in by Wednesday evening."

Dan agreed that Thursday would be all right, though he sounded far from thrilled about it. "Please don't make it any longer than that, Logan."

Sending a quick prayer heavenward that nothing would occur to make him into a liar, Logan promised he'd be there by a week from Thursday.

The next morning, Lacey drove to the main house—by herself this time—to call Jenna and tell her about the wedding.

Jenna was thoroughly pleased at the news. "I'm so glad, Lace. I really do think it's the best thing."

"Well, I hope so. Because I'm doing it."

"And what then? That big, beautiful house of Logan's in Meadow Valley?"

Lacey gulped. "Yep. Can you believe it? Wasn't I the one who swore I'd never move back to my hometown?"

"Never say never," Jenna teased.

"Ain't that the truth."

"And Meadow Valley is a beautiful place to live."

"Well, *you* always liked it there."

"It's kind of ironic." Jenna's voice held a wistful note. "All I ever wanted was to spend my life there. And all you ever wanted was to get out. And look at us now."

"No, Jen," Lacey said, "you wanted Mack more than you wanted to live in Meadow Valley. And me? Well, look who *I* ended up wanting."

Jenna laughed. "Mr. Meadow Valley himself. What did I tell you?"

Lacey was nodding. "Pure irony."

"You'll be all right," Jenna said. "You'll have the man you love and your baby. And there are four bedrooms in that house of Logan's—five if you include the upstairs family room. I'm sure one of them is going to make a great studio. You'll be totally absorbed in some new painting project again before you know it."

"Right," Lacey said. At that point, the idea of starting a new painting seemed far off in the distant future somewhere.

Which was nothing to worry about. After all, it had only been a few days since she'd had her baby. Right now, all she could think of was her child and her new life with Logan.

"Lace," Jenna said, "be happy. Take care of yourself."

Lacey promised that she would.

"Call me if you need me. Any time. For anything."

"I will. I promise."

After she hung up, Lacey realized that neither of them had brought up the idea of Jenna and Mack flying west for the wedding, though Mack was a multimillionaire who set his own schedule and Jenna's job right then consisted of renovating the old mansion they owned in Key West. They could have easily managed the trip.

But it wouldn't have been practical, Lacey told herself. It was such short notice, after all. And Jenna *was* seven months pregnant. Maybe she didn't feel up to any serious traveling at this point.

*It wouldn't have been practical....*

Lacey sat back in her cousin's leather desk chair and shook her head at the phoniness of her own excuses.

Practicality wasn't the issue.

The issue was that she didn't want the woman Logan had loved for fifteen years at her wedding—even if that woman did happen to be her own wonderful big sister.

Lacey had a feeling the idea didn't hold much appeal for Jenna, either. Or maybe Jenna was just being considerate and would have come in a minute if Lacey had only asked her.

Whatever.

Someday, they would all have to deal with this uncomfortable situation.

Someday.

But not right now.

Right now, there was too much to deal with already. A new baby. A new husband. A new life in her old hometown.

She got up from the chair, pushed it under the big desk and went out to thank Tess for the use of the phone.

All the local Bravos showed up for the wedding. Cash and Abby and their little boy, Tyler. And another cousin, Nate, who brought his wife Meggie and their toddler, Jason James. Meggie had a cousin of her own named Sonny. Sonny had a wife and two kids. They all came, too.

The honorable Reverend Applegate, who, as it turned out, had presided at the weddings of Cash and Abby *and* Tess and Zach, performed the ceremony. He kept it simple and brief.

Lacey gaped in disbelief when Logan slipped a diamond ring on her finger. Now, where had he found the time to go out and buy that? He must have read her thoughts in her expression, because he leaned close and whispered, "I bought it in Meadow Valley, the day before I flew out here to get you."

She stared down at the lovely bright stone glittering on her finger, then whispered back, "Pretty sure of yourself, weren't you?"

He answered with a question of his own. "Do you like it?"

And she had to confess, "I do. Oh, Logan. Thank you. I like it very much."

The Reverend Applegate coughed to get their attention. "And now," the reverend intoned, "You may kiss the bride."

Logan kissed her. Pure heaven, Logan's kiss. She threw her arms around him and kissed him back.

The Reverend had to cough again to remind them that they'd been kissing long enough. As they drew apart, Lacey heard chuckling from more than one of the guests. And sniffling, too—Edna or Tess, probably.

After the ceremony, they all sat down to dinner at the long table in the dining room. Tess and Edna had put out the best china and silver. There were candles, twelve in all, thin white tapers in antique silver candlesticks. In their warm light, the china gleamed and the fine, old family linen gave off an ivory glow.

The cousins and their wives took turns toasting the happy couple.

"To Lacey and Logan…"

"To the bride and groom…"

"To happiness…"

"Eternal love…"

Logan laid his hand over Lacey's. She twined her fingers with his.

It will all work out, she told herself. I love him and he…well, he cares for me. And he wants to take care of me. And there's Rosie. She needs us both. I'll take Tess's advice, she promised herself, as Zach stood to propose another toast.

I'll do everything I can to give love a place to grow….

# *Chapter Nine*

They left for California early Monday morning, Logan following behind Lacey in his rental car to Buffalo, where he'd made arrangements to drop the car off.

In Buffalo, Logan took the wheel of the SUV. They made surprisingly good time the first day, considering that they had a newborn as a passenger. They stayed in Salt Lake City that night, in a nice hotel that provided excellent room service. They ate by candlelight, in the sitting room of their suite.

Lacey said, "This is getting to be a habit with us, romantic dinners with candles on the table…." She had her shoes off by then and she reached out her toe and hooked it under the cuff of Logan's trouser leg.

He gave her a smoldering look from under those sinfully thick, dark lashes of his. "If you keep that up, you won't get a chance to finish your dinner."

She laughed, a thoroughly naughty laugh, a laugh that made his dark eyes smolder all the more.

Of course, it was too soon after Rosie's birth to make love in the fullest sense. But Lacey had always been an imaginative woman. She liked giving pleasure as much as she enjoyed receiving it.

On their wedding night, by the time they finally got into bed together in the cabin, she'd been too tired to think of anything but curling up close to Logan and trying to catch a few winks before Rosie woke and demanded feeding again. But in the morning she'd felt a little friskier. She'd been able to remind her new husband of how much he appreciated what she could do with her lips and her hands.

She'd reminded him more than once since then.

He said she was insatiable.

She patiently explained to him that, no, *he* was insatiable. She was merely helpful.

"Eat your dinner," he commanded gruffly.

She shrugged and picked up her fork.

Later, after Rosie had been fed and diapered for what seemed like the hundredth time that day, Logan took Lacey's hand and led her to the king-size bed. She had planned, once again, to show him just how helpful she could be.

But her body, evidently, wasn't quite so willing as her mind. She closed her eyes when her head hit the pillow. And that was it. She didn't open them again until Rosie started crying for her next feeding.

Tuesday, they ended up in Winnemucca, Nevada. They shared a pizza in the room and fell asleep watching television—with the sound down very low, of course, in order not to disturb their slumbering daughter.

Wednesday, they were on the road good and early. In Reno, at a little after eleven o'clock, they made a brief stop at the airport to pick up Logan's Cadillac. And by early Wednesday afternoon, Lacey was pulling her SUV into the tree-shaded driveway of Logan's two-story house in Meadow Valley, just a block and a half from the old Queen Anne Victorian where she had grown up. Logan nosed his Cadillac in beside her.

He had their luggage and all the baby's things out of the back of the SUV and stacked in the skylighted two-story front foyer in no time at all. "I thought we'd put Rosie in the east bedroom, the one that overlooks the back deck. It's the closest one to the master suite, so that'll minimize the running back and forth."

"Sounds fine," Lacey said. "The closer the better."

Rosie was right there in the foyer with them, lying on her back in the bassinet that Tess had given her, making little cooing sounds and staring up toward the skylight.

"She's happy," Lacey said. "Let's get moving before she decides she's hungry again." She picked up a big suitcase.

Logan took it from her. "No heavy lifting for you."

She made a face at him. "I'm fine."

"Take that stack of baby blankets and come on. You can start putting things in drawers while I carry it all up there."

"We'll have to fix this room up for a baby," Logan said half an hour later, as Lacey was changing their daughter on the queen-size bed in the room Logan had chosen for her. "We need a crib, and a changing table—"

Lacey nodded. "And a dresser or two, some cute kid's-room curtains, new paint—the works." She pressed the tab on the diaper and straightened Rosie's little pink T-shirt. "There. All clean."

Logan said, "Listen…"

She put the baby on her shoulder and smiled at him. "What?"

"I want to check in at my office for a while. Will you be all right?"

"Sure."

"The refrigerator should be fully stocked." He had called his housekeeper, Mrs. Hopper, before they left Wyoming, to ask her to have everything ready for them.

"I'll be fine," Lacey said.

"I need to…have a talk with my partners. I thought maybe I'd take them to dinner, if I can catch them and they can make the time."

Dinner? That was hours away. "You'll be gone until sometime in the evening, then? Is that what you're saying?" She really did try not to sound as bewildered as his sudden decision to take off for so long made her feel.

"Lace. I've left them high and dry for two weeks— after giving them virtually no notice that I was leaving and no reason why. I only said I had some personal problems that couldn't wait. I owe them an explanation and I want to get it taken care of as soon as possible."

Lacey forced an understanding smile. "Hey. It's okay, really." And it was. If only she didn't feel so disoriented suddenly. As if she'd woken up and out of nowhere found herself in some other woman's skin.

Lord. Married to Logan. The mother of his baby. Standing here in his beautiful house on Orchard Street with its spacious rooms and high ceilings, its skylights and arched windows, its walk-in closets in every room—the house where he and Jenna were supposed to have lived.

Logan was watching her, a frown marring his brow. "I'm sorry," he said. "If you're really uncomfortable with my leaving right now, it can wait until tomorrow."

Lacey shook herself. What was the matter with her? He was a doctor. If she couldn't get used to his being gone for long stretches of time, she'd be in big trouble.

And this *was* her hometown, for heaven's sake. If she got too lonely, she could call an old friend—one of the twins, her high school buddies, Mira or Maud.

But then again, maybe not. Not right away, anyway.

The twins *had* mellowed a lot in recent years. They no longer automatically despised anyone who embraced what they considered to be "establishment" values. But they still considered Logan something of a stuffed shirt. And Logan didn't think too highly of them, either.

She didn't know if she was ready right yet to listen to what they'd have to say to her when they learned that not only had she given birth to Mr. Straight-Arrow's baby, she'd gone and married him as well.

"Give me Rosie," Logan said. "I'll rock her for a while and you can go on in and lie down."

She granted him her best rebellious scowl. "Get out of here. Rosie and I can manage just fine."

Relief brought a smile to that sexy mouth of his. "You're sure?"

"Positive."

He leaned toward her and brushed a kiss at her temple. A moment later, he was gone.

* * *

Logan found Dan on duty at the office.

"Great. You're here." The other doctor clapped Logan heartily on the back. "Safe and sound. And a day early, too. Listen, I've got five of your patients scheduled for this afternoon, but since you're here now…" He let the suggestion finish itself.

"No problem. I'll take them."

"Good. And we'll need some consulting time, tomorrow morning, if possible. Get it out of the way. You've got a few surgeries to schedule and a mountain of charts we need to go over."

"Tomorrow morning's fine. Where's Helen?"

"She's already taken off for rounds at Miner's." All three had privileges at the local hospital, Miner's General.

"But she's coming back here later?"

"I think she said she'd drop back by around four-thirty, see if she could pick up the slack for me if I get too far behind. That shouldn't be a problem now, though, with you here."

"Right. No problem now—but I do need to ask a favor of both of you."

Dan rolled his eyes, but in a good-natured way. "Do not tell me you're taking off for another two weeks."

"I'm not. I just want to explain the details of my trip to Wyoming. Can you clear off your calendar enough to let me buy you dinner tonight?"

"Tonight…" Dan said, considering. "I don't know. I'll have to check with Fiona." Fiona was Dan's wife of twenty-five years, a slender, gracious woman who chaired a number of volunteer organizations and loved to entertain. "Wednesdays are supposed to be our night out, just the two of us."

"Tell her it's all my fault and ask her to please forgive me. In fact, you're on call tomorrow night, right?"

"Right."

"You and Fiona can have it. I'll take the emergencies. We have to talk, Dan. As soon as Helen gets here, I'll ask her to join us, too."

"Is this…bad news?" Dan looked stricken.

Logan couldn't blame the other man for his reaction. Logan had joined the partnership just a few years ago, when the previous third partner had retired. As the junior member of the team, his partners rightfully expected him to take up the slack for them, to make their jobs easier. Since he'd learned that Lacey was pregnant, he hadn't been doing what they expected of him. It was only logical that Dan would now anticipate more of the same.

Logan hastened to reassure him. "No. It's not bad news, I promise you. It's just something you both need to be brought up to speed on, that's all."

Dan's expression relaxed. "Well. Good enough, then. I'll tell Fiona I'm all hers *tomorrow* night—and maybe tonight we could try Frau Angelica's? They say the rack of lamb there is out of this world."

"I'll get Cathy to call and make us a reservation." Cathy was their extremely efficient receptionist. "Seven-thirty?"

"Better make it eight. I've got rounds of my own after I get through here."

"And I haven't been in to take a look at my desk yet, but I can guess that the in-box is stacked sky high."

"You imagine right." Dan affected a sigh.

"It's settled then. I'll have Cathy make the reservation for eight."

* * *

Reality check, Lacey kept thinking—or rather, *un*-reality check. The afternoon had somehow turned into one long *un*reality check.

Her baby was demanding. But not *that* demanding. Rosie slept a lot. And while Rosie was sleeping, Lacey had plenty of time for wandering around Logan's house, meandering from one big, bright, beautifully appointed room to the next, wondering vaguely if this could really be her life.

Or if somehow, she had turned into Jenna.

Not the *real* Jenna, the strong, self-directed woman who had finally accepted her abiding love for Mack McGarrity and discovered that what she wanted most was a life at his side.

No, not that Jenna. But the other Jenna, the sweet, unassuming hometown girl who'd always known exactly how things would go for her: high school and then college in Los Angeles—just to get a taste of the big world out there. And then back to Meadow Valley to open a cute little shop, marry her high-school sweetheart and have a half-dozen kids.

Lacey could see Jenna's touch everywhere in the house. All the curtains and area rugs, the towels in the bathrooms, even some of the furniture could have been bought at Linen and Lace, the shop Jenna had owned over on Commercial Street. A lot of the things no doubt *had* been bought there.

Logan had made an offer on the house three years ago. Lacey remembered Jenna mentioning the purchase. And over the months that followed, Jenna had helped him decorate it. They'd been dating again then, Jenna and Logan. And there had been a kind of unspoken understanding between them. That, eventually, he would ask. And she would say yes.

And then he *had* asked.

What neither of them had counted on was Mack McGarrity striding back into the picture, adding that key extra element that turned everything upside down.

Now, Jenna lived in Florida with Mack.

And Lacey lived with Logan in the house Jenna had decorated with the idea that someday it would be *her* house, too.

Strange. Bizarre. *Unreal.*

During the endless afternoon alone, while her daughter slept, Lacey went into each of the two unused bedrooms in turn. She stretched out on the beds and gazed at the ceilings. She looked in the closets and then stood at the windows, trying to picture herself creating a workspace there.

But in the end, she found herself staring at the curtains, or at an obviously expensive, hand-knotted rug on the hardwood floor.

She would stare and she would think: Jenna's choices.

Lacey never did decide which room to take. Probably the one in the southwest corner—it had windows on two sides and that meant more light.

But whichever room she chose, she would take down the pretty window treatments and banish the bed with its matching linens, its attractively contrasting tumble of throw pillows. The gorgeous area rugs would have to go. She would paint the walls eggshell white, install rice-paper blinds and leave the floors naked and shining, so that she could walk barefoot and feel the warm give of the wood beneath her soles.

After lingering for hours in each of the two unused bedrooms, she went down to the main floor. She wandered the dining room, the living room, the family room, thinking how lovely it all was, thinking…

*Un*reality check.

She stayed in the kitchen a long time, opening and closing the doors of the huge stainless steel refrigerator, turning the big knobs on the chef-style range, gazing at the LaCuisine forged cutlery, mounted so cleverly on the wall over the green marble counter by means of a magnetized knife block.

Eventually, she opened the flatware drawer and stared at the forks.

And it happened.

One of those turn-around moments. The kind that occurs when you think you're driving south in some place you've never been before. You pass a landmark, something startlingly familiar.

And all of a sudden, you find you know right where you are. You've driven this route and you know it well. And, wonder of wonders, you're going north—which is the direction you actually wanted to go.

Yes. A turn-around moment. Lacey looked at the forks in Logan's flatware drawer and all at once, she wasn't thinking of Jenna, or wondering if somehow she had taken over Jenna's life.

All at once, she was thinking strictly of herself. Standing naked in this very kitchen, tearing into a four-layer devil's food cake and feeding it to Logan, who happened to be just as naked as she.

By then, she was smiling.

And when she thought, *un*reality check, it was more with humor than with hurt.

\* \* \*

At Frau Angelica's, after their entrées had been served, Logan embarked on the task of telling his partners everything he thought they needed to know.

He started out by saying that a few weeks ago, he'd learned that he was going to be a father. He'd gone to Wyoming with the intention of marrying the mother of his child.

"The baby, a little girl, was born Friday, the second," he explained. "And Lacey and I were married just this past Saturday."

He paused, to give the other two doctors a chance to say something.

Dan spoke up first, announcing way too cheerfully, "Well, this is certainly exciting news!"

Helen, who was in her mid-fifties but looked at least a decade younger, took a judicious sip of merlot. "Yes, Logan. Congratulations."

"Thank you."

Dan asked, "A daughter, you said?"

"Yes. Margaret Rose. We call her Rosie."

Helen said, "That's lovely. And your wife? Lacey…?"

"Bravo. Her last name was Bravo." He gave out that information fully expecting it to ring some bells.

It did. "Bravo?" Dan's right eyebrow shot toward his receding hairline. "I wonder. Is Lacey any relation to—?"

Logan let him have it. "As a matter of fact, Lacey is Jenna's younger sister."

Dan's jaw dropped. "Oh," he said. "Well, isn't that…" He didn't seem to know how to finish, so he coughed into his hand instead.

Both Dan and Helen had met Jenna on a number of occasions. They had each said they liked her immensely. Dan's wife had seemed very fond of her, too. As a matter of fact, Fiona had thrown a big engagement bash for Jenna and Logan. It had been a great party—and then three weeks later, Jenna had run off with Mack McGarrity.

Dan lurched to life and tried again. "This is just…such a surprise," he said.

A painful silence followed, during which Helen took on the task of buttering a kaiser roll and Dan evinced great interest in his rack of lamb.

Logan could almost hear their thoughts.

*Hmm. Jenna left him. And that's when the sister came on the scene. An affair on the rebound. And the woman became pregnant. Now he's married her. I suppose he's made the best of a bad situation. But how long can it be expected to last?*

Helen set her butter knife on the corner of her bread plate. "I'm sure you're going to be very happy." She bit into her kaiser roll.

Logan did not flinch and he did not allow his eyes to shift away. "Yes. Lacey and I *are* very happy. And of course, we have the most beautiful baby in the world."

Helen finished chewing and swallowed. "I can't wait to meet both your wife and your daughter."

"And you will, I'm sure. Very soon."

Dan had recovered his equilibrium enough by then to exclaim, "I'm just stunned." He reached for the bottle in the center of the table and began topping off their glasses. "This calls for a toast." He set the bottle aside and raised his glass high. "Ahem. Here's to you, Logan. And to your bride. And your new daughter."

Logan thought of the long series of toasts at the Bravo table during his wedding dinner. He had liked those toasts better than Dan's. They'd seemed a lot more sincere.

Still, he had to admit that his partners were taking this pretty well.

And then again, why shouldn't they? The situation *was* something of an embarrassment, but nothing that couldn't be easily handled with the judicious application of proper damage control.

Helen raised her own glass and chimed in, "Yes, Logan. To your new family." She knocked back a big gulp of merlot.

Dan braced an elbow on the table and rubbed his chin. "I have an idea. Why doesn't Fiona give you and your bride a little party?"

Helen sat up straighter. "That's an excellent suggestion." She swung her sharp gaze Logan's way, then looked at Dan again. "But not a *small* party. A big one. A big party in honor of Logan's new family. Get Gabriella Rousseau to cater it. She's the best."

The corners of Dan's mouth drew down. His wife and her hostessing skills were a big asset to him, and he was always protective of her territory. "That's Fiona's department. She'll choose the caterer."

Helen dipped her perfectly groomed blond head. "Of course. It was just a thought."

"And I'll pass it right on to her."

"Great."

Dan was smiling, way too pleasantly. "You're quiet, Logan. Is a party a problem for you?"

A party, with most of the local medical community invited, no doubt, was probably not Lacey's idea of a great time. But he could talk her into it.

He'd have to warn her to be on her best behavior. She did have that wild side—the side his partners would most likely be hearing about once the gossip mill kicked in.

But for this, she'd tread the straight and narrow. For his sake. Because she did love him.

He had seen it in her eyes.

And heard it from her lips on the day that their daughter was born.

"Logan?" Dan was waiting for an answer.

"I think a party is an excellent idea, Dan. Thank you."

"No problem. Now, tell us some more about your new wife."

Logan set down his wineglass, thinking, she's reckless and a little wild and absolutely captivating. He said, "Well, she's…a very adventurous woman. She's not afraid to take chances. She goes after what she wants."

"And what *does* she want?" Helen asked. The question was a particularly irritating mix of sly interest and condescension.

"She's lived in Los Angeles the last few years, pursuing a very promising career as an artist."

"An artist. How fascinating…"

Logan wished he were anywhere else right then but here at this restaurant discussing his private life with his professional colleagues.

He wished he were home. With Lacey.

Lacey.

All at once, he found himself holding back a fool's deep sigh as a swift series of images flashed on the screen of his mind.

Her incredible face, mottled and slick with sweat, grinning at him between the V of her spread legs on the night that their daughter was born.

What had she said right then?

It came to him: *"I feel so utterly demure…"*

And then later, not long after the birth, laying her palm against his cheek, confessing that she loved him.

And the night she finally said yes, giving him that grin of hers again across the rough pine table in that tiny, dark cabin, declaring, *"I have something of a reputation myself, in Meadow Valley…."*

Right then, he could almost wish himself back there with her, in that cramped little cabin, just the two of them and Rosie.

"Logan?" Helen was frowning at him. "Are you with us here?"

"Of course."

"We have to make some decisions. When should Fiona have that party?"

Logan pushed his tender thoughts aside and ordered his mind to focus on the all-important subject of damage control. "Let's give Lacey until her six-week checkup, how about that? Say, any time from mid-August on."

Dan asked, "Then Fiona *can* start making plans?"

"Absolutely."

Helen brought out her Palm Pilot and began punching buttons.

Logan glanced surreptitiously at his watch. Nine-fifteen.

What was she doing now? Nursing Rosie? He loved to watch that, her breast so white and full, traced with sweet blue veins, pressed against his daughter's plump cheek.

Or maybe she was lying in his bed, waiting for him? She might even be sleeping.

Since the baby, she seemed to have given up her passion for staying up until all hours. She'd learned to steal a nap whenever the opportunity presented itself.

Helen glanced up from the electronic device in her hand. "How does Saturday, the fourteenth, sound? Is that still too early?"

Dan was consulting his Day Runner. "For me, the fourteenth would probably be a go. Of course, I'll have to firm it up with Fiona."

Logan shrugged. "The fourteenth sounds fine to me."

Lacey had saved the master bedroom for last. She'd been in there to unload her suitcases, before Logan left. But after that, she hadn't crossed that particular threshold again. She'd waited until nine-thirty at night to return to it, first lingering over her solitary dinner, then hanging out in the family room for a while, watching a movie on HBO.

When she finally did enter the master suite, she went straight to the bath.

She showered in the enormous shower stall, glancing more than once at her soft, just-had-a-baby stomach and frowning, thinking that she'd have to put herself on some sort of exercise plan. Once she'd showered, she treated herself to a long, luxurious soak in the big spa tub.

After a while, resting her head back and closing her eyes, she let herself remember a few choice details of the five glorious days that had ended up creating Rosie and thus bringing her back here.

*Un*reality check.

Yes.

But what a beautiful time that had been.

Lacey heard Rosie crying just as she was drying herself off. She went and got her daughter and returned to the master suite to sit on Logan's wide bed with her.

Lifting her breast free of her robe, Lacey brushed the side of Rosie's tiny mouth with the nipple. Unerringly, that mouth found what it sought. Rosie latched on.

It didn't even hurt anymore, as it had the first few days. Now, there was only a pleasant tugging sensation and a sweet feeling of warmth and fullness as her milk came down and began to flow. Lacey smiled and whispered to her daughter, stroking the soft, bumpy head, which already seemed to have lost its pointiness and smoothed out into the shape of a very average-looking baby's head.

As Rosie settled into the rhythm of feeding, Lacey scooted back up against the headboard. She stared around her at the rich, deep textures of the bed linens, at the burled walnut bureau and bedside tables, at the royal blue walls and creamy white ceiling.

It was a very masculine room. Not a ruffle or a frill in sight. It didn't look like Jenna.

It looked like Logan.

And the rest of the house?

"You know what?" Lacey said aloud, stroking her daughter's head some more. "During this day of *un*reality checks, it has slowly become clear to me that I like it here. And I could live here quite comfortably."

The only rooms she'd want to change were Rosie's room and the room she'd choose for her studio.

Yes, the house bore Jenna's touch. But it was a very light, very loving touch. And really, Lacey was finding that seeing her sister's touch everywhere bothered her less and less with each hour that passed.

Perhaps, Lacey thought with a grin, it was because she had made her own mark here. A much more elemental mark than Jenna's.

Lacey had raided that big Sub-Zero refrigerator downstairs, in the middle of a warm September night, after she and Logan had spent hours making love. He'd hoisted her up on the cool green marble counter and made love to her again.

And here, in this bedroom—she had absolutely wonderful memories of what had happened here. If she closed her eyes and let her imagination take her, she could almost hear their sighs, their moans, their low, lazy laughter.

It *had* been a good time, those brief days in September. A beautiful time. A perfect, magical time. And at the end of it, she'd discovered that she'd found her love.

And now she was back here. In her hometown. Logan's wife.

*Un*reality check?

Maybe.

A big change, definitely. Major adjustments to be made, no doubt about that.

But she had her love. And her little girl.

A roof over their heads, food on the table. A room to work in, when she was ready to paint again.

It was a lot. And she was grateful for it.

"We're going to do fine, Rosie," she whispered to her daughter. "We are going to do just fine."

After they discussed the party, there were a number of other issues the partners decided they might as well deal with as long as they had each other's attention. Logan didn't sign for the check until after eleven.

And he didn't pull into his driveway until half an hour after that. The light in the master suite, which faced the street, was still on, a golden glow in the velvety darkness of the summer night. Logan stopped in the driveway as the garage door was rolling open. He stared up at the spill of warmth and brightness and felt something painfully sweet wash through him.

Urgency followed.

To be in there, where she was. To crawl into bed with her and turn off the light and…

He dragged in a breath. It didn't really matter what happened next. They might just drop off to sleep until Rosie woke them. Or Lacey might decide to show him how *helpful* she could be.

Then again, maybe she was angry with him by now.

He frowned. It *had* been—he glanced at his Rolex—almost ten hours since he'd dropped her off and headed for the office. He hadn't planned to be gone quite this long. Not on their first day home.

He'd also kept meaning to call her, just to check on her, to see how she and Rosie were doing. But every time he reached for the phone, something always cropped up that had to be dealt with right then. Somehow, he'd never gotten around to calling home.

Home.

Strange. He'd never thought of the house that way before.

It had always been just that. The house. *His* house. A place to live. An expensive, attractive possession of which he was justifiably proud.

But now…

Now, it had Lacey in it. And Rosie.

Now it had his *family* in it.

And somehow, that made all the difference.

Logan blinked and realized he was sitting in the driveway, the Cadillac's big engine purring softly in his ear. The garage door was all the way up and had been for over a minute now.

He hit the gas and shot into the garage so fast that he had to slam on the brakes to keep from hitting the far wall. The tires squealed and the car bounced on its cushion of shocks. He punched the button hooked to his visor and the garage door went rumbling down. Jumping from the car and slamming the door behind him, he entered the house through the laundry room door and jogged through the dark family room and breakfast room, headed straight for the front foyer and the stairs to the upper floor.

Lacey had put Rosie back in her crib at a little after eleven. She'd found a novel in a hall bookcase and settled back into bed to read.

Not too long after that, faintly, she heard a car pull up outside.

Logan.

She set her book aside, heard a low rumble—the garage door going up. After a minute or two, she heard a faint squealing sound—as if he'd hit the gas too hard and had to stop too fast. The garage door rumbled down again.

She sat forward, straining to hear. There it was. The door to the laundry room closing.

And then, seconds later, footsteps moving fast up the stairs. There was a certain urgency to them. As if he couldn't wait.

Couldn't wait to get to *her*....

He appeared in the doorway, hesitated there, seeking, then finding her, hope and tenderness and a kind of dark joy suffusing his features, burning in his eyes.

She thought, Why, Jenna was right.

He loves me.

He loves me in his actions. And he also loves me deep in his most secret heart.

*And that, the love deep in his heart, he doesn't even know about.*

"I'm sorry I'm so late." His voice was low, a little rough.

It's all right, she thought. But her throat felt so tight, the words wouldn't quite come.

So she smiled to show him he didn't need to worry. It was a shy, quivery sort of smile. Her heart was beating very fast, as if she'd run a long, hard race, one she'd known that she would lose—and reached the finish line to find herself victorious.

"You're not angry," he whispered. It seemed to mean the world to him.

She shook her head and felt her smile bloom wider on her mouth.

He swore, a passionate oath. And then he came to her.

She held out her arms to take him in.

# Chapter Ten

Four weeks and two days later, at ten in the morning on the thirteenth of August, Lacey got a clean bill of health from Dr. Enright, the obstetrician Logan had recommended.

The doctor fitted her for a new diaphragm and told her to feel free to resume sexual relations with her husband. Lacey smiled to herself. She and Logan had been having "sexual relations" all along, thank you. They'd made love in just about every way but one.

Now they could do that, too.

Lacey winked at the doctor. "Well, Doc. Looks like Friday the Thirteenth is my lucky day."

"Get that diaphragm first," Dr. Enright advised. "Give your body a little rest before the next baby."

From her carrier in the corner of the examining

room, Rosie let out a happy gurgle. Lacey smiled at the sound. She did love her baby. And she wanted another. And another. And another after that. And so did Logan. But the doctor was right. No need to rush it.

She stopped in at the pharmacy on her way home to fill the prescription for her new diaphragm. After that, she visited a little deli she and Logan liked. She got dark bread and roast beef sliced paper-thin, and pastrami and a loaf of rye. And horseradish and fat dill pickles, too.

The twins were coming for lunch. She had talked to both Mira and Maud by phone since she'd moved back to town, but she hadn't invited them over until now. They had been thoroughly stunned when she'd told them that she'd married Logan Severance—and, as Lacey had expected, neither of them had approved of the match.

"You *married* him?" Mira had cried. "I can't believe it. You and Dr. Do-Right? Uh-uh. I mean, I know it was hot and heavy with you two back in September. And I can see why you might want to keep the baby. But *marriage*. To *him*? Did you have to go that far?"

Lacey had tried not to let Mira's reaction upset her. She'd explained calmly that she loved Logan and she believed he cared deeply for her in return. She was happy. Things were working out fine.

Mira had scoffed. "Ex-squeeze me. What is this? Bizarre." She warbled out a few bars of something that sounded like the theme from *The Twilight Zone.* "It's straight out of *The Stepford Wives,* if you ask me."

Lacey gritted her teeth. "Oh. Now I'm something out of a horror movie, a soulless clone of my former self? Thanks a bunch, Mir."

Mira backed off. A little. "Look. I'm sorry. It's just…whoa. I'm blown away. I haven't heard from you in months and then—"

"What's that got to do with anything? There have been lots of times when we haven't talked for months."

"You know what I mean. It's a shock. You call me up out of nowhere and say you've had a baby and married your sister's ex. It's a lot to take in."

"Well, deal with it. I went through some big changes myself over this."

"No kidding."

"It's the right thing for me. Mira, I love the man."

"Are you working?"

Leave it to Mira, Lacey thought. Mira knew right where to slide in the knife. "I just had a baby, remember?"

"You're not working."

"I'm fixing up a room. For my studio."

"But you're not working."

"I will be. Soon."

Mira demanded, "What does Xavier have to say about this?"

Xavier Hockland was a professional artist, a well-known and highly respected one. His shows always sold out. He worked in oils, for the most part. Like Lacey. And he had been her teacher and mentor until several months before—when he had learned she was pregnant and told her she had to make a choice: her baby or her art.

"Xavier is out of the picture," Lacey said.

"Why?"

"He just is, that's all. I don't want to talk about him."

"Fine. What about Barnaby, then? And Adele?"

Barnaby and Adele were also artists, and friends of Lacey's in L.A. Barnaby rented a huge loft downtown, where he was storing a number of Lacey's paintings for her.

"I called them both," Lacey told Mira defiantly, "a couple of days ago. They congratulated me and wished me well."

"They don't know Logan Severance."

"What is that supposed to mean?"

Mira was silent, a silence that spoke volumes. After the quiet hummed through the line for several long seconds, she deigned to speak again. "I could become very worried about you, you know?"

Mentally, Lacey counted to ten. Then she suggested, "We'd better talk about you. How's the band doing?"

The band was the twins' passion and had been for over a decade. Mira played lead guitar and Maud played drums. They also had a bass player and a guy on keyboard. But the band really *belonged* to Mira and Maud. It had gone through a series of name changes over the years. The last Lacey had heard, they were calling it Mirror Image.

"You're switching subjects on me," Mira accused.

"You're right. I am. How's the band doing?"

Mira hesitated, but then let out a big sigh and answered Lacey's question. "We've been playing the Eureka Lounge Friday nights for a couple of months now."

"Hey. Way to go."

"But you know how it is. Maud has her job at the GiantValue Mart, Sunday through Thursday, as always. Eight to four. And I'm still waiting tables four nights a week."

"What? Is that whining I hear?"

Mira chuckled. "Maybe what *I* need is a rich husband."

"Was that a dig?"

Mira laughed "Sure sounded like one, didn't it? Do you think I'm just jealous?"

"You? No way. You're not the jealous type."

"God, Lace. I can't believe you married him."

"Well, I did. Get used to it."

"I'm working on it."

They had talked for several minutes more. And when they hung up, it was on a reasonably cordial note. Lacey had called Maud right afterwards, figuring that she might as well get it over with.

Maud took the news in the same manner as her identical twin—only more so. She was shocked. Amazed. Blown away. And not the least bit pleased to learn that one of her best friends had "sold out" and married "Mr. Super-Straight Upwardly Mobile Big Shot M.D."

"He was fine for Jenna," Maud said. "And at least he always treated *her* with respect. But you know how he's been with you, Lace, all these years. How could you forget? Always after you, always telling you how to live your life, acting as if your career as an artist was just a big waste of time, some foolish, silly dream. How could you have…"

There was more in that vein. Finally, Lacey had been forced to lay down the law.

"He's my husband now, Maud. You are my friend and I'll always love you. But if you keep talking against him, I can't deal with you anymore."

Maud had hung up on her.

And then called back a week later to apologize. They'd talked a couple of times since then. And yesterday, on the spur of the moment, Lacey had invited Maud over for lunch, then called Mira right afterward and asked her to come, too.

As she put the pastrami and roast beef into the meat drawer of the refrigerator, she muttered to herself, "Please. Don't let this visit be a total disaster."

It wasn't.

There *were* a number of potentially rocky moments, but Lacey had made up her mind ahead of time not to let the twins get to her.

Of course, they couldn't resist making cracks about the house.

"Straight out of *Better Homes and Gardens,*" Mira said. "Totally *not* you, Lace."

Lacey had only smiled. "I like it. Jenna did most of it and I love my sister's taste."

"*Très* weird," said Maud. "Shouldn't you be, like, bothered, just a little, that she was his ex and she did the decorating?"

"Maybe I should. But I'm not."

"And just what does your big sister think of all this, anyway?"

"All what?"

"Come on. You know. You and Dr. Do-Right. Married. With a baby."

"She's happy for us. In fact, she thought I should marry him."

"Too strange."

"And she sent a complete layette for Rosie." The layette had arrived two days after they'd returned to Meadow Valley. Lacey had called and thanked her sister.

Jenna had called twice since then. But Lacey had cut both calls short. Once, because Rosie had demanded attention. And the second time, because Lacey had heard Logan's car pulling up in the driveway. She'd told her sister, "Logan's home. Gotta go."

Jenna had said, "Call me."

And Lacey had promised she'd do just that.

They hadn't spoken since, though, and that had been over three weeks ago.

"Anybody in there?" It was Maud.

Lacey laughed. "Sorry. Just thinking."

Maud grunted. "This is all pretty strange and unusual, if you ask me."

Mira muttered, "Bi-zarre." Then she shrugged. "But then again, Dr. Do-Right is one good-lookin' dude. And I gotta admit, I can relate to that fridge and the stove. Only the best, huh?"

"Right," Lacey agreed easily. "Only the best."

They did admire her studio, which she had fixed up just as she'd planned, with bare floors and white walls and rice-paper blinds.

"Now, *this* is you," said Maud. Her full red lips turned down at the corners. "It looks awfully…perfect, though. No clutter, no globs of paint on the worktable, no brushes soaking in jars. Have you been using it?"

She hadn't. And it was starting to bother her just a little. "I'm getting there."

Maud and Mira exchanged a glance, but before they could start in on her, the baby monitor Lacey had carried with her as she gave the twins the tour began emitting fussy little cries.

"She's awake." Mira's big dark eyes were gleaming. "I can't wait to meet her."

"And speaking of little darlings…" Lacey switched off the monitor and turned to Maud. "…I thought you'd bring Devon." Devon was Maud's two-year-old. "I haven't seen him since last September. He was barely walking then."

"He's into everything now," Maud said. "And talking? You can't shut that kid up."

"Where is he?"

"Deke's got him." Deke and Maud had married right out of high school. Everyone had predicted that it would never last, but they were still going strong. "Deke's got Fridays off now, and he actually volunteered to baby-sit. I didn't argue. My mama didn't raise no fool."

"Bring Devon next time?"

Maud shrugged. "Sure."

Lacey led them to the baby's room, which now contained everything the discerning infant could desire, including a crib with a music-playing mobile above it and a double bureau appliquéd with balloons and teddy bears. The changing table had open shelves above it, so the diapers and receiving blankets were right within reach. The curtains and bedding sported clouds and rainbows on a sky-blue background.

"Wow," said Mira. "*This* is way cool." She was looking up at the ceiling, which Lacey had painted deep blue and decorated with a whole universe of planets, bright stars and silvery moons.

"So you *have* been painting," Maud teased, as Lacey picked up the fussing baby.

"You bet."

Mira turned her attention to the baby. "This girl is gorgeous. Let me hold her."

"Me, too," said Maud.

The twins passed the baby between them, each cuddling and cooing to her and calling her adorable. Then Lacey sat in the rocker to feed her. Finally, after a quick diaper change, they went downstairs. The twins took turns holding Rosie as Lacey got out the deli meats and breads.

Then they all made their own sandwiches. The twins had two each, roast beef *and* pastrami. They'd always loved to eat. Their lush, size-twelve figures attested to that fact.

"Umm," groaned Mira, as she bit into a fat dill pickle. "Heaven." She frowned at Lacey. "What? The nursing mother is only having one sandwich? Is this wise?"

Lacey patted her stomach, which had endured an endless number of crunches in the last few weeks. "I've lost most of what I gained with Rosie. Five pounds to go and I'll be back to my starting weight."

Mira crunched her pickle. "You only live once is what I always say."

"Exactly." Lacey grinned to herself, thinking of the night to come. Friday the Thirteenth, her lucky night.

"Eeeuu," cried Maud. "I know that look."

Lacey widened her eyes. "What look?"

"Sex look. So weird. You and Dr. Perfect really have a thing, huh?"

Lacey only smiled.

Mira bit into her pastrami on rye and chewed with lusty enthusiasm. She swallowed. "The world never changes. Opposites go on attracting."

Maud waved her pickle. "Just paint," she commanded. "Get up there in that big white room and paint."

Lacey said, "I will," and told herself that she meant it.

\* \* \*

Logan came home at a little after eight.

It was perfect timing, really. Lacey had dinner all ready: herbed roast chicken, bow-tie pasta with olive oil and basil, and a salad of romaine, watercress and radicchio. Rosie had been fed and changed and put to bed.

Lacey was just getting out of the shower, humming to herself, feeling school-girl giddy and a little bit foolish, sighing at the thought of what was going to happen in the next few hours—if Logan didn't get held up by some emergency, of course.

There was always that possibility. But oh, she did hope there'd be no emergencies tonight.

She finished drying herself and pulled on the white silk robe that Logan had bought her a few weeks before. She liked to think of him, stopping in at that lingerie shop over on Commercial Street with the idea of buying some little wisp of nothing for her. She liked to picture him consulting with the saleswoman, describing her: "She's blond, about this tall…" She liked to imagine him touching the satins and the laces with those fine big hands.

And she also liked the feel of the silk against her bare skin, that slinky, shivery, flowing feeling as it clung to her body, caressing each curve. She tied the sash around her waist and turned to the mirror over the black marble sink.

A big tortoiseshell clip held up her hair. She reached behind her and unsnapped it. Her hair spilled down her back. She shook her head, set the clip on the marble counter and reached up to comb her fingers through the heavy coiling strands.

That was when she caught sight of him.

He stood in the doorway to the bedroom, his tie hanging loose and the cuffs of his white dress shirt rolled to just below the elbows. He'd already gotten rid of his jacket, probably tossed it on the bed, or across a chair in the other room. He'd undone the top button of his shirt. She saw the shadow of his evening beard on his square jaw, and a hint of dark chest hair, in the V of his collar.

She met his eyes. Her heart caught, stuttered beneath her breastbone, then began beating slow and very hard, as if her blood had thickened somehow and it took a stronger, deeper beat to push it through her veins.

He raised a dark brow. "Well?"

She turned to face him, leaning back against the marble counter, gripping it with her hands, feeling that sweet loosening all through her, a warmth that pooled in her center and spread out from there. "I love it when you come home. Did I ever tell you that?"

Could those dark eyes of his get any darker? They seemed to, right then. "I thought maybe you'd call today, tell me how it went with Dr. Enright."

"I didn't want to bother you."

His mouth curled up on one side, a half smile, both ironic and tender. "You wanted me to wonder, to think about tonight."

"Well, maybe I did—a little, anyway. And I wanted to tell you in person."

"To tell me what?"

She slowly untied the sash of the robe. His eyes grew darker still.

She let the sash drop to the floor. The silk fell open.

He leaned in the doorway, folding his arms over his broad chest.

She touched her fingers to her collarbone, then traced a path downward, following the open facings of the robe, her fingers gliding between her breasts, over her stomach, lower still. When she reached her thighs, she let her hands fall to her sides and whispered, "Dr. Enright says I'm fine."

"Fine?" His eyes were dark as midnight now. "That means fully recovered?"

"That's right. Ready for anything…for everything…."

He went on watching, his gaze a brand, as she lifted her hands again to grasp the facings of the robe.

He was already striding toward her when she let the robe drop to the floor.

# Chapter Eleven

When he reached her, he wrapped his arms around her and pulled her close. She sighed, reveling in the feel of him, the heat of him, the strength in his hands splayed on her bare back. She rubbed her cheek against his shoulder, breathing in the scent of him, which she could never put words to, but which she would have known anywhere.

She closed her eyes as he bent his head and pressed his lips to her throat. He drew on the skin.

She moaned, and then grasped his arms enough to pull away from the suckling kiss. "Stop that. You know if you put a mark there, it'll show."

He laughed, a husky, hungry laugh that set all her nerves humming. Then he pulled her close again and breathed against the reddened spot. "You like it."

She sighed some more. "I do. But remember that party Fiona Connery's giving us…"

He swore. "Tomorrow night."

She whispered in his ear, "We want them all to know we're happy, but…"

He laughed again, and lightly nipped the forbidden spot. "But not *that* happy."

"Exactly. So watch it."

"All right." He nuzzled lower, latched onto her left breast just above the nipple. She pulled him closer, moaned without shame, giving in to the kiss that marked her. Her milk flowed a little, wetting his shirt. Logan didn't mind.

He pulled back, studied his handiwork and then whispered gruffly, "There. No one will see. Now, come on."

She gave a glad cry as he scooped her up, one hand at her back and one under her knees, raising her high against his chest. He turned for their bedroom.

She clung to him, lifting her mouth to his. They kissed all the way to the bed.

He laid her down carefully, resting his hand on her belly for a moment, then sliding it down. He dipped a finger into the nest of dark gold curls at the juncture of her thighs. She closed her eyes, moaned deep in her throat and opened for him.

He stroked her, slowly, tenderly. She moved, unashamed, lifting herself toward his caress. After a moment, he slid that finger inside. She lifted herself higher still, and with an eager cry tried to reach for him.

But he stepped back. With a moan of disappointment, she opened her eyes to find that he hadn't really left her. He was only pulling off his tie, tossing it on a chair, and then getting rid of his shoes and his socks.

Barefoot, he came to her again, to the edge of the bed. She rose to her knees and began working at the buttons of his shirt, her fingers quick and eager, pressing herself close to him, kissing a path down his chest as each button gave way.

She pushed the shirt off his shoulders, tossed it aside. He was already unhooking his belt. She took care of the hooks at the waistband of his slacks and then pulled the zipper down in one slow sizzle of sound. Together, they pushed the slacks away. He stepped out of them, and his briefs as well.

She took his arm. "Come here. Come here to me…."

They fell across the bed together, legs in a tangle, mouths fusing, tongues playing. She wrapped her legs around him and felt him at her entrance.

Right then, she remembered. She stiffened.

He pulled back, looked down at her. "What?"

She lifted up, kissed his beard-roughened jaw. "You know I want more babies…"

He kissed her in return, but on the mouth, biting her lip a little. "It's too soon, I know."

The kisses always felt so good, so right, so wonderful. His mouth closed over hers. She let him have her tongue, tasted the inside of his mouth, so slick and wet and lovely. And then he did the same to her, his tongue entering, sweeping the moist surfaces, retreating only to enter again.

Sometimes, when he was kissing her, she wondered how she had lived without the taste of him. How she had gone all those years, knowing him, often irritated or even angry with him, and somehow managing never to realize that her anger and irritation only masked her own hunger. They were desire denied.

He touched her again, his hand finding her, parting her, stroking her, delving in.

She gasped. "I should…I have…"

His hand moved faster.

She gave herself up to it, her body gathering, rising. His kiss deepened. She cried into his mouth. He drank that cry as fulfillment shimmered through her.

Sometime later, she rose from the bed. "I'll be right back," she promised.

He made a low noise, part regret at her leaving him, however briefly, and part acquiescence to the necessity that she go.

He caught her hand, pressed his lips to it.

She pulled away with reluctance. "I promise. Right back."

In the bathroom, she took out her new diaphragm, spread on the contraceptive cream and, after only two tries, slid it into place. She rinsed her hands and returned to the bedroom.

He was waiting for her, sitting up on the edge of the bed. He held out his hand. She went to him. He guided her onto his lap. She hooked her legs around him, crying out when he filled her, then letting her head fall back, awash in the wonder of once again being joined to him.

For a time, they didn't move, except for the slow, measured care of each breath. And then they couldn't help themselves. He raised his hips, pushing deeper as she pressed down.

And soon enough they fell together across the tangle of bedcovers. She rode him, moaning. He clutched her hips and pushed in hard. Then they were rolling, so he was on top. He braced his arms to either side of her and lifted his broad chest up, at the same time pressing in deeper down below. His eyes burned into hers.

"My love," she whispered. "Oh, yes, my love…."

He whispered something in return. It might have been her name.

And then there were no words. Only the two of them, only heat and desire and the pulse of fulfillment, starting at the point of joining and moving out, singing along every nerve, until they shuddered together and cried out as one.

The food was a little bit dry by the time they sat down to eat, both of them in their robes, at the dining room table, by candlelight. Logan had no complaints, though. He told her it was the best dry chicken he'd ever tasted. He opened a bottle of Pinot Grigio and Lacey allowed herself a half a glass, enough to raise and clink against his. They didn't need words for the toast. Their eyes said it all.

Lacey had taken exactly three bites and one sip of wine when the fussing started, little cries and bleats issuing from the monitor she had brought downstairs and parked on the sideboard.

She and Logan looked at each other and sighed.

"Could be worse," she said. "She could have decided she was hungry half an hour ago."

Lacey got up, gave her husband a kiss, and went to take care of their baby.

It was early, a little before ten, when she and Logan settled into bed again. She cuddled up close to him.

He smoothed her hair off her cheek and kissed her—

a warm, chaste, peck of a kiss. "You make me so happy, Lacey Severance."

She dropped off to sleep smiling.

And woke in the middle of the night with an idea.

She turned toward her husband. Sound asleep. Good. And the monitor on the nightstand stood blessedly silent.

She slid from the bed with the stealth of a thief, careful to disturb the covers as little as possible. Once she was on her feet, she crept to the bathroom and got her robe. She stopped by the bed again, just long enough to get the baby monitor—or that had been her intent.

But somehow, she found herself hesitating there, wanting to bend across the bed, press her lips against Logan's temple, breathe in the warm, delicious scent of his skin.

And more than a kiss, she was tempted to crawl back in beside him. She would cuddle up close and rub her foot along his calf, her hand up his arm, over the strong muscles of his shoulder, onto his powerful chest with its mat of dark, curling hair.

She loved that, waking him in the middle of the night with caresses, loved the low sounds he made, his warm, sleepy kisses, the way he would…

No.

She was going to her studio and she was going right now.

She scooped up the monitor and tiptoed toward the hall.

She worked for an hour, lining out quick, rough sketches in pencil. Of Mira and Maud mostly, sitting at the kitchen table, Maud waving her pickle, Mira taking that first lusty bite of her pastrami sandwich.

It felt good to be working again.

The twins were right. She needed to make time for this, she needed to get in here on a regular basis, just an hour or two a day for right now, kind of ease into it gradually, slowly get herself back up to speed.

At a little before three, Rosie started crying. Lacey put her sketch pad aside, grabbed the monitor and turned off the lights.

When she got to the baby's room, she found Logan already there. He stood over the crib, his back to the door. Lacey paused at the threshold, warmth spreading through her. He'd pulled on a pair of pajama bottoms, but left his torso bare. As he bent over the crib, moonlight streaming in the window etched each muscle in silvery relief.

He lifted Rosie from her nest of blankets, raised her to his bare, beautifully formed shoulder and rubbed her tiny back, whispering, "Hey, there. It's okay. Daddy's here…"

He turned. Through the darkness, their eyes met.

Lacey moved into the room, setting the monitor on the bureau as she went by. "Here. I'll take her."

Logan passed her the squalling bundle. She carried the baby to the changing table to check her diaper. "Dry. Must be hungry."

Settling herself and the baby in the rocker, Lacey pushed the facing of her robe out of the way and cradled her breast, holding the nipple ready. Rosie latched right on and went to work.

"Where were you?" Logan was standing over her.

She looked up, gave him a smile. "In my studio. Sketching out a few ideas."

"At three in the morning?"

She'd been rocking slowly. Now she toed the floor and stopped the gentle movement of the chair. Something in his voice bothered her. Something…disapproving. Something that reminded her way too much of the Logan she had grown up telling herself she despised.

"Yes," she said levelly. "I was working in my studio. At three in the morning."

He was silent for a moment, staring down at her, his eyes gleaming through the shadows. She felt his possessiveness of her as a physical presence right then. That possessiveness aroused her. He wanted her so much, he didn't want to share her, except perhaps with their child.

A dark thrill coursed through her, to think that his need for her was that strong.

At the same time, she knew his possessiveness could pose a threat to them both, to what they had as a couple, to the life they were working together to build.

"Did those friends of yours come by today?" It almost sounded like an accusation.

"Yes," Lacey said. "Mira and Maud were here for lunch. You have a problem with my friends paying me a visit?"

He shrugged, the movement casual, his expression anything but. "It's interesting, that's all. Those two come for lunch—and all of a sudden, you're up at three in the morning."

*"Working,"* she said, stressing the word. "In my studio."

"You should get your rest when you can." His voice was low, soft—and yet she heard the command in it.

She decided it would be wisest to go straight for the throat about this. "I love you, Logan. But I won't be owned by you."

His eyes didn't waver. Still, she saw the flicker of unwilling understanding in their depths. He put his hand
on the rocker back, holding it still. If she had tried to
rock right then, she most likely would not have been
able to.

She drew in a breath, closed her eyes briefly, focused on the physical, the warm wonder of her baby
drawing on her breast, the feel of the silk robe he had
given her, pleasurable as a lover's caress against her
skin.

"I do love you," she whispered, gently now. "You
don't *need* to own me."

Logan stared down at his wife's upturned face, wanting her, hard with the need for her, though at least she
couldn't see that. The chair hid it from her view.

Lately, it had occurred to him that he had everything
a man could ever ask for now. His wife. His daughter.
A family that made his fine house a home.

And more. He had the nights.

With a woman who wanted him as much as he
wanted her.

Sometimes, he thought of how empty it had all been
before. An emptiness he hadn't even seen for what it
was.

Always, there had been that emptiness. His mother
had died when he was so young. His father, Dr. Logan
Severance Sr., a good man but a distant one, had been
left to raise him alone. His father had pushed him to
work hard, to be the best. And Logan hadn't minded
being pushed. He had wanted, when he was very young,
to please his father.

And as he grew older, he found he wanted to be the
best for the sake of excellence itself. For the feeling of

satisfaction it gave him to know that he'd done what he could, given his all to any task he'd taken on.

The first moment he laid eyes on Jenna he'd known she was the one for him. Pretty and sweet and bright and fun to be with, she'd wanted a big family. Well-mannered and dignified, she would make the perfect doctor's wife.

He had loved her. But she hadn't filled the emptiness. And it hadn't mattered, because he'd had no idea that anything was missing.

As if his life had been this grayness, this…predictable procession of days.

And now, there was…color.

Color, which to him equaled Lacey.

Lacey in a silk robe and nothing else, waiting for him at the end of a long working day, turning from the mirror in their bathroom, blue eyes soft and hungry, opening the robe, dropping it to the floor….

The uncomfortable truth was that sometimes, lately, he couldn't help wondering how long it would last.

She said that she loved him. He believed that she did. For now.

But she *was* Lacey. Impossible, unpredictable, incredible Lacey.

He *could* lose her.

So easily. Maybe not to another man. For some reason, he didn't fear that kind of rival.

But to her stubborn dream of a life as an artist. Yes. That damn dream could very well take her away from him.

"Logan…" She was still looking up at him, waiting for him to speak, to say the reasonable thing.

He let go of the chair. "I woke up and you weren't there. I got worried, that's all."

"It's important to me, to start getting back to work. Rosie makes her demands. And you know I want to be there for you, when you get home. But any time neither of you needs me, and I get the urge to pay a visit to my studio…" She let the thought finish itself.

He nodded, said the words she needed to hear, the fair words, the reasonable ones. "Of course. I understand."

She smiled, and his heart did something physically impossible inside his chest. "All right, then," she whispered.

Rosie let out a small, sweet sigh. Her little eyes were shut. She'd stopped nursing. Logan looked down at his sleeping daughter, at his wife's breast, the just-released nipple shining and taut. "Come back to bed," he said, and knew that his longing was there in his voice.

Lacey nodded, answered huskily, "Yes. In a few minutes. I should at least try her on the other side first."

So he waited there with her in the dark as she put his daughter to her other breast. Rosie woke enough to begin nursing again. But in three or four minutes, her tiny mouth went loose once more.

"She's done." Lacey slid the robe back in place and lifted Rosie to her shoulder. Next, there was the diaper to change. And then finally, Lacey put the baby in the crib and tucked the blankets around her.

"Come to bed."

She hung back. "Logan…"

"What?"

"I do love you. So very much. Please believe me."

He pulled her into his arms then, held the silk, the softness, the warmth of her close. She tipped up her head and he kissed her, a deep kiss, one that he broke only to whisper with more urgency than before, "To bed. Come on."

She went willingly then, pausing only to collect the baby monitor from the bureau as they went by.

## Chapter Twelve

"It's so lovely to meet you at last," said Fiona Connery, reaching for Lacey's hand. "Where is the baby?"

"Rosie's at home," Lacey replied, "with a sitter."

"Ah. Well." Fiona twined her fingers with Lacey's in a proprietary fashion and swept out her other arm in a gesture that indicated the whole of her large, beautifully appointed house and each and every one of her well-dressed, well-off, well-behaved guests. "Probably a good idea. What fun would a one-and-a-half-month-old have at something like this?"

Lacey agreed. "Maybe next time—or better still, the time after that."

Fiona leaned close. She wore a subtle, expensive perfume, one that suited her—floral, with a hint of musk. "Now, I shall drag you around for a moment, showing you off." She captured Lacey's free hand, then pulled both hands wide and stepped back. "This is a gorgeous dress."

Lacey smiled—modestly, of course. The dress was a simple, just-above-the-knee black velvet sheath, sleeveless, with a scoop neck. She'd bought it a week ago, specifically for Fiona's party. It had been easy to choose. She'd simply imagined what her sister might wear to an event like this.

Fiona spoke to Logan, who stood behind Lacey. "Your wife has great taste."

"I think so, too."

Lacey cast a glance back at him. He looked sexy and protective. She wanted to grab him and press herself against him and whisper something thoroughly inappropriate in his ear.

But Fiona was already pulling her toward the wide arch that led to the living room. "Come on. You have to meet Daniel. And Helen—or have you already met Helen?"

"No, not yet."

"She's a dear. You'll love her." Fiona sent a reassuring smile over her shoulder in Logan's direction. "Don't worry. You'll have this lovely wife of yours back soon enough."

Logan waved them on their way.

The next few hours weren't bad at all. Lacey smiled and laughed and talked about her baby and how happy she and Logan were. When asked about her life before her marriage, she spoke briefly of her work as an artist—*very* briefly, as a matter of fact. No one seemed that interested in what she'd been doing with herself before she married Logan, and that was fine with her. Her aim was to make a good impression, for Logan's sake. And she felt, as the evening progressed, that she was doing a pretty fair job of it.

She did have to turn down a couple of offers to get involved on charity committees. Fiona asked if she'd like to help out with Miner's General's Auxiliary. And the wife of a doctor who had his office in Logan's building wondered if Lacey might want to join Helping Hands, a group of doctors' wives who raised funds for such worthy causes as AIDS and breast cancer research.

She explained to both women that she would love to help out, but she couldn't right at the moment. She said she needed to get back to work in her studio before she took on anything else. With a new baby, and all the other changes that had taken place in her life lately, somehow there were just never enough hours in a day.

Fiona and the other woman smiled graciously and assured her that they understood. Lacey wasn't sure they did. And she felt just a little bit guilty at having to say no.

For about a minute and a half.

Then she reminded herself that she'd never claimed to be the ideal doctor's wife. She was an artist. After her family, her work had to come first—at least until she got herself back on track. And then, well, she'd see about taking on a little volunteer work.

It was just after eleven when she and Logan thanked their hostess for a terrific evening.

Fiona begged them to stay longer. "Don't go yet. The fun is only beginning."

Lacey put on an appropriately regretful expression. "We'd love to stay. Unfortunately, Rosie will be waking up soon, if she hasn't already. She'll be hungry. And guess who has to be there to feed her?"

"Ah," said Fiona, "I don't want to let you go, but I do understand." She leaned forward and kissed Lacey on the cheek. "It is so good to meet you at last. And I want to see more of you. How about lunch next week? I could drop in at your house, just long enough to meet little Rosie. Perhaps then…you *do* have a sitter you can call?"

"Well, I—"

Fiona ran right on. "I was thinking that we could get out for an hour or two, just you and I, that we could really get a chance to put our heads together. How would that be?"

Put our heads together about what? Lacey wondered.

Logan said, "Mrs. Hopper can watch the baby for a couple of hours, don't you think, Lacey?"

The housekeeper, who came twice a week, probably could watch Rosie—and no doubt would quite willingly. Mrs. Hopper loved babies. And Lacey always paid her extra whenever she agreed to baby-sit for an hour or two while Lacey ran errands.

Fiona pressed on. "How about a week from this coming Wednesday? That should give you plenty of time to work things out with a sitter. Say right around noonish?"

Lacey felt slightly railroaded, but then wondered why. It *was* only lunch. Wasn't it?

Logan and Fiona were waiting to hear her reply.

She put on her most gracious smile and said she'd love to join Fiona for lunch. And a week from Wednesday would be fine.

The twins came to visit again on Friday. Maud brought her little boy, Devon.

Lacey exclaimed over how much he'd grown.

She was also able to inform the twins that she'd spent several hours in her studio since their last visit.

"I have no big projects in the works yet, but I have a lot of ideas. I've been drawing again. It's slowly coming back to me."

"Way to go, Lace," cheered Mira.

Maud agreed, "We're proud of you. Keep it up."

They asked her when she'd be coming to the Eureka Lounge to hear the band again. "It's August," Maud reminded her. "Almost a year since the last time you heard us play. We've been adding in a few of those great old blues and soul classics to some of our sets, 'Stormy Monday' and 'When a Man Loves a Woman.' Mira's doing lead vocals on them. And you know how she can wail."

Lacey said she'd try, but with the baby and with Logan's demanding schedule, it was always a challenge arranging a night out.

Maud made a face. "We didn't say you had to bring *him.*"

"But I want to bring *him,*" she replied. "I have high hopes that someday the three of you will learn to get along."

Mira groaned. "Gag me with a stethoscope—and don't hold your breath. He thinks we're a bad influence on you. He's *always* thought so. Remember back in high school, when we broke into the science lab before the advanced biology classes got their vivisection lesson and let all those poor doomed frogs out of their terrariums? He told your mother that she should forbid you to hang with us ever again."

"That was high school."

"You're trying to tell us he's changed his mind about us?"

Lacey coughed. "Well..."

"Don't try," Maud advised. "You'll only be lying and we won't believe it. Just come hear us play—and bring *him* if you have to."

Lacey said she would come—eventually.

The twins shared a significant glance and left it at that.

That evening, Lacey mentioned the idea to Logan. "They play on Friday nights, so I was thinking that maybe we could—"

He was shaking his head before she'd even finished making the suggestion. "I'm not much for heavy metal music, Lace."

She started to set him straight. "The twins' band isn't heavy metal..." But then she remembered that it had been at one time. "Well, maybe it *was*. Seven or eight years ago. They've changed a lot since then, though. I think you'd like them now."

He gave her one of his irritatingly superior doubtful looks and said that maybe, some evening, in a few weeks...

Wednesday, Fiona arrived right at noon. She held the baby and declared her "an absolute doll."

"Daniel and I have two of our own, did you know? Patrice and Daniel, Jr. Patrice is at Stanford. Daniel, Jr. is at UCLA. I miss them, but I do manage to keep busy." She laughed. "Do I ever. Being a doctor's wife is a full-time job."

And that, as it turned out, was the theme of Lacey's lunch date with Fiona: being a doctor's wife is a full-time job.

Fiona asked her again to join a couple of committees. Lacey said she just might do that. Later. Right now, as she'd already explained, she had her own work to catch up on.

Fiona accepted Lacey's refusal with a dazzling smile. "Don't expect me to stop asking you."

Lacey laughed. She really did like Fiona. "Fiona. You are not going to charm me into doing things your way."

Fiona put on a wide-eyed expression and splayed her beautifully manicured hand against her chest. "Me? Try to charm you? Never. You and Logan *will* make it to the Health Aid Society's annual banquet, won't you? It's on the fourth of September. Everyone turns out for it. Daniel and I will be there, of course. And Helen and her husband. It's important that the practice be well-represented."

Lacey was able to say yes to that one. "Logan mentioned the banquet. He told me he wanted to go. So when the invitation came, I went right ahead and sent in the check for two tickets."

Fiona beamed. "Good. I'm so glad." She reached across and patted Lacey's arm. "We'll make a proper doctor's wife out of you yet."

Lacey decided she was going to have to be more direct. She pushed her empty plate aside, rested her forearms on the table and leaned toward the woman across from her. "Fiona. Be honest. I'm sure you've heard about me."

Fiona sat back. She was blushing, a blush that looked thoroughly enchanting on her. "Well, now. What can I say when you put me on the spot like this? Meadow Valley has grown a lot in the past couple of decades. But at heart, it's still a small town, isn't it?"

"Yes, it is. And if you've asked around, you must have learned that I've never been a 'proper' anything."

Fiona waved a hand. "Oh, now. A childish prank or two…"

"I'm never going to try to be someone I'm not, Fiona. I love Logan and I'm proud to be his wife. But I am not Jenna. I'm me."

"I understand that. I do."

"Good. Then you and I will get along just fine."

Fiona sat forward again. "Of course we will—and you know, the Aid to the Indigent fall rummage sale is almost upon us. September eleventh and twelfth, can you believe it? If you could see your way clear to making a few calls next week to ask for donations, and then another set of reminder calls the week of the sale, just to let people know again that we do need their donations—"

"Fiona, don't you ever give up?"

"Never. What about those calls?"

Lacey shook her head—and said yes.

Fiona said, "Wonderful. And if you'd just agree to a few hours on Saturday the eleventh, manning a booth, well, I cannot tell you how grateful I would be."

Lacey suppressed a sigh. "Okay. I'll take a booth— if you promise me that'll be all for a couple of months, at least."

"I promise."

"All right, then."

"Excellent—and where is our waitress? I want a fruit tart, just for a little extra treat."

"I think Fiona likes you," Logan said later, when Lacey told him about their lunch.

"Maybe she does," Lacey admitted. "She's also determined to show me the way to be a real asset to you and to the practice."

"Don't let her railroad you," he advised. "Just do what you want to do."

That pleased her. Fiona might hope to make her over into the perfect doctor's wife, but Logan didn't appear to be in on the scheme. She winked at him. "Have I ever done anything but exactly what I wanted to do?"

He laughed then. "Not that I can recall."

"I have an idea," she suggested brightly. "How about a visit to the Eureka Lounge this Friday night? You can hear Mira sing the blues."

His expression darkened. "What brought that up?"

"I'm learning from Fiona. When you want someone to do something, you have to ask them. Repeatedly, if necessary."

"I don't think I'm ready to hear Mira sing the blues—not this week, anyway."

"Why did I know you'd say that?"

"I haven't a clue."

"I'm not giving up."

"I'll consider that a warning."

"Please do."

He pulled her close and planted a kiss on the tip of her nose. "You have an extremely self-satisfied look on your face, Mrs. Severance."

"That's not self-satisfaction. That's contentment. All in all, even though I've yet to drag you to the Eureka Lounge, I'd still say this marriage of ours is working out pretty well."

"I couldn't agree with you more," he said, and kissed her again, this time on the mouth.

They went up to bed not long after that and made slow, delicious love. Lacey thought, as she dropped off to sleep a little later, that she'd never been happier. She had her love and her baby and little by little, she was getting back to work.

Xavier Hockland called the next day.

# *Chapter Thirteen*

"I got your number from Barnaby," Xavier said in that slightly bored, thoroughly arrogant tone Lacey remembered so well. "I asked him if I could just drop by his loft and show Belinda Goldstone the work you did last winter. He said I had to check with you first."

Belinda Goldstone. Lacey's pulse accelerated. Belinda Goldstone was one of L.A.'s premiere art dealers. She owned a gallery where she hung only the works of top contemporary artists.

"Lace. Are you there?"

Lacey swallowed. "I'm here."

"I heard you had that baby."

*That* baby. What was the matter with him? "Her name is Rosie."

"And you adore her." Xavier sighed.

"Yes, I do. She's one of the two best things that ever happened to me."

"The other being?"

"My husband, Logan."

Xavier said nothing. Lacey waited him out. Finally, he asked, "Have you done any work at all in the past few months?"

"Xavier. Let's not get started on that. What I'm working on, or when, or how much time I'm giving to it is no longer your concern. What's this about Belinda Goldstone?"

He let a few seconds elapse, just to show her he was controlling the conversation, before he said, "I had lunch with her yesterday. She asked about you."

Lacey was frowning. "I hardly know her. I've met her at two or three openings, that's all—just to shake her hand and say, 'How are you?' Why would she ask about me?"

Xavier sighed again. "Until you decided to throw it all away, you *were* my protégée."

Lacey knew that wasn't all of it. "Okay. So she asked about me. And you told her I'd thrown it all away. End of conversation."

Xavier made an impatient sound. "All right, all right. Word gets around. There has been some buzz about that series of figure studies you were working on before you took off to…complete your gestation period in the wilds of Wyoming."

"So she asked about the series I was working on last winter, is that it?"

"Yes."

"And you told her…?"

Another pause, then he gave out grudgingly, "That

they were fabulous. Sensual. Arresting. Powerful. I laid on the adjectives. They were only the truth."

Lacey's heart had started pounding hard again. "And she asked if she could see them?"

"Yes. I told her I'd check into it. Will you call that damn Barnaby and tell him it's all right if I show them to her?"

Lacey resisted the urge to throw back her head and let out a long, loud yelp of glee.

"Lace? Will you call Barnaby?"

"Yes, Xavier, I will."

"Thank you."

"Thank *you*."

"You're welcome," Xavier said. "And there's one other thing…"

"Yes?"

"Perhaps I was a little out of line, about that baby."

"Her name is Rosie. And yes, you were out of line."

"You're happy."

"I am."

"And Barnaby said the man's a doctor. That he has money."

"What are you getting at, Xavier?"

"Happiness and money. These are good things for an artist. Some opt for struggle—they buy into the myth that suffering will somehow improve the work. This is delusional. Struggle only wears one down. The work gets done in spite of suffering, not because of it. A place to work, and few outside worries. That's what an artist needs. Happiness and money can help a lot in that regard. When you told me about the baby, I understood you were going to be dealing with it on your own. Now

I can see that isn't the case, so perhaps I was too quick to offer my advice on the subject."

"Xavier, is this an apology?"

"I never apologize. I'm just pleased to hear you're doing well. Have Barnaby call me."

"Yes. Yes, I will."

At first, Lacey told no one about Xavier's call—except Barnaby in L.A. It was her little secret she kept just to herself.

Belinda Goldstone had asked to see her work.

It might mean nothing.

Or it might mean a great deal.

She wouldn't know until Xavier—or Belinda Goldstone herself—called back. *If* one of them called back.

Until then, well, she certainly did feel terrific about herself. She found it easier to concentrate when she went into her studio. Her confidence had just gotten a big boost, and that did wonders for her ability to focus when she worked.

And beyond progress in her work, it was pure self-indulgent delight just to fantasize a little about what this might mean. To imagine her paintings hanging in Belinda Goldstone's gallery.

In her fantasy, of course, the show would sell out before the opening. And her beautiful paintings of Logan would…

Logan.

That did give her pause. She had yet to tell him that there were nine nudes of him—his face carefully disguised, of course—stored in Barnaby Cole's L.A. loft.

She probably *should* have told him before now.

In fact, she realized, she couldn't afford to put off telling him any longer. If anything did come of Belinda

Goldstone's visit to Barnaby's loft, she wanted her husband to be reasonably prepared. It only seemed fair that he should know about the existence of the paintings before she sprung the news that Belinda Goldstone wanted to hang them in her gallery.

She told him two nights after Xavier called, over a dinner of roast beef, baby carrots and new potatoes—a meal that was one of his favorites. She'd decided it wouldn't hurt to coddle him a little before she hit him with the information she probably shouldn't have kept from him in the first place.

He took the news amazingly well. He seemed surprised, but not offended. And he had a number of questions.

"You say it's impossible to tell that I was your…" He frowned, seeking the right word.

She provided one. "Inspiration?"

"Okay. I'll go with that. Will anyone be able to tell that I *inspired* you?"

"Well," she hedged. "People who know you might guess. But I promise, they won't know for certain. The face in each painting is hidden—with a mask, or by shadows, or because the figure is turned away from the viewer."

He was still frowning. "Exactly how nude is nude?"

"Logan. What is that supposed to mean?"

He tried again. "I guess I'm asking, are they… tasteful?"

She had to laugh. "*Tasteful* wasn't exactly what I was shooting for."

He set down his fork. "Let me put it this way. What shows?"

She understood. And laughed again. "How can such a sexy man be such a prude?"

"Just answer me. What shows?"

"No genitals. How's that?"

He picked up his fork again. "A relief."

They ate in silence for a minute or two. Then he said, "There are nine of them?"

"Uh-huh."

"How long did it take you to paint them?"

"I painted the first one here in Meadow Valley, when I was staying with Jenna, at the beginning of October."

He glowered at her. "Right after you sent me away."

She let the implied accusation pass and stuck to the issue. "Yes. And I finished the ninth one in L.A., in early April, about a month before I left for Wyoming."

He drank from his wineglass and set it down. His expression had softened. "I guess that means I was on your mind a lot, all those months."

"Yes, Logan, you were." She cut a bite of meat, concentrating on the small task, then glanced up through her lashes at him. "You know that you were."

His eyes were very dark. "You were on my mind, too."

"I'm glad." She waited, thinking, *It's going to happen now. He's going to actually get the words out. He's going to say that he loves me.*

But the moment passed. He watched her with desire, with tenderness, with a hint of exasperation—and with what she knew to be love.

He just didn't say it.

"Why are you telling me now?" he asked quietly.

She poked the bite of meat into her mouth and chewed, thinking, *Well, what did I expect? The man is hardheaded, but he's certainly no fool.*

So what now? She could lie and keep her little secret to herself. He might never have to know.

But if Xavier or Belinda Goldstone *did* call…

So much for her secret.

She finished chewing. He waited, his eyes never leaving her face.

She swallowed. "You remember the artist I went to L.A. to study under? I think I talked about him a little, last September."

Logan thought for a minute. "Hockland, right? Xavier Hockland."

"Yes, Xavier Hockland. He called, the day before yesterday with some good news…or it *could* be good news."

Logan had set his fork down again, but he didn't speak. He was waiting for her to tell him whatever it was she had to say.

She sucked in a breath. "Xavier had lunch with a certain very well-known art dealer, Belinda Goldstone, a few days ago. She'd heard about the paintings—through the grapevine, you could say. She asked to see them. He wanted my permission to show them to her."

"Xavier Hockland has the paintings?"

"No, they're at Barnaby Cole's. I've told you about Barnaby, haven't I? He's a friend. He has a big loft. Downtown. And Xavier wanted to take Belinda Goldstone there, to see them."

"And?"

"And I said yes, that it was fine with me if Xavier showed her my paintings."

"What else?"

"Nothing else. Yet."

"A reputable art dealer wants to see some of your paintings. You gave Xavier Hockland permission to show them to her. And that's all."

"Yes," she said. "That's all. As of now. Naturally, I'm hoping more will come of it."

"Like what?"

She realized she couldn't read him. He seemed distant. Or at least he had in the past few moments. Distant and a little bit cold. Strange. She'd anticipated that he might be distant and cold, even angry with her, when he learned of the existence of the paintings. But she never would have guessed that this other bit of news would upset him.

"Logan. What's the matter?"

"Nothing. Just tell me. What exactly are you hoping for?"

His disdainful tone grated. She answered with heat. "What do you think I'm hoping for? That Belinda Goldstone will want to hang my paintings in her gallery, that I'll have a major show and that the show will sell out. What do we all hope for, Logan? Appreciation. Acceptance. To get paid and paid well for the work that we've done."

He was sitting very still. "You're angry," he said.

She pushed her plate away. "No. Yes. It means a lot to me, that's all, that someone like Belinda Goldstone wants to see my work. I'd like to think that you're pleased for me. But you don't seem pleased. You don't seem pleased at all."

"I *am* pleased."

She stared at him across the table, wanting to believe him, but not quite able to.

He slid his napkin in at the side of his plate and pushed his chair back. "Lace…" His eyes pleaded. His tone was gentle again.

Her heart went to mush.

She let her shoulders droop. "I guess I am a little sensitive about this."

In two long strides he was beside her, taking her hand, pulling her up and into his waiting arms. "I'm sorry," he whispered as he stroked her hair. "I didn't mean to hurt you...."

She wrapped her arms around him, pressed herself close. "It's okay. Never mind. You're right. Nothing's really happened yet, anyway. And it could very well turn out that nothing will."

He tipped her chin up and his mouth came down to cover hers. With a low moan, she slid her arms around his neck.

A few minutes later, they went upstairs.

The next day was Sunday. Logan didn't have to work. They spent a long, lazy morning reading the Sunday papers in bed, with Rosie between them, gurgling and cooing and waving her tiny, plump hands above the blankets.

Later, they dressed and put Rosie in her car seat and drove down into the Valley to buy a few things for the house—some new deck chairs and an entry hall table. That night, they left Rosie with a sitter and went out to dinner at a place they both liked over on Commercial Street.

It wasn't until Monday morning after Logan had left for his office that Lacey found herself rethinking their exchange of Saturday night. As Rosie napped, she sat in her studio with her sketch pad in her lap and brooded over the words her husband hadn't said.

Simple expressions of encouragement and understanding, like...

Good luck.

Or, I'll keep my fingers crossed for you.

Or, Of course, Belinda Goldstone will call.

Or, You're a damn good artist and it's about time you got a break.

Eventually, Rosie woke. Lacey heard the fitful cries from the monitor on the windowsill and came back to herself with a start.

She looked down at the sketch pad in her hands.

Blank.

Well, she thought, that's what brooding will get you. Nowhere.

Was she overreacting?

Probably.

As she'd admitted to Logan the other night, she *was* sensitive on this subject. Probably way *too* sensitive.

The wisest thing to do, she knew, was to let it go for now. And when the subject came up again, she'd try her best to approach it calmly and rationally. She'd make a concerted effort not to allow her own insecurities to get all mixed up with whatever might be bothering her husband.

Rosie cried louder.

Lacey set her sketch pad aside and went to take care of her baby.

Two days later, on Wednesday, at eleven in the morning, Mack called from a Key West hospital.

"It's a boy," he announced. "Eight pounds, two ounces."

Lacey let out a glad cry. "Oh, Mack! Congratulations. I can hardly believe it. His name. What's his name?"

"Ian Alexander. The Alexander's for my stepfather—"

"And Ian after our dad. Great choice."

"We think so."

"Is Jenna…?"

"She's right here. A little tired."

"I'll bet. I promise I won't keep her long."

Jenna came on the line. "Lace. Hello."

Lacey's eyes blurred with sudden moisture. She swiped at them with the heel of her hand. "Hey. A beautiful boy, huh?"

"Yep. You're an auntie."

"Oh, Jen. I can't believe it. I…I want to see him."

"Then come. Bring Rosie. And Logan. Come see us."

"Oh, Jen. You know I'd love to…"

Both sisters were silent. Lacey knew that Jenna was thinking the same thing that she was.

*Logan would find some reason why they couldn't go.*

Jenna hitched in a tight little breath. "It's all right," she said, her voice weary. "I understand. Maybe someday…"

"Yes," Lacey agreed. "Someday soon…" Why did that feel like such a complete lie? "…and I should let you go now, shouldn't I?"

"I'll call you, in a day or two, after we're out of this hospital and back home where we belong."

"Yes. Oh, please do."

"We…we don't talk enough anymore, Lace."

Lacey closed her eyes and murmured, "I know."

"What? I can hardly hear you."

Lacey spoke right into the mouthpiece this time. "I

said, I know. We don't talk enough. I keep meaning to call you, but…" But what? There was really no excuse.

Except that she and Logan had a good life. And Jenna wasn't part of it. Jenna was someone Lacey and Logan never talked about.

Logan certainly never mentioned her. He'd loved Jenna for over a decade, had wanted to marry her. She had helped to make his house a beautiful home. Yet it was as if he'd prefer to pretend that she simply didn't exist.

Then again, maybe Lacey had it wrong. Yes, Logan never mentioned Jenna. But Lacey never talked about her either.

Jenna said, "Let's not allow ourselves to drift apart."

Lacey brushed away more tears. "It's a deal."

"I love you."

"Oh, and I love you, too."

Jenna laughed then, a tired sound, but a cheerful one. "My husband is grabbing the phone from me now. He seems to think I've talked long enough. I'll call…"

"Okay. Bye."

Mack came back on. "Think about it," he said. "Come for a visit. Talk it over with that husband of yours. I think it's about time we all started letting bygones be bygones."

It was good advice and Lacey knew it. "All right," she said.

"What was that?"

"I said, all right, Mack. I'll talk to him."

## *Chapter Fourteen*

That evening, Lacey told Logan that Jenna and Mack's baby had been born.

He said, "Be sure to congratulate them for me."

They were sitting in the family room, on the long sofa there. She toed off her shoes and folded her legs under her, to the side. "I thought I'd send them a baby swing. I love the one we got for Rosie. Keeps her happy for long stretches of time."

"A baby swing sounds good to me."

She leaned her head against his arm, which rested along the sofa back. Her heart was racing. But she kept her voice offhand. "Oh, and Jenna asked us to come to Key West. For a visit. Mack mentioned the idea, too."

She felt his bicep flex beneath her cheek. "Lace, I

can't get away right now. Not so soon after a two-week trip to Wyoming."

She sat up straight and sought his eyes. "All right. Then when?"

He hesitated, but finally gave out reluctantly, "Maybe next spring."

In the spring. Six or seven months. That wouldn't be so bad, if she could get a definite commitment. "The spring then. In April? I'll tell Jenna when she calls."

He was already shaking his head. "Let's just wait until April and think about it then."

"But Logan—"

"I can't make any promises about seven months from now." His tone had cooled, and there was an underpinning of steel in it. "That's all there is to it."

Okay, Lacey thought. We've danced around this long enough. Now, we'd better get down to a little honesty on the subject. "Logan, what's the real problem here?"

"I told you. I can't—"

She didn't let him finish. "Is it that you still feel uncomfortable at the thought of seeing Jenna and Mack again?"

He didn't answer for a moment. Then he admitted, "Yes. The idea does make me uncomfortable. But Jenna is your sister. And I suppose we'll have to see her and McGarrity now and then."

"We'll *have* to see them?"

He looked at her levelly. "That's what I said. Please don't ask me to pretend it's something I'm looking forward to."

She stared right back at him, eye-to-eye. "I'm not asking you to pretend anything. I'm asking you to start thinking about putting all the old garbage behind you."

"Fine. I'll do that. To the best of my ability."

She let out a long breath. "To the best of your ability?"

"That's what I said."

She bit her lower lip, released it. "That's just great." She found she didn't want to sit there with him, not right then. She slid her feet to the rug and padded to the big window that looked out on the redwood deck. The outside lights were on, illuminating the new deck furniture they'd bought the other day, as well as the old willow tree that grew right next to the backyard steps. The willow's leaves were still summer-green. But soon enough, those leaves would begin to turn.

It was September again. In a few weeks, it would be a full year since she had knocked on his door, offering a shoulder to cry on and a four-layer devil's food cake.

A full year. In that time, she had learned that she loved him. She had borne his child. And she had come to believe that he loved her.

And was that the real problem here, the one she was trying to get them both to deal with?

She believed he loved her. But he had never said he did.

In some ways, it seemed that Jenna's gentle, loving spirit stood between them still. And never more so than now, when he refused to take the steps required to put old hurts away for good.

She heard him approach. He put his hands on her shoulders. She stiffened, but then made her body relax beneath his touch. She felt his breath, warm across the crown of her head. "Lace. Just give it a little more time, all right?"

"How much more time?"

He didn't answer, but his hands tightened a fraction on her shoulders, a signal that he wanted her to lean back against him.

She folded her arms over her stomach and remained fully upright. "Logan, you say you're happy with me."

"I am."

"Then why can't you let the past go? Why can't you forgive my sister for…choosing another man over you?" She turned beneath his hands, so she could face him. "I don't call her anymore, Logan. Because I feel uncomfortable myself, about the whole thing. I don't want it to be like this. I don't want to lose touch with her. She's my sister. And she's my friend. And I love her very much."

"I never said I expected you to cut off contact with her."

"No. But you…you don't want me to talk about her. You behave as if you'd just as soon forget that she and Mack even exist."

She paused, waiting for him to argue with her, to reassure her, to tell her he didn't mind talking about Jenna at all. That he most certainly did not want to forget she existed.

But he didn't argue.

She made her final point. "You won't go and visit her."

He did have a reply to that. "I will. Eventually. You just have to back off a little. Give me a little more time."

More time. "You already said that."

"And I think it's a reasonable request."

She stared at him, thinking, I love you. Do you love me?

Should she ask him?

Somehow, she just couldn't bear to.

It seemed to her that a declaration of love ought to be freely given. It wasn't something a woman should pull out of a man—like a splinter or a shameful confession.

She warned in a gentle voice, "Don't take too much time, Logan. Eventually I'll simply go to Key West without you."

"I understand," he said.

"Do you?"

"Let it go, Lace."

"All right. I will. For now."

Two days later, when Jenna called, Lacey told her it would be a while before she and Logan visited. Jenna didn't ask why. She said she'd look forward to their visit whenever it came. And that any time Lacey needed her, all she had to do was call.

The phone rang again not two minutes after Lacey hung up from her conversation with Jenna.

It was Barnaby Cole. "I had to call you. My fingers were just itching to punch up your number."

Lacey laughed, but her heart had started beating hard and fast. "What?"

"They just left."

"I take it you mean Xavier and Belinda Goldstone."

"You take it right." Barnaby's voice, always deep and booming, seemed even deeper than usual, and charged with excitement. Lacey could see him in her mind's eye, a chocolate-skinned, muscular giant of a man, hunched over the phone, fiddling with the small gold hoop he always wore in his left ear.

"How long were they there?" she demanded.

"Over an hour."

"And? What happened? Barnaby, stop torturing me. Tell me, before I have a heart attack."

"Tell you—?"

"Everything."

"Everything." He chuckled, that low, rolling chuckle of his that Lacey had always loved. "All right. Let's see. They came up the freight elevator, since that's the only way to get here. Xavier made the introductions. The art dealer said the same thing that everybody says. It must be fabulous to have all this space—but the neighborhood is so dangerous, didn't I worry a little about my own safety? I said—"

"Barnaby. Stop it."

He chuckled some more. "Stop what?"

"When I said 'everything,' you know what I meant."

He pretended innocence. "Oh. You want to hear about your *paintings*...."

"That's right. So tell me. Tell me right now."

"Well, let's see. I'd taken them out of the storage racks and propped them against the walls of the studio, in the order you told me to. I led both the Goldstone woman and Xavier back there. She took one look at them—"

"Oh, God." Lacey ordered herself to breathe. "What?"

"—and she turned to Xavier and me—we were standing behind her. She waved at us, a shooing gesture, with the back of her hand. 'Leave me alone,' she said. 'Give a woman some space.'"

"So? You and Xavier—"

"We went out to the kitchen area. I bought an espresso machine, did I tell you? We made lattes."

"You and Xavier made lattes, while Belinda Goldstone looked at my paintings."

"That's right. She was in there forever."

"And when she came out?"

"She was very quiet. I offered her a latte. She said she had to get back to the gallery."

"And that's all?"

"You should have seen her face."

"Why? What was wrong with it?"

"Nothing. She loved what she saw."

"You *think* she loved what she saw."

"No. I *know* she loved what she saw. She'll be calling you, just wait."

"Wait?" Lacey let out a wild laugh. "*Wait?* I'll go crazy…"

"Call Xavier. Maybe she said something more to him after they left."

She did call Xavier. He didn't answer, so she left him a message.

He called back two hours later, after she'd nursed Rosie and changed her diaper and spent the rest of the time pacing the floor.

Xavier said virtually the same thing Barnaby had said. That he was sure Belinda Goldstone would be calling her soon.

"Soon? When is *soon?*"

"It's Friday, Lace. And it's after three. The working week is over."

"Oh. Great. That's just great."

"I'm sure she'll call you Monday. Or sometime next week."

"I might have a nervous breakdown before then."

"A nervous breakdown would be counterproductive. My advice is to work."

"Work."

"Yes. And do…whatever mothers do with their infants. Go someplace wonderful for dinner. Make love with your husband. Live your life and live it well."

"If Belinda Goldstone happens to call you—"

"She won't. Not about you. It's between you and her now. I gave her your number."

"She asked for it?"

"Yes. So settle down. Wait. She will call. She'll ask you to meet with her. She'll offer to become your dealer. And she'll want to discuss your first show with her gallery."

"You're talking about it as if it's really going to happen."

"Because it is. Wait and see—and calm down. You deserve this, Lace. Remember that. You've worked long and hard to get to this point."

Lacey decided not to tell Logan about the calls from L.A. She had no real news yet, and he'd seemed so cool on the subject the other time they'd discussed it. She decided it would be wiser to wait until she had something concrete to say.

By the time he came home, after eight, she had settled down considerably. She'd even spent a couple of hours in her studio working on a painting she'd started of the twins.

He brought flowers. And his eyes were tender and hopeful.

He didn't mention Jenna or the argument of the night before. But he did say, "I missed you all day. I couldn't wait to get home and get my arms around you."

He gave her the flowers and then hardly allowed her the time to put them in a vase before he was pulling her close and raining kisses on her upturned face.

"I love kissing you. It's something about the way you smell, like no one else, so damn sweet..." His lips moved down to her throat. He began to draw on the skin.

She laughed, putting up a playful struggle. "Remember. Tomorrow night. The Health Aid Society Banquet."

He growled against her neck and took his bruising kiss lower.

A few minutes later, he was leading her toward the stairs, stopping in the breakfast room and the hall, first to remove her big shirt and then her skinny tube top, which he'd already slid down so it was bunched around her waist.

On the stairs, he helped her out of her shoes. He took away her capri pants in the balcony hall. By the time they reached their bedroom, all she had left was a pair of red bikini panties.

He got rid of them, too.

Then he guided her down onto the bed and he kissed her all over, until she moaned and writhed and forgot all about the love words he never said and the sister he wouldn't visit and his cool, distant responses when she'd hinted at a breakthrough in her career.

The next night, at the Meadow Valley Country Club, Lacey and Logan shared a table with Dan and Fiona and Helen and her husband, Bud. After the food and the speeches, there was dancing. Lacey whirled in her husband's arms and thought that being the wife of a handsome doctor did have its moments—especially when the doctor in question was Logan.

They danced for a half hour without stopping, waiting on the floor as each number ended, and then picking up the rhythm again when a new song began. Finally, though, the five-piece combo took a break.

Lacey whispered in her husband's ear, "We're going to have to leave soon, I'm afraid."

He knew what she meant. "Are you all right?"

"So far." Her breasts were beginning to feel just a bit uncomfortable. "But I'd say that Rosie's probably getting hungry and I would prefer not to have a leaking accident—and don't look now, but that nice pharmaceutical supplies salesman is headed our way. I think it's time I paid a visit to the ladies' room."

Logan held her closer and murmured for her ears alone, "Great. Leave me when I need you most."

She kissed him on the cheek. "I'll be back. Then we'll go."

The salesman was closing in as Logan reluctantly released her.

Lacey followed the arrows to the club's black and white marble ladies' room, which was, surprisingly enough, unoccupied. She proceeded down to the end stall.

She'd barely shut the door and engaged the latch when she heard the main door open again. High heels tapped against the marble tiles.

"No one here." That was Helen Sanderson's voice, pitched low, but quite clear. Voices carried easily, amplified against the cool marble walls.

Lacey froze, feeling awkward and a little silly, wondering if she should announce her own presence, then thinking how gauche that would sound. She heard a stall door open, then another, and then two sets of footsteps again, this time entering the stalls.

"She really is lovely," Helen said. Two latches clicked shut. "And quite charming, as well."

"Yes." That was Fiona. "Those gorgeous big blue

eyes and that angelic face—you did hear the story, didn't you?"

Dread. Lacey felt it. Like a lead weight in her stomach. She knew what was coming.

And it was.

"Of course," Helen said. "Jenna Bravo's sister. An affair that resulted in pregnancy. A marriage was probably the best choice, under the circumstances. And they certainly do appear devoted to each other."

Lacey leaned her forehead against the cool metal of the stall door thinking, *It's too late to speak up now.*

She lifted her head, straightened her shoulders. *Buck up,* she silently instructed herself. *The things they're saying are only the truth.*

"Yes," said Fiona. "I think it's all working out rather well. It's obvious Logan is thoroughly taken with her. I think a lot of it is—oh, how to say it—physical? But there's nothing necessarily wrong with that, now is there? Over time, I'm sure the relationship will deepen and mature."

One toilet flushed, and then the other.

Lacey thought, *That's all. They're going to shut up now.*

They weren't.

Helen said, "I understand you've been taking her under your wing."

"I have," Fiona replied. "I really do enjoy her. And I think, as time goes by, she'll settle down. She did have a few problems as a high school girl. Wild antics and crazy pranks. And she ran away a lot, from what I've been able to find out. But all that's in the past. Nothing to worry about now, from what I can see. I'm trying to guide her along a little, to get her involved with the auxiliary at Miner's General and a few other important pet projects of mine. She insists she doesn't have the time, that she's going to *make* something of herself as an artist."

"So I heard." The stall latches clicked again, the women's shoes echoed on the marble tiles.

Lacey remained absolutely still. She thought, I will be quiet. I will be tactful. I will do what my sister would have done under these circumstances. I will wait here with my mouth shut until they leave.

Water ran in the basins. Fiona declared, "Marrying Logan is the best thing that ever could have happened to her. She's been living hand-to-mouth in Los Angeles the past several years, hoping her *art* would someday support her." The water stopped. Lacey heard the whisk-thump of paper towels being pulled from dispensers. "It's sad, I think, a bright, sweet girl like that, with such big dreams and no hope of their ever coming true."

That did it. It was just one condescending remark too many.

Lacey whirled and hit the flush button, though she'd never gotten around to using the toilet. Maybe it was small-minded of her, but she found the corresponding hush from the sink area gratifying in the extreme.

Then she turned back to the door, clicked open the latch and exited the stall, shoulders back and chin aimed high.

Fiona and Helen turned from the mirrors with matching expressions of mortified horror.

Fiona found her voice first. It sounded slightly choked. "Uh. Lacey. Oh, my..."

Lacey granted Fiona a blinding smile as she stepped

up to the sink and flipped on the goldtone faucet. She squirted soap onto her palm and stuck her hands beneath the water, sending a second smile, as dazzling as the first, in the doctor's direction.

She said sweetly, "You two really ought to find a more private setting for your intimate conversations."

Fiona started to speak, and then coughed instead. Helen merely continued to look dismayed.

Lacey turned off the water and yanked a towel from the dispenser. "I'll tell you what. Sometime in the next year or so, I'm having a major show of some of my most recent paintings, in Los Angeles—have you heard about my show?"

Both women, in unison, swung their heads from side-to-side.

Lacey wadded her towel and tossed it in the trash. "Well, you have now. And of course, you will both be invited. Can I count on you to come?"

"Ahem, well…" said Helen.

"I…really…I…" stammered Fiona.

"A simple yes or no from each of you will do."

Fiona blinked. And then she actually said, "Of course I'll come, Lacey."

And Helen said, "Well. Thank you for inviting me. I'll do my best to attend."

"Terrific." Lacey fluffed her hair and straightened her midnight-blue sequined sheath—no leaks yet, thank God. "I can't tell you how much I'll enjoy having both of you there." She turned, edged around the dazed-looking Fiona and headed for the exit door, pausing before she went out to remark pleasantly, "This has been a great party. But the chicken Kiev was just a tad dry, didn't you think?"

Fiona and Helen looked at each other. They both nodded.

"Yes," said Fiona.

"A little dry," Helen concurred.

## *Chapter Fifteen*

During the drive home, Lacey told Logan all about the incident in the ladies' room.

He did not look pleased when she related the things Fiona and Helen had said, but then a half-smile curved his lips as she described how she'd marched out of the stall and spoken right up to them.

And then he said what she already knew. "You probably would have been wiser to have spoken up right away— or to have left it alone and kept quiet until they left."

"I agree, but you know how I am." She leaned across the console and touched a finger to his lips. "And I saw that smile. You don't completely disapprove of the way I reacted."

He caught her hand, kissed the fingers, then let go to execute a turn.

"And besides," she said. "I *like* Fiona. And Helen's basically okay, too. They can be a little stuffy, but they're still good at heart—a lot like you, actually, in that respect."

"Oh, I'm stuffy, am I?"

"If the lab coat fits…but it's okay. I love you anyway. And if I hadn't stood up to those women right then, I would have had to do it later, or ended up resenting them. This way, we all know where we stand."

"No doubt about that." He cast her a look. "And what about this L.A. opening you invented out of thin air?"

She hesitated, not sure she wanted to get into the subject of the call she hoped to receive from Belinda Goldstone.

He prompted, "Well?"

"I think I'll play that by ear."

He sent her another glance, an amused one this time. "I guess you will."

She waited a little nervously for him to say something else about the supposed art show. But he didn't. So she let it go. She'd stick with her original plan and tell him after she knew more—if it turned out there actually *was* more. It was always possible that both Barnaby and Xavier had misread the art dealer's reaction.

Maybe, in the end, there would be no call from Belinda Goldstone. That thought made her feel more than a little deflated.

But then she reminded herself of the painting she'd been working on, the one of the twins. It was coming together pretty well. She *was* working again. She *did* have talent and she wasn't going to give up, whether Belinda Goldstone offered to be her dealer or not.

* * *

Rosie was hungry when they got home. And Lacey was more than ready to feed her. Logan paid the sitter and drove her home.

When he returned, they took Rosie to bed with them. They snuggled in, all three of them, and turned on the television in the sitting area to a channel that was playing an old Hitchcock thriller. Rosie fell asleep first, cuddled between them.

Lacey dropped off soon after that. She woke a little later to find her husband snoring softly and her baby still sound asleep as well, sucking her tiny fist. On the television, Tippi Hedren screamed under brutal attack by a flock of furious crows. Lacey found the remote and pointed it at the television.

The screen went black. She kissed her baby and brushed her husband's dark hair off his forehead.

"And Fiona thinks it's mostly physical," she murmured fondly. Then she pulled the covers close and joined her family in sleep.

Fiona called the next day to apologize. "I was completely out of line to speak that way of you. I've just been agonizing that you're going to hate me."

Lacey said, "I don't hate you, Fiona. I like you. And I agree with a lot of what you said last night."

"You...you do?"

"Absolutely. Marrying Logan *is* the best thing that ever happened to me. And since *I'm* the best thing that ever happened to him, I'd say we're an excellent match."

Fiona took a moment to digest that bit of logic. Then she chuckled. "Lacey, my dear, you are a breath of fresh air. Tell me, can I still count on you for Saturday? The Aid to the Indigent rummage sale?"

Lacey assured Fiona that yes, she'd be there to handle a booth.

"And about those reminder calls…"

"I made the first set already. And I'll call everyone again in the next couple of days."

"You are an angel."

"Well, I wouldn't go *that* far."

At one o'clock Monday afternoon, Belinda Goldstone called.

At first, she spoke in hushed, awestruck tones, praising the nine figure studies she'd seen in Barnaby Cole's studio, calling them fresh and exciting and "hauntingly sensual."

Then she got down to business. "As I'm sure you've guessed by now, I would like to represent your work. Now, I know this is a lot to take in all at once, but as it turns out, I have an unexpected hole in my gallery's schedule."

One of her artists, she explained, had moved to New York.

"The SoHo scene has gone to his head," Belinda grumbled. "The wretched little ingrate has jumped ship to go with a dealer there. He was scheduled to show in March. I'd like to put you in his slot. We'd hang the paintings I saw at Barnaby Cole's studio, of course. And do you have anything else that's ready to show…or *could* be ready by then?"

Lacey felt slightly dizzy. Six months. Six months until her first major show, a *one-woman* show. With Belinda Goldstone's gallery.

"The silence is deafening," said Belinda. "Am I pushing too fast? We could wait until next October. Would that be better? That will give you a full year to—"

"No. No, March should be fine."

"You sound unsure."

"I'm not. It's just…what you said. A lot to take in. But I have a few other paintings stored at Barnaby's. You could take a look at them. And I've been working on some things more recently, too." She was thinking of the painting of Mira and Maud, of some ideas she had that would center on Rosie—and the sketches she'd done of Logan, asleep in the cabin in Wyoming. She'd been planning to do more with those very soon.

"We must meet in person as soon as you can manage it," said Belinda. "You'll see. The next six months will fly by. We have to get started. We have to firm up the business end. And I want to visit your friend Barnaby again—but together this time—to discuss the work you have at his studio. When can you come?"

Lacey heard herself announcing that she could come right away.

Logan didn't get home until after nine that night.

Lacey fed him and listened to the details of a doctor's day: the seven-year-old who had almost died of an asthma attack, the sweet elderly widower who refused to take his meds, the thirty-five-year-old woman who had fallen off her roof trying to coax her cat down out of a maple tree.

"Compound fracture of the left tibia." He shook his head. "What a mess. Shouldn't an adult woman know better?"

Lacey wiggled her eyebrows at him. "You're asking me?"

They laughed together. The previous September, right at the end of their five-day affair, Lacey had put her foot through the ceiling of one of the upstairs bedrooms in the house that had been her mother's. She'd been searching the attic for Jenna's cat, which had vanished not long before. She'd ended up with a broken foot—and the cat had shown up over a week later, in another part of town.

"What is it with women and cats?" Logan asked.

Since the question sounded thoroughly rhetorical, Lacey only shrugged.

Once Logan had eaten, Lacey poured him a brandy and led him upstairs. They sat on the sofa in the sitting area of their bedroom.

He swirled his brandy, sipped and set his glass on the coffee table. "Should we check on Rosie?"

"I'd say we have approximately…" she glanced at her watch, and then at the baby monitor across the room, on the nightstand by the bed "…a half hour, and we'll be hearing from her."

"Better enjoy every second of quiet, then."

"My sentiments exactly."

He laid his arm along the sofa back. She snuggled up close and leaned her head on his shoulder.

His lips brushed the crown of her head. "It's good to be home."

"Um…" She rubbed her cheek against the starched cloth of his dress shirt, thinking how she liked this time the best, in the evenings, when he came home to her and they sat together—talking, laughing, sharing what had happened in their respective days.

"So tell me," he said, "what's been going on around here?"

It was the moment she'd been waiting for, time to tell him her news.

Her pulse had picked up. She was a little nervous, a little worried about how he would take this, given the way he'd reacted the last time she'd mentioned the dealer who just might be interested in showing her work.

Logan laughed, a low, pleasant sound, warm and deep in her ear. "What? Total boredom? Nothing to report?"

She ordered her silly heartbeat to slow down. "As a matter of fact, I do have some news."

"What?"

She raised her head from its comfortable niche on his shoulder. It seemed wiser, somehow, to look at him when she told him.

He frowned. "What? Is something wrong?"

"No. No, not at all."

"Then…?"

Her mouth had gone as dry as a long stretch of desert road. She gulped, licked her lips.

"Lacey? What's the matter?"

"Nothing. Really. I only…"

"You only what?"

She said it. "Belinda Goldstone called today."

He just looked at her.

She gulped again. "Belinda…offered me a show— my *own* show—at her gallery, six months from now."

"Your own show," he repeated, each word slow and cautious.

She nodded. What was he thinking? She couldn't tell. She barreled ahead. "She needs to meet with me right away. So I said I'd fly down to L.A. tomorrow, and stay at least until Saturday. We'll get to know each other a little, make some decisions about what to include in the show—well, I mean, beyond those nine paintings I told you about, the ones of you?" She made herself pause, aware she was talking way too fast.

A black hole of silence followed. Cold fingers of dread tracked their way down her spine. He wasn't taking this well. He wasn't taking it well at all.

She didn't know what else to do, so she babbled out more information. "And Friday night, as it turns out, there's a show opening at Belinda's gallery. So I said I'd be there for that. It will be a great way to get the word out that she'll be handling my work."

She stopped again, for a breath—and because it seemed that she ought to give him a chance to talk.

He didn't talk. He just went on staring at her. She couldn't bear that. She prattled on. "I'd love for you to go, too, if you could manage it. I booked a flight for me and Rosie today, while I was making all the other arrangements, but I'm sure I could find one for all of us, if you'd come. I'm leaving tomorrow, staying with my friend Adele. But if you come, we can just go ahead and get a—"

He raised a hand. She fell silent in mid-sentence. "Let me get this straight," he said. "You're dragging Rosie to L.A. with you. And you're leaving tomorrow." His voice was utterly flat.

She stared at him, shocked by the look of pure disdain in his eyes.

"Well?" he demanded.

She made herself answer in a low, careful tone, all her former manic brightness fled. "Yes, Logan. I'm leaving tomorrow. And as for Rosie, well, what else would I do? She's nursing, so I have to be around to feed her."

"You're dragging her all over L.A. with you, to meet an art dealer? And to some art party?"

"No. I'm not dragging her anywhere. I have it all worked out. Adele loves babies. She's promised to baby-sit."

"All right. So you're flying to Los Angeles tomorrow to meet Belinda Goldstone. You're taking our daughter with you, and some artist friend of yours has promised to watch her."

"Logan, if you'd only—"

"Just tell me. Have I got it right?"

She pulled back to her side of the sofa, shock giving way to anger—anger that tightened her stomach and brought a hot flush to her cheeks. "Yes," she said, her tone as flat as his. "You've got it right."

"I suppose you knew about this the other night," he accused, "when you came up with that crack about your L.A. opening to put Helen and Fiona in their places. You knew then, didn't you, and you never said a word to me?"

The anger inside her burned hotter. She kept her voice low with great effort. "No, Logan. I didn't know. I *hoped.* But I didn't know any of this until Belinda called this afternoon."

That stopped him. For a few seconds, anyway. But he wasn't about to let the fact that he'd judged her unfairly slow him down for long. He shook his head—in disgust, or disbelief, or some distressing combination of the two. "You could have talked to me before you made your plans."

Stay cool, she told herself. It's not going to help if you start yelling at him.

"I know," she said, each word precise, strictly controlled. "I probably should have talked to you first. But I got excited. I agreed to meet her right away. And then I didn't want to call you and try to discuss it while you were taking care of patients. It just seemed wiser to go ahead and make my plans, and then explain everything when you got home."

He made a low sound in his throat, a sound that dismissed her, a sound that disregarded everything she'd said. "This is totally irresponsible of you. Rosie is barely two months old. And you are nursing. You can't leave her for long."

Lacey kept her mouth shut. Rosie often went as long as four hours between feedings. And there *was* such a thing as a breast pump, after all. But she knew her husband wouldn't hear her if she told him those things. No point in wasting her breath.

He sneered, "I've never met this—what did you say her name was?"

She sighed. "Adele Levenson."

"How do I know that this Adele Levenson is someone reliable?"

That really grated. She couldn't keep quiet, couldn't hold back the sarcasm. "Well, I don't know, Logan. How about because I say so and I'm your wife—and you *trust* me?"

He looked away, picked up his brandy glass, gulped down a too-big sip. She sat, waiting, watching him regroup, knowing just how his mind worked.

He'd come on way too strong, and he was realizing that now, remembering what he was. A *reasonable* man.

"Listen," he said at last, gently now. "You've got to look at this logically. It's just not a good time for something like this. You have a two-month-old baby. And responsibilities here. I thought you told me that on Saturday, you were helping Fiona out at one of her charity events."

She had to suppress a groan of disbelief. "Oh, Logan. Do you *hear* yourself? You're saying I should turn down the most important career opportunity that's ever come my way because I promised Fiona I'd help out at a rummage sale."

Now he looked wounded. "The rummage sale is something that you agreed to do."

"Yes, I did. But I'll call Fiona first thing tomorrow. I'm sure she'll understand. Everything—all of this—can be worked out. As I said, I have friends in L.A. who will help me with Rosie. And we have Mrs. Hopper. She's a jewel and you know she'll take good care of you while we're away, unless—" she tried one more time "—you decide to come with me?"

"I can't get away now. It's impossible."

"All right, then you'll stay home. But as I just said, we can work it out. It'll be a challenge, yes. But not an insurmountable one."

He had that intractable look on his face, an expression she'd always disliked—and never more so than now. "It's not good for Rosie," he said again. "You can't just run off and leave her with your flighty artistic friends."

She held on to her patience—by a thread. "Logan. Just because a person is an artist doesn't necessarily mean they're flighty. Or irresponsible."

"I don't know these friends of yours."

She closed her eyes, dragged in a breath. "We're going in circles."

"I don't want you to do this."

"I got that. Loud and clear. And my question is, *why?*"

"I've told you. For a number of reasons."

"Yes, you have. A number of trumped-up, fake, completely meaningless reasons."

"Meaningless? I'd hardly call it meaningless that I want my wife at home with me, and I want to know that my daughter is being well cared-for."

"Oh, come on. I'll be gone for five days. And Rosie, as I've said about ten times now, will be fine."

"It's not a good idea."

Oh, how she longed to start shouting. But somehow she managed to hold her anger and frustration in check. She leaned closer to him. "Why won't you tell me what's really going on here? Please. I want to understand."

He sat back, reached for his brandy again. "I've told you my concerns. They're completely reasonable."

"Reasonable," she repeated.

"Yes," he said, "reasonable."

"You know, it wouldn't be hard at all for me to learn to hate that word."

He emptied the glass and then set it down a little too hard. "I don't want to discuss it further. Call that dealer and tell her you're not coming."

Her mouth dropped open. "What did you say?"

"You heard me."

"Tell me this isn't happening. Tell me this is some nightmare I've stumbled into, that in a moment or two, I'm going to wake up."

"Just call that damn dealer."

"No."

He glowered at her.

She wanted to fling herself at him and pound on his chest. She wanted to scream rude, *un*reasonable invectives, to rant and rail at his impossible, pigheaded, unbearable male arrogance.

But she didn't. She held her temper and she spoke with low and hard-won control. She said, "I love you, Logan. We have a good life together. Yesterday, I told Fiona that you were the best thing that ever happened to me. And I meant it. You came to me in Wyoming when I didn't even know how much I needed you, and you refused to go away. You stayed at my side to see our daughter safely born. You convinced me to marry you. And I have been grateful, so grateful, that you did. Because on the whole, we're good together. I have been happy being your wife.

"You've never said that *you* love *me*. But I've learned to accept that. I've told myself that you love me by your actions, and that someday, when you're ready, you'll come to me and say your love in words."

He started to speak.

"No," she said, "wait. I'm not finished. I have gone into your world and learned to enjoy it—the upscale business parties, the charity dinners, the good works everyone seems to expect from a doctor's wife. I've made, or am making, space for all that in my life. For your sake. And I would like very much for you to return the favor. So far, you haven't."

"I—"

"No," she said. "Wait."

His eyes spoke volumes—angry, hard, ugly volumes—but he kept his mouth shut.

She said, "I've asked you to come with me to hear

my friends play their music. You've put me off. Okay, I told myself, he'll come eventually. Just be patient. Give it time. I've wanted you to come with me to visit my sister. You put me off again. I've said to myself, All right, he loved her and she hurt him and I'll give him some time on that, too."

Lacey stood. "But this, I can't give you time on. People only get so many great chances in life. For me, this is one. It really won't wait. And there's no reason, other than your completely *un*reasonable possessiveness, that it needs to wait. I am not going to turn Belinda Goldstone down. Rosie and I are leaving tomorrow. We'll be back Saturday afternoon. And that is all there is to that."

# Chapter Sixteen

Logan recognized the look on his wife's face.

On this issue, there would be no compromise.

She was going to Los Angeles tomorrow and nothing he could say would change her mind.

He'd told her all of the reasons she *shouldn't* go, and she refused to hear them.

Rosie chose that moment to let out a cry.

Logan glanced toward the baby monitor, then back into his wife's flushed, furious face. Lacey stayed where she was for a grim few seconds, staring down at him with fire in her eyes. He stared right back at her, his will meeting hers. Rosie let out another wail.

Lacey spun on her heel and left him there.

His beeper went off about two minutes later. He removed the device from his belt and checked the number: his exchange.

Five minutes after that, he stopped at the threshold of Rosie's room where Lacey sat in the rocker, nursing their child. She hadn't turned on the light. A wedge of brightness from the hall fixture behind him spilled across the floor, not quite reaching the chair where she and the baby rocked.

"Emergency," he said. Ordinarily, he would have given her some explanation. He would have said, That asthma patient's had another severe attack.

But not tonight. Tonight he didn't want to explain anything to her.

"I don't know when I'll be back."

She looked at him. Her eyes were somber and far away. In the dim light, they seemed strangely without color. "All right," she said. "I won't wait up."

He turned and left her in the dark.

In the morning, over an otherwise silent breakfast, she told him that her flight left from Sacramento at four that afternoon. "I'll just take my SUV and use the long-term parking."

"No. I'll take you."

She would have smiled at him in pleasure at the gesture, if only he hadn't been looking at her through eyes as cold as a midwinter night. "Thanks, but it isn't necessary, honestly. I can just—"

"I said, I'll drive you. Is there some reason you'd prefer I didn't?"

"Of course not. I just thought that it might be hard for you to manage the time away from the office on such short notice."

"If I couldn't manage it, I wouldn't have offered."

"All right, Logan. Thank you. I'll ride with you."

"When is your flight back?"

"I should arrive in Sacramento at four-thirty Saturday afternoon. I'll leave you the flight number and Adele's number and Barnaby's, too."

"Fine."

He didn't speak again until it was time for him to leave for the office, when he said, "I'll be here to pick you up at two."

"I'll be ready."

He left without granting her his usual fond goodbye peck.

She had plenty to do that morning. She got her portfolio in order, tucking in some sketches that would help her to explain her works in progress to Belinda. She wrote out detailed instructions for Mrs. Hopper, packed for herself and Rosie and then called Fiona.

Fiona wished her well, and made her promise that she'd help out with something called Food for Friends. "We have our big food drive next month, for Thanksgiving."

"Count me in."

"I knew I could. Good luck in L.A."

"Thanks. It's a big step."

"And your paintings will be hanging in a gallery in March?"

"That's right."

"Remember, you're getting Dan and me tickets to the opening."

Lacey promised she wouldn't forget.

She called the twins next, first Mira, then Maud.

Mira let out a shout of glee when she heard the news.

"Call the minute you get back," she instructed. "Maud and I will want to know everything."

Maud's reaction was a mirror to her twin's. Their unbridled enthusiasm helped to cheer Lacey up—as the disagreement with Logan dragged her down. She tried to put images of his scowling face from her mind as she hurried to get ready.

The ride to the airport was as silent as breakfast had been. Rosie fussed some and Logan demanded suspiciously, "Is she feverish?"

Lacey reached over the seat to press her palm to Rosie's brow. "Feels normal to me."

Her husband shot her a glance in which skepticism vied for dominance with brooding hostility. She bit her lip to keep herself from saying something she'd later regret.

At the terminal, Logan helped her check her luggage, then carried Rosie's car seat, diaper bag and Lacey's bulky portfolio to the boarding area for her.

She and Rosie boarded early. Logan helped with that, getting the steward to find a place for the portfolio and strapping Rosie's car carrier in the seat next to Lacey's.

Then he muttered a gruff, "Goodbye," and turned to go.

Rosie rested on Lacey's shoulder, cradled on her left arm. She reached out with her right and caught his elbow. "Logan?"

He faced her again, unsmiling.

She pulled him to her and kissed him, a quick, hard kiss, on the mouth. "See you Saturday."

"Yes." His eyes were distant, his voice without inflection. "I'll be here." Rosie made a cooing sound. He

laid his hand on her small back. "Bye, Rosie." Those
words, at least, had feeling in them.

Lacey watched him walk up the narrow aisle away
from her, until he disappeared through the exit. Then
she strapped Rosie into her seat.

Adele met Lacey and Rosie at LAX and drove them
straight to her shingled bungalow-style house in Pasa-
dena. The two women spent the early evening playing
catch-up, filling each other in on their separate lives in
the months since Lacey had left L.A.

Adele Levenson was in her mid-fifties, with a cap of
wild gray curls and a body of Rubenesque proportions.
She wore flowing dresses in dramatic colors: hot tur-
quoise, emerald green, yellow as bright as lemons in
sunlight. She'd been married and divorced and had three
grown children living in different parts of the state. She
confessed that she'd enjoyed her marriage—at least the
first ten years of it. And she'd loved raising her children.

"But I love this, too." She gestured with a wide
sweep of both arms. "My own house. Time just for me.
The luxury of working whenever the mood strikes."

They spent a couple of hours on the sunporch in
back, which Adele used as her studio. Lacey admired
the new landscapes Adele showed her, struck as always
by the way Adele's watercolors shimmered with vivid
color and gorgeous washes of golden light.

"You just get better and better," Lacey told her friend.

Around nine, after Adele had served a dinner of lamb
chops and wild rice and Lacey had put Rosie down to
sleep in the spare room, the two women went out onto
the big stone front porch. They sat on the porch swing
in the moonlight and listened to the sounds of night

birds and the whispering whoosh of cars going by down the drive.

"You seem…a little sad," Adele said. "A little pensive. It's in your eyes. And in your voice. Is it something you'd like to talk about?"

Lacey shook her head.

"I'm here to listen, if you need me."

Lacey reached out, put her hand on Adele's bright sleeve. "Thanks. I'll remember that."

At a little after ten, Lacey excused herself. She went to the bedroom she shared with her daughter, took out her cell phone and dialed the house on Orchard Street. After four rings, the answering machine picked up. Lacey listened to her own voice instructing her to leave a message.

Then she said, "Logan, it's me. I just… wanted you to know we got in all right. We're at Adele's now, all settled in for the night. I…I love you. Don't ever forget that."

She hung up feeling foolish, wondering if he'd had to work late, or if he'd rushed out to the hospital to handle some emergency. Or if maybe he'd been standing right there as she left her message, listening to each word that she said, unwilling to pick up the phone and talk to her.

The next day, Adele insisted that Lacey use her car. "It's ridiculous for you to rent one. I never go out that much anyway. We can share while you're here."

So Lacey drove Adele's comfortable old Chrysler into downtown L.A., where she met with Belinda at Barnaby's place. Belinda liked the seven other paintings Lacey showed her. And she seemed honestly enthusiastic when Lacey described her ideas for the three or four more pieces she thought she could finish before the show in March.

"Come see me at the gallery, tomorrow," Belinda said.

Lacey agreed to be there at eleven. Then she gave Barnaby a big hug and promised she'd find some way to get together with him before she left for home. She raced back to Adele's, her breasts aching and full, to feed Rosie her lunch.

That evening, after she'd told Adele good-night, she called Logan again. And got no answer. She left another message, a brief one, "It's me. Everything's going fine. I love you. I'll see you Saturday."

Strange, she thought when she hung up. Last winter, it was Logan calling me, leaving messages I never answered.

And just look at us now—the situation reversed.

She'd thought they'd come so far, in the two months of their marriage. But now she wondered if they'd made any progress at all.

She loved him.

She would always love him.

But she was beginning to ask herself the scariest kind of question: Would they get through this with their marriage intact? Could she, perhaps, have been right from the first about the two of them, that they were two people distinctly *not* meant for each other?

The way it looked now, either she gave up her dreams for him, or she would lose him. What kind of choice was that?

And why would a basically good man—and she did believe that Logan *was* a good man—force her to make such a choice?

* * *

Logan got in after midnight.

The house seemed too empty, too damn gray and dreary, without Lacey there. He'd stayed away as long as he could, eating dinner out, then heading back to the hospital to check on a couple of patients in critical care.

After the hospital, he'd made a last stop at the office. There was always a stack of stuff on his desk crying out to be dealt with. He spent a couple of hours plowing through the pile.

And then, because he couldn't think of any more ways to avoid it, he returned to the house on Orchard Street. He went straight to the answering machine on the counter in the kitchen. The message light blinked at him.

He pushed the button—and he heard her voice.

He played the message three times, longing coursing through him like a pulse.

*I love you,* she said, just as she had the night before. Only then, she had added, *Don't ever forget that.*

*I love you....*

*Don't ever forget that....*

The words echoed through his brain, along with all the things he kept trying not to think about, those hard things she had said to him the night before she left.

*This really can't wait. And there's no reason, other than your completely unreasonable possessiveness, that it needs to wait.*

*I have gone into your world and learned to enjoy it. I would like very much for you to return the favor. So far, you haven't.*

*I've asked you to come with me to hear my friends play... To visit my sister... You've never said that you love me...*

Logan leaned on the counter and pressed his head between his hands. "Stop, damn it!" he shouted at the silent, empty room.

It worked, more or less. It silenced the remembered echo of her voice.

But it didn't make what she'd said any less true.

Thursday evening, Adele invited Xavier and Barnaby and Xavier's wife, Sophia, to dinner. Barnaby had a previous commitment he couldn't get out of, but Xavier and Sophia came. It was a good evening, full of laughter and interesting talk. Xavier held Rosie, declared her a beauty and said she smelled like peaches. He and his wife left at a little after ten. He had an early flight to New York the next day.

At ten-thirty, after she'd bid Adele good-night, Lacey called her husband for the third time. He didn't answer. She left a three-sentence message that ended with *I love you.*

Then she got into bed with her daughter and tried to sleep.

It was no good.

At ten-forty-five, she called home again.

After three rings, her husband surprised her. He answered.

"Hello." The way he said that single word made her heart ache. He sounded so lonely, so very far away.

And something in that hollow, distant voice reminded her poignantly of his father. Lacey hadn't known Logan Sr. particularly well. She remembered that he had dark eyes, like Logan's, and that he rarely smiled. He'd been a very serious man, a man who set high standards and expected his only son to live up to them.

And live up to them Logan did. Perhaps too well in some ways.

"Hello," Logan said again, an impatient edge creeping in.

"Hello, Logan. It's me."

He hesitated, then said her name, "Lacey…"

Now, that's more like it, she thought. That sounded almost tender.

But then again, maybe she was just a victim of a bad case of wishful thinking. "Did you get my messages?"

He took a moment to answer, as if he suspected she meant to trick him with such a question. Then he said, "I got them. Last night and the night before."

"You didn't call back," she said, thinking: Brilliant. State the painfully obvious.

He cleared his throat. "You didn't say anything about wanting me to call you back."

Ohmigoodness, were they a pair or what? She sighed. "Next time I'll make my desires clearer—I also called about fifteen minutes ago."

"I just walked in the door."

"I see. Well, then. I guess you didn't get that one."

"Right. I didn't. How's Rosie?"

"She's doing great. She's asleep now, otherwise I'd let you talk to her."

A silence, then he chuckled. To Lacey's ears, the sound was like soothing balm spread gently on a throbbing wound.

He asked with reluctant humor, "Learned to talk in two days, has she?"

Tears misted her vision. She blinked them away. "Children can really surprise you. Especially the bright ones."

"Lacey…"

She clutched the phone tighter. "Yes? What?"

"Uh—how's it going there?"

"Um—good. Really good. I met Belinda. I have a positive feeling about her. She's exciting, but soothing at the same time. If that makes any sense."

"You'll have to explain it to me in more depth… when you get home."

Home. That sounded lovely. "Yes. Yes, I'll do that. She, Belinda, I mean, she liked the other things I showed her. Some older paintings I had at Barnaby's. And she seemed excited about my sketches. Of course, we both agreed you never can tell. You can have the most wonderful ideas, but then, in the execution, everything falls apart. Or it all changes, and it's not what you thought it would be when you started…which isn't necessarily bad. It might be *better* than what you conceived in the planning stages. It might—" She realized she was babbling and cut herself off. "Anyway, we'll just have to wait and see what else I come up with. And Belinda's open to that, which is another thing I like about her."

"So you're saying, it's all working out."

"Yes. That's exactly what I'm saying."

He was silent. And so was she. For a moment, they just listened to each other breathe.

Finally, he asked softly, "Lace?"

Hope. She could feel it growing inside her, effervescent as the bubbles in a glass of champagne, warm as sunlight streaming in an open window. "Yes?"

"I…"

"What, Logan?"

"I want you to know…" The sentence wandered off unfinished.

She clutched the phone and waited.

At last, he said, "Look. We'll talk. About a lot of things. When you get home."

She sighed. She had wanted more. A heartfelt apology for the way he'd behaved. An impassioned declaration of undying love. A vow never, ever again to doubt her devotion.

But *we'll talk* wasn't that bad. In fact, *we'll talk* sounded pretty darn good.

"All right," she said. "We'll talk. When I get home."

"And good luck at that big opening tomorrow night."

She laughed. "Thanks, but it's not anything terribly challenging. I'm just putting in an appearance, and then going right back to Adele's in time for Rosie's midnight snack."

"Whatever. Good luck."

"Thank you." She couldn't resist offering one more time. "You could come. You could fly down tomorrow. I'll pick you up at the airport. You can meet Adele. And I'll take you to Barnaby's loft, show you those incredible nude studies of you that everyone's talking about. And then tomorrow night—"

"No," he said, but in a tender tone. "Let's let it go this time."

*This time.* That sounded pretty good, too. As if there'd be a next time, when he *would* come with her.

"Logan. I love you."

"Good night, Lace."

"Good night."

"The sun has come out in your eyes," Adele said the next morning. "Something good happened, right? You're feeling better about things."

Lacey sipped her orange juice—the thick, pulpy kind. She'd just squeezed it herself. "Umm. I love orange juice. I love oranges. Doesn't the word seem to just *go* with the fruit? Remember those still lifes you did a few years ago? Oranges in a wooden bowl? I loved those. They were so…orange." She sipped again.

"So," Adele said, "I'm right. You're feeling better."

"Let's say I've discovered there's hope."

"All right. Let's say that."

"Also, I'm leaving tomorrow and I've hardly had a moment with Barnaby."

"So do lunch."

"I should go downtown, to his studio again. I want to see what he's been working on."

"More of that cogs in a machine stuff, from what I understand."

Barnaby painted occasionally, in oil and acrylic. But his real talent was in sculpture. He worked in metal with a blowtorch. His twisted, tortured metal forms had garnered him more than a little recognition on the national art scene.

Adele got up and poured herself more coffee. "Call him. I'll watch your little rosebud for you."

"Adele, I adore you."

"Good. I'll try to be worthy of such passionate affection."

Lacey found a parking space about ten feet down from the front door of Barnaby's building.

"My lucky day," she said to herself, as she anchored her purse securely onto her shoulder and fed a few coins into the meter.

The buildings around her were big, square industrial

structures of chipped concrete and dirty glass. The sidewalk under her feet had cracked and buckled, with time, and from the effects of more than one earthquake, she had no doubt. Trash lined the gutters and piled up in the doorways. The few lost souls on the street looked dirty and desperate and in need of a good meal. There wasn't a tree in sight.

But it all looked beautiful to Lacey.

Because things were going to work out with Logan, she could feel it.

She had it all.

A man she loved heart and soul, a beautiful baby, several dear friends, a talent for doing work she loved— and the distinct possibility that someone would pay for that work in the near future.

And on top of all that, the sun was out, but then, this was L.A., where the sun was *always* out.

She felt like singing, so she did, a few bars from a great old Otis Redding song, "I've Been Loving You Too Long."

She sounded awful. Like a cornered cat, Mira always said.

She laughed, tipping her head back, feeling the sun's benign kiss on her upturned face. "Never was much of a singer…"

Someone had left the street door to Barnaby's building open a crack. She shook her head at it. The neighborhood was a dangerous one. It wasn't wise to leave the doors unlatched for any L.A. desperado to wander in. However, there was a bright side. It saved her the trouble of ringing the bell and waiting for Barnaby to buzz her up.

She pulled open the heavy door and stepped into the shadowy vestibule.

She never saw what hit her. One minute she was turning to make sure the door was firmly shut behind her—and the next the world went black.

## Chapter Seventeen

At one-fifteen in the afternoon, Cathy the receptionist stuck her head into the examining room where Logan was going over a medical history.

"You've got a call," Cathy said. "Someone named Adele Levenson on line three. She said it's about—"

He didn't need to hear more. It had to be about Lacey or Rosie. "Thank you, Cathy. I'll be right there." He spoke quite calmly. But his heart had gone into overdrive. It felt damn near tachycardic, beating with a rhythm ragged and way too swift.

Slow down, he thought. It's probably nothing serious. Some minor problem. Nothing that bad…

His patient smiled at him when he excused himself. He slipped out the door and went to his private office, where he dropped into his desk chair, grabbed the phone and punched the button that blinked red.

"Hello. This is Logan Severance."

A woman with a gentle voice spoke to him. She said things that couldn't possibly be true.

Lacey had been mugged. Some street punk had attacked her. Her friend Barnaby had found her and called an ambulance.

He heard himself ask, "Head injury, you said?"

"Yes. She was hit on the back of the head. From what I understand, someone knocked her out, grabbed her purse and ran."

"Is she conscious now?"

"No—I don't know. I talked to Barnaby just before I called you. As of then, she hadn't come to."

His heart pounded. His mind swam. He thought, "My God. Rosie…" and realized he'd spoken aloud when Adele Levenson answered him.

"It's all right. Rosie's here with me. You don't have to worry about your little girl."

"What hospital? Where is my wife?"

Adele told him.

He grabbed a pen and wrote it down. "I have your phone number, but I don't know where you live."

She gave him the address.

He scribbled that down, too. "Will you be there, at this number?"

"For a while. I think that's best, with the baby. Lacey borrowed my car, anyway, so I'll have a little trouble trying to go anywhere. But in a few hours, if there's no news, I might try to get a ride to the hospital."

"Do you have a cell phone?"

She said she did. They exchanged numbers. Then he

said, "I'll book the earliest flight I can get. And I'll call you back as soon as I know when I'm coming in."

It took six hours, from the moment Logan hung up the phone until he was striding into ICU at Twin Palms Hospital in Los Angeles.

A neurologist spoke with him. Logan listened, feeling damn near disembodied, one part of his mind screaming, *This is Lacey*—Lacey *we're talking about*, as the information came at him.

She was in a coma.

Lacey. In a *coma*…

The word kept repeating itself in his head. Coma, coma, coma, until it sounded like nonsense syllables, nothing real, nothing that could happen to Lacey, with her bright, inquisitive mind and her naughty sense of humor. Not to Lace, with her musical laughter and her sweet wildness in bed.

"Signs are good, Dr. Severance," the neurologist said.

"Good?" Logan repeated. It was another nonsense syllable.

Good, good, good, good…

"Yes. Very good. Your wife is breathing on her own. We intubated and had her on a respirator for a few hours, then tested and found the respirator unnecessary. EEG and CT scans have revealed nothing out of the ordinary. Of course, we've set up arterial and CVP lines to measure blood pressure and oxygen levels.

"So far, we have minimal cerebral swelling, and we've seen no necessity for invasive procedures. We're going to be monitoring her closely for the slightest change. As I'm sure you're aware, she could wake any minute."

Logan knew the rest of it, the part they never said if they could help it.

Yes, she could wake any minute.

But she might *never* wake.

With head injuries resulting in coma, you waited.

"Can I see her?"

"Of course. Come this way."

He did what the husbands of very ill wives do.

He sat by her bed and he held her hand. He watched hungrily for each slightest movement—the twitching of an eyelid, the tiniest flutter of a muscle in her smooth, white neck.

He spoke with Barnaby Cole—and Adele, who had finally found a ride to the hospital and brought his daughter along. He held Rosie and he fed her milk pumped from the breasts of his unconscious wife.

And he hated himself.

At ten that night, Detective Carla Cruz from the LAPD called him out to the hall. She told him that they'd caught the man who'd attacked his wife. A junkie with a habit to feed. They'd also recovered Lacey's purse, which they were keeping, temporarily anyway, as evidence.

"Whatever cash she might have had is gone, along with any credit cards," Detective Cruz told him regretfully. "But the wallet is still there, as well as her driver's license, some pictures and various store membership cards. And then there are lipsticks and a compact, a small address book—"

"Jenna," Logan said, the name popping into his head and coming right out his mouth.

"Excuse me?"

"I…you said you found an address book in her purse. I was just thinking of someone I should call."

"I'm sorry. That book will be locked up in Evidence now. You can't get to it."

He thanked the detective. She advised him to call the credit card companies and cancel Lacey's cards. And she also said she'd be back in the next twenty-four hours to check on the witness.

Logan understood. They'd want to interview Lacey, if and when she emerged from her unconscious state.

Somehow, that thought soothed him. To imagine cool, efficient-looking Detective Cruz coming back, interviewing Lacey—who would be sitting up in bed by then, blue eyes alert, full lips softly smiling.

As soon as the detective left him, he pulled out his cell phone. He had Mrs. Hopper's number stored there. He dialed the Meadow Valley area code and then punched the proper auto-dial button.

When the housekeeper answered, he told her what had happened and listened to her expressions of shock and concern. Then he asked her to go to the house and get Jenna's phone number from the kitchen drawer address book.

She called him back twenty minutes later.

He thanked her, disconnected the call, and punched up the Key West number the housekeeper had given him.

Jenna and Mack and their ten-day-old baby, Ian, arrived at Twin Palms Hospital eleven hours later. They'd chartered a jet. Money—and Mack McGarrity had plenty of it—had its uses.

Jenna came into Lacey's room alone, leaving her husband and their baby in the lounge down the hall. Logan was sitting with Lacey, holding her hand, talking to her softly, telling her that she was doing well, that she would get better, that her baby was fine….

He glanced up and Jenna was standing there, her straight blond hair smooth as always around her oval face and her eyes—blue, but a softer, less vivid blue than Lacey's—filled with tears.

He felt relief, that she had come. And affection—the kind of warm feeling one bears a sister. Or a dear friend.

As for the hurt, the bitterness of her leaving him— he could hardly remember it.

The bitterness had been gone for a long time now. Months, really.

Maybe since that September night when Lacey knocked on his door, chocolate cake in hand, determined to console him—and ending up doing so much more.

Changing his life, opening his heart, turning his gray world to full color.

Jenna came to stand beside him. She looked down at her sister "Oh," she said. "Oh, Lace…"

Carefully, mindful of the lines taped to the back of it, Logan let go of Lacey's hand. He laid it with infinite gentleness on top of the blanket.

He stood.

Jenna turned to him. She held out her arms.

He went into them, seeking solace, seeking reassurance—desperately needing the touch of someone who could understand.

Something inside of him broke wide open. He felt terror and relief, combined.

He couldn't hold back. In a ragged whisper, he breathed his confession against Jenna's shining hair.

"I…never told her. Never said, I love you, Lace. I…held it away from her. I feared the power it would give her, to know how I felt. I let her wonder…if I still loved *you*."

"Logan—"

"No. Please. That's not all. I tried to take her painting away from her. I…I tried to keep her just to myself. She wanted me here, with her, when she came to L.A. She asked me to come any number of times. I should have been with her, when that bastard attacked her. But I wouldn't come. And now, if I've lost her. If I've—"

"Shh," Jenna pulled him closer. "Listen. Listen to me…."

He took her by the arms, looked into her eyes. "Did you hear me? Did you hear what I said?"

She nodded. "I heard. And if you've tried to keep her from her painting, well, shame on you. But about the other. Logan, I think she knows that you love her."

"No. I wouldn't let her know. Wouldn't let her be certain. Even the last time we talked, when I knew how wrong I'd been about so many things, I still couldn't get the damn words out of my mouth. I held back. I said, 'we'll talk, when you get home.' The last thing she said to me was 'I love you.' And all I said in return was 'Good night, Lace.'"

"Logan, she did know."

"No, I—"

"Logan, I told her."

That made no sense. "You…?"

"Yes. I told her. When you were both still in Wyoming. She called and asked my advice about marrying you and I said, 'Do it. He loves you. He's always loved you. He just doesn't know it yet.'"

He gripped her arms harder, his fingers digging in. "Don't tell me good-hearted lies. I need the truth now."

Jenna neither flinched nor wavered. "I'm giving you the truth. My sister knows what love is. And she knows that you love her."

He let go of Jenna's arms and sucked in a breath through a chest that felt as if bands of steel constricted it. "That's something, at least." He turned to Lacey again, took her limp hand. "Do you know?" he asked in a broken voice. "God, let that at least be so. It won't make what I did any more acceptable. But it's better than nothing." He reached up, smoothed the translucent skin of her pale brow.

Jenna took the chair on the other side of the bed. They settled in. To wait some more.

Two hours later, Lacey opened her eyes.

Logan whispered her name.

She turned her head, seeking—and finding him. "Logan," she said, her voice ragged, dry, very low, each syllable an effort—and a triumph. "Logan." And she smiled.

# *Chapter Eighteen*

The next day, they moved her out of ICU.

She got a nice, private room in a medical/surgery wing. After a battery of tests and a lot of poking and prodding by an astonishingly large number of nurses and neurologists, they removed all of the tubes from her arm.

Her prognosis was excellent. She had scored a solid "eight" on the Rancho Los Amigos scale, which measures recovery in brain injured patients. An eight meant her responses were "purposeful-appropriate," that she was alert, conscious of who she was and where she was, as well as able to recall past and recent events— well, most of them anyway. In twenty-four hours, if no complications arose, she would be released.

In the early afternoon, soon after they'd moved her

to her new room and given her lunch, Detective Cruz came to speak with her. Lacey shook her head in apology and told the detective she recalled almost nothing about the day she'd been attacked.

"I remember sitting at the breakfast table in my friend Adele Levenson's kitchen. And drinking orange juice. Adele agreed to watch my baby while I went downtown to see my friend, Barnaby Cole, at his loft. I know I went there. I know I was mugged there, because I've heard everyone talking about it. But actually *remember* it? I'm sorry. I don't."

Detective Cruz reassured her that her attacker was in custody. And a pipe wrench had been discovered in the alley behind her friend's building. The wrench had bits of Lacey's blood and hair on it and also a very clear thumbprint matching that of the man they had apprehended in possession of her shoulder bag.

"I think he'll be going away for quite a while," the detective predicted.

"I have only one question for you, Detective."

"Hit me with it, Ms. Severance."

"When can I get my purse back?"

"I suppose we don't need to hold it much longer, since we're no longer dealing with the possibility of a homicide."

"You mean I'm going to live?"

"It would appear so," the detective said dryly. She gave Lacey a card. "Drop by the precinct when they let you out of here. You can pick it up then—or have your husband do it today, if you'd like. And be sure to give me a call if anything else about the incident comes back to you."

Lacey promised that she would.

Not long after the detective left, the nurse brought Rosie in for a feeding. A few minutes later, Jenna and Mack arrived with Ian. Lacey got to take her nephew in her arms for the first time, while Jenna held Rosie. The sisters agreed that their children were the best, the most attractive and the brightest in the world.

"I can't believe you're really here." Lacey held out her hand and Jenna took it. "It's almost worth getting beat on the head with a pipe wrench, just to look at your face and hold this little boy."

"Hey," Mack complained teasingly, "what about me?"

"You know I'm *always* grateful to see you," Lacey told him.

"We'll stay for as long as you need us," Jenna vowed.

"Watch what you promise me. I may never let you go."

As the sisters admired their babies, Adele and Barnaby appeared. Adele carried a huge bunch of daisies in a big crystal vase. "These are from Xavier and Sophia."

Barnaby presented an arrangement of yellow daylilies. "Belinda Goldstone sent these."

Lacey beamed at the flowers. "Daylilies. They're beautiful. And Xavier knows how I love daisies. Put them all on that ledge up there by the TV, where I can see them."

The flowers were duly set on the ledge. There was no space anywhere else. The room had begun to look like a florist shop. Jenna, Adele and Barnaby had each brought in their own offerings earlier. About an hour before, a lovely creation of birds of paradise and antheriums had arrived from Dan and Fiona. And a bouquet of white roses had come from the Wyoming Bravos.

For a few minutes, Jenna and Mack and Adele and Barnaby all gathered around Lacey's bed. They talked in hushed, happy tones of how good it was to be here, with Lacey awake now, on the road to full recovery.

Too soon, Jenna handed Rosie to Adele. She turned back to Lacey. "Better give me that baby and get some rest."

Lacey rubbed her nose against her nephew's sweet wrinkled neck. "I just don't want to let him go…"

"Come on."

"Oh, all right." She passed the warm bundle into her sister's arms and lay back with a sigh, smiling drowsily, thinking that the lump on the back of her head could still ache like the devil and wondering where her husband had wandered off to. From that first time she woke up yesterday, he had been there whenever she opened her eyes—attentive and so gentle. And a little bit…what? Subdued, maybe. Or even sad.

They needed to talk. They just hadn't had the chance.

And where was he now?

"Where's Logan?" she asked. "I haven't seen him since they wheeled me out of ICU."

"I believe he mentioned some errand he had to run," Jenna said. She sounded just a little too mysterious.

"All right." Lacey looked from her sister, to her brother-in-law, to her friends. "What's up?"

Mack advised, "Take a nap, Lace. He'll be here when you wake up."

One by one, they all tiptoed out. Lacey was asleep before the door shut behind them.

Sometime later, Lacey heard whispering. Very familiar whispering.

She opened one eye and then the other. And then she blinked. "Mira? Maud?"

Giggling in delight, one on one side of the bed and one on the other, the twins grabbed her in a three-way hug.

Lacey hugged back as hard as she could. "Oh, I can't believe it. Tell me I'm not dreaming…"

"You're not dreaming," Maud promised, hugging tighter.

"How did you get here?"

"Logan sent for us," Mira declared.

"Got us plane tickets," added Maud.

Mira pulled away and winked. "First class, doncha know."

The dimples on either side of Maud's mouth twinkled merrily. "The only way to go…"

Mira giggled some more, kissed Lacey wetly on the cheek, and then dropped with a grunt to the chair next to the bed. "I sang for him, on the ride here from the airport. 'When a Man Loves a Woman.' He was duly impressed."

"You bet he was," agreed Maud. "He says he's bringing you to hear us play, the first Friday you guys get back home."

Mira said, "The man is transformed. It's a miracle. What did you *do* to him?"

Lacey lay back on her pillow and grinned. "If I told you, I'd have to kill you."

The sisters groaned in unison, then demanded to know everything that had happened since Lacey came to L.A. Lacey obliged them, filling them in on all the details of her visit with Adele and her meetings with Belinda. She told what she knew of the attack that had landed her at Twin Palms Hospital.

"But you're coming home soon," Mira said hopefully, once the story was told.

"In the next few days, I think."

The twins fell on her for more hugs. Lacey surrendered to their lavish affection. They stayed for an hour. But then they decided they were hungry. Logan had given them a rental car. They wanted to check out L.A. a little and get a sandwich—or maybe two. And they'd be back around again to see how she was doing in a few hours.

They strutted to the door, pausing long enough to blow her more kisses, and then they were gone.

A nurse poked her head in and asked if Lacey needed a Tylenol. "No, thanks. I'm okay."

She closed her eyes and settled back, a contented smile curving her lips.

She didn't even hear him enter.

But she knew he was there when his lips brushed hers.

With her eyes closed and her mouth still pressed to his, she lifted her arms to encircle his neck. "Umm…"

He deepened the kiss, but not too much, his tongue entering just enough to caress the moistness beyond her parted lips. Then he pulled back. She let him go with reluctance, sighing a little, her eyelids fluttering open.

"Oh, look at you. You shaved."

"And showered, too. I needed it," he said gruffly.

"Any way you come to me, you are a sight for sore eyes."

He kissed the tip of her nose, then pulled back again. "I have something to say."

She looked at him sideways. "This sounds ominous."

"It's not. It's…damn hard, that's all. For a man like me."

"A man like you?"

He nodded—and lightly ran his index finger down the curve of her cheek. "An arrogant man. A proud man. A man who always knows he's in the right."

"Surely you're speaking of someone else."

"No, I'm not. And you know I'm not. Lacey, I—"

She reached up once more, this time to put her fingers to his lips. "Oh, Logan. I know."

He caught her hand, kissed it, then folded their fingers together. "Your sister told me you knew. But you do want to hear it." A hint of a smile came and went on that wonderful mouth of his. "Don't you?"

She couldn't seem to keep from sighing. "Yes. It's true. The words do mean something. They mean…a lot."

He said it, very slowly, with just the right blend of tenderness and passion. "I love you, Lacey Severance. I love you with all of my heart. I…thought I knew it all. I thought I knew how to love. I believed that I loved your sister. Because I had decided she was the right woman for me. But I didn't even know what it was, to love. I…hell. Maybe I just never learned."

She thought of his cold, distant father. Of the mother he had never known.

He said, "I don't know how long I've loved you. I don't think it matters. Maybe forever. Maybe I've been fighting it for years. But when I finally had you, when you married me and were my wife, I…didn't want to admit to myself how important you had become. And more than that, most of all, I didn't want to lose you. I've been so afraid of losing you…

"Sometimes it seems to me that I was never really alive, until that day in September when you first came to me. And during those months after you broke it off, I was so damn miserable. You can't know what it felt like when I got your letter about the baby. And I knew I would *have* to marry you. That what I wanted with every beat of my heart was also my duty. God, I was happy. I was in heaven."

"But you—"

He kissed her hand again. "Let me say the rest. Please."

She nodded. "Yes. All right."

"I saw your painting as a threat, to me, to what we had together. And the twins—they scared me, too. Anything you loved and wanted, anything you cared passionately for that wasn't me or Rosie. Those things seemed to only be ways I could lose you. And visiting Jenna, the idea of that scared the hell out of me. I knew that as soon as I saw your sister's face again, the truth would no longer be something I could avoid. I would recognize her for what she is. My longtime friend. And my wife's sister. And that's all."

"Oh, Logan. I just… I want to kiss you."

"Wait. In a minute. I have to finish this. To say that I never told you I loved you because I felt a little less scared of what losing you could do to me, as long as I thought you didn't know. As long as I kept it from you, as long as I didn't give you that power. And I hate myself, for not coming to you the other day after we talked on the phone and you asked me for the last time. If I had come, you wouldn't have been alone when you went downtown, you wouldn't have—"

"Stop. Stop. Enough."

"Lacey—"

She shook her head. "No. It is not your fault that

some desperate fool whacked me on the back of the head. You can't have the blame for that. Do you understand?"

Slowly, he nodded. "All right."

"Good."

She watched his Adam's apple bob up and down as he swallowed. And she thought of that afternoon at the end of June, when he'd come to Wyoming to find her and she'd watched him swallow the ginger ale she gave him and wanted to press her mouth against his throat.

"Bend down to me," she commanded, reaching for him again, hooking her arm around his neck.

He came close, and she kissed him, a deep, sucking kiss on his strong, tanned throat.

When she let him go, he rubbed the spot. "That's going to leave a mark."

"I know."

"I don't believe you did that."

"Believe it."

"I love you, Lacey Severance."

"I know. You said that."

"I'll say it a hundred times."

"You'll say it a thousand, a thousand times a thousand. And so will I. We'll say it to each other every day. Morning, noon and night. Until we're old and tired, and...and *still* we'll say it. Until they lay us in the grave. Oh, Logan, please believe me. We're going to have a wonderful life together."

"Swear it."

"I swear it. Now, bend down again. We'll seal it with a kiss."

He bent close. Their lips met.

Logan closed his eyes.

Even the darkness behind his lids seemed to pulse with color. He smiled against his wife's soft mouth, at last fully understanding exactly what he'd found with her.

Love.

The end of loneliness.

And the beginning of his very own happily ever after.

\* \* \* \* \*

*Everything you love about romance...*
***and more!***

*Please turn the page for Signature Select™*
*Bonus Features.*

# BRAVO BRIDES

BONUS
FEATURES
INSIDE

## A Day in the Life...
## of Christine Rimmer

*Note to readers: People often ask me about my day-to-day life as a writer. I can see in their shining eyes that they imagine my world as glamorous and exciting, that they picture me well-groomed in cute clothes, dashing off my books in a haze of white-hot inspiration.*

*Um. Not quite.*

*My real life goes a little more like this....*

I wake suddenly to a pitch-dark bedroom. Stifling a groan, I lift my head and look at the glowing red numerals on my digital clock—5:34 a.m. In one minute, the alarm will go off, reminding me that it is, indeed, an Exercise Morning (three of these a week—or there are supposed to be). Husband lies still and silent next to me. Breathing in that way that is really indescribable, but you know it when you hear it: still asleep.

Hmmm...

Carefully, so as not to disturb him, I extricate an arm from the tangle of bedcovers and flip the little button on the top of the clock in that precise split second before the numeral four becomes a five. Ha. No alarm. Only a deep and velvety silence.

It is just possible that I can shut my eyes now and drift back to sleep for an extra few—

"Well? Are we going?"

So much for a few extra minutes of sleep. My husband is awake, after all. We rise, we dress, we head for the gym.

After the gym? Surprise, surprise: a shower. After the shower, a minimal grooming ritual that does not include makeup—or anything remotely resembling panty hose.

I ponder the panty hose equation: lack of panty hose = a very good thing. Nine out of ten professional authors cite not having to wear panty hose as the greatest side benefit of writing for a living—nine out of ten *female* authors, I mean. As a rule, men are not polled on the panty hose question.

So, all right. I'm exercised, clean and dressed in ratty jeans and a baggy shirt. Ready for my daily battle with the written word. I trudge to the kitchen for coffee. Two cups. With milk and sugar...

I greet my teenaged son who is not going to school today due to some minor holiday or other. He tells me he's spending the day at his girlfriend's. Girlfriend's mom will be there. Girlfriend's mom has a day off from work. Why is it regular people occasionally get days off from work? Is this fair?

I sigh, remind myself of what my grandma Smith always said: "Whoever told you it was going to be fair?"

I smile sweetly and give him permission to go. He leaves and I then send my husband off to work.

Alone at last.

E-mail. Very important. And checking to see how my books are doing on *Amazon.com*. And on *BarnesandNoble.com*. And of course, I must slip over to *eHarlequin.com* and check out what's happening on the Silhouette Special Edition board....

Suddenly, with no warning, it is 9:00 a.m.

I should have breakfast. I do. At my desk. As I chomp my Oatmeal Crisp and peel my banana, I consider the book I'm scheduled to begin today.

Openings, after all, are everything. The opening line, especially, must be perfect.

"I want you," he said. "Name your price."

What he actually wants is for her to open one of her topnotch preschools on-site at his casino—well, and he wants *her*, too. But that's not what he's talking about in the opening. That he wants *her* is definitely implied, though not stated.

Do I need his name in that first line? Is it too pointlessly mysterious not to just go ahead and call a Bravo a Bravo?

Probably.

"I want you," Fletcher Bravo said. "Name your price."

Better. Yes. But why am I seeing him leaning across some big, gleaming desk?

Probably because he is.

But what kind of desk? Glass? Some rare, exotic inlaid wood?

Two hours fly by as I surf online, trying to find exactly the right desk—or if not the desk, at least exactly the right exotic wood. I do find it: macassar ebony. And then, after more thought, I reject the choice as *too* exotic.

And if you're dozing off about now, maybe you've figured out that I am creating a time sink. Favorite author pastime. Research and ruminate and nothing gets written.

Lunch at my desk and back to the page...

Fletcher Bravo rose from his sleek leather swivel chair. He braced his lean hands on his black slate desktop and canted toward Cleo Bliss. "I want you," he said. "Name your price."

A thoroughly unwelcome thrill shivered through Cleo. She had to remind herself not to shift nervously in the glove-soft guest chair.

*Calm,* she thought. *Serene. Under no circumstances can he be allowed to sense weakness.* She met those eerily compelling pale gray eyes of his with a level, no-nonsense stare.

8

Well, okay. Not too bad. I continue on. Five pages is the goal during the first week of a new manuscript. It's hard, slogging work. I don't know these people and I have no idea how I ever imagined that I could write books for a living....

And then, much too soon, I hear the faint rumble of the garage door opening through the wall behind my computer screen. Can it be? Five o'clock already? I'm nowhere near five pages and my husband is home.

My son arrives soon after. We do the things that families do: dinner, a little television, maybe reading in bed. Around ten, it's lights out. I drop off to sleep like a rock tumbling down a well.

And then, hours later, I wake with a start. It's 3:00 a.m. and I have an idea for a future story. Seriously, I would rather be sleeping. But okay, fine.

I get my pencil and paper from the bedside drawer, scribble a note to myself in the dark. That should do it....

Not. I lie there, staring at the dark ceiling above, spinning a story in my head. I look over at the clock again, and somehow it's past four and I'm still wide-awake, telling myself a story that won't go away.

Oh, well. At least it's not an Exercise Morning.

# Backstory: Mr. and Mrs. Mack McGarrity

*Note to readers: Here's a taste of what we authors call Backstory—the important stuff that's happened in the past of the main characters....*

10    Mack McGarrity met Jenna Bravo when they were both students at UCLA. She was twenty-one, in her junior year, pursuing a business degree, lonely for the small-town life she'd left behind. He was twenty-five, an obsessed go-getter, just about to take his bar exams.

As luck and love would have it, they rented rooms in the same building—and both "adopted" the same stray black cat, which *she* called Byron and *he* called Beelzebub, Bub, for short. Both of them were what you might call loners at that time; Jenna, because she felt like a fish out of water in L.A.; Mack, because of his driven, focused obsession with getting ahead.

They fell in love practically on sight, when Jenna showed up at his door to ask him what he was doing with "her" cat. From the first, Jenna felt Mack answered something in her that she hadn't even known was calling out. Mack felt she was exactly the woman for him: sweet, funny, bright—and pretty in an understated way. Not only did he want her desperately, he could see she'd make a fine wife for the successful corporate lawyer he would soon become.

Within two months of the day they agreed to share that roaming black cat, they were married and blissfully happy. The only shadow on their first happy months together was cast at Christmas when Jenna wanted to spend the holiday with her family in her hometown up north and Mack wanted to stay in L.A., just the two of them. He did go with Jenna to her hometown in the end, under protest.

Mack hated that visit. His wife's widowed mother was kind to him, but still he felt that she resented him for stealing her favorite daughter away. Jenna's old boyfriend, a local golden boy and pre-med student, kept hanging around. And Jenna's younger sister, a juvenile delinquent if there ever was one, constantly picked fights with her mother and sulked—when she wasn't staying out all night. Mack felt relieved to get back to L.A.

He passed his bar exams in June—and got several good offers from major law firms right away. He took one that necessitated a move to New York City. When he told Jenna they were moving right away, she wasn't near as happy as he'd expected her to be. She seemed to think he should have consulted with her before making the decision. But she did go with him. He was making good money and they were able to afford a nice apartment. He told Jenna she could sign up for courses at Columbia or NYU if she wanted to.

Of course, he was busy. Really busy. He didn't have much time for his wife and he knew it. But a man didn't carve a niche for himself with a major law firm without putting in long hours. He had no choice but to live, eat and breathe his work.

Jenna went into a depression. She longed for the mountains of home. If L.A. had seemed like another planet to her, New York was an alternate universe. At this time, she developed her interest in genealogy. She began tracking down Bravos all over the country. She actually discovered a branch of her family right there in New York City: a third cousin who was a professor at NYU.

But even finding she had family nearby didn't help. Except at bedtime and early in the morning, Jenna rarely saw her husband and she missed her mother and her brat of a younger sister. She simply longed for home.

And for a baby. She kept thinking that a baby would give her something to do that mattered, something worthwhile on which to spend her empty days.

But Mack said no when she told him how much she wanted a child. He said he didn't have time to be a father right then. He had a place to make for himself—and for her, too—in the world. And he wasn't even sure he'd ever want to bring a child into a world like this one.

Jenna's resentment toward Mack grew. In bed at night, she turned away from him. When they spoke, there were always harsh words exchanged.

Then Jenna's sister called. Their mother was ill. Jenna packed a bag, put Byron in a carrier and she and the cat flew back home.

She never returned to New York, even after her mother recovered and her sister, greatly relieved to learn that Jenna didn't want to leave home again, set out to make her own place in the world, leaving their recovering mother in Jenna's care. Jenna and Mack exchanged a few heated phone conversations in which he demanded she return, and she said she just couldn't because there was nothing in New York for her.

Finally, he actually took time off from his precious job and flew to California. He ordered her to return home with him. And she told him New York was not—and never would be—her home.

He made no offer to stay there with her, to hang out a shingle on Main Street and become a small-town lawyer as she had hinted he might be. He couldn't do that. He hadn't sweated and slaved through law school just to give it all up before he'd even really succeeded. He returned to New York.

Jenna sent him the divorce papers in the mail. She didn't want anything from him—except Byron. And that really got to him. He had money now, damn it. And he would have been willing to toss some her way. And *he* wanted Bub, too. So he got a colleague in his firm to handle his side of the divorce. And she got herself a lawyer in California. Papers flew back and forth for a while.

And then along came the class-action lawsuit that would make Mack a multimillionaire. It was all about a faulty steering system in a very popular minivan. His firm turned it down. But Mack thought it had merit. He took it on himself, quitting his firm and going out on his own. It became his obsession. And he gave up on Bub. He told his lawyer to let Jenna have the damn cat.

The suit was all he lived for. All he thought about. The last set of papers he was supposed to have signed to make his divorce final just never got dealt with. Twice, his lawyer reminded him to come in and sign them. Mack put the lawyer off, paid his bill—and the lawyer sent him the papers in the mail with a reminder to sign them and forward them on.

He stuck them in a file cabinet and forgot about them.

He won the lawsuit. His percentage amounted

to ten million dollars. It was a big deal, all over the newspapers. Even Jenna, making a new life for herself in her hometown of Meadow Valley, read about it. Over the next few years, his practice grew and so did his nest egg, because it turned out he had a real feel for investing.

By then, for Mack, driving himself to make more and more money began to seem foolish, like a waste of precious time. He decided to "drop out"—well, as much as a brilliant, focused man ever could drop out.

He moved to Florida. He continued to manage his own investment portfolio from his home office. And now and then he took on a legal case or two, but only if it interested him—and usually pro bono, since the cases that interested him were often cases in which the client couldn't afford to pay.

He thought of Jenna often. Maybe with something that could be called longing. She was the only one he'd ever felt close to in his life. And because of his ambition, he'd lost her. Maybe, if he found a way to get another chance with her, he wouldn't let her go so easily. And maybe that's why he's never gotten out those final divorce papers, signed them and sent them back to her.

# THE BRAVO FAMILY

## A Family Tree

Here's a genealogy of this prominent family so you'll know who's who and how they're all related.

# THE BRAVO FAMILY

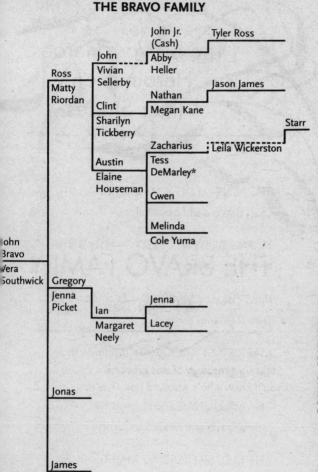

John Bravo
Vera Southwick

Ross
Matty Riordan

John
Vivian Sellerby

John Jr. (Cash)
Abby Heller

Tyler Ross

Clint
Sharilyn Tickberry

Nathan
Megan Kane

Jason James

Austin
Elaine Houseman

Zacharius
Leila Wickerston

Starr

Tess DeMarley*

Gwen

Melinda
Cole Yuma

Gregory
Jenna Picket

Ian
Margaret Neely

Jenna

Lacey

Jonas

James

BONUS FEATURE

(Broken lines indicate previous marriages)
*One child from a previous marriage: Jobeth

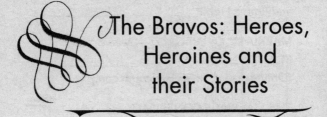

# The Bravos: Heroes, Heroines and their Stories

THE BRAVO BILLIONAIRE—Jonas Bravo
and Emma Hewitt

MARRIAGE: OVERBOARD—Gwen Bravo
McMillan and Rafe McMillan
(Online read at www.eHarlequin.com)

THE MARRIAGE CONSPIRACY—
Dekker (Smith) Bravo and Joleen Tilly

HIS EXECUTIVE SWEETHEART—
Aaron Bravo and Celia Tuttle

MERCURY RISING—Cade Bravo and
Jane Elliott

SCROOGE AND THE SINGLE GIRL—
Will Bravo and Jillian Diamond

FIFTY WAYS TO SAY I'M PREGNANT—
Starr Bravo and Beau Tisdale

MARRYING MOLLY—Tate Bravo and
Molly O'Dare

LORI'S LITTLE SECRET—Tucker Bravo and
Lori Lee Billingsworth Taylor

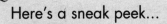

Here's a sneak peek…

20

# *BRAVO UNWRAPPED*
## by
## Christine Rimmer

*Coming in December 2005 from Signature Select.*

## CHAPTER 1

$She shouldn't be so put out with him—and she wasn't, not really.

Not any more than she was put out with her life in general in the past five days. Or maybe not so much put out as *freaked* out. Since the stick turned blue, as they say. Since the panel said "pregnant."

Six years since she called it quits with…B. She'd moved on. He'd moved on.

And then, seven weeks ago, she'd run into him. Your classic Friday night at that great club in NoHo, the underground one with the incredible sound system. Fabulous music and one too many excellent Manhattans and they ended up at this place. She wasn't careful—with B, that had always been her problem: failure to be careful.

Or one of her problems, anyway. To be painfully frank, there were several.

So she'd slipped up, she'd reasoned, feeling like a drunk off the wagon, a junkie back on the stuff. Once in six years. That wasn't so bad, she kept telling herself. Oh, no. Not so bad. Not to worry. She wasn't taking his calls. He was out of her life and she'd make absolutely certain that what had happened in September would never happen again....

And then, just when she'd pretty much succeeded in convincing herself that one tiny slipup did not a crisis make, she'd realized her period was late.

Very late.

Thus, the disastrous encounter with the pregnancy kit five mornings ago. Now, everything was all messed up all over again.

And speaking of again, she was doing it. Again. Thinking about B, and what had happened with B *and* the result of what had happened with B—all of which was *not* to be thought about. Not tonight. Not…for a while.

The limo rolled up to the iron gates that protected the Carlyle estate. The gates swung silently back. The stately car moved onward, up the long, curving drive that snaked its way through a forest of oak and locust trees, trees somewhat past their fall glory and soon to be winter-bare.

At the crest of the hill, the trees gave ground and there it was: Castle Carlyle, a Gothic monstrosity of gray stone, a Norman conqueror's wet dream of turrets and towers looming proudly against the night sky.

\* \* \*

Roderick opened the massive front door for her. Roderick was tall and gaunt and always wore a black suit with a starched white shirt and a bow tie. He'd run the castle since before her father bought the estate from an eccentric Dutch-born millionaire twenty years back. L.T. liked to joke that Roderick came with the castle.

"Ms. B.J. Lovely to see you," Roderick said with a faint, slightly pained smile. He wasn't very good at smiling. Loyalty and efficiency were his best qualities.

"Roderick," she said with a nod, as he relived her of her bag and briefcase. "The oak room?" she asked. Roderick inclined his silver-gray head. She told him, "I'll see myself in."

"As you wish."

Her heels echoing on the polished stone floor, B.J. proceeded beneath the series of arches down the length of the cavernous entry hall, past a dizzying array of animal heads mounted along the walls. For about a decade back when B.J. was growing up, L.T. had amused himself hunting big game all over the world. Being neither a modest nor a subtle man, L.T. proudly displayed every trophy he took—whether it was a handsome buck with a giant rack, or one of an endless string of gorgeous girlfriends known in the press as his Alpha Girls.

The oak room, named for the dark, heavily carved

woodwork that adorned every wall, branched off toward the end of the entrance hall. The room boasted a long bar at one end, also ornately carved. L.T., wearing his favorite maroon satin smoking jacket over black slacks, sat in a leather wing chair near the bar, a Scotch at his elbow and one of his trademark Cuban cigars wedged between the fingers of his big, blunt-fingered right hand.

His current Alpha Girl, Jessica, had found a perch on the arm of his chair. Jessica was, as usual, looking stunning. Tonight she wore red velvet, her plunging neckline ending just below the diamond sparkling in her navel. As B.J. entered, Jessica threw back her slim golden neck and trilled out a breathless laugh.

24

L.T. and his Alpha Girl weren't alone. On a brocade sofa across a Moorish-style coffee table from the pair sat the one person B.J. did not want to see.

Buck Bravo, in the flesh.

...NOT THE END...

*Look for the continuation of this story in*
*BRAVO UNWRAPPED by Christine Rimmer,*
*available in December 2005 from Signature Select.* ✑

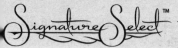

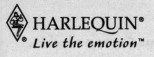

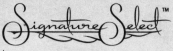

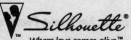

# A bear ate my ex, and that's okay.

Stacy Kavanaugh is convinced
that her ex's recent disappearance
in the mountains is the worst
thing that can happen to her.
In the next two weeks, she'll
discover how wrong she really is!

# Grin and Bear It
# Leslie LaFoy

**Clip this page and mail it to Silhouette Reader Service™**

| IN U.S.A. | IN CANADA |
|---|---|
| 3010 Walden Ave. | P.O. Box 609 |
| P.O. Box 1867 | Fort Erie, Ontario |
| Buffalo, N.Y. 14240-1867 | L2A 5X3 |

| Name | (PLEASE PRINT) | |
|---|---|---|
| Address | Apt.# | |
| City | State/Prov. | Zip/Postal Code |

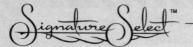

# COMING NEXT MONTH

**Signature Select Spotlight**
**IN THE COLD** by Jeanie London
Years after a covert mission gone bad, ex-U.S. intelligence agent
Claire de Beaupre is discovered alive, with no memory of the brutal
torture she endured. Simon Brandauer, head of the agency, must
risk Claire's fragile memory to unravel the truth of what happened.
But a deadly assassin needs her to *forget*....

**Signature Select Saga**
**BETTING ON GRACE** by Debra Salonen
Grace Radonovic is more than a little surprised by her late father's
friend's proposal of marriage. But the shady casino owner is more
attracted to her dowry than the curvy brunette herself. So when
long-lost cousin Nikolai Sarna visits, Grace wonders if *he* is her
destiny. But sexy Nick has a secret...one that could land Grace in
unexpected danger.

**Signature Select Miniseries**
**BRAVO BRIDES** by Christine Rimmer
Two full-length novels starring the beloved Bravo family.... Sisters Jenna
and Lacey Bravo have a few snags to unravel...before they tie the knot!

**Signature Select Collection**
**EXCLUSIVE!** by Fiona Hood-Stewart, Sharon Kendrick, Jackie Braun
It's a world of Gucci and gossip. Caviar and cattiness. And
suddenly everyone is talking about the steamy antics behind the
scenes of the Cannes Film Festival. Celebrities are behaving badly...
and tabloid reporters are dishing the dirt.

**Signature Select Showcase**
**SWANSEA LEGACY** by Fayrene Preston
Caitlin Deverell's great-grandfather had built SwanSea as a mansion
that would signal the birth of a dynasty. Decades later, this ancestral
home is being launched into a new era as a luxury resort—an event
that arouses passion, romance and a century-old mystery.

**The Fortunes of Texas: Reunion**
**THE DEBUTANTE** by Elizabeth Bevarly
When Miles Fortune and Lanie Meyers are caught in a compromising
position, it's headline news. There's only one way for the playboy
rancher and the governor's daughter to save face—pretend to be
engaged until after her father's election. But what happens when
the charade becomes more fun than intended?